FLUTTER

L. E. GREEN

DEDICATION

For Meemee, Tangee, family & friends.

TABLE OF CONTENTS

CHAPTER 1

BOSTON, MA HIGH RISE

The night was warm with a slight chilling breeze squeezing through the buildings, imposing upon the Boston horizon of dark blue and black. Dark slithering clouds wisped about the night sky, moving quickly from a violent wind, preceding a rain storm destined to batter down upon the city. The wind smelled like ice; the city lights blinded the stars, and only the moon and a few bright planets were in sight. Built in 1964, the 52–floor Prudential Tower sat in the background declaring its presence, the city's most iconic monument. A few horns beeped here and there as car tires of the passing vehicles slapped the road and bumped against the destructive potholes. Yet traffic moved smoothly courtesy of the completion of the infamous Big Dig. Finally, the dreadful Big Dig had subsided after a solid 25 years of construction but not without being $12 billion over budget, not without four related deaths and or countless injuries, lawsuits and political corruption scandals. Out–of–towners flowed into the city for the night's excitement, ready to take part in the adventurous Boston nightlife.

Two miles away, a woman stood on the ledge of another skyscraper. No one noticed her nor cared, but she was there watching the world hustle and bustle beneath the tips of her toes. From afar, she almost looked like Antony Gormley's Naked Man statues of New York City. Many of these statues were placed on the ledges of high buildings. Panicked citizens had called 911 believing they were actually suicidal maniacs ready to plummet to the pavement. Farther away, she looked like an antenna fading into the black of the sky. She could see the Prudential Tower light up in green LED lights, GO CELTS! It blinked G–O–C–E–L–T–S! Each letter appeared exactly one second after the other. Then all together, GO CELTS blinked three times with a three second pause between each cycle. A few lights were out in the G and T letters and almost read CO CELIS! Those lights had been out since the start of the season and hadn't been fixed.

The Boston Celtics were playing against the New York Knicks. Most of the police force lurked around the TD Garden Center to intimidate the drunken patrons into compliance and order. The last game between the two rivals had resulted in a murder, a rape and a bonfire in the parking lot. The police walked to and fro, pacing about as they swung around their batons. They checked their radios, keeping side chatting brief as they maintained watch, anxiously waiting for the guaranteed commotion which would ensue at the final buzzer. Win or lose, there would be a riot. Win or lose, there would be pepper spray in the air. The police prepared their gas masks. The infamous Boston/New York team rivalry was at the center of everyone's minds tonight. There was no time to focus on a random, ledge–walking psycho with a bad attitude and mysterious purpose.

This mysterious woman, Abigail was a peculiar, young lady. She was slightly annoyed by the missing lights and wondered how many fools would misread the electric banner. Abigail counted the blinking green LED light cycle at least five times before she remembered her initial focus. As she stood on the ledge she could feel the wind sweeping past her feet, almost with enough force to pick her up from the rubber of her black Gortex boots which she had borrowed from her friend and coworker, Roger. Her hair was black and shaped into a lazy style Mohawk where her bangs hung long over the front of her face. She had on dark eye makeup, to match her black Dickies cargos, a black top and a black oversized leather jacket, frayed at the edges and elbows. She stood on the ledge, thinking of where her mysterious life had taken her and what had led her to this moment. It was the moment she looked forward to yet regretted at the same time.

Abigail never told Roger most of the thoughts that went through her mind. She wanted to embrace who she was and what had happened to her but there was no time. Her fate was sealed at that very moment. Figuring out what was going on in her life and in her head was more complicated than a teenage girl realizing she has a crush on a boy she used to despise, who is also getting her period and figuring out how in the hell to use a tampon. She was on the verge of a mental crisis.

There she was, standing at the ledge, thinking of life's mysteries that had created this kink in her path— her choices and decisions driven by her fears and uncontrollable desires, all of which changed the meaning of her existence. Everything around her— the people, the air, the texture of things — now seemed worthy of investigation. There was so much she didn't understand. So many thoughts in her head were in turmoil: Love fighting with lust, confidence in war coupled with insecurity, and pain fighting with joy. Abigail was very unsure of herself. This moment was another reminder of how her body was not under her own control. Her conscience seemed to have declared mutiny against her flesh. She had lost control and wanted it back. Abigail looked down at the pavement. It called to her. From afar it looked like the soft black foam padding in a gun case. Only Abigail would make a connection like that.

Abigail brutally ripped the jacket from her body tossing it to the tar covered roof. She turned around, jogging away from the edge in a slow steady pace. Her heart was pounding so hard, she could hear it in her head and feel it in her chest. Her breathing was rhythmic and timed. She walked back about 50 feet from the edge. She turned and faced the edge again. She closed her flaming blue eyes and reopened them. She began to run toward the edge of the building. Fast, hard footsteps pounded against the concrete roof. Little puffs of dirt spewed out from under her feet, pushed out from under the rubber soles of her boots. Her last step was against the very edge of the building. It's a 12 inch step but she took it gracefully without breaking a stride. This is where she committed to regain control. She was fearless. She jumped.

TWO WEEKS EARLIER
CHAPEL AND CASE

Dennis rushed to finish up a few phone calls and paperwork for a minor project he had worked on with PNC bank. He rushed through the office to the fax machine, placed a few papers in it and tapped the side of the machine, hoping it would operate faster.

"Come on!" he whispered impatiently. One by one, ten sheets of paper scanned through the machine. When they were done, he grabbed them. He then took the receipt and rushed back to his desk. His suit jacket was tossed around the back of his office chair. He looked at his phone, anticipating a call. The phone rang.

"You got it?" Dennis listened for an answer. "Good! We'll catch up on Tuesday in the board room. Thanks." It was 1:00 pm and Dennis was leaving for the day. He packed up his belongings and shut down his computer. He took the elevator down to the first floor, walked through the lobby and into the garage that could be entered and exited through a door attached to the lobby. When he-arrived at his car, he saw Alan Jiang waiting in a truck, parked behind his own car.

"Hurry up Chump!" Alan yelled over the rumble of the engine.

"Let me get my bag." Dennis grabbed a bag from the trunk of his car, locked the door, and tossed the bag into the back seat of Alan's truck. He opened the front door of the truck and climbed in, closing the door behind him.

"Buckle up!" Jiang reminded him to secure his seat belt. They left the garage and jumped on the highway which wasn't far from the office.

Alan Jiang and Dennis Matthews were traveling on Interstate 95 North in eastern Massachusetts, heading towards Alan's cabin in Falmouth. They rode along the highway in a 2007 dark green, four–door Toyota Tundra. The truck had a dent in the rear driver side panel. Jiang wasn't very good at driving in reverse or parallel parking. He had backed into a "No Parking" sign on Newbury Street a few weeks earlier. His only intention was to quickly pick up a gift for his wife from a boutique she repeatedly talked about. He was late coming home from work and needed an alibi. Showing up with a gift always smoothed things over.

"How far are we?" Dennis wondered.

"We have about 20 minutes left," Alan seemed tired. His eyes were heavy after a long workweek. His voice was scratchy yet firm.

"Can you believe Charles?" Dennis reminisced about the meeting they had earlier that morning. Dennis, too, was tired from a long night of research. His eyes had dark circles. He kept blinking to refocus them. It had been a long time since he had seen the sun.

"Charles has no idea what he is doing and no clue what he is talking about. I have bailed him out so many times; but I think this time, I'm going to let him fall flat on his face." Alan was clearly frustrated. A crease formed between his eyebrows and his nostrils flared.

Dennis agreed, "He didn't even look at the packet. How could he ignore the numbers so easily?"

"He is too passionate about that company," Jiang took his eyes off the road for a moment. "He believes too much in the idea and doesn't give two shits about the numbers not adding up. He won't get another dime from us." Jiang swerved when he realized his truck was drifting into another lane.

Dennis wasn't nervous at all. He continued saying, "And I'm trying to figure out how we will recover the funds we have already invested in that monstrosity of a company." Dennis nibbled on his finger nails. "I'm hungry." His stomach growled.

Alan's crinkled angry face softened. He said, "We can stop for dinner as soon as we get to Falmouth, or I can also have dinner delivered to the house. It's your call."

"I heard about a place named Mackie's." Dennis was suddenly excited. "I hear they have really good seafood."

"Sounds good!"

"I'll look it up." Dennis picked up his iPhone and ran a search. He checked a few text messages and read an email. "It's three miles from your cabin."

******

Alan Jiang was the CEO at Chapel and Case Investment Company. He was 39 and considered an up and coming business mogul. He had lifted many companies out of the red with his creative consultation strategies, motivational speeches, and his sacred list of angel investors. He had quickly worked his way up the corporate ladder, rising faster than any other CEO in the area. Alan had graduated from Yale's MBA program at the age of 34 and had been promoted to CEO of

Chapel and Case two years ago after having worked there for only three years. He served on the Boston Minority CEO board whose major purpose was to recruit minority business professionals from the best higher education business programs in New England. The board also sought to mentor them on a monthly basis by checking in, providing support and employment as needed.

Alan had been married to Katherine Smith for two years. She worked at Carter Consulting firm located in downtown Boston. They had met during a lunch break at a hot dog stand on the Boston Common. They dated for three years before marrying. Katherine was a short, red–headed woman with a long, thin face. Some of her colleagues called her "The Kraken" behind her back. She was known to be extremely cold hearted and very business oriented. Whenever she walked into a room, someone would invariably whisper, "Release the Kraken!"

Katherine barely cracked a joke or smiled in the office place. She never meddled in Jiang's affairs. She never gave him advice nor did she expect to take advice from him about her business affairs. "Let me fail and learn from my own mistakes," she would say whenever she thought he was about to make a comment. She was extremely curt and tough at work, but at home she was very gentle and family oriented. She backed off when she knew her husband was having a macho moment. She could read him like a book. She knew when to step in and when to back away and let her softer, feminine instinct take over.

Katherine wasn't much of a cook; she didn't have much time to practice. She worked extremely hard for her employer but knew she would never become a partner there. She was also well aware of the comings and goings of Alan's many mistresses. She never let them bother her because she figured it was love that brought them together, but her wit that sustained them. Her understanding of mergers, investments, and corporate takeovers set her strategy for their marriage. She had sworn to herself never to be the strong corporate woman who worked late everyday because she had no one to go home to at night.

******

Dennis Matthews was enrolled in the Isenberg School of Management at the University of Massachusetts, Amherst three years ago when he first met Alan Jiang while applying to become an intern. Alan was asked by Dean Rogers of the School of Management to come in and give a presentation about developing, running and sustaining a Massachusetts–based finance institution. In attendance were representatives from MassMutual, Babson Capital and State Street Bank, all speaking about how they had started as finance majors and worked their way up to the corporate penthouse. Some were candid about their climb— the pitfalls, the money, the backstabbing, and the women. When Alan spoke, he spoke with poise and was captivating. He didn't address students' questions about women, money and fast cars, but he did express his commitment to long nights of study and research, the strain on personal relationships, and the joy of success that always seemed just beyond reach and which became harder to reach each day.

Alan was born in the United States and didn't have an accent, which was surprising to the crowd. They expected him to have a Chinese twang to his voice. In fact, He spoke better English than a few of the professors. He spoke fluidly, with a commanding seriousness that made others listen without interruption. He wasn't the most suave corporate mogul in the room, but he was the most successful and sometimes thought the other businessmen attending these sessions must have just wanted a day out of the office.

When Alan concluded his brief speech and presentation, Dennis was so impressed by Alan's story that he approached Alan directly after the speech to pick his brain a bit more. They got to talking and quickly bonded over sports and investment chatter. Alan got to know Dennis and eventually thought of Dennis as his protégé. Dennis saw Alan as a mentor. Alan took Dennis under his wing and never looked back. *I'll show this kid how to really run a business.* Alan was proud of Dennis. He was evolving into someone Alan had dreamed he would become.

Alan hadn't been very trusting of Dennis at first. He didn't want to expose his secrets to some random kid who had initially come off as annoying. Alan had always suspected that other corporations were capable of planting intellectual property spies anywhere they could, and he didn't put Dennis above any of it. Dennis was sharp beyond his years. *He should have studied at Harvard,* Alan always thought to himself. He watched Dennis with a close eye. Alan had even hired a private investigator to research Dennis' background to make sure he was legitimate and not harboring any secrets. Alan learned some horrifying details in Dennis' past and was determined to help this young man succeed in the finance industry.

Dennis hadn't told anyone about his upcoming fishing trip. He was too excited about going and didn't think to call his mother who would probably worry about him being on the ocean in a small boat. On the roof of the truck was a gray storage bin full of hunting and fishing gear which Alan had purchased from various online sporting goods stores. His favorite store was Cabelas, but he often purchased items from Bass Pro shops and Dicks Sporting Goods. Alan had strapped the gear to the bars on the top of the truck before he left to pick up Dennis. Occasionally, the bin would shift although it was quite secure and was not going to fall off. The road was so bumpy at times that it made Alan question his strapping skills.

He would hear the bin shift and look up to the roof of the truck.

The truck towed a galvanized trailer with a boat named "The Polaris," a 20 foot Mako 204 with a center console and a pearl white, fiberglass V–hull with a horizontal red stripe for decoration. Alan's wife had named the boat before their first ride out to sea. It carried a 200 horse power black Mercury Engine with a bright red logo and a sliver stripe. The Polaris was a $29,000 boat Alan won for a second place finish at the 2009 Master Angler Classics tournament in North Carolina. Alan was excited to bring Dennis bluefish and striped bass fishing. He wanted to teach Dennis how to balance work and play, with an emphasis on the work and play as the reward when the hard work was complete.

Alan followed the GPS faithfully and successfully reached Mackie's Bar and Grille at Pier 6. The restaurant was a reddish brown shack that sat ocean side. It was a nice break from the drive. They found a parking space on the side of the road and pulled in. Parking in the parking lot was a bit difficult since they were towing a boat. Dennis and Jiang exited the car and stretched their legs. It wasn't a long drive but it was long enough for the joints in their knees to get stiff. The two men walked into Mackie's. It looked like an old boat house with wooden panel walls. There were family pictures on the wall and pictures of the owners with famous people who occasionally stopped in to have lunch or dinner. There was a picture of the original owner with a young Ted Kennedy at the beginning of his political career.

They chose the table near the window overlooking the ocean. *What a view.* Alan ordered grilled shrimp and a lobster roll with a gin and tonic. Dennis ordered crab cakes, clam chowder and pasta salad with a soda. The smell of the fresh ocean water was in the air. Dennis had never been able to relax and enjoy the beauty of the sea. He was excited just to be able to finally smell the ocean breeze without inhaling pollutants. During dinner, they spent the majority of their time talking about the earlier meeting, women and sports. Dennis was intrigued by anything Alan said. He knew Alan had the magic bullet of success and he would do just about anything to learn how Alan ticked.

Jiang asked, "How did you find this place? The food is pretty good."

"A friend of mine, Garrett, he told me about it. I spoke to him on Facebook yesterday and he said, 'if you ever get a chance, check out Mackie's' so here we are. His parents have a timeshare out here. They come once a year in August, so he's pretty familiar with the area."

Jiang was always a skeptic. He didn't like people knowing where he was. He knew Dennis wasn't familiar with much of anything outside of Boston so he wondered if someone had put him up to coming to this place. He loved Dennis like a little brother, but didn't put anything past anyone. *Everyone is an opportunist given the right persuasion and opportunity.* He wondered if Dennis had become buddy–buddy with another executive at the firm. Alan often had to stop his mind from wandering. He figured, "If I can imagine it, then someone has already done it or is going to do it. So act first."

"Garrett... from where?" Alan questioned.

"Oh from B school. We chat once in a while." Dennis had picked up on Alan's natural instinct to question motives. He smiled. "Don't worry. It's no one you know or who knows you. He gave up business and became an art student. He has no interest in the world of finance and I didn't tell him exactly when I was coming this way. You are paranoid about the smallest things, man. Chillax!"

Alan smirked, but he didn't find it funny.

It was mid–afternoon when two men finally got on the water. They were off the coast of Portland, Maine blue and striper fishing on Alan's boat. Alan knew it was a little early in the season, but he was more excited about just being on the water. Alan showed Dennis how to set the proper knot for the eight ounce diamond jig. He explained how to use the fishing pole and what to do if he caught a fish. Alan had herring and chicken breast that he would attach to the hooks if they decided to go with bait instead of a jig. Alan loaned Dennis an older pole with a Penn reel on it. It's the pole he had used up until two years ago. *That pole has done some great fishing.*

"The sea is a little rough today. I'm surprised you're not sea sick," Alan joked as he dropped his line to the ocean floor. "No no. Let the jig hit the bottom, *then* crank it up about 20 times before you drop it again."

"I did!" Dennis scrunched his face. His arms were fatiguing.

"No, you didn't. I watched you, and I counted."

"Well, maybe you lost count. You're getting a little old, you know." Dennis smiled a wide smile while squinting his eyes.

"Your ass is right behind me, fucker!" Alan smiled back.

They laughed.

Dennis had something on his mind. "What do you think about Moore?"

"You mean Erin? Erin Moore?" Alan was no longer thinking about the fishing. "I must admit she is brilliant. I just don't like the fact that I can't read her. I don't know whose side she is on or if she is even listening. She nods and scrunches her eyes while taking notes at every meeting. She makes really good decisions and tough ones too. She takes her time and doesn't care if anyone tries to rush her."

Dennis agreed. "She is very smart. It's almost scary how wise and creative she is. The board loves her. If they ever decided to jerk you, she's next in line."

"Yes I know. I see it," Alan responded.

"Do you think the board is gonna jerk you?"

"Dennis, everyone gets jerked at some point. One minute, you're their star player, the next minute you're riding the bench hoping you will be substituted in. Then, the owners are wondering why they are paying you so much and they're not using your services anymore. I see them whispering behind closed doors. I don't care whose business they put on the table. Each one gets the same scrutiny as the next."

Slowly the sky turned dark and large dark gray clouds move in overhead. There was a crack of lightning that shook the men in their boots. Dennis grabbed his chest in horror. He tried to laugh it off, but then another thunderous boom followed. Alan didn't want to take any chances.

"Well, this was unexpected. Reel up!" Alan shouted nervously.

Dennis and Alan reeled up their lines vigorously just as the rain began to pour. Alan drove the boat. He was extremely nervous thinking about how he didn't pay enough attention to the weather reports. He turned back and headed to the Falmouth shore. They were about 20 minutes out, and the sea got rougher. Alan was sure he could make it back so he stayed on the course. *I have been on rougher seas than this.* But Dennis had not. They shouted inaudibly. Alan tried to signal Dennis to put on a life jacket, but Dennis didn't understand. He was too afraid to walk over to Alan and Alan was too afraid to stop driving the boat. Lightning cracked again as the rain flooded out Alan's warnings to Dennis. The sky turned blacker than ever as they sped off over the rough sea.

THE NEXT DAY

Saturday morning, London Bradley was a young woman on a mission to do some fishing off the Portland coast for stripers. She arrived in her army green 2001 Jeep Wrangler at about 10:00 in the morning and pulled out her equipment. She put on her neoprene Cabelas suit so that she could wade in the shallow ocean water as she fished. She slipped her legs in one by one and pulled the straps up over her shoulders, then slipped her feet into the waterproof boots she had purchased a few weeks earlier. She gathered her long black hair into a ponytail and slipped on a cap. London grabbed her bait from the floor behind her seat, took out her tackle from the trunk, put her phone in the chest pocket of her jacket and headed across the rocky path that lead to the beach. It was a short walk from where she had parked to the little cove.

Her uncle, Benjamin Simms, was supposed to meet her there within the hour. He had to run a few errands for her grandmother before he could reach the beach where London had asked him to meet her. She argued with him repeatedly that the season was a little early, but his friend at work had told him blues and stripers were biting since a week before due to the warm winter that year. All winter, London and her uncle had friendly arguments about who would catch the most fish or the largest fish this season, so she made sure she was there early, hoping to catch the first saltwater fish of the season. Last year their fishing buddy, Oscar Youngblood, won the title for saltwater fishing. Benjamin took the overall freshwater fishing title; and London, who called herself the "BASS MASTER," earned the bass fishing title in their friendly competition.

As she got closer to the water, the rocky path slowly turned into a small, sandy beach. She had been there many times and was familiar with the depth of the water. There were fissures in the sand from the previous night's storm where rain had washed over the beach. London was careful to walk around them for fear she would trip and twist her ankle. She received a text from her uncle. "BE THERE IN 15."

She knew she'd better hurry and at least get a few casts in to increase her odds of catching the first fish. She was so competitive with her uncle and other fishing partners; she prepped all her tackle at home the night before and hoped she would get right to it. She dropped her tackle box and bait bucket on the shore and placed herring on the hook. She turned on her iPod, plugged in the ears, and then went directly into the water until it was about waist high. The neoprene suit kept her warm as she released her first cast into the water.

Ten minutes of casting and London hadn't caught a thing. She didn't even get a nibble. Her bait was beaten up from repeatedly smashing against the rocks, so she decided to change the bait. As she changed the bait, she looked toward the path and noticed a familiar figure coming toward her. Although she wanted to beat him to the punch, her uncle Benjamin had reached the beach sooner than she had expected. He, too, was dressed in a neoprene suit. She was happy to see him.

"Any luck?" He shouted as he walked closer.

"None yet." She rushed to get her bait secured on the line.

"You're supposed to be the Bass Master– or does that only apply to freshwater bass? Are you having trouble with sea bass?" He laughed loudly, almost snickering.

"HA HA HA! You wait old man! The Bass Master will prevail."

He smiled, noticing that she was anxious to get back into the water, and said, "No worries. The professional is here." He put his tackle box on the beach and opened the bait bucket. In the bucket he had eels. "You aren't using the right bait. Use these." He smiled.

"Well why didn't you tell me to pick up eels instead of letting me buy all these herring?"

"Because I knew you wanted to beat me so I wasn't going to let you in on my secret until I got here."

They both laughed. London took the herring off her line and replaced it with an eel. Her hands were getting cold but she was ready to get back to the task. They both walked back toward the beach and immediately stopped in their tracks.

Benjamin dropped his pole in the sand and said, "Call 911!"

London dropped her belongings and began to dial 911 in her phone. Her hands were shaking. Meanwhile, her uncle ran back to his truck and returned with a camera.

London stared at the water as she called, "Yes... I'm at Yellow's Point in Portland. It's a little cove across the street from Jerry's Pizza Palace. You need to get here ASAP."

Her uncle Benjamin snapped pictures.

"You have to get here quickly! A body just washed up on the shore."

CHAPTER 2

ALAN'S FUNERAL
FIVE DAYS LATER

The 200-year-old basilica held approximately 300 guests attending Alan Jiang's funeral. Cherry blossoms were sprinkled along the steps of the main entrance. Reporters from various television stations were on the perimeter and were roped off away from the family. The pipe organ could be heard blocks away. Many of Jiang's colleagues and friends came to pay their respects. Without question, everyone respected him, and it was clear where the power would shift after this day. Alan's parents were somber as they walked into the church. Jiang's mother was a stout Chinese woman. She had straight, silver hair and rosy cheeks. His father was tall and strong looking for his age. His hair was gray. He wore glasses and peeked over them from time to time, whenever he was unsure of something he saw. Jiang's father seemed unshaken as he helped his wife up the front stairs.

The other Chinese people with Jiang's parents must have been other family members and close family friends about whom Jiang never spoke. There were about 30 people in attendance. Jiang didn't want people involved in his family life. He didn't want them to be watched or be used as a means to influence Jiang's decisions, so he lived as if he was estranged from his family. Secretly he loved them very much and created false business meetings to pay them an occasional visit. The parents and family stood outside of the front door awaiting the arrival of Alan's wife.

Erin Moore pulled up in a limo. She exited the limo with Darren Hall, another executive from Chapel and Case. Moore was wearing a simple, all–black dress with four inch stilettos. A slim gold belt was tightened around her waist. Her blonde hair was pulled back in a sloppy bun. She wore a pair of small gold hoops, conservative makeup and a gold Tiffany necklace. Darren Hall had on a dark gray Armani Suit with a white handkerchief in the jacket pocket. He wore a pair of Armani eye glasses with a slight burgundy tint. He was rather flashy for corporate America and had been warned to keep his color choices to gray, blue and black. Many thought he might have homosexual tendencies, but Erin Moore had been sleeping with him for two years. There was even a pregnancy scare rumored about the office. When the former CFO heard about it, he and the board had a serious conversation with the couple. Nine months later, there was no baby in sight. Erin whispered something in Darren's ear once he was out of the limo.

She reached over and helped him straighten out his tie. "You look stunning."

"As do you." Darren winked.

"Let him know we are here, and we will head back as soon as it is over."

Hall nodded and pulled out his phone. He began to text someone and put the phone away by time they reached the stairs. He straightened his tie. On their way into the sanctuary, Erin and Darren acknowledged Jiang's parents and expressed their condolences. She handed Alan's father a card from Chapel and Case containing a check for $10,000. Erin Moore noticed a tear drop down the face of one of the Chinese women standing behind Alan's parents. She reached in her purse and handed the woman a tissue, then nodded and walked in. Erin and Darren chose a row on the right side of the room next to a few corporate colleagues they knew from business dealings, both shady and legitimate. They shook a few hands before settling in and finally sitting down.

Another limo approached. It carried Alan's wife, Katherine, and Katherine's mother, father and her brother, Jake.

"You ok, Katie?" Jake was very protective of his big sister. She nodded and looked to make sure no one heard him call her Katie. Jake hugged and kissed her on the forehead. Jake had just returned from Afghanistan three weeks earlier. He had been seeing a psychiatrist for post–traumatic stress disorder. Jake felt that he didn't need to see a psychiatrist, but the service was free and mandatory as instructed by his superiors. He had intended to marry his girlfriend of five years when he returned to the States except she had gotten pregnant by another man while he was gone. Jake went into a rage when he received her letter in the mail the day before he was set to return home. His rampage put him on watch and thus the mandatory appointments with a psychiatrist were required. He insisted he didn't need it. *What man wouldn't go on a rampage over something like that?* But the army had insisted, just in case.

Katherine was trying to be strong because she knew many business colleagues were in attendance: CEO Joshua Gorman from Eckerson and Bland Investments, COO Mary Aboku from Interspire Inc., and Henry Lloyd from Blackstone Construction, who were responsible for just about all the new construction projects in the Northeast. Katherine wasn't sure if crying would make her look weak or if not crying would make her look inhumane. She decided to hold her tears. Seeming inhumane was never a bad quality in the business world. Seeming weak was never a good idea. She was extremely sad and wondered how she would ever manage to keep her tears hidden, so she wore a black hat with a veil just in case she lost control of her emotions. She had on a sleek black dress with black leather shoes with silver studs on the heels. She wore a silver brooch on the lapel of her blazer. Her red hair blazed from underneath her black hat.

Katherine reached the top of the stairs where Alan's parents stood. She gave his mother a kiss on the cheek and a soft hug. Mrs. Jiang was extremely fond of Katherine. Katherine loved to spoil her mother–in–law with expensive purses, shoes and perfume. She spoiled Mrs. Jiang even more than she did her own mother. Last Mother's Day, Katherine took her mother and Mrs. Jiang to St. Martin where they stayed at the Sonesta Maho Casino and Resort. They had an all girls weekend on the beach; they explored the fancy boutiques and the cuisine on the French side of the island. Katherine's mother wept softly and hugged Mr. and Mrs. Jiang. The funeral director came over to the family. She wanted them to process into the sanctuary.

"Are we ready to pay Alan his final respects?"

No one said anything.

"Whenever you are ready we will be ready. Take your time," she smiled and backed away.

Mr. Jiang gave the final nod before they walked in as a family. Suddenly, Katherine was grabbed by the family lawyer Joseph "Terri–bull" Terbull. He was also called THE BULL for short because of his cut throat tactics in the court room and in negotiations. Joseph was heavy set and dark skinned with even darker circles under his eyes. He had a scar from his right eyebrow down to his nose. Some said it was the result of a fight with a client who didn't pay him. The truth was that he had been in a car accident the night after he passed the bar exam. He and a few buddies went out to drink. His friends, Mitch Loomis and Travis Carry, were also in the car. Mitch was driving on I90 heading back to Framingham. When he got back onto the city streets, he ran a stop light, swerved to miss another car and crashed into a mailbox. They were so afraid when they came to that Joseph followed his first instinct, hopped out of the car, moved Mitch, backed the car up and drove it to his house. He hid the car in his garage and his wife drove them all to the hospital. They told the cops they had been jumped when coming out of a bar and left it at that.

"Dennis Matthew's parents want to know what we plan to do to investigate further," Mitch informed her at every step.

"No! Tell them not to investigate, and I will give them $500,000 to leave it be. This is not something they want to mess around with. Send them my condolences. I can't imagine how they are feeling right now after losing a son. Send the money tomorrow and tell them that we know it will never replace Dennis in our hearts. He was a good kid whom Alan loved dearly, and our hearts go out to their family. Make them agree to leave it alone."

"Got it. I will start with 250 and then sweeten the deal up for them up to half a million and let them know it's best for them to let their son rest in peace and allow the police handle things from there."

"The police are incompetent."

"Agreed. Come on inside. Let's worry about this later. You look amazing by the way."

"Thank you, Joseph."

Before Katherine turned around, she caught a quick glimpse of a woman that she knew Alan had been seeing on the side. Katherine's expression tensed as she turned to walk into the building. Alan's mistress was Jennifer Kalis Martin. Katherine had hired a private investigator to research the woman. The investigator had turned in an extensive report that was 30 pages thick and did not leave any stone unturned. Katherine was just as skeptical as her husband. She figured if he was going to open up to this woman, then he'd better not let his dick make silly decisions that would destroy the empire they planned to build together. Katherine wanted to know everything about this woman and even more importantly, she needed to be sure Alan didn't have silly plans to leave her for this juvenile fluff.

Jen was a brown haired and short young woman in her last year of pharmacy school in Boston. She was from Poughkeepsie, New York, and was a biology major at Boston College. Jen had three sisters, no brothers and a cat named Harris. She lived in Hyde Park with her friend, Martha Howes. The investigator provided dental and medical summaries. *Good, no diseases.* She was a red belt and avid Tae Kwon Do enthusiast. She had a part–time job at Best Buy, but she quit a few months after meeting Alan. Jen was top of her class and had just completed an internship with Johnson and Johnson. Jen had met Alan at a pharmaceuticals conference entitled, *THE FUTURE OF PHARMING.* The title was rather tacky. Jen was interested in the finding her place in the field. Alan was interested in investing in the field. Jen bumped into him when trying to take a picture of a chemical model of a new cancer drug, Orpenzia.

"Excuse me. I'm sorry, I didn't see you."

Alan smiled, "I saw you. I just didn't know you would keep backing into me, so I apologize. I should've moved. Did you get the shot?"

"Well… not yet, but there's no rush. The model is pretty static. I don't see it taking a lunch break any time soon."

They both giggled.

"I'm Jennifer," she reached out her hand.

"Alan Jiang," He shook her hand. "What brings you here?"

The rest was history. Eventually Alan asked her out to lunch, lunch turned into dinner and vacations and sex. Jen taught Alan a few tricks his wife would never tolerate. She was into role playing and kinky sex acts. Alan also enjoyed her company enough to stop seeing all other women and just focus on his wife and Jen. Jiang gave Jen an allowance of

$1,500 a week. She had refused at first, but he had continued to shower her with gifts anyway, so she decided why not? Alan was upfront about having a wife and his feelings for her. Jen was upfront about continuing to see other men. Alan didn't like it very much, but that was how this game was played.

Jennifer grew to love Alan and he loved her, but she wasn't a fool. Initially, she thought he would never leave his wife for her, and she concluded that he wasn't really the type of man she saw herself settling down with. But over time, in the deeper part of her heart, she wished they could stop the running and hiding and just be together. Though it was too late to trust him, she had fallen in love with him but knew her place and never overstepped her boundaries with Alan or his wife. She knew Alan's wife was aware of her, so it was a mutual understanding among the three. *We don't see it and we don't talk about it.*

FRANKIE'S PUB

From across the street, Abigail watched the commotion of the funeral unfold. Abigail worked in *Frankie's Pub,* an Irish pub with about 15 tables and eight booths on the right side. Centered on the left wall was a huge mahogany colored bar about 15 feet long with copper fittings on the corners. The wall behind the bar was stacked with various top shelf and house liquors. The door to the kitchen was just to the right side of the bar. The floor was constructed of thick maple hardwood, glossed over in a half inch polyurethane coating. In the center of the floor was a large green shamrock painted years earlier. The pub had pictures of Celtics, Bruins, Red Sox team players and memorabilia from just about all Massachusetts professional sports teams posted on the "Wall of Fame." There were even pictures of the old Springfield YMCA, the birthplace of basketball. An 8-foot-long black awning displayed "FRANKIE'S PUB" with a shamrock separating the two words.

Abigail stood about five feet, eight inches tall and had a slender build. She had thick, long, black hair, which hung down to the middle of her back below her shoulder blades. She had a tanned complexion. Her ethnicity was hard to determine, but Frankie, her boss, would have guessed she was part Asian as her eyes were slightly slanted. She had a beauty mark under her right eye. Over the same eye, her eyebrow had a slit in it from a past injury. Her brown eyes were dark and cold, especially when she wasn't smiling or when she was deep in thought.

She watched the scene outside through the window as various limos and cars were driven to the front, unloading pretentious passengers who represented various types of executives, investors, coworkers, professors and family friends. Emotionless, her eyes glanced over to Alan's widow and her parents congregating in front of the basilica's main entrance. The dark clouds hovered low today. Abigail was cleaning glasses behind the bar while watching the important men and women entering and leaving the basilica. They were all sharply dressed in black and dark shades of blue and gray. She thought they looked like corrupt government officials sneaking into a covert Illuminati meeting.

Abigail was captivated by all that she saw and wanted to know more. With all of the news crews outside, she figured TV stations must be airing this live. *Where is the remote?* She found the remote and changed the station until she saw Samantha Callahan reporting. Samantha was a tall, slender blonde woman whose signature style was to wear something pink every day. She always wore too much makeup and was caught a few times cursing at the camera man, unaware that she was still live on national television. Abigail and her coworker, Roger, continued their daily cleaning rituals as they watched the latest news unfold across the street and on TV at the same time.

"We're here live outside at the funeral of international investment phenomenon Alan Jiang, CEO of Chapel and Case Investment Company. His body was found five days ago, washed up on the shores of the Atlantic Ocean in Portland, Maine, with a gunshot wound to the head and neck. Apparently, he was on a fishing trip..."

Roger poked his head out of the dishwasher, "That's fucked up." Roger was a drop out from the Massachusetts Institute of Technology, MIT for short, located in Cambridge, Massachusetts. Roger stood about 5'11" with light brown hair and a "boy band" haircut. He had bangs that hung over his face and made him look immature and younger than he really was. He lived with his mother and was an introvert with everyone else except Abigail and Frankie, the owner of the pub. After two and a half years at MIT, he had decided he wasn't interested in learning things he already knew about mechanical and chemical engineering. Ironically, he still couldn't figure out how to fix the dishwasher. Roger banged on the side of the machine.

"This damn... Hey, Elvis. Can you get those tables in section four for me? I think I can fix this." Roger often called Abigail, Elvis.

"No Problem." Abigail's attention was still stuck on the black limos across the street. Frankie came into the room from the back. Frankie was a broad faced Irish man who always worked out and wore a white tank top.

"Do your own damn tables, Rog." Frankie interjected.

"I'm trying to fix this washer," Roger said with a struggle.

"You've been fixing it for six months. You just don't want to wash dishes by hand. Do something productive so I don't feel like I'm wasting my money paying you for work you delegate to Abby."

"I don't mind, Frankie." Abigail tried to support Roger.

"I'm serious, Roger. I'm gonna pay Abigail your wages."

"Frankie, you're always complaining! One day I'm gonna get sick of your complaints, old man."

"And do what?" Frankie was ready for any challenge Roger was willing to offer.

"You know I could kill you with this little pinky here?"

They all laughed.

Abigail looked back and forth from the television report to the funeral. Samantha Callahan was mumbling about another body found 10 miles down the coast from Jiang's body. They showed footage of the young man's mother collapsing at his funeral a day earlier. There weren't many details mentioned about the homicide investigation, and most of the executives remained quiet about the murders when questioned by reporters. Death never seemed to stir up Abby's softer emotions. She didn't get why people got so upset about it. She figured, "We all die. No point pretending that one day, there'll be a cure for death. We can't stop it. But, one thing we *can* do is rush it along." This man's life was over; someone felt it was time for him to die and made sure it happened.

As the pre–funeral bustling went on, Abigail didn't say a word. She curiously watched these posh snobs tip toe in and out of the church. *Half of these people don't give a shit about this man,* she thought to herself. She could tell they were having frivolous conversations on their way in and out of the basilica. She saw a few people on their cell phones, barely taking their eyes off the screen to say hello to the family on their way in. The news report flashed a few pictures of the victim's face across the screen, some family photos and a picture of his company. There were a few comments about the Chapel and Case stock price fluctuating up and down, gaining and losing, back and forth all week. Investors weren't sure if this was a good thing or a bad thing that Jiang was out of the picture.

Would they miss out on the next big price increase, or was the company doomed? No one could tell.

From behind the bar Abigail dried her hands with a towel. She tossed it to the side and grabbed her hoodie from a hook against the wall.

"I'm gonna grab a smoke. Gimme a minute," Abigail said as she zipped up her hoodie and grabbed a pack of cigarettes and a lighter from the top of the bar. She exited the pub. There were a few patrons inside, but Frankie could handle them alone. When she got outside, she leaned against the building slightly shivering from the cold rain falling over every little piece of exposed flesh. She loved the smell of the rain, it was refreshing. But Abigail's focus was on that funeral. She couldn't resist getting closer to inspect the mournful day of the Jiang family. She fed off the sorrow that sat thick in the air. Sorrow seemed to follow her, or maybe she followed it. No one could be sure, but she was intrigued by the mourner's discomfort and wondered if she would ever feel that much emotion for anyone.

Katherine walked quickly and caught up to Mrs. Jiang. She grabbed her hand and assisted in escorting her to the front row. On the way a few people reached over and touched them or hugged them. Mrs. Jiang began to weaken at the knees and grabbed hold of Katherine's hand to maintain her balance. Jiang's family slowly processed up the aisle as the organist played *Morning Has Broken*. The organist was an older black man named Johnson. No one knew if Johnson was his first, last or middle name, but every knowledgeable funeral director knew that Johnson played the best pipe organ in the area. The Jiang family did not skimp on this funeral. They paid Johnson $2000 to play for up to three hours. The total cost of the funeral was $450,000 which was easily covered with Jiang's $20 million life insurance policy.

Inside the basilica, the room was full of people who knew Katherine and Alan from work, school and business. Some neighbors showed up and a few folks from the golf club were in attendance. The room was decorated with cherry blossoms, lilacs and white roses. A burgundy rug guided the eyes towards Jiang's coffin which was a cotton white shiny vessel at the front of the room. Flowers and mixed height white candles surrounded the casket; the candle light flickered and reflected, creating a halo effect. There wasn't much natural light coming in through the stained glass windows due to the lack of sunlight. Each of the windows carried a stained glass image of Jesus and the 12 apostles, even Judas. Each of the apostles had a white dove somewhere in the glass image, signifying the presence of the Holy Spirit. However, the window depicting Judas didn't have a dove, but instead a crow and a small satanic figure wrapped around his left leg.

All of the rows in the basilica were filled with people except for the first five rows on the left side of the church, reserved for family and closest friends. At the center of the aisle was Alan's body pale and stiff, stitched back together by the finest morticians. Mourners processed, passed by his body, and touched his hand. Some made the sign of the cross over their chests as they paid their respects. Katherine dropped a tear and wiped it away swiftly before she turned her face towards the crowd. She looked at the crowd and tried to pick out the faces of friends and foes. *There has to be someone in here happy that he is gone.* She tried not to think about it, but it had crossed her mind so many times. *Which one of these bastards killed my husband?*

Abby stood outside smoking as she leaned against the glass windows. She was there for about 10 minutes analyzing the guests. She stood, wondering if any guilty parties would show up; and if so, she wondered who they were. Was the wife in on the killing? She knew there was something corrupt brewing by the way everyone's whispers on the way in were followed with fake hugs, smiles and kisses. Abigail decided she was bored with it. Her questions would never be answered by stalking the funeral guests. She wished she could go inside and view the body, but came to her senses as soon as the silly thought crossed her mind. She finished her cigarette and flicked it into the street puddle. It let off a soft hiss as water hit the flame. She walked back into the pub, thinking about looking back only once but never doing so. More limos arrived at the basilica carrying guests to the funeral.

Chapel and Case was closed for the day for all employees except for maintenance and security workers. Maintenance staff was given a partial day and free to leave at 2 pm. Security, unfortunately for them, was necessary 24 hours a day. Last Christmas security staff was sent home at 1 pm in the afternoon. The next morning when people came back to work there was a 10 foot snowman sodomizing another snowman in the rear with his four foot crystal penis. The Thanksgiving before that, someone had strung a few raw turkeys from the company logo. The turkeys wore bowties and wigs and hung down in front of the doors. Security staff didn't mind having to stay. It was always easier to secure a building when no one was inside, and most of the time they watched TV and cracked a few jokes among themselves. Erin Moore provided a lunch of pasta, salad, water and soda for all employees who were left working in the building to keep their spirits up while on duty.

When the funeral was over, guests were invited to share hors d'oeuvres in the courtyard behind the basilica. On a table covered in white linen was caviar, foie gras, crackers, brie, goat cheese, raw oysters, steamed dumplings, Swedish meatballs wrapped in duck bacon, arugula salad, beef and tuna tartar with quail egg on top. The guests' tables were also covered in white linen with flowers and wine on top. Jiang's mother did not say a word. She just smiled and nodded as the guests came and went. The father walked around shaking hands with guests. Katherine tucked herself away in a corner and scanned the crowd from behind her veil. Occasionally, guests would stop by to offer condolences, but most recognized that she had intentionally secluded herself. She quietly watched.

Directly after the ceremony, Jennifer Martin took a taxi back to her apartment. Being the mistress of a top executive was exciting until something important happened and you have to take a back seat. Reality set in. She saw his family, but never met them. She didn't know much about any of them, yet Katherine was being embraced by Alan's loved ones. It was a lonely journey and she knew it had been a bold move on her part to even bother showing up. She had no one to share her grief with. Her heart was broken and no one really understood what she was going through. No one has sympathy for a mistress in distress.

During the taxi ride, she looked out the window and reminisced about the fun times with Alan and their many sneaky getaways. She remembered their trip to Montego Bay when Alan slipped and fractured his ankle on the water falls. He told his wife it was an accident that happened while on the company ski trip. She remembered the trip to Paris and dinner at the Eiffel Tower. She thought it was the perfect moment for him to confess his love and promise to leave his wife for her, but instead he gave her a pair of two carat diamond earrings. She smiled and accepted the gift as a reminder of how insignificant she was in Alan's deck of playing cards.

After about 20 minutes in the cab, Jennifer arrived at her apartment building. She went up the stairs after checking to see if there was any mail for her. Slowly she took one step at a time, feeling weak and tired from the long day of mourning. She entered her apartment, kicked off her shoes and sat on the couch. She wept for a few seconds and shook her head, thinking about Alan. Her phone rang. It was her friend, Missy.

"Hey, Missy." Jennifer was happy she had called.

"Jen, are you ok?" Missy was concerned. She hadn't heard from Jen in a few days.

"As good as I can be right about now. Sorry I haven't answered your calls and texts. I just needed some time to think about things."

"Have you talked to anyone?"

"I can't really talk about everything with anyone. It would be a major scandal that I can't deal with right now. I saw his wife there. She knows about me, but I didn't think she would recognize me. She looked at me like she knew exactly who I was."

"Oh boy. I wouldn't be surprised if she did know. I don't think you should be alone. I'm gonna come by in an hour. We can talk about everything then. Talking over the phone probably isn't a great idea. So, I'll be there soon."

"You really don't have to. I'll be okay."

"Listen, I know you will be okay, but you need company and a few glasses of wine. We can get drunk and cry together." Missy laughed. "I'm gonna swing by. Be there in an hour or less."

"Thanks Missy. I really appreciate it."

Back at the basilica, by about 4:00 pm, the funeral and gathering was over and the crowd had mostly cleared. The news stations were gone as soon as most of the guests left. No one gave any comments about the funeral, about Alan Jiang or his mysterious murder. Even the workers left behind to clean up kept pretty quiet about what was going on inside. In a week no one would be talking about Alan Jiang. All that lingered were a few rose petals and cigarette butts from a few smokers who rushed in and out to have a quick smoke during the eulogy. After the reading, a few of the guests from the funeral ventured into Frankie's to check it out and have a couple of drinks before going on their way.

CHAPTER 3

WHEN FRANKIE MET ABIGAIL
FOUR MONTHS EARLIER

Frankie was a bald, Irish former thug in his mid 50's. He had a graying goatee and huge muscles that bulged through the tank tops he liked to wear on a daily basis. He had a three inch scar on the back left side of his head from when he was stabbed in a fight at the age of 25.

Frankie would never forget the night he met Abigail. It was an unexpected encounter. She had scared the shit out of him with her unexpected arrival one cold rainy night. It was a very late night in Boston and the rain had been pouring down for the past few hours. It had been unusually warm that winter. There were about four huge snow storms followed by oddly warm weather in the low 50s which was unusual for late February. The overabundance of rain had caused drains to clog all over the city. There were flash flood warnings broadcast over the television for the Boston metropolitan area. Despite the warnings, the pub was having a decent night. Some people showed up after work before the rain had begun and never left. Maybe the rain deterred them from leaving too soon. The busy night had created a need for more frequent runs to the trash bin in the alley. By the end of the night Roger, Larry and Frankie were slaving over the kitchen and bar floor, trying to clean up as swiftly as possible.

Frankie looked at Roger and said, "Rog, I'm taking the trash out back."

"Yup!" Roger yelled across the room.

Frankie left Roger and Larry in the bar. It was about midnight, and all of the patrons had left. It was time for a serious cleaning for the next day. Frankie began the clean up by carrying the overflow of trash to the dumpsters in the back alley. Some of the bags were very heavy and half torn. They leaked a smelly trail of mashed food and beer from the kitchen to the back door. He knew he would have to give the floor a thorough mopping later. Frankie tossed bag after bag from the door to the dumpster, trying his best not to get wet but needed to make sure that the bags landed in the bin. He paused for a moment when he saw two bare feet on the other side of the bin. Frankie questioned the accuracy of his aging eyes. He cleared his eyes and was sure there was a person back there. She coughed and Frankie was startled.

"Oh shit. Holy Mother…" He put his hand over his chest as if he was about to have a heart attack. He looked closer. "Hey! Hey!" The rain pounded against the pavement, muffling the sound of his call.

There was no answer. He tilted his head to see if he could get a better look at the figure scrunched tightly into the sticky corner. He couldn't see and knew he had no choice but to step out into the rain for a better look. He looked up as if to curse the rain. He stepped out into the alley and went over slowly. Frankie was instantly soaked and freezing from the water bouncing off his skin and soaking into his tank top. He saw a frail looking Abigail shivering in the corner attempting to hide under torn plastic and paper bags. He lightly jogged over.

"HEY! You okay? Can you hear me?"

She barely raised her eyes.

Frankie yelled, "You gotta get out of this rain."

Frankie spotted a trail of blood streaming away from her body. With the rain splashing into it, a red stream ran down a cement crack and underneath the dumpster. She was losing a lot of blood. Frankie pulled back the bags of trash and noticed a bullet wound in her shoulder and thigh. In addition, she had a bruise on her forehead. Her shirt and pants were soaked with blood around the wounds. She was too weak to stop him from touching her. Abigail knew she needed help and had to trust her instincts that this was her last chance to get it. She didn't have one speck of energy to resist and she had no clue where she was or what was going on.

"Oh shit. You've been shot!" Frankie carried her inside and upstairs through a door where no one would see her. Above the bar was kind of an apartment consisting of an open space, two rooms and a bathroom with a toilet and shower. It was where Frankie stayed. Frankie carried Abigail to a small room with a twin sized bed and laid her down. He didn't tell Roger or Larry what he was up to. He would tell them in the morning. He didn't want to hear Roger's jokes or Larry's complaints.

He asked, "Little girl, what are you into?"

Abigail was too weak to respond. She tried to speak but her lips resorted to a rapid quiver. Everything she tried to say sounded muffled. Her heart was palpitating and her limbs were burning as the blood attempted to flow back into her extremities. Her arms and legs were completely cramped. Her feet were blistered and bruised. Frankie quickly stripped Abigail down to her underwear. He hadn't seen a young woman's body in a long time, but he was not thinking along those lines. Her skin was smooth and pale; her veins were visible under her skin. Frankie was nervous but he had to do something about the wounds. By this time, Abigail had passed out from exhaustion.

The wound in her shoulder wasn't a big deal. The bullet had grazed her shoulder and was out of her body. Frankie cleaned the wound, took some floss and sewed it back together with a few stitches. He had some experience in dressing wounds from his participation in illegal activities in the past. Frankie had removed about 50 bullets from bodies in his lifetime, but it had been a while since he practiced his skill. The bullet in her thigh was a little deeper than he would have liked, but he removed it with ease. She had lost a lot of blood, but she was a good patient. She laid still and allowed Frankie to do what he needed to do without much movement or resistance. Frankie didn't want to have a naked bloody girl anywhere near his establishment, but something made him feel like she would be ok. He had seen worse and felt bad about leaving her there.

"I have to take the underwear off you, girly. I'm not a perv ok? But you need to get warm as fast as possible and all your clothes are soaked." Abigail was out for the count. Her flesh was turning pink again, but not fast enough. Frankie covered her in a blanket before he pulled her underwear down. He reached behind her and unstrapped her bra. *I can still do this without looking.* He placed her underwear on rail of the bed. He ran into his room and grabbed a plaid comforter and a pair of clean socks. He placed the socks on her feet and covered Abigail and tucked her in for the night.

Frankie was completely distraught. He was shaking and second guessed his decision to let this girl stay upstairs. This was sneaky and scary. He didn't want any trouble and he felt like she would be just the reason to bring drama that he wanted to avoid. Frankie left her room and poured himself a shot of whiskey. He quickly downed it; then he took another. Anyone else would have called the police and reported the victim but the last thing Frankie needed was an investigation and cops snooping around his pub or the alleys that surrounded the place.

The basement of Frankie's pub was the site of an underground fight club. Frankie started the club as a means to settle occasional bar fights that would ensue after the guys had a few drinks too many. Some of Frankie's most faithful patrons were also participants in the club. Most people knew what was going on, but as long as Frankie paid his debts and followed the rules, he was allowed to keep going. The club had about 20 regulars from various walks of life. Some were teachers, others were police and firefighters. One man was a minister at the Baptist church up the block.

The basement had a padded wall on the far side. It was large enough that Frankie and Roger had installed a set of bleachers. The ring was sectioned off by gray mats Frankie picked up from the YMCA before it did a massive renovation a few years back. The mats were stained with blood from years of scuffing and fighting. Frankie padded the ceiling with additional insulation to muffle cheers and painful grunts. He didn't want people to hear anything upstairs. He also made an escape hatch that lead directly to the back alley where he had found Abby.

Frankie had made his money fighting and also skimmed 5% off the top of the winning bets made on the big bet days. The club was open two days a week and the days alternated depending on the week of the month. The first week of the month fighting happened on Mondays and Wednesdays. The second week of the month fighting only occurred on Tuesdays and Thursdays. The third week of the month, they only fought on Tuesdays and Fridays. Big bet nights were reserved for the fourth Saturday of the month. All bets had to be finalized by noon on Saturday. No betting was allowed on the floor and no bets under $100. Frankie's friend Larry handled the bets. Larry often helped run the bar as well. They alternated the fight nights to throw off anyone looking to cause trouble.

One night incumbent Mayor Cusher came into the bar. He was trying to appear more people friendly than how his image was being portrayed in the media. His first term as mayor was ending, and he was campaigning for reelection. He walked in with his campaign manager and other constituents.

"Are you Frankie?" the mayor asked.

Frankie wiped his hand on a towel and reached out to shake the mayor's hand. "Yeah that's me. This is my place. Been here for 10 years this May." Frankie was skeptical.

"I'm Mayor Cusher. I hear good things about you." He smiled.

"Thanks. Can't say the same for you though," Frankie said with a smirk on his face.

They all laughed.

"Listen, Frankie. It's no secret I'm running for a second term. I want to know what you need as a local business owner; it is someone like me who has the ability to make things happen. I have the ability to do a lot of things that could help your business be a bit more successful."

"I need a damn tax break!" Frankie joked.

"You can get one. You are a local business and you employ citizens of this city."

Frankie nodded his head and folded his arms.

The mayor continued, "Ok how about this. When is your entertainment and liquor license up?"

"In December. I've been trying to get the process started but I've been getting the run around from the licensing commission."

"Say no more." The mayor cheerfully patted Frankie on the shoulder. "Post a couple signs in your window for me. Talk to your people, and I'll take care of that license for you."

Frankie's face lit up with delight. He responded, "You got it! Have a scotch."

By the end of the night, Mayor Cusher was drunk and fighting in the basement rink. He lost the fight but was extremely pleased with the hospitality he received from the men in the pub. He won the election and celebrated with a "THANK YOU" banquet at Frankie's Pub aired live by 14 News. One of the first things Mayor Cusher did was extend Frankie's liquor license for another five years free of charge. He also forgave a few parking tickets and covered some other business for Frankie. Frankie and Cusher remained friends to this day.

Frankie's fight club was the best networking space in the city. It was a great little money maker and was fun. He made a lot of friends because of this place and was not about to lose it over any additional drama that a young injured woman could bring to his pub. He didn't know anything about her. He didn't know if someone left her there or followed her. He figured that someone must have wanted her dead, but whom? His head began to hurt with the influx of thoughts and questions that muddled through his mind. Frankie took another shot.

Roger and Larry were still downstairs cleaning the bar. Frankie almost forgot about them. He changed his shirt, which was now covered in rain water and blood, before he went back down. Roger noticed something wasn't right with Frankie's mood when he reappeared. He had worked long enough with Frankie to know when trouble was in the air. He walked over to Frankie.

Roger asked, "You ok, old man?"

"Go home, Roger. You too, Larry. Come in early tomorrow. We'll talk then." Frankie scratched his forehead trying to think of what he should do.

Larry was concerned as well and asked, "Are you sure? You don't look good right now."

Frankie grabbed the mop, "I'm fine. I'll finish up here. Just go on home and we'll chat in the morning about everything, but I'll need you both to be completely discrete."

Roger grabbed his jacket and walked out the door. Larry followed. Frankie took another shot, turned out the lights and went upstairs to the upper level apartment. *This is gonna be bad.*

THE NEXT DAY

The sun beamed over the window sill, gently warming Abigail's face. It woke her. The flesh of her cheek was rosy again, a drastic difference from the previous night's experience with hypothermia. She could feel her toes again, but the pain in her shoulder and thigh was not subtle. She felt an ache that crawled up her left side, making her bend her body to adjust to it. She stretched. The pain in her body was a sharp throb that intensified with the slightest movement. She realized she was totally naked underneath the shaggy blanket and immediately became anxious. The world around her was blurry and unfamiliar. She saw a figure moving and decided to lie still until she could be sure what it was and if she was safe enough to admit she was awake. Soon her sleepy eyes cleared enough for her to notice what she saw before her was the back of a young man. Things still were not fully clear. This was the first time she ever saw Roger. He was placing a tray of food on a table. The tray had a thick turkey sandwich, bottled water, an orange and a bag of chips. Roger turned around. He noticed her eyes had opened ever so slightly.

"You ok? I'm Roger. What's your name?"

Abigail was a little disoriented. Keeping her eyes fixed on Roger, she tried to get up but she was weaker than she had thought. She grunted from pain shooting through her body.

Roger sat on the edge of the bed. Abigail wanted to move away but her body was too weak. He said, "Hey hey home girl.

Relax." He gently patted her on the leg, "You've been asleep for about a day and you still seem tired. Get some rest and then some food. I left a sandwich over there. You need to eat. I'm gonna leave a buzzer right here. If you need me you hit it. It will vibrate in my pocket and I will come up ASAP! And, since you don't seem to have a name, I'm gonna call you Elvis. That's my fish's name and you resemble her." Roger smiled. Abigail didn't find his joke funny. "Seriously, you're in a good place. It's safe here. Frankie's a good man. He's cool. He'll take care of you. Just rest and we'll sort everything out when you're feeling better." He smiled again and said "You really do look like Elvis." Roger laughed. He got up, walked out and shut the door. Abigail tilted her head back. It sank slowly into the warm pillow. The lights fade out when she closed her eyes. She couldn't get enough sleep. Her body needed to heal and only rest would suffice.

Roger, Larry and Frankie had a few regulars come into the pub that day. Today was meatloaf day for anyone who wanted to eat. Frankie kept his menu simple by only cooking one type of food on each day. Monday was corned beef and cabbage day. Tuesday, Frankie served burgers and fries. Wednesday was buffalo wing day. Thursday they served baked chicken and rice. Friday was meatloaf and mashed potato day. No need to guess that today was Friday. Frankie and Roger served about 50 dinners that night and endless rounds of beer. Frankie felt like Abigail came at a perfect time. He had been thinking about hiring someone else to help around the pub and her extra hand of help was perfect. Roger worked really hard but couldn't manage the floor alone and Roger never took a day off. Larry would come in and help from time to time, but Larry's main job was to manage the fight club while Frankie kept the bar running upstairs. Frankie thought many times that he would close the fight club, but the money he made supplemented a lot of his overhead and he got a lot of side favors by running it. *Maybe I'll give it a few more months.* He said that to himself every few months.

A few members of the police force were regular pub patrons. They would come in and shoot the shit with Larry or Frankie. The police and detectives that came in tried to keep a close relationship with Frankie. Frankie was well respected. He had changed a lot in the past few years. Frankie used to be a hired hand for the Bulger crime family. He had broken a few faces for a nominal fee. Frankie was always loyal and when he was done, he quit. No one threatened him or asked questions, but there was a rumor that he had quit when he fell in love with a woman in the South End. She was a short, very thin Asian woman who worked in a launderette owned by her parents. Loving her was the only thing that scared him. He felt helpless around her.

After visiting the launderette once a week for a month, Frankie mustered up the strength to speak to her. She was very shy but liked Frankie too. Her parents were very strict, but allowed her to meet with Frankie only at a café they could see from the living room window. This went on for five months before the parents stopped watching from the window. Finally he stole a kiss and fell in love. Frankie wanted to marry her, so he bought a ring, but he never got a chance to give it to her. The woman died from what the police determined to be a mugging. Frankie was distraught and kept to himself for a year.

If there was anyone in the know, it was Frankie. He knew just about everything that was happening on the streets. He wasn't much of a snitch, but if it benefited him in anyway, he would point the police in the right direction if they asked the right questions. *Never volunteer information.* He felt anything good for the business didn't count as snitching. When two officers came in today, Frankie wasn't very friendly. He hoped there wasn't an investigation into a missing young girl who was shot and spotted in the area. Frankie was eager to close. He and Roger periodically checked on her. She slept like a baby.

The evening arrived and Abigail woke to a faint base line ringing in her head. It wasn't from the pub, but a car that drove by. She had a headache and the noise made her bite down on her teeth. She was in serious pain. She saw a small table with food and water next to her bed. She was fully rested but weak and the pain in her thigh was worsening. She saw her underwear on the bed rail. She quickly put on her underwear and fought against the sore muscles in her body. She sat on the edge of the bed looking around and examined her wounds. The door opened. She was frightened and quickly recovered her body with the comforter. Frankie walked in. She looked around as if she would like to escape but could not.

"Hey, girly. Relax. I didn't mean to barge in; I thought you were still asleep. You had two bullet wounds. The one here in your shoulder went straight in and out. This one on your thigh, I removed it for you. I'm no doctor, but I've been shot a few times my damn self." He pointed to a few scars on his stomach. "Do you remember what happened? Are you from Boston?"

Abigail shook her head.

"Where are you from kid? What's your name?"

Abigail seemed lost; she was torn. *Who is this man? Can I trust him?* Her instinct told her to trust no one, but her body reminded her she was too weak to have any options. She had no choice but to let Frankie take her away and have his way with her.

"When you're ready to talk, let me know. Against my better judgment... you can stay here until you figure things out. I need an extra hand around anyway. I'll pay you. It's up to you. Do what you want; just don't bring trouble over here. You look like you're gonna be a handful." Frank turned his back to leave the room. "When you get the strength, wash up and come down for dinner. That food over there is stale." Frankie picked up the stale sandwich and left the room. Immediately after Frankie stepped out, Larry peered into the room and stared Abigail up and down before he turned away and closed the door. Abigail met his eyes confidently.

Larry was obviously uncomfortable with the idea of Abigail staying at the pub. Larry asked Frankie, "What the hell are you thinking?"

Frankie answered, "I don't know. I felt it was the right thing to do."

"You can't just bring wounded runaways around here. You know we have enough heat already. You know nothing about her!"

"Well she's here now! What do you want me to do? You want me to toss her out back out on the streets?" Frankie was upset.

"Yes! Give her a sandwich or something if it makes you feel better and send her ass out the back door. Figure it out, but she needs to go. I'm not trying to be mean. Maybe if someone wasn't trying to kill her, I wouldn't care so much. You have to think about what you're doing."

"I know. I have. She stays." Frankie walked away.

"I hope you know what you're doing," Larry said as he followed Frankie back to the bar.

Abigail's ears were tight on that conversation. She heard the whole thing and figured she would have to keep her eyes on Larry. However, she knew he had a point. They didn't know her or anything about her. She hoped to leave before she overstayed her welcome. She also didn't remember much about how she arrived in the alley and didn't want to bring this man or his place additional trouble. It seemed they were having problems of their own.

Abby had a small bag strapped over her shoulder when Frankie picked her up. Neither he nor Roger had gone through her stuff. He hung the bag from the edge of the bed. The bag was black leather with a shoulder strap and a flap that covered the opening. She grabbed it and quickly ruffled through it. Her things were intact. She knew there wasn't a need to do a full investigation of the contents of her purse. There was nothing in there that would spark her memory of what happened. She knew who she was but the events of the past few days eluded her. Actually, the more she thought about her past, the less she recalled. Abigail saw her clothes hanging in the corner on what seemed to be a towel rack. She made an attempt to stand up. Her weak leg gave in. She almost fell but managed to stay on her feet by shifting her body weight to the other leg. Her feet were cold. *Where are my shoes?*

Abigail put on some sweat pants, socks and a Red Sox t shirt left at the foot of the bed. Her clothes from the other night were still wet. She felt warm but the pain continued to distract her desire to run. She saw water on the table. She was starving. Her belly ached and growled from the natural need for food. She grabbed the glass of water and downed it. Some of the water missed her mouth and ran down the sides of her face. It was warm but it was refreshing. She didn't remember water tasting this good. She hobbled over to the window and looked out. She didn't see anything suspicious, but she didn't know what she was looking for. *I give up.* On the sill, she saw a rubber band and used it to tie her hair back.

Abigail opened the door to her room. She saw an open area that looked like it used to hold dance classes. There were a few punching bags and weights. The hard wood floor was a bright shiny maple. She investigated the bathroom before she realized she had to pee badly. The toilet was relatively clean for a man's house. She used the toilet and washed her hands. The small mirror above the sink had small splatters of tooth paste and soap on it. She splashed her face with water. *I need to bathe.* She smelled a faint aroma of cooked food. She couldn't resist the desire to eat and followed the smell to the ground floor of the bar. Walking down the stairs was torture. Abigail limped her way down, step by step. She held on to a rail. When she reached the main floor, she looked around the corner and saw Frankie and Roger sitting at the table having a dinner consisting of meatloaf, mashed potatoes and corn. She stood still.

Roger smirked when he saw her glance at the food. "Good morning, Elvis. Come get some chow."

"Yeah you haven't eaten in a day. Don't be shy, take a seat and eat."

Frankie stood up as Abigail approached the table. He pulled out a chair for her. He went into the kitchen and made her a plate. Abigail didn't speak. She inspected the pub from corner to corner.

"Where are you from, Elvis?" Roger tried to be friendly. "Can you speak? Do you have a family?"

Frankie came out of the kitchen and slapped down a plate and a glass of water in front of Abby. Her eyes widened like a child. She was starving. There was a big heap of meatloaf with gravy spilling over the top of a hump of mashed potatoes. "Roger, get out her face! Eat up, you need it. And take one of these." He pushed a bottle of Motrin across the table. She immediately took the medicine and ate the food. She stuffed her face as if she hadn't eaten in weeks. The meatloaf was juicy and flavorful. The corn was sweet and buttery. Her mouth watered as she devoured every morsel on her plate. Frankie looked at Roger. Roger shook his head and continued eating his food.

As time went on, Abigail made a decision to stay for a while. Frankie showed her around the kitchen and paid her for working the bar. He taught her how to mix drinks, showed her how to change and connect the beer tap, and showed her the register. She was a quick learner. During all this time they spent together training, she still didn't speak for a week. She nodded and absorbed everything Frankie told her, especially his warnings about the male patrons. Her first word was "Fuck" when she burned herself in the kitchen with hot grease. It was an exciting moment for the guys since they were only used to hearing moans and groans from the pain she felt in her leg and shoulder from the bullet wound. They clapped and whistled.

"SHE SPEAKS!" Roger shouted.

Frankie followed with, "Break out the champagne." For now, Frankie and Roger were her only refuge from whatever she was running from. She decided this was a great place to lay low so she could sort things out. She was doing fine, but the only thing she could not escape from were her recurring vivid and violent nightmares.

The night was moist and calm. The rain left a humid mist upon the street, just light of being classified as fog. Abigail and Roger cleaned up the bar from top to bottom. At the end of the night, Abby put up the last chair, hit the lights and headed to her room. Roger headed to the back door to leave.

"I can tuck you in if you like," Roger said just before she turned up the stairs. He winked. Abigail stuck up her middle finger and slipped away.

CHAPTER 4

THEY COULDN'T SLEEP

Roger Atkins spent most of his late nights working on engineering projects in his garage. He spent most of his spare change shopping on Amazon buying DC motors, cables, gears and various parts he would need to see his vision come alive. He liked to be alone most of the time and always had some sort of project that required private focus time. He was very secretive about his designs; he wouldn't share them with anyone at all. Most of his projects consisted of robotic vehicles, other motorized gadgets and protective gear for law enforcement. Many of his experiments were defective and many sat incomplete because there never was enough time to finish before the next bright idea came streaming into his mind. Roger's engineering career had been over before it started.

At MIT he was at the top of his class. He was envied by many of the students and was extremely popular among the students and faculty at the school. By Roger's sophomore year, he had won various awards, including the most prestigious MIT Student Engineer of the Year Award, which landed him an internship at Deere's engine manufacturing facility. This was the first time the award had been given to a sophomore. It was rare that the award didn't go to a senior student.

One day, Roger called the dean of students and had a long talk about his mother's health and how he needed to leave for a year and return the next fall. He convinced the dean to allow him to retain his scholarship for when he returned a year later. The dean agreed in writing to hold Roger's scholarship until he returned. Roger never returned. Truth is, Roger felt like MIT was not the place for him. Many students felt threatened by his abilities and refused to befriend him. It was true that his mother's health was not the best, but it hadn't been good for many years now; this was just his excuse. Roger had received a few threats from students and unknown sources for his unmatched success. Some students, faculty and parents felt that he deprived other students of a chance at recognition. After all of this, Roger took a hiatus from engineering projects for a few years. Since he had left MIT, Roger lost his engineering mojo. He just couldn't build anything that worked.

Roger lived at home with his mother, Terry Atkins, in a three bedroom, two–floor Cape Cod home built in 1964. Roger's mother had renovated the house when they moved in, but the house was overdue for a serious update as witnessed by the '80s Italian lacquer furniture and wooden beads hanging in the entry ways.

Roger's room was on the ground level. He had posters on the walls of Halle Berry and Melissa Ford. One wall was practically covered by a shelf full of '80s action figures. He had three *For Her Pleasure* Trojan condoms between Heman and Chitara of the ThunderCats. For many months, he considered asking Frankie about renting the room above the bar where Abigail was now staying, but he didn't think Frankie wanted company. Although he enjoyed living with his mother, he thought he needed some private space once in a while. Roger also liked having the space to work on his designs where no one would snoop or be annoyed with the noise. He also needed a significant amount of space and storage to be able to create and invent. *Maybe when Frankie closes the fight club he'll let me stay in the basement.*

Roger and Abigail became good friends as the months passed. He had never been very open about his past or let her know too much about his personal life. He was slightly embarrassed that he didn't have much of a life outside of Frankie's pub. Roger and Abigail didn't initially like one another. It probably started when he first called her Elvis. He knew she didn't like it, but she would never give him the satisfaction of letting him know that it irked her nerves. Abigail barely made eye contact with Roger for the first two weeks she was there. She didn't crack a smile until the day he tripped over the mop and cracked his chin on the counter. That was the first time she spoke to him.

"You ok?"

Maybe she cared. Roger was humiliated, "It would help if you weren't smirking," he said as he blushed with embarrassment.

Roger placed a rag on his chin to catch the blood. Abigail drove him to the emergency room that night. As they waited in the waiting room, it was the first time she opened up and told him about the strange nightmares that were keeping her up at night. Her voice sang to him like a bird whistling at the morning sun after a night of thunderous rain. He didn't have a more interesting story to share, so he just listened and there, he fell in love with her. He didn't know if he was listening to her story or imagining himself kissing her on the cheek and neck, smelling her hair, and enjoying her body. Roger did, however, grab enough information to understand why Abigail kept to herself. She was trying to set things straight in her mind. Half the time she was trying to put the pieces of her life together and just thinking. Frivolous conversations weren't Abigail's priority.

After Roger got six stitches in his chin, she drove him home. They sat outside in the car for hours as she gave him a more vivid description of some of her dreams. Roger's eyes were open wide while listening to the details. He didn't have a clue what they meant but was sure that having similar dreams over and over meant something important. He figured they must be connected. *Write them down,* he thought. Eventually he opened up to her about his ongoing experiments. She was actually interested and wanted to know more about them. He was honest with her that they didn't work, but working on things made him happy. She thought it was cool.

The time was just past 2:30 in the morning. Roger had spent his night playing with a mini robotic device that he had built a few months earlier. It was supposed to be a prototype for an unmanned solar powered cargo transportation device that would safely and securely transport hazardous or sensitive material from one warehouse to another. If the smaller prototype worked, a larger one should work without a problem, or so he thought. No matter how many times he played with it, it kept overheating and sparking. He had reworked the design numerous times but the prototype would not travel more than three feet without a malfunction. He was getting bored with it so he turned on his laptop and checked his email. *No new messages* - in his Gmail account. He checked his Facebook account. He had a few spam posts on his wall and a few friend requests from fellow geeks from the *Robotic Pulse* fan page. He often posted his ideas and got feedback from other self proclaimed engineers and inventors. *This is boring.*

Roger left his room and went into the kitchen. On his way, he saw his mother asleep in the recliner with the TV still on. He walked into the room and turned off the set. He was careful not to wake his mother. Roger then went into the kitchen and grabbed a glass of water. He gulped it down quickly, went into the bathroom, urinated and went back to his room.

Finally, Roger pulled out his phone and sent Abigail a text message, "YOU UP, ELVIS?" She didn't respond. Roger laid in his bed and closed his eyes.

"I can't fucking sleep!"

Frankie was in his room doing pushups. He had a lot on his mind, starting with the fight club, Abigail, bills... He wanted to tell Larry that it was time to call it quits and just focus on legit business deals only. He and Larry argued about the state of the club five months earlier when it cost Frankie a $20,000 payment to the Albano family.

One evening Mousy Albano had challenged Frankie to a fight. They had argued over a $2,500 debt Mousy owed Larry. Little by little, the argument got personal; and Mousy bet double or nothing that he could kick Frankie's ass. Frankie hadn't fought in a while but was sure he could win. By the end of the fight, Frankie had a fat lip and Mousy had a ride to the hospital. Mousy didn't come out of a coma for 10 days. His father and a few goons bum rushed the pub and demanded $15,000. So, Frankie paid out the money. Plus he had lost $5,000 in winnings. After that incident Frankie decided never to fight again. Larry considered the event extraneous and unpredictable.

Frankie also spent a significant amount of time thinking about Abigail as well. He was concerned for her safety and besides being overwhelmed with it, he wasn't sure that running the fight club was the best situation for her. The club was completely connected to underground activity and he was positive that whoever shot her was also connected to something shady. *Any moment one of those bastards could come in here.* Frankie began to feel like Abigail was a daughter to him. He was protective of her and thought of her safety at all times.

Anytime a man groped her or said anything inappropriate, he would kick them out immediately. One time Frankie had stepped out to buy a few bags of ice when the ice machine was down. When he came back, he caught the tail end of a situation where Abigail had dragged a man out of the bar by his collar and kicked him in the groin. Even though she could handle her own, he took care of all disrespect directed toward her. The man was never allowed back in the bar even though he had been a loyal patron for five years.

Frankie was also concerned about the noises he heard coming from her room from time to time. He usually slept with his TV on, but occasionally he would hear moans and groans coming from her room. At first he thought she was in the room masturbating so he would turn up the TV and try to ignore the sounds. When the noise persisted, he decided to check up on her and realized she was having nightmares. He peeked into her room and saw her tossing and turning in the bed. She gritted her teeth and scratched the bed. She would shout, speaking in languages he didn't understand. Once he grabbed her to wake her and she scratched his face. Even then she didn't fully wake up. From then on, he would ignore such nighttime sounds.

That night, Frankie's mind raced incessantly, obsessing over his responsibilities and the difficult decisions that needed to be made each day to keep the pub fully operational. The mysterious Abigail was only one more thing adding fuel to the tormenting fire in his mind. He prayed for the morning news to come on, looking forward to the new day, but sunrise was still a few hours away.

The TV played real estate infomercials as he pushed up and down against the hardwood floor. He did 100 pushups without stopping. He picked up a pair of 45 lb weights and began doing bicep curls. He did sets of 20, alternating arms. Staying strong and physically fit was a passion of his; it was also a means for him to calm down or think. Frankie was used to his fitness regimen. He had followed it for 25 years. It started as a part of his job requirement in his former life, and remained an important piece of his daily ritual. After the biceps, Frankie focused on his shoulders and then his triceps. He broke a sweat. Little by little his t–shirt began to soak with sweat. It gathered at his chin and eventually dripped down to the floor. Once Frankie was done, he sat on the edge of his bed to meditate and pray. Frankie didn't talk to God much, unless he felt he really needed a judgment free friend. He felt that God was the only friend who could listen without interruption. A talk with God was declared the immediate solution to remedy this headache now pounding between his ears.

Frankie had suffered from depression for many years. He was haunted by the faces of people he had killed or hurt in his past. When he quit the hired hand business, he had seen a psychiatrist who prescribed him Zoloft. He didn't like the side effects and quit cold turkey. For three months he had nightmares and found himself walking the ledge of many buildings contemplating life and death. He understood how tormenting nightmares could be to a person. He felt Abigail's pain and worried if she would find herself, one day, pacing along a ledge. Those depressing days were brutal, and Frankie feared that he would slip back into depression if he didn't make some difficult choices soon.

Abigail sat on the edge of her bed. She saw the text from Roger. She ignored it and carried on with what she was doing. Abigail was rummaging through her purse again. She had laid out her license which read:

ABIGAIL PAIGE
652 SCOTT STREET
UNIT 6
UTICA, NY
She put the license away.

She had a small stack of cash totaling about $250, a key, eye shadow, dark brown lipstick, and a small black King James bible– both new and Old Testament. She flipped through the pages from back to front. The only thing she saw in the book was a note on the last page in red ink that read E2 ON THE FIRST FOURTEEN. *This doesn't mean shit to me right now.* Her frustration level soared to critical.

She put her stuff away again and laid down to go to sleep. She let out a deep sigh. Then her phone rang. It was Roger. She picked up with a sleepy voice. "Hey Roggie bear."

"Hey Elvis. Just checking to see if you were ok. You seemed a little bothered today."

"I'm bothered every day."

"You just ignore my texts now?"

"Yes!"

They giggled.

She asked, "What are you working on now? I hear a catastrophe brewing in the background. It sounds like something wants to explode over there."

"If I explained, you wouldn't get it."

"Well maybe I can come by and check it out tomorrow."

Roger was a little shocked and happy. He always wanted to spend time with her but never had a chance and here it was. "Ok. If you're not being cynical, then that would be really cool. As long as you don't laugh. Half of my ideas don't work."

"Half of my brain doesn't work, so we're pretty even."

"Still can't put the pieces together?"

"The rabbit hole goes deeper and deeper every day. Does *E2 on the First Fourteen* sound familiar to you?"

"Not in the least. Where's that coming from?"

"Good question. It was written in this... oh never mind. I'm hoping something will jar my memory but it's more complicated than that, I guess."

"What about the dreams?"

"I still have those from time to time. It's been getting worse. I try to keep my iPod playing while I sleep. It helps sometimes but once the batteries go…"

Another spark went off on one of Roger's experiments. "OW! Shit!"

Abigail laughed. "Let me let you go before you kill yourself. Any final words for the eulogy?"

"SHUT UP!"

"Duly noted. Good night!" They hung up.

Abigail laid her head down on the pillow and tucked herself in. She liked to feel the fleece from the blanket run over her legs when she was tired. Her initial goal was to avoid sleep as much as possible, but her body needed rest. Her head continued to sink into the pillow. She fought the urge all night but couldn't resist the desire to close her eyes. Her body was getting more and more comfortable. Sleep weighed over her body, sucking her in like a drain. Her head tilted to the side. Slowly she drifted into a deep slumber.

Abigail's head moved frantically from side to side as her world spun from a dark city night into a murky rain forest, thick with trees and dense fog. She lay on the muddy soil in a fetal position, naked and cold. The black ground crept up over her body. She peeled her body out of the position and stood up. Her legs wobbled as if it was her first time walking. The trees towered over her, leaning inward with their upper branches tangling overhead. Black snakes slithered down the trucks and hissed all around. She stood in the midst of the shiny black bark that oozed down like crude oil over a rusty pipe. She snapped her neck around upon hearing a faint sound coming from the bushes. Suddenly, she heard feet pounding against black broken leaves, vines and twine.

"Get her!" voices cried out from between the brush.

She began to run, dodging the vines that reached out for her arms and legs. One vine caught her and twisted around her neck stopping her in her tracks. Four more vines grabbed her arms and legs, lifting her up off the ground, sprawling her out above the jungle floor. Her wrists and ankles bled from the places where the vines attached themselves to her body. Thorns pierced into her skin. Loud drums played in her head faster and faster as she hung above the slithery ground. Suddenly, the vines let go and she fell; but she landed flat on her feet, which smashed against the wet leaves and tree roots. She ran again and tripped. Her heart pounded against the back of her chest. The leaves closed in around her, getting thicker. It was getting harder to move through the thicket. She looked back and saw jungle natives in pursuit. She stood up again and ran.

Black oily ooze flowed out of her mouth to the back of her neck and down her spine. She screamed in agony, stretching her arm, gripping at her back as far as she could reach. The oil burned and eventually caught fire as she continued to run. She screamed again and the scream sounded like the screech of a bird of prey. She turned and looked at the men behind her to see if they were gaining ground.

"Ado a balidah," she yelled at the men behind her.

They were closing in on her. She was suddenly hit with an arrow in her shoulder. She screamed in pain. The world became blurry. They must have poisoned the tip of the arrow. She looked back again to see where she was; the native men were gone but two men in suits were now chasing her. She ran until she came to the edge of a cliff. The men were getting closer; she had no choice. She jumped off the cliff into a cloud of smoke. The smoke engulfed her body. When it cleared, she could see the ground approaching fast. Right before she hit the ground, she woke. She sat up straight. Abigail was breathing hard and sweating.

"What the fuck?" She threw her head back on the pillow and caught her breath.

Larry Crawford was a tall, big bellied Irish man standing 6'3" who lived a simple, lonely life. He had a one bedroom apartment in Cambridge, not too far from the Boston line. His apartment was in an old lingerie factory that was built in 1826. He lived on the third floor which had four other apartments on it. The interior of his apartment was an IKEA showcase and could serve as a model space in the IKEA department store. His apartment was very neat and clean with exposed brick walls and hardwood floors. The apartment looked like a sports bar lounge with sleek modern furniture and sports memorabilia. He was a collector. In separate frames hanging from the walls, he had a Larry Bird jersey, a Drew Bledsoe Jersey, and a signed Bobby Orr Boston Bruins jersey. On the mantle, he had various signed baseballs, gloves and cards in glass cases. On the side was a wet bar with a granite counter top and various top shelf spirits.

He had 14 foot high ceilings and a simple ceiling fan. Larry's bedroom was equally as neat and organized as the rest of his apartment. His closet was carefully arranged. The shoes were neatly stacked on racks. His dress shirts were folded and color coordinated. His slacks and jeans were hung on hangers. All of his clothes fit into the closet. He didn't have very many. His bedroom had a queen sized bed covered in a fitted sheet with two white pillows and the blankets neatly folded at the foot of the bed. He had a 42 inch Toshiba flat screen TV on a stand, a cable box and no other furniture. Needless to say, Larry was very particular about his apartment. He didn't have much furniture, so that way he could keep track of what he had. He hated clutter in his living space and refused to allow anyone to enter his apartment while wearing shoes. No eating was allowed out of the kitchen.

Larry tapped away on his computer seemingly preoccupied with crunching numbers for the pub. In secret, Larry had a hidden agenda. He sat in his apartment on the couch with his bifocal glasses drinking a glass of milk, rum and ice. His eyes were glued to the screen. He typed into the Google search engine "ABIGAIL PAIGE," searching for missing persons' reports to see if Abigail's name or photo had surfaced. *Nothing!* He tried another search "MISSING WOMAN UTICA, NEW YORK." Nothing came up. He sipped his drink and grunted. He tried again, "RUNAWAY ABIGAIL PAIGE UTICA, NEW YORK." *Nothing! That slippery bitch.*

Larry had become obsessed with getting to the bottom of Abigail's mysterious appearance and didn't trust her situation one bit. She had been around for a while and Larry didn't understand why her memories hadn't returned by now. *She's lying!*

He grew to think she was tolerable, but didn't feel she was worthy of his complete loyalty and adoration, especially since she was curt and often sported an attitude he cared not to entertain. He made a concerted effort to be sure he didn't get too attached or too emotionally involved. He couldn't understand why Frankie, who was so street smart, could be so weak for this girl. *She could ruin everything.* He didn't even bother questioning why Roger allowed himself to get attached. *Horny bastard!*

The soft blue glow of the computer screen illuminated his chubby semi wrinkly face. He kept thinking of search combinations he hadn't tried. "MISSING PERSON'S REPORT UTICA, NY." *Again, nothing.* He was silently enraged. He clenched his fist and took a sip of his drink. He was determined and focused. The time slipped away. Hours passed and Larry wouldn't give up on finding a lead or a clue.

"Maybe I should hire a private investigator." But he had a feeling that wherever she was coming from, she had covered her tracks well. He thought that maybe she was lying about her memory loss. It made sense. Maybe she didn't want to be found and was intentionally hiding in the pub, away from everything she knew. Even if she was telling the truth, his research would prove that as well. He couldn't really figure her out, but he insisted that understanding the mysteries of Abigail Paige was going to be his number one priority. He was determined to prove to Frankie that she was not good for business or for him. She had changed Frankie into a person he didn't understand anymore. Larry didn't like it.

The sky was a bluish black as the sun set its course to rise for the day. Abigail counted the cracks in the ceiling until the six o'clock morning news came on. She turned on the TV and waited for the weather report. It was 73 degrees. She decided to go for a short run to buy herself time. She put on her sneakers and sweats, grabbed her keys and headed out the door.

CHAPTER 5

BOSTON POLICE STATION 10:00 AM

The Police station buzzed with detectives, officers and criminals. Many of the detectives had recently arrived for the day and were just punching in. Detective Sydney Brown pulled up to the precinct, ready for the impending argument of Boston baseball versus New York baseball. Detective Brown was a 38 year old New York–born homicide detective for the Boston Police Homicide Unit. He was six feet tall with a medium build, short brown hair and a short beard.

He had worked for the department for the past eight years as a detective after serving as an officer for the previous five years. He had started in the Narcotics Unit but quickly found out that homicide was his niche. He pulled his 2009 black Toyota Camry into a parking space, locked the door and walked to the front door.

"Here it comes," he thought to himself.

"How about those Yankees?" the man at the front desk yelled out. His name was Barkley Duckworth, a soon to be retired officer who decided to spend his last six months on the force behind the front desk.

"Good morning, Duck," he said full of annoyance. It was best to avoid the question. He rolled his eyes and walked to the second floor and into the staff lounge. It was empty for a change. Brown was relieved. He filled a mug with Folgers decaf. One of the rookies was usually on assignment to keep coffee hot and ready. After filling his cup and adding sugar, he headed back to his desk, hoping to avoid an argument about last night's baseball game. Though he did everything in his power to quietly return to his desk, Detective Chris Duffy noticed Brown's effort to slip by.

"Oh Brownie. Where are you going?" Duffy teased.

"Stuff it Duffy, I don't wanna hear it."

"Just hand over the spoils, Brownie. This is the debt you pay for being a Yankee fan."

"It's not about winning the battle…" Brown insists.

The crowd of cops and detectives chime in, "It's about winning the war." They laugh.

"No! It's about winning the game! Shut up with that crap. Pay up you sore loser!" Duffy gloated. Brown handed over two fifty dollar bills. Duffy held the money up to the light, "I gotta check the authenticity of these bills. Can't trust a New Yorker these days."

"Shut up or next time you're getting your money in pennies and scratch offs. Enjoy your insignificant victory. They don't happen very often, Duffy. So we know you have to soak it in when you can." The crowd laughed as Brown bitterly walked away. *FUCKING BASTARDS!* Detective Brown sipped his coffee as walked back to his desk. Piles of papers were added to his desk since he had left yesterday evening. As he shuffled through some of the papers, he was interrupted by Meghan Finch.

Meghan Finch was ready to work. "Good morning Detective Brown."

"Good morning, Detective Finch." He barely made eye contact as he shuffled through some papers on his desk. "I can't believe this." He was upset about the amount of paperwork left for him to review.

"I know you haven't had much time at your desk, but we have to go. A call just came in from Tammy. There's a new case that's come in and Downy wants us over there now."

"Hope it's a good one. Debrief me on the way." Detective Brown and Detective Finch head out quickly.

Meghan Finch was a new detective that had been assigned to shadow Sydney Brown for three months per order of her precinct. She was 5'4", strong and red–headed with a few freckles on her nose and cheeks. Meghan had been a police officer at the precinct for about four years before she began their homicide detective training program. Finch was known to be pretty tough. She did, however, have to take a month off after being punched in the face at a Beanie Man concert. Her nose was broken, and when she passed out from the blow, her face hit the pavement and her cheek bone was fractured. This happened her second year on the force. The assailant was a drunken UMass student named Darcy Small who had just lost his mother that morning. His friends took him out to clear his mind, and things didn't go very well. Meghan sympathized with the kid and convinced the judge to lighten the sentence if he promised to attend counseling for three months and volunteer at the Every Woman's Center on campus. They sent biweekly reports of his progress and hour logs to Finch's lawyer.

Finch had about a week left under Brown's supervision. Things were going pretty well and she was ready to embark on her full–time career in the homicide unit. Brown trusted Meghan enough to let her take the lead on the last investigation, which she led successfully. In the last investigation, Finch ruffled a few feathers when she investigated a robbery that led to the arrest of Sean Pearson, the youngest son of Jackson Pearson, a real estate tycoon who was in the process of negotiating the purchase of a highly sought after site by the Boston Harbor. The case against his son was solid. There were four witnesses, 30 minutes of footage, matching serial numbers, and a snitch. The case got even more interesting when Finch was offered $500,000 to "lose evidence." She refused.

Meghan was engaged to a young man, Anthony Fowler, who was a debt consolidation specialist at Eastern Bay State Credit Counseling Corporation. Anthony and Meghan met at a Starbucks as she was walking the beat with Officer Hanson Granby. Anthony wasn't shy about asking her for her phone number after she had given him a quarter to cover the rest of his tab. His bill was $3.17. He found the three dollar bills with ease but fumbled around to come up with the last 17 cents. Finch reached in her pocket and pulled out the quarter.

"I got it," Finch said. She dropped the quarter in his hand and smiled.

"Thanks," he said.

"Don't mention it. It's not a problem."

"It's nice when a woman doesn't mind paying the bill," he said as he smirked.

She smiled and said, "Not when it's a cheap date."

"So then let's make a real date. I'll even pay this time."

She hesitated at first but finally agreed.

For their first date, Meghan agreed to meet Anthony at the Locke–Ober, a seafood restaurant in downtown Boston rather than having him pick her up. At this point in the dating game she didn't feel comfortable with him knowing where she lived. Anthony was mesmerized when she showed up in a spring yellow sleeveless dress, gathered at the waist, with nude colored three inch heels. She had on a pearl necklace, a pearl bracelet with matching earrings. Her hair was pulled back into a ponytail. Anthony met her at the door. He was wearing a light blue button shirt, khaki colored slacks and loafers. He fit the description of tall, dark and handsome. He greeted her with an orchid flower and kissed her on the cheek. He loved the soft scent of her perfume. She smelled clean, sweet and fresh. Anthony had liked her in the uniform but was love struck after seeing her in that dress.

He whispered in her ear, "You look amazing."

She replied, "Thank you." He had put a smile on her face.

He gently touched her on her waist and guided her into the lobby.

Anthony made reservations for 7:30 pm. Once they were seated, Meghan ordered a classic Caesar Salad and the Honey Glazed Salmon with a baked potato and pea shoots. Anthony ordered the house salad with broiled scrod, mashed potatoes and broccoli. They agreed to share a bottle of Sauvignon Blanc.

Anthony fell in with her love after their first date. He had made up his mind that she was going to be the one he would marry. Meghan was cautious about giving in to her feelings, but after their vacation to Costa Rica, she was hooked. Six months later they were engaged, and he moved into Meghan's house. Meghan and Anthony's relationship progressed and they set the date for their wedding for Mother's Day weekend of the following year. Several weeks after the engagement, Anthony was heading home from a long day of work and taking his mother on errands. He was five blocks away from the house when three joyriding teenagers ran a traffic light going 70 miles per hour. They hit Anthony's car in the driver's side door. His car flipped over three times before it came to a halt on its roof.

Meghan was made aware of the accident about 30 minutes after it happened. She drove to the site of the accident and went into hysterics. Detective Tammy was on the scene. She and Finch were decent friends at that time. Tammy took Finch to the hospital to wait with Anthony's family. Anthony sat in a coma for two days before he stopped breathing. Finch still wore her engagement ring.

From her first day in homicide training, Meghan Finch had impressed Sydney Brown with her competency, accurately detailed descriptions and organizational skills which surpassed his own. She thought outside of the box on each case and helped bring cases quickly to a tight close. She developed a virtual checklist of "things to look for and do" an evidence log which listed: ITEM IMAGE, NAME, LOCATION, DIMENSIONS, and DESCRIPTION columns. She uploaded the spreadsheet to a cloud drive and showed Brown how to edit and immediately upload the file so there would be immediate access at the precinct while they were still on the scene. She collected information on her phone and immediately uploaded the content to be analyzed later. The chief could also review the files as they were in the process of being created. Her method of on–site data collection was adopted by 10 other districts within the month. During her training, they covered six homicides, either leading the investigations or tagging along with other investigative teams.

About a month earlier, Detective Finch and Detective Brown's relationship elevated and became intimate. Sydney started the flirtatious interactions with playful text messages before and after the shift. He figured testing the water with subtle flirts would give Finch a route to easily ignore him or reciprocate if that's what she wanted to do. Finch initially hesitated to flirt back because she didn't want anything to seem afoul or have things seem like she was losing focus of why they were working together. Her attraction was growing stronger but despite her lingering feelings for Anthony, she couldn't resist. *What would it hurt?* Eventually, the flirtations turned to light touches on the neck, ear or hand. He would find reasons to move her hair off her shoulder or take a quick sniff of her perfume whenever he reached past her.

One evening, Finch showed up to Sydney's house looking for an ear. It was somewhere close to 12 am and she was having trouble sleeping. She drove around the city for an hour before she sent him a text. "YOU UP, BROWNIE?" She was partially shy about being forward with him. *What if he has a woman over?*

Sydney had been up cleaning his gun and watching sports highlights on ESPN. He was wearing a white tank top and gray sweats with white Hanes socks. The Giants were pissing him off all season, but they had beaten the Patriots in the playoffs; and he couldn't wait until he ran into Chris Duffy on Monday to rub it in. When he received the text from Meghan his heart raced. He was a little anxious because he wasn't sure why she was asking whether or not he was awake. She never texted him this late, so he was concerned. It wasn't 30 seconds before he replied, "YES. YOU OK?" He hoped she would respond swiftly and she did.

"NEED COMPANY," she wrote back.

He mistook her text as a question and thus answered, "I WOULD LOVE IT…" He was genuinely concerned for her well being, but also hoped she was looking for a little more than a shoulder to cry on. He couldn't be sure with her; she was so complicated and hard to read. It aggravated him and enticed him at the same time. Sometimes he would look for signs but she would never give in. He didn't know when things were going to be business or pleasure, if she would be Finch or Meghan, hungry or horny. Either way he was there to support her intentions and was willing to let her decide where things would go. She was destined to be an awesome coworker if nothing else. "COME BY. I'LL BE UP IF YOU LIKE." He was eager to see her.

"BE THERE IN 5." Meghan wasn't far away. She didn't intentionally drive close to his house, but once she realized how close she was to Sydney's house, she was inclined to message him. Her eyes were getting heavy anyway and the ride home was going to require a bit more stamina than she could afford at the moment. Meghan drove a gunmetal gray 2007 Honda Accord. She connected her iPod through the audio port. It had played the R&B artist Brandy's album Full Moon, almost to its completion by time she felt tired. She was ready for a break.

Meghan was frustrated with the Pearson case and harassing messages she received from anonymous sources concerning the details and individuals involved. One man would call from time to time saying, "Watch your ass, bitch." or "Take the deal and fuck off." She tried to get a trace on the calls, but her efforts were unsuccessful.

After a few shots of Glenlivet 18, all reservations were eliminated. The first time they had sex, Finch made the first move. She was attracted to Sydney Brown from the first time she had met him a year ago, but she had kept it to herself until that particular evening when she needed company. Ever since then they would sneak off in between assignments and find places in the precinct they could have private time.

Finch's first interrogation consisted of a case dealing with four young adults suspected of kidnapping and murder over an unpaid drug debt. The victim was 23 year old Dale Walker. Dale Walker was a known felon with a rap sheet that went back to assault and battery charges received at the age of 13. Boston detectives were familiar with this kid. Brown wanted to see how Finch handled an interrogation where most of the evidence was circumstantial. They needed a confession or a witness to verify their hunch that these four were at the center of the murder. Finch's strategy was to start by putting two of the four suspects in separate rooms, and then group the other two in a separate room to appear as if they were conspiring against the others. Brown sat back and watched it all unfold. He refused to help with the questioning and would only interfere if things got out of hand.

Patrick "Patty" Quibby was in room 4C. He sat in the room with his arms folded. He wore an over sized black shirt that read MONEY, POWER, RESPECT. Finch took the folder of evidence and beefed it up, grabbing a few papers out of the recycle bin. She walked in and sat down.

"Patty. Patty, right?"

"Yes." He didn't give her eye contact.

"My name is Detective Meghan Finch. I'm leading the investigation on this case and I just need a few more details to write this report before it's complete."

"I'm not sure what this is about or how I can help you. Why am I here?"

"Dale Walker. He was murdered two evenings ago. I just needed a few more details here so we can wrap this up."

"Dale? I haven't seen Dale in like three weeks."

"Are you sure?" She reached in her folder.

"That's a picture of you and Dale outside of the McQuick's on Lincoln a week ago. I have pages and pages of phone calls between you and Dale's cell phone this Monday. Here is a list of the text correspondences between you and him the day he first disappeared..." She tossed a thick folder on the desk.

"So what!? I ain't got shit to do with that boy getting murdered."

"I'm not here asking for you to tell me what happened. I already know. And your friend Drew gave us a five page statement..." She pulled out some papers in the back that had nothing to do with anything, but Patty was too stupid to look closely.

"WHAT!?"

"I was just gonna ask you your address so we could complete the paperwork to charge you with first degree murder."

"DREW? Nah. Drew wouldn't even..."

"Drew is here in the other room waiting for a ride home. He's identified you as the shooter and wishes to take a plea deal."

"Bullshit. I had nothing to do with it."

"Well, I have his statement and the D.A. is making quick deal with him. They're hashing out the details right now."

"I don't believe you. You don't have a case."

"No? Your friends, Felix Ricks and Carmen Shirley, are here, too. Carmen and Felix are dating right?"

"So?"

"They are in another room writing a statement right now, as well placing you at the scene and identifying you as the shooter"

"Bullshit!"

"Really? I'll show you. Oh and Carmen's pregnant, or maybe you didn't know. She'll do anything in her power not to have a baby in jail." Brown helped escort Patty to the room where Drew is being held. Prior to this, Finch had come up with a story where Drew named Patty as one of his alibis. Finch approached the room with Patty. She told him to stand aside and watch. She opened the door and pulled out a picture of Patty and said, "Is this him?"

"Yes. That's him right there."

"You fucking liar!" Patty yelled out and charged the room but Brown and a few others grabbed him and brought him into the room. He turned his head toward the other side of the office and viewed Felix and Carmen in the room talking with another officer. This made him even more upset and fueled his anger like a steam engine. The detectives antagonized Patty.

"You sure you have nothing to tell us?" one officer teased.

"Your friend has a lot to say." Another detective chimed in. Patty was extremely furious. His hands were shaking. His eyes were watering up. He and Drew had their story straight, and Drew had double crossed him, *That bastard snitch!*

Finch played them all. While Drew thought that he was only identifying Patty as his alibi, Patty thought that Drew was identifying *him* as the shooter and when he saw Carmen and Felix his guilt made him imagine they were snitching him out. Finch's clever scheme opened the floodgates. Carmen and Felix caught the tail end of the ruckus. They saw Patty being escorted away and figured Felix and Drew were making a deal against *them*. After the commotion subsided, Patty, Felix, Carmen and Drew were in a race to the finish to see who could come up with the best plea deal by ratting out the others. It turned out that Carmen and Felix really had nothing to do with the crime. They thought they were riding to the corner store to buy cigars to smoke marijuana. When they all reached the store, Patty and Drew saw Dale and an argument developed. Carmen and Felix went back to the car to wait. The other three walked out into the parking lot and continued to argue over money. Patty and Drew started shoving around Dale, causing Dale to supposedly pull out a knife. Drew pulled out a gun. Drew was the shooter.

Meghan was eager to take off to the next assignment but not without a physical check in with Brown. Just before they made their way to the next assignment, Finch and Brown slipped off into a storage closet on the north side of the precinct. This side of the precinct had been under construction for a few weeks. Brown had a spare key to the closet and they would use it whenever the urge came during working hours. Brown wanted to tear her out of her clothes as rapidly as possible. She couldn't wait to have him against her even if for a brief moment. A quick slip away in a closet was not beneath either one of their standards. Their love affair was very discreet, and Finch made sure of it. She suspected that Brown was developing deep feelings because the way he touched her was changing in passion and purpose. She tried to keep it business but that line was crossed a while ago.

FRANKIE'S PUB MORNING

Frankie decided to close the bar for the next two days so that the bar could be thoroughly cleaned for the new season. He also needed to think about the future of the bar, the fight club, and how he would deal with "the mysterious Abigail" who came into his life and made him rethink a lot of things. Abigail spent the morning cleaning the kitchen. She decided it was time for a small break as she waited for Roger to arrive. He was on his way. Frankie asked them to go to the store to buy more supplies that they would need for cleaning and for other miscellaneous items they would need for normal business operations. As she waited for Roger, Abigail sat in the back corner reading the Boston Globe. She flipped through the pages uninterested in most of the news. Eventually she focused her attention on an article that described a house fire that had killed three people and the family dog. DORCHESTER BLAZE KILLS THREE. Roger suddenly knocked on the door. Abigail jumped up and opened the door.

"Elvis, you ready?" he asked.

"Yes." she answered. "Let's go." Abigail grabbed her backpack off the edge of the bar before she left. She took out her keys and locked the door. Abigail and Roger stepped out onto the sidewalk while chatting.

"We really gotta get this place clean today before Frankie flips out," Roger said as he watched his feet press against the concrete sidewalk.

"Especially the basement. I can smell the stench upstairs through the vents sometimes," Abigail said.

"Gross. You have a good nose. I would seriously vomit from the smell of old sweat and blood... Anyway, I'm working on something and you sort of promised you would check it out so... How about tonight?" Roger asked shyly.

"After work? Sure. Long as you promise not to set me on fire with your little contraptions."

"HA HA HA! Maybe setting you on fire would make you more appealing." Roger wished he was brave enough to flirt with her. Abigail smiled.

Unbeknownst to Abigail and Roger, detectives Brown and Finch drove past them with Finch behind the wheel. Finch and Brown were on their way to their latest case. Detective Brown sipped his coffee which he had transferred from the mug to a thermos. Finch's phone rang. She looked at it and ignored the call. She took a deep breath and turned up the radio.

"Who's that?" Brown asked.

"My mother–in–law."

"Yikes. What's up with that?"

Finch ignored the question. "Tammy is on the scene. I told her *not* to let Fisher touch anything. All we need is his grimy little hands contaminating the crime scene. They want us to park in the garage to avoid making a spectacle. Security will let us in."

Finch and Brown arrived at the Chapel and Case building, the company formerly run by Alan Jiang. They passed the front of the building and pulled around the corner to the parking lot in the back. A security officer had been waiting for them. He walked up to Finch's window and bent over to address her. His tattooed hand rested on the door.

"Detective Brown?"

"I'm Finch. He's Brown."

"Sorry. I'm Turner West. I was told to let you guys in and make sure we keep things quiet. I'm gonna swipe you in and escort you to the lobby." He took his security badge from around his neck and waved it past the sensor. The bar rose. "Park in Jiang's reserved space over there." Finch drove her car through. She took a right turn and pulled into the parking space. She and Brown exited the car. Brown left his thermos in the car and tightened up his tie as he walked around the car. He shook hands with West.

"Nice to meet you."

"No one ever took the space?" Finch inquired.

"No. Ms. Moore already had a better spot. No one has filled her position yet. I'm not sure they are actively looking. I'd assume whoever takes her old job would take the space." He led them through a door. "The lobby is right through there. I have to head back to the lot."

"Thanks." Brown and Finch echoed in unison.

Brown and Finch headed through the lobby. The lobby floor was made of white marble tile with light gray mineral swirls. There were little speckles of gold and silver, which reflected the sun that beamed through the enormous sized windows that comprised the lobby walls and ceiling. In the center of the floor was the Chapel and Case logo inlaid in gold and platinum colored tiles. They showed the guards their badges as they walked towards the elevators. Brown and Finch discussed the case as they rode in the elevator. Brown cleaned his glasses with a cloth, put them back on and adjusted them to fit his face properly.

"So... Where did they find it?" Finch asked Detective Brown as she watched the green floor numbers display on the screen.

"On the window sill... of his office," Brown shrugged.

"On the what?" She laughed. "You gotta be kidding me. How did that happen?"

Brown was just as confused. "Not a clue in the world. Hopefully we can find out when we get up there. I just wanted to get there before Fisher, but that didn't work out so much."

On their way up, Finch sent Detective Tammy a text. "COMING UP NOW. BE THERE IN A MINUTE."

"Yeah maybe we shouldn't have started our investigation in the storage closet earlier." He smirked. She punched him in the arm and smirked a little. For Finch, business was business. She didn't like to discuss anything about their relationship while on the job. This was the first time she let it slide. *I'm getting soft.*

THE 34ᵗʰ FLOOR

Brown and Finch arrived at the 34ᵗʰ floor. When the doors opened, they saw Detective Tammy waiting for them at the elevator. "Finch. Brown."

Tammy was in charge of the forensics team and was very thorough. Like Finch, she was very detail–oriented and organized.

"Tammy." Brown gestured his hand to let her lead the way. "This way."

Officer Alicia Tammy and Detective Brown had worked on a few cases together over the years. She was the only person he ever trusted to handle the forensics on his homicide investigations. Tammy was a thin, African American woman who had worked at the precinct for six years. She sported a curly afro for the past year after swearing off relaxers and hair straightening chemicals. Tammy met Brown while handling her first case on the job. She was transferred to Boston after she was pulled in from Worcester to work on a high profile case. She had just finalized a divorce and needed to move on with her life.

Tammy's divorce was no surprise to her family. Her husband, Martin Tammy, had been abusive for many years after he returned from his tour of duty in Afghanistan. Many nights she would wake up to find him outside in the cold, confused about where he was or punching the tree in the yard until his hands bled. Another time, she found him in the kitchen smearing his body with oil and flour. The final straw was when she caught him at 3:00 am walking around the house with a cleaver threatening to cut off his own penis. She immediately took their kids and left the house. She felt bad for him. He needed help but was on a five month waiting list to see a psychiatrist, and his mind was quickly deteriorating.

The move to Boston was the perfect situation at the perfect time. She moved herself, her two daughters, Kyla and Marie, and their cat, Punchy, in a day. She left Martin with the house, the car and the joint bank account. Six months later, Martin killed himself by swallowing a half gallon of bleach. Tammy and the girls were devastated, but she knew that leaving was the safest thing she could think to do at the time.

There were cubicles in the center of the office floor virtually covering 90% of the level and various sized offices on the perimeter of the floor by the windows. Most of the people had been removed to conference rooms and cafeteria. Police were on the opposite side of the floor, but it was hard to see from the other side of the room.

"So far no one has seen anything."

"The only people we asked to stay were people who either worked late the night before or arrived early that morning. There were about 15 people we quickly questioned, but none of them had seen anything out of the ordinary."

"What about maintenance?" Finch asked.

"I wish. A few maintenance workers were questioned; but once again, they didn't see anything that night or this morning."

"Where are the other employees?"

"We got them out before they could figure out what we had seen and take pictures. The guard was first on the scene. He's in the office with Fisher." They continued cutting through the cubicles.

Through the glass, they could see Detective Fisher talking to the security guard. "Oh God, here we go. Fisher is gonna mess things up." Finch was annoyed.

"Fisher will be leaving soon. He is not getting anywhere with the guard and hasn't finished his BU... no Brandeis case. I'm not sure why Chief Downy sent him of all people to cover for you. I already told the guard not to say anything until you guys got here. He keeps saying things are classified and Fisher is pissed."

"I like him already."

They opened the office door. Fisher and his team were taking pictures.

"Find anything interesting, Fish?" Brown pretended to care.

"Just an incompetent guard and an unidentified forearm on the ledge." Fisher pointed to the ledge. They looked over to see a man's severed forearm on the ledge of the building. "I was able to gather that the window cleaners work this area once every two to three weeks."

Finch jumps in. "So, that explains why we are just getting the call now. Nice!"

"I'm getting the idea that Chief Downy wants you guys to take over here." Finch wasn't surprised at all.

"Homicide." Brown had an answer ready for the comment he knew would come.

"Except there's no body to prove homicide, just an arm, buddy. Sounds more like a missing person than a homicide," Fisher said in response.

"I'm sure a body will turn up."

"Either way, I have to get outta here and get back on that Brandeis case." Fisher handed the cameras memory card to Finch.

"How's that going?" Finch asked as she inspected the memory card.

"Pretty well. We should be wrapping things up. Hopefully warrants will go out this afternoon. So, I'm outta here. Let's go. Good luck with those Yankees, Brown." Fisher smiled and walked out with two other officers.

Brown shook his head. Finch was surprised. "I've never seen him jump off a case without a fight."

"I'm not asking questions." Brown located the coroner.

Finch dropped the memory card into her pocket. She took out her phone to take her own pictures for upload to the cloud drive and take notes. The coroner approached them.

The coroner was Michelle Cox. She had worked for the force for about ten years and was always Brown's first recommendation. He was happy to see her on the scene working with Tammy. Cox shook their hands. "Good to see you guys."

"How's it going?" Finch asked as she folded her arms.

"Pretty well. Have you taken all your pics? We wanna get this off the ledge and down to the lab ASAP. We think it is Robert Benson's."

The guard jumped in, "I *know* it is Robert Benson's arm."

Cox introduced them, "Sorry. This is Sam Petit, the guard on this floor."

"I'm Detective Brown. This is Detective Finch. Who is Robert Benson? And how do you know this is his arm for sure?"

Petit was happy to explain, "Robert Benson is COO of this company. He's been missing for what... a week or two?"

"And no one said anything?" This didn't make sense to Brown.

"They knew. They wanted to keep it quiet," Detective Tammy jumped in. "This place has been buzzing with reporters since the death of Alan Jiang and they've been concerned about the stock price I assume."

"Whose decision was it to keep things quiet?" Brown asked.

Tammy answered, "The family... and the board of directors of course." She went back to dusting for prints.

Petit confirmed, "She's right. The board held a meeting with all managers, supervisors and security informing us that he went missing. They told us if anyone asked to say he was on vacation while the family did their own private investigation. Most figured he went into hiding after the murder. That was most of the mailroom chatter I heard."

Finch thought for a moment, "Oh yeah! The Alan Jiang murder thing. Remember that? That lines up pretty nicely *if* there is a connection." Finch made a note in her file.

"If... But that's a good if." Brown knew to trust Finch's instincts.

ALAN JIANG: CEO

ROBERT BENSON: COO, MISSING ABOUT TWO WEEKS

SAM PETIT: GUARD ON DUTY

"That's definitely his hand right there," Petit insisted with confidence. He slightly gagged when he looked at it. He patted his head with a paper towel as sweat dripped down his forehead. The nausea raised his temperature. He felt heat running underneath his uniform. He unbuttoned his collar.

Brown asked, "Are we done taking pictures."

The officers nodded.

"Get that thing off the ledge for us." Brown directed the assisting officers to bring the arm closer. The two officers, wearing protective coveralls and gloves, reached out and grabbed the arm. It was tied down to a brick so that it would stay on the ledge and not be blown away. They carefully lifted the arm, bringing it into the room. They placed it on a black bag on the desk.

Brown took a closer look scanning his eyes across the flesh of the severed stiff forearm hoping to find clues. He felt a bit sick from the rotting smell but stomached it very well. Maggots were starting to form.

Finch needed more information and asked, "What time are you on shift?"

Petit responded, "The office opens at nine, but a few people like to get in early, so I get here at eight in the morning."

Brown jumped in, "What are your normal duties?"

"I usually hang out by the elevators. I walk the aisles once every 20 to 30 minutes. I take lunch at 11:30 or 12, a 15 minute break at 2:30 and I leave at 5:00, once everyone is gone. Sometimes people stay, but I leave at 5. Overtime has to be approved."

"Have you or anyone worked overtime this week?" Finch asked.

"I didn't, but I'm not sure if others did."

"What usually happens on the floor? Was anyone acting strangely?"

"Well, I never go into private offices unless asked to. That arm could have been out there for a week and I wouldn't know. And I haven't seen anyone doing anything out of the ordinary."

"Does another guard come in after you?" Finch asked.

"No. This place is cheap. They wouldn't pay another person to walk the floor when no one is here. This level gets locked up at 8:00. No one gets in; no one gets out unless you have security clearance."

Brown asked, "Who has security clearance here?"

Petit answered, "I don't know exactly who. I would think head of security and the big wigs around here. Anyone from the board may have it, but I'm not 100% sure."

"How did you find the arm?" Finch asked as she filled in the online worksheet.

"I didn't find it. I got a call from one of our window washers, Eddie Cons. He was completely terrified and hysterical."

"Where is he now?"

"He was throwing up when I got here. So I sent him home, but he is on call and willing to speak."

"Let's get back to this arm here. How do you know it is Robert Benson's arm for sure?" Brown wanted to get his questions answered.

Petit walked closer and pointed. "That middle finger. See how it's short? I remember him giving a speech about eight months ago to the employees here. And he told us a story about a butterfly that was caught in his dorm window back when he was at Harvard. He opened the window to free it and the window slammed back down on his finger cutting it off at the tip. I'm not sure if he was making a point about helping the helpless, or getting burned by those you help."

"Was there a ring here? Look at that tan line. Did he wear a ring?" Brown asked good questions and always made good observations.

"Harvard ring. Class of 97. It slipped off once and my buddy, Jake, found it. That cheap bastard gave him 10 bucks for finding it. It was a $5000 ring!" He covered his mouth with the paper towel in his hand. "Sorry. This is kind of hard."

"It's ok. Get some air." Brown sent Petit out of the room.

In the meantime Finch sent a text to Chief Downy. "HERE. EVERYTHING IS GOING WELL. UPDATING FILES ON THE CLOUD NOW." She went back to her notes and was impressed with the way Brown handled the guard. Finch nodded as she took notes:

ROBERT BENSON: COO CHAPEL & CASE
MISSING TWO WEEKS
SPEECH 8 MONTHS EARLIER
SHORT MIDDLE FINGER: CUT IN WINDOW
HARVARD RING MISSING
CLASS OF '87

Some things may have seemed irrelevant, but she wrote everything that could possibly lead to a motive:
SAM PETIT: GUARD
BENSON LOST RING– JAKE FINDS RING
REFERS TO ROBERT BENSON AS "CHEAP BASTARD"
WORKS 8–5PM NOT A MINUTE MORE
20 MINUTE LAPS
EDDIE CONS: WINDOW WASHER FINDS ARM ON LEDGE

Brown looked around to take a second to think. "I'm gonna need that window washer's name, number and address." Brown was ready to go. Finch was focused on taking notes. She preferred to do it over Brown. He was used to memorizing and writing by hand. They often argued about the best way. Brown thought that too much typing would make him overlook subtle gestures by the guilty and mini clues left behind. Maybe he had a point. By time they left, Meghan could barely remember the guards face. Luckily, she took a picture of him as she visually scanned the room.

CHAPTER 6

ROGER'S HOUSE
THE ATKINS' RESIDENCE

Roger and Abigail spent the day cleaning the pub from top to bottom. Larry came in to help out. He didn't speak much. His goal was to get it over with and head back home. They wanted to get everything done today so they could have the next day completely to themselves. The most difficult area to clean was the club in the basement. The stench of old blood and sweat lingered through the vents. The smell had been easing its way up toward the bar. Occasionally, the odor could be smelled in the night air as the breeze carried the scent up the walls and through the vents. After the cleaning session, Roger and Abigail decided to go to Roger's house. They arrived at his house later on that evening around 9:00 pm.

Roger's mother always expected him to arrive late. Sometimes she waited up just to see how his day was going. They walked through the hall, past a fish tank on a table. There is a funny looking goldfish in it. Elvis. Ms. Atkins had food ready for him in Tupperware on the kitchen table. She sat with big pink rollers in her hair and a bath robe which she never seemed to take off. She wore the same robe every day for the most part. She sat in the kitchen reading a book, snickering at the funny parts. When Roger walked into the kitchen she was happy to see him. "Welcome to earth, Rog."

She looked at Abigail. Abigail took off her hood. Ms. Atkins put down her book. Her eyes were fixed on Abigail.

"Good evening." Abigail was nervous. Roger always complained about his nagging mother, but this was the first time she was seeing the woman in the flesh. She looked a lot different from the way Abigail imagined her. Abigail thought she had a very pretty face, but carried herself as if she was older than she really was. On the table was a bottle of Jack Daniels. Ms. Atkins had a glass and finished the last sip.

"I see you have company. Little late wouldn't you say?"

"Mom, this is Elvis. I told you about her." Roger was a little embarrassed. "No worries ma, she's asexual." He bent over and kissed her on the head.

"Asexual? Well, that's special. Nice to finally meet you, Elvis," Mrs. Atkins smiled.

Abigail rolled her eyes at Roger. "I'm Abigail. Abby is fine, too."

"Oh. Ok. I've heard your name a few times. Ms. Atkins will do. If I had known you were bringing company, Rog I would have put more food aside. Let me make you a plate." She rose from her seat.

"No. It's ok, Mom. We had burgers on the way. We will be fine. We're just going to my room to play with my toys."

"Hmm. Ok, well, I'm heading to bed. I have a long day of show case showdowns, big wheels and Court TV." Ms. Atkins leaned over and kissed Roger goodnight. "Nice to meet you, Elvis. And Roger, please don't set the house on fire." She left.

Roger put the food in the container in the fridge, and then picked up his backpack. He headed to his room. Abigail followed and looked around. The house was very clean but old fashioned. *This woman is stuck in the '70s.* In the corner of the living room was a shrine to Elvis. Abigail mumbled. "You gotta be kidding me." She saw a few pictures of Roger and his mother when they were younger. Roger was a cute kid.

They reached Roger's room and entered. He closed the door behind them. Roger exposed another side of his life to Abigail. She never imagined his room to look like this, but she thought it was pretty cool. "Welcome to my lab. No work tomorrow. After a day like today, a day off is what we need."

Abigail looked around and is fascinated with a gadget on the desk. "What is this?"

"Whoa, whoa." Roger grabbed it from her hand. "Careful, Elvis. This here is my baby."

"Sorry."

"It's ok. Maybe you can help me with this." Roger pulled a roll from under his bed. He unrolled it as Abigail took off her hooded sweat shirt. Her shirt underneath got caught in the sweat shirt and went up too. A part of her midsection showed, exposing her muscular stomach and a small part of the bottom of her bra. Roger watched but looked away quickly. She didn't notice. *Oh my God help me.* He turned away from her to stifle a certain erection. "I have the idea, but there is something missing here that I can't figure out."

Abigail smiled as she scanned the drawing. "You're a creepy fella."

"Don't judge me."

"Relax. I think I know what you are trying to do. It looks good. Ok, so. I think I have an idea how you can fix this. Look at this gear here..." Abigail gave Roger a few suggestions on his design. Roger hadn't figured Abigail to be as smart as she was; he just wanted to spend time with her but as they talked out the design, he realized how much she was helping. Abigail was very bright; she just never had a reason to display her mental talents. She probably could have fixed the dishwasher months ago. She and Roger sat in the room studying his design for about an hour before they touched the machine again. Roger and Abigail completely reworked the drawing. Roger felt it was now time to make a model.

Roger played with a clay model of the new concept. Abigail helped. Roger couldn't resist watching her from time to time. She moved her hair away from her face. Roger would sometimes get lost in her eyes. She caught him once in a while and he would brush it off with an Elvis joke. Eventually, they disassembled the initial machine. Piece by piece they rebuilt it, replacing gears and rewiring the entire unit. Abigail and Roger picked apart Roger's experiment and reconstructed it into a working product. The wooden floor in his room was covered with burn marks, screws and wires. In the wee hours of the morning, Roger and Abigail's remote controlled vehicle zipped across the floor.

The sky was dark purple from the suns approach. Roger finished brushing his teeth and returned to the room. Abigail had fallen asleep in his bed. Her headphones were in and her iPod was playing. Roger had given her a t–shirt and shorts to sleep in. He tucked her away for the night. Sitting on the edge of the bed, he watched her sleep for a moment and smiled. Here she was in his bed, and he had no intention of spoiling things by sneaking a kiss even though the thought had crossed his mind a thousand times. He laid out a pillow and blanket on the floor and fell asleep by the side of the bed.

BROWN'S APARTMENT

Sydney Brown entered his apartment after a late run to the gym. He opened the door and closed it behind himself. He was exhausted. He tossed his jacket and towel on a chair and went into the kitchen. He checked his phone, hoping to have a message from Meghan; but there was only a message from Chief Downy. He checked the message.

"Brown, I've been checking the shared files and have a few questions. Tell Finch excellent work and thorough assessment thus far. I want a debriefing in the morning and I want more information on this window cleaner I'm reading about."

FRANKIE'S APARTMENT ABOVE THE PUB

This was one of the many nights Frankie could not sleep. He and Larry had argued earlier about the club, and all the things he wanted to say were running though his head. *Larry has a point. If we go legit, will I be able to afford it?* Frankie punched his hanging punching bag ferociously. The sweat ran down his face and soaked his t-shirt. He punched until his arms were rubbery and tired. He finally stopped. His age was catching up to him. It was time for bed. Water would have been nice, but water wouldn't do the job that he really needed done. He went over to the mini fridge and poured a glass of whiskey. He took a sip, swirled it around in his mouth and finally swallowed it down. He exhaled with relief. He took his time with the whiskey, enjoying every peaceful sip, and embraced the gentle burn as a reminder that he was still alive.

MORNING
DETECTIVE FINCH'S HOUSE

Finch was lying in the bed, but did not enjoy a solid hour of sleep the entire night. Her mind raced about Chapel and Case, Anthony, her mother in law, Sydney… The time was 6:13 am. The sun slowly slipped through the vertical blinds of her windows. She rolled over and got out of the bed. "UGH!" She wore short gray sweat pants and a white tank top. Her hair was in a ponytail. She walked into the kitchen, put on some coffee and went out onto the back porch. She took a few deep breaths of the chilly morning air before she reached down and took a joint out of a side board. She had a lighter on the floor next to the door frame; she lit the joint and began to smoke it.

She liked to take one or two puffs of marijuana from time to time but never more than that. She just needed to get the edge off. A sleepless night always made her jittery and unfocused. She thought about the new case. It would be her last case as a trainee. Hopefully it didn't carry on too long.

Finch took a third and forth puff of the joint, which wasn't very typical of her. She put the flame out and then she tucked the joint back into the side of the house. She went back into the house and went to the kitchen. She took a mug out of the cabinet and poured a cup of coffee. She wanted to let it cool, so she went to the front porch and grabbed the morning paper.

Back in the kitchen, Finch sat at the kitchen table. On the side she had two Morningstar veggie sausage patties and her coffee.

"GOOD MORNING, SUNSHINE!" Finch received a text from Brown. She ignored it.

Detective Finch continued to eat as she skimmed through the paper to see if anything had been leaked to the press. She didn't see anything about the case. She did see one article about Chapel and Case:

CHAPEL AND CASE STOCK STABLE AFTER CEO DEATH

She thought to herself, "Good. Nothing about Benson. Let's keep it that way until we get more information."

After her quick snack, she cleaned the kitchen and put everything away. She went into her bedroom and moved around the room quickly, looking for socks and shoes. She reached into her dresser drawer and pulled out an Adidas workout set comprised of a tank top and fitted Capri pants. It was 6:30. She laced up her sneakers, grabbed a jacket, and left the house. "Good morning," she greeted a passing neighbor as she jumped into her car and headed to the gym. She worked out every other day for about one and a half hours beginning each workout with a 45 minute run on the elliptical machine and alternated upper and lower body workouts.

She returned home just before eight, took a quick shower, dressed and left to meet up with Detective Brown.

EDDIE CONS' APARTMENT

It was 9:00 am when Finch and Brown arrived at Eddie Cons' Apartment door. They had hoped to get in touch with him the previous day, but for one reason or another, he wasn't home and didn't return their calls until 11:00 pm that evening. He ranted about something to do with his mother and sister, but Brown was too tired to listen. Finch on the other hand would have asked Cons to slow down so she could shake off the sleepiness and get her computer ready to take notes. Finch and Brown knocked on the door.

"Why are you so quiet this morning?" Brown sipped coffee from his thermos.

"Nothing to say," Finch barely looked him in the eye. She sent out a text message. Brown tried to sneak a peek but was unsuccessful. Finch knocked again. They looked around inspecting the halls. The place seemed like a quiet building but it smelled like old people and fried chicken. Finch's phone vibrated. She read the message and put her phone back in her pocket. "Where is this guy?"

"I called him before we got here. I don't know what the hell is going on." Brown knocked again. A short man with a bald head opened to the door. "Mr. Cons? Eddie Cons?"

"Yes. Come in." They walk into the apartment. The man is a hoarder. The apartment is covered in clothes, papers and old Chinese food containers. "Just step wherever you can find a place to put your feet."

"We'll be quick. We just wanna know what you saw, and then we will be out of your way." Finch was afraid to touch Cons' belongings. She was disgusted and ready to leave.

Eddie asked, "Can I offer you two to some tea? Coffee?"

"No no. No thanks. We just wanna get started." Brown wanted to speed this along as much as he could. He saw Meghan's face and she gave him a signal with her eyes that she was uncomfortable.

"It's no trouble, but yes, let's get started. I'm sure you have better things to do than hang out with me. I don't get much company here, you can probably see why but..."

Finch said, "Tell us a little about yourself."

Eddie asked, "Like what? I'm an interesting fella. I can go on forever."

"Well we don't have forever," Finch declared. She was getting frustrated. "How long have you worked at C&C?"

"For three years. I was voted Window Washer of the month!"

"How many washers are there?" Finch asked.

"I think we have about 20, maybe 18 or so."

Finch kept questioning, "Who was on shift when you found the arm?"

"There were five of us, Sally, Charles, Garcia, Clark and myself, but they weren't anywhere near the arm."

"Do you think anyone would have wanted *you* to find the arm?" Finch filled in her spreadsheet as she questioned.

"What? I don't know. I don't think so. I don't have problems with anyone." Eddie scratched his five o'clock shadow and chewed at his knuckles. "I don't know anything about Mr. Benson."

"How do you know this is about Benson?" Finch listened carefully.

"Because the arm was outside of his office and the guard told me it was Benson's arm. Are you trying to say I had something to do with this?" Eddie was nervous. He stood up straight pacing back and forth in front of his couch.

Brown interrupts, "No. We aren't accusing you of anything. We're just being thorough. Relax. So, tell us what happened yesterday at the office. Tell us what you saw, what you did, everything."

Meghan's thumbs were clicking away as she took notes. She listened carefully and snapped pictures of the apartment in between the typing frenzy. She believed that the condition of his apartment may have implications about his personality and habits. There are some things that may seem irrelevant but Finch wasn't sure that the irrelevant facts could be determined until after the case was solved.

Eddie moved a few things over before he sat on the couch. "Well, it started as a routine cleaning. We clean the whole building everyday but in sections. The building is so big; I don't get back around to that window but once every two to three weeks or so. Sometimes four weeks depending upon weather conditions and bird shit emergencies." Eddie takes a sip of his tea. He shakes his head and puts on his glasses. "It's normal to see an occasional dead birdie on the ledge, no problem; but a human arm? You can tell the birds had been picking at it... the maggots, the smell. I just couldn't keep my food down after that. I got hot and woozy and I threw up."

Finch interjected, "Describe the location of the arm. Where was it when you found it?" She listened and took more notes in her phone.

EDDIE CONS: WINDOW WASHER/3 YEARS
HOARDER
ANXIOUS
5 WORKERS ON SHIFT: Sally, Charles, Garcia, Clark, and Cons

Eddie fixed his glasses again, "I found the arm on the ledge! It was tied to a brick. I never touched the damn thing. I screamed like a bitch though." He laughed. No one else found it funny.

Brown asked, "So, how did you alert others about the arm?" Brown propped his hands on his hips and listened carefully.

"I radioed in to dispatch. They called the guard over and I went back to the roof and I threw up there too. Everyone else was asked to leave the floor but they called me into the office. I threw up again! This time I made the bucket." Eddie got up from the couch.

"Oh yeah. I uh, took a picture before I went back up to the roof."

Finch was appalled, "You took pictures?! Where are the pictures?"

"On my cell." Cons picked up his phone from the couch.

"Mr. Cons, this stuff is classified until…"

"I know I know. I promise I didn't show anyone, and I won't. Shit. I can't anyway. The phone fell in the bucket after I threw up in it and now the damn phone isn't working." Eddie flipped open his cell phone showing it to Finch and Brown. Brown rolled his eyes and huffed in disgust. Brown snatched the phone opening up the back and removed the memory card. They headed towards the door. He tossed the phone on the couch.

"Hey hey! I need that! You can't just take my memory card like that." Cons was flustered and anxious.

"We'll mail it back to you. It's police evidence," Finch smirked on her way out.

"But I have personal…"

"I'm sure it's nothing we haven't seen," Brown opened the door. Brown and Finch stepped out and closed the door.

Eddie ran over and opened the door. "I need that back by tomorrow!"

"Forget about it. You'll get it when we're done." Finch didn't even turn her head to address him. They disappeared around the corner.

ATKINS' RESIDENCE 10 AM

Abigail and Roger had a late night playing with Roger's inventions. They made a lot of progress on a few of his machines and moved on to a more complicated project. Roger wanted to make a safety vest for police and security officers complete with bullet proof protection, LED signaling lights and straps for extra clips, a flashlight and flares. A few months earlier, a state trooper pulled over a speeding drunk driver. While he was in the breakdown lane, he was struck by an oncoming car and died. Massachusetts then instituted the *Pull Over* law which stated that if a driver passed an emergency vehicle or officer in the breakdown lane, the driver must pull over to the next lane or drastically reduce speed if pulling over safely was not possible. If drivers could not see the officers, Roger thought it would be safer if the officer wore a protective vest to signal to drivers that he or she had exited the car and was on the road. It was just an idea, but Abigail thought it was clever.

Roger woke up first when his mother glanced into the room.

"MA!"

"Just checking if you were awake! Sheesh!" She closed the door again.

"I have to get my own place." Roger went and watched a little bit of the news with his mother. Because he was extremely excited to spend this much time with Abigail, he couldn't resist checking up on her every few minutes. Occasionally he would simply look in the room to watch her sleep, hoping he could catch her waking and be the first person she would see in the morning. He finally left her alone, letting her sleep while he took a shower and then prepared breakfast.

Deep in the jungle night, Abigail's feet sunk into the muddy terrain of rock, sand and fallen foliage. She was lost as the jungle forest closed in around her. Lightning cracked in the cloudless sky splitting rocks and setting fires in the ground near her bludgeoned feet. Streams of blood ran down her arms and pooled into the palms of her hands as black fur seeped from the pores of her skin. She grunted her teeth in pain. The black fur grew longer and thicker, wrapping around her body like a cocoon. Thorn covered vines from the ground tangled around her feet ripping into her skin. She struggled to break free but could not get away. Around her, little blue eyes appeared in the night shadows, watching her like prey. She could see their fangs dripping with blood, sweat and saliva.

Suddenly, the vines pulled her feet from underneath her causing her to fall. Her body smacked against the ground before the vines lifted her up into the air. She hanged upside down. The beasts with drooling mouths and blue eyes, charged as native drums played. They stood up straight like men as smoke emitted from their heads. They jumped, growling, swinging their claws at Abigail, missing her face by inches she could see they had hands instead of paws. The fur wrapping her body also wrapped around her mouth and crawled into her nose and the smoke from the beastly beings rose into her nostrils. She could not scream; she struggled for air.

A man whose face was black as coal came from the midst of the beasts. He was dressed in all white. He took a mahogany colored spear with a stony tip and pierced Abigail in the center of her back. Her body curled as the rod delivered an electric current, cutting deep into her spine. Black blood drained down. The vine wore weak and began to tear. The beasts below waited. Their eyes went black. They drank the blood that dripped from Abby's hanging cocoon. The drums beat faster. The beasts growled in anticipation of Abby's inevitable plummet. One ordinary butterfly fluttered from below, past the smoke and blood scented air it fluttered upward ascending towards Abby. Abigail's eyes focused and followed the light purple winged insect as it eventually landed on her nose and immediately turned to ashes. The vine tore. Little by little she lowered and squirmed, watching the last thread give way. She fell.

Abigail jumped out of her sleep from another frightening dream. Gasping for air, she was shaking, sweaty and cold. The pillow was damp. Roger entered the room just as she woke and sat on the bed next to her. She was happy to see him. She was slightly embarrassed because Roger had never seen her coming out of a nightmare before; she felt vulnerable and weak. Roger was sympathetic and concerned for her. He only wanted to be closer to her and care for her, but he had nothing to offer her except for a friendly embrace. She was accepting of whatever he had to offer.

"Hey. Elvis. You ok?" He knew she must have had another one of those dreams that she had told him about in the past. As far as he knew, she was having the nightmares more frequently and they were becoming more and more vivid each time. He put his arm around her and gently rubbed her shoulder and neck with his hand. He slightly touched her hair, pushing it away from her face as she closed her eyes and calmed down. She took a few deep breaths until her heart beat slowed to an acceptable pace. He wanted to kiss her, but he was afraid. "Are you ok?" He asked again.

"Yeah. Shit. Sorry. I kind of forgot where I was for a minute." She put her head on his shoulder but picked it up again quickly. *It's Roger.*

"Bad dream again?"

"I wish they would stop. More importantly, I wish I knew what they meant. I'm assuming they mean something but maybe they don't mean anything. Maybe I'm thinking too deep about it."

"Maybe not. Maybe your mind is trying to help you remember some things in your past. Things you may have tried to forget."

"I can't imagine that what's happening in my dreams could have ever been real."

"Maybe they're symbolic. Like a puzzle. You just have to focus and put the pieces together."

"I'm trying, Roger. It's just not triggering anything that I can think of."

"I hope you figure things out soon."

"Thanks. I do, too. Anyway..."

"Yeah well, what do you wanna do today? You hungry? I made you breakfast."

"Yes. I can smell it. I'm starving. Thank you. Is it okay if I take a shower first? I feel a little icky."

"Of course. Meet me in the kitchen when you're done. I left a red towel for you in the bathroom." Roger stood up and walked away. Abigail watched the muscles in his back flex from behind his tank top. *When did Roger grow muscles?* She thought about how much Roger had matured since they first met. His jokes and insults slowly turned into compliments, kind words and small acts of chivalry. She didn't really think about them until today. When she looked back, for the past month or so he had been treating her differently. She thought about it for a moment but shrugged it off as a misinterpretation of signs at a confusing time in her life.

Abigail picked up her backpack, walked out of the room, entered the bathroom and shut the door.

POLICE HEADQUARTERS

Finch and Brown drove back to the station separately. Chief Downy wanted a face to face debriefing of the information that had been collected at Chapel and Case. There was a lot of pressure coming down from the mayor and commissioner about cleaning this up quickly and quietly. The cloud service was great for collecting data, but Downy was still old school and wanted to hear about the detectives' gut feelings and wanted a face–to–face interpretation and update. And though he had immediate access to her notes, he believed that not all information should be shared via an Internet–based shared file system.

Finch and Brown parked in the lot and walked in together. They did not speak to one another as they went up the stairs to the second floor. Brown sipped coffee from his thermos. The staff was very busy as there had been a shooting in Mattapan and another in Dorchester that same night. It was speculated that two rival bike gangs were hashing it out over race winnings. Two men had been arrested thus far.

Finch knocked on the chief's glass door. He waved for them to come in.

"So what do we have?" Downy got straight to the point.

Brown spoke, "We have a left forearm of a john potentially 5'11 to 6'1 in height. We made an observation of a tan line on one finger which we figured sported a ring at some point. The guard confirmed it was the arm of the Robert Benson, according to what he knew about the short finger and tan line of the ring."

Finch butted in, "We are still trying to get DNA samples to confirm, but we are pretty sure that we have his arm. Benson was the COO of Chapel and Case and has been missing for about two weeks."

Downy wanted more information, "Tell me about Benson."

"We haven't got much information on him yet. We've been chasing down this window washer who found the arm," Brown said.

"And we met with him this morning. Confiscated some evidence that we will bring down to the lab." Finch was nervous because she knew that getting information on Benson was essential, but they still didn't have enough to evidence to close the case.

Brown added, "Finch made an observation that this may be connected with the Alan Jiang murder case in Portland. It could be sheer coincidence, but it's odd that both the company CEO and COO end up missing."

"But remember, sir. We still don't have a body, so technically this is a missing persons case, not a homicide," Finch wanted to be clear.

Downy said, "I know; but by the looks of it, we will find a dead body soon enough. No one is walking around with that type of amputation, without seeking medical care and living to tell the story. Check the local hospitals within a 50 mile radius and see if anything comes up. Ask if anyone with an amputated arm came in. I know he was ID'd by the guard, but get me some DNA. I feel like this case is going to go off the deep end."

"Thanks." Finch was no longer nervous.

Downy said, "Excellent job on the spreadsheet. I may have you host a training session on this in a couple of weeks after everything calms down."

"Definitely! Anything you need." Finch was feeling better after hearing Downy's comment.

They left the office.

Finch said to Brown, "I'm gonna go to my desk, do a little research and call those hospitals."

"Ok, no problem. You know where to find me."

They turned their backs to each other and walked away.

BATHROOM

The lower half of the bathroom was constructed of white ceramic subway tile. The upper half was painted canary yellow; the sink and tub had stainless steel fixtures. The bathroom had a two by three foot window with textured translucent glass held tight between the frames. Abigail reached into the tub and turned on the water. She took the clothes she intended to wear and placed them on a little chair on the side of the room. She grabbed her tooth brush, brushed her teeth, took off her clothes and got into the steamy water.

As she showered, the water steamed up the bathroom to the point where her vision was only inches in front of her. Abigail was wet and naked and soapy. She whipped her head around as if she had heard someone moving behind her. She looked left and right. She had heard something but couldn't place its location. She remembered her dream where she was free falling into the fog. She heard a faint growl and a wolf's howl. She rinsed off, stepped out of the tub and made her way to the other side of the bathroom, finding the door. Her heart was pounding. She thought someone or something was behind her. She opened the door and a swift breeze released the steam from the room. She quickly reclosed the door when she remembered her nakedness would be exposed. Abigail was afraid and panting as if she had just run a mile and could barely catch her breath.

Her nightmares were now interfering with real life. They were emerging from the night and now clouding her mind, obscuring what was real from what was not. Abigail could only imagine what would happen if it got worse. She was losing her mind. She leaned against the door and banged her head three times hoping she could knock some sense into herself.

Roger knocked on the door. "You find everything ok, Elvis?"

Abigail tried to pull it together. "Yes. I'm fine. I'm okay. I'll... I'll be out. Just give me a minute. I'm almost dressed."

"Ok. Just checking up on you."

They both stood on either side of the door, wanting to say more, but didn't. Roger hesitated, but then shook it off and walked back into the kitchen.

Abigail grabbed the towel to dry herself. She dried her legs and worked her way up her body. She then applied lotion to her feet, legs and arms. Roger's bathroom had two mirrors almost directly across from one another which created the eerie optical illusion of reflections like one would see in a House of Mirrors at a county fair. *Who would do this?* She looked at her hair and brushed it to the side. She rarely wore it back. She looked closely at her face, inspecting it for pimples. Then she noticed something she had never seen before. She could see a reflection of her back in the mirror behind her, a sight she hadn't seen in God knows how long. Though there was a mist in the room and condensation on the glass, she could see that there was a string of tattoos running down her spine. "What the hell?"

She took a towel and wiped down the window so she could get a better look. She investigated the markings by twisting her body around. Her everyday garb of hoodies and turtle necks covered up her back and she had never noticed the markings. She grabbed a hand held mirror from the shelf. "What the hell is this?"

Amazed at her discovery, Abigail quickly got dressed and ran to the kitchen. Roger could tell something was wrong but didn't say anything right away. She met him eye to eye with a glance. She took off her shirt. He wasn't sure where this was going and began to sweat. She turned around. She moved her wet hair over her shoulder. Roger dropped a spoon on the stove and slowly walked over. He examined the tattoos. He put his left hand on her shoulder and lightly ran his index finger down her back.

"What are these?"

"I don't know! I didn't even know they were there until just now."

"You never saw them?"

"No! When was the last time you looked at your back? And that little ass mirror at Frankie's… I don't remember anything about these."

The tattoos were small icons no bigger than a quarter, stacked one above the other. Roger continued to touch them lightly with his hand.

"Hold on." Roger ran into his room and grabbed his iPhone. He began taking pictures of the small tattoos on her back. One by one he snapped the pictures so that she could get a better view of each picture.

Finding those markings made Abby even more uncomfortable with her memory loss and her body. "Who tampered with me? Who did this?" she thought to herself. Even Frankie hadn't noticed them when he dressed her wounds the night he found her in the alley. Once again, she felt vulnerable in front of Roger. She had showed Roger another mystery about herself, and now a new project had begun. Roger downloaded the pictures onto his computer and printed them out. Abigail looked at the images one by one, but none registered any meaning to her. Unfortunately, the process of rediscovering who she was only made the nightmares worse.

ANOTHER DREAM

Abigail took a midday nap after her breakfast, a half movie and a few minutes of staring at the images on her back. When she fell asleep, she slipped into another nightmare. She was strapped to a medical table on a mountaintop. Her arms, legs and midsection were strapped down to the table. Her mouth was stuffed and tied. She looked left and right investigating her surroundings. Her body is bloody and bruised. A Harpy Eagle, known for its deadly talons, swooped down and landed on her stomach. Its long black talons pierced into her belly, ripping into her organs. She tried to scream but there was no sound. The eagle flew away and the wounds in her stomach turned black.

Black patterns spread out across her body, growing away from the holes in her midsection. She was terrified. Suddenly the sky turned black, lightning cracked, and the ground fell from beneath her. She was falling. She felt a familiar electric jolt run through her body and she clenched her teeth. Her eyes turned blue with each jolt. She heard a voice say, "Awake." She opened her eyes and she was in a medical room. She was sweating. The markings were gone. The straps were gone. She was naked. She rose out of the bed effortlessly, noticing the funny look of the walls of the room. She could see shapes of other bodies against the wall. She reached out to touch the body of one of the beings. The man opened his eyes and roared at her. She jumped and awoke.

Abigail sat on her bed sweating and panting. Again her dreaming had disrupted a peaceful and necessary rest. The setting sun flickered over the treetops and what was left of its light snuck through the blinds. She stood up, stretched and looked through the dusty white plastic strips. A cat passed by. It noticed Abigail's glance. It hissed at her. She hissed back and caught herself. "What am I doing?" She stretched again and rubbed the top of her back between her shoulder blades, touching the highest of her tattoos.

CHAPTER 7

FINCH'S HOUSE

It was late afternoon and Finch had just arrived home. She was barely out of her jacket when she received a text from Brown. "MISS YOU! JOIN ME AT FRANKIES." She didn't want to sit home alone. After a long day of work, a drink at Frankie's was a nice bonus. She decided to take a shower. After the shower, she changed into a t–shirt and running pants. She sprayed her body with some sweet smelling body splash just before her phone rang. It was her mother–in–law. Finch ignored the call as usual. She wanted to answer but couldn't find the energy to have an hour long discussion about anything that had to do with Anthony. She had been ignoring the calls for the past three months.

Suddenly Finch looked directly in front of her. She stood there for a while and stared at absolutely nothing. There was nothing there, but she sensed something was there. She turned around, looked behind herself, thought for a moment and shook it off. She went into the bathroom and washed her face. "I'm going crazy in this house."

Finch went to her back porch. She took out the small joint that she kept hidden and lit it up. She took two hits from it and took a couple of deep breaths. It was a short moment in heaven. She needed it. It was a temporary fix before a potential sex–filled night with Sydney Brown.

She grabbed her keys and ran out of the house.

FRANKIE'S PUB

Brown sat at the bar, drinking a Guinness and milk. He had been quietly watching a boxing match he had seen before, so his attention wasn't 100% into it. He and Frankie spent the night engaging in small talk. Frankie was tending the bar alone. Technically, he had closed the bar for the night, but if he was on the floor and an acquaintance of his stopped by, he didn't mind opening up the bar and sharing a few drinks.

"Where is my girlfriend?" Brown joked about Abigail.

"Who? Abby? She doesn't work every day you know."

"Tell her I miss her." Brown smiled as he took a sip.

"You better worry about your own unfinished affairs old man and get Abigail out of your head." They giggled.

"I hear you're thinking about closing the club," Brown pried.

Frankie didn't want to talk about it with a cop, but he figured it was okay. "Man. I been trying to close the place for the past couple months. I just can't convince Larry... I don't need the heat anymore man. I know you guys know about it and look out for me. I respect that, but it's not worth the headache. You know what I'm saying?"

Brown agreed, "Yes. I'll tell you something. You are a respected man, but the police force gets older; and new, younger guys come in. You don't know them; they don't know you. They don't understand how important these relationships are; they're just looking for stripes and recognition."

"I know. I saw some new kid in here, sniffing around like he had big balls. I wanted to knuckle his ass up. Scaring my customers just to be a prick. What was his name? I can't remember. What a prick!" Frankie poured himself a shot of Jameson whiskey. "So, what's new? We haven't seen you here in a while."

"Not much new. It's the same old shit. Work and women! Keeps you busy!"

Frankie agreed, "Ha! Ha! Busy and broke!"

The door opened and Finch walked in the door. The two men look at her. "Hey guys."

Frankie found her attractive, "Now that's a nice one right there."

"That's my partner."

"You're a lucky man." Frankie winked and reached for a glass.

Finch sat down at the bar. She immediately ordered a drink. "Let me get a double Crown Royal on the rocks." The drink was the best compliment to how she had felt all day.

"So...Meghan..."

"So...Sydney..." They both giggled. "I can't even take you seriously right now."

Brown leaned toward her and whispered in her ear, "You're cute." Brown didn't get much time to flirt with her in public, but he seized the moment whenever he could. "I don't tell you enough." They had the bar to themselves; the night was lovely, the setting was romantic enough to make Meghan more open with her flirtations as well. Finch smiled and looked away, shyly. Frankie handed her the drink and walked away giving them privacy.

"What's up with your mother in law calling and you ignoring her calls? What's going on?"

"We don't talk about that, remember?" Finch reminded him that their time together was about them and no one else, not even Anthony.

Sydney shrugged his shoulders and conceded. He finished his drink. Frankie placed the bottle of Crown Royal and a glass with ice in front of Brown and winked. Frankie went back to shining glasses on the other side of the bar. He got a phone call from Larry and walked into the kitchen to take the call.

"You get that memory card over to the lab?" Finch swiftly changed the subject.

"Let's not talk about work!" Brown wanted to focus the discussion in another direction.

"Agreed." They toasted glasses and smiled at one another.

"So, let's talk about us." Brown was a little uncomfortable because he wasn't sure how Meghan would react. She could turn her soft side off and on like a stop light. She intimidated Brown a little but not enough to keep him at bay. He was sick of the hiding and the secret life they shared. He wanted more, but all the cards were in Meghan's hands. And she knew it.

"What about us, Sydney?" She gulped down the Crown Royal out of nervousness. She knew what he meant, but it wasn't a conversation she was ready to have. She poured another shot.

"I mean us maybe being a little more serious about this you and me thing. I have feelings for you, you know that." He sipped. "I'm tired of... sneaking around in closets or for a late night rendezvous'. I want to dress up and see you in a sexy dress — take you out, buy you things, and have all of this be okay."

"I'm sure the department would like to know you've been fucking your partner, Sydney." Meghan's defense was to be an asshole. She knew he didn't look at her that way. She couldn't look him in the eye. She had strong feelings for him, too.

"I don't 'fuck' you, Finch."

"Then what is it that you do to me? What else would you call it?" She really didn't want to hear his answer but didn't know what else to say to start an argument that would give her an excuse to end the conversation.

"Okay, yes. Sometimes we fuck. Fine! It is what it is, but if you can't tell the difference between the times it's just sex and when I'm making love to you, then maybe I'm fucking up over

110

here and I *should* leave you alone. Because I thought…" Brown moved in closer. "I thought you were making love to me too."

They were both feeling loose from the drinking. Finch had let him get closer than she ever had in public. He ran his hand through her hair and kissed her on the jaw line two soft times. He moved around and gently kissed her on the lips. She was afraid, "Syd, you know my mind is not straight right now. This is too much for me." She pulled away and took another shot. "That's the last one for the night. I have to drive."

Brown wouldn't give up, "Come stay with me tonight. I can't let you drive home, and…"

"I'm fine. I can drive." She meant it. "I can't stay tonight," she lied.

"No. You can stay, but you choose not to. Just stay with me tonight. Please. I need to feel you."

Frankie stepped out of the kitchen and back onto the floor.

Brown sensed he was ready to close up and said, "Sorry, Frankie. We stayed a little longer than we thought. We're gonna head out."

"Take your time. No rush." Frankie was upset after his conversation with Larry. "I have to stay open for a while. Larry's on his way over. He should be walking in shortly. So, I'll still be here."

Finch jumped in, "Thanks, but we really must head out. We have a long day tomorrow." She pulled out her wallet. "What do we owe you?"

"Keep it. It's taken care of."

Brown interjected, "Come on Frankie. Take something."

"Next time," Frankie insisted. "Don't worry about it. You're a good friend."

Brown nodded, "Next time. Thanks again. See you soon."

Sydney and Meghan walked out of the bar just as Larry walked into the bar.

Larry and Frankie's friendship started long ago when they were each 15 years old. Larry was a very quiet and mild tempered kid who lived on the same block as Frankie. He was taller than the rest of the boys and was built stronger. People used to tease him that he was lying about his age. Once, he and Frankie were teased by some boys from the football team. The football team learned the hard way that a quiet demeanor didn't mean a weak punch. Frankie and Larry polished off six football players in two minutes. They never had any more trouble from the team or from anyone else for that matter.

Upon finishing high school, Larry and Frankie each went in different directions, keeping in touch about four times a year. Frankie started running errands for local Italian mob families. Larry went to Bunker Hill Community College and received his associate's degree in Business Administration and then finished his bachelor's in business at UMass Boston. He worked as an auditor for about four years and a personal accountant for another six years.

In 2002 Larry was arrested for soliciting an underage prostitute in Revere. The morning his divorce was finalized, he went on a drinking binge and didn't show up for work. He took three Percocet pills, downed a whole bottle of vodka, and sped through the streets. He finally crashed into a pole on Main Street. Someone called the police. He awoke just as the police arrived and realized he was in an alley with the prostitute performing oral sex on him. He tried to explain that he was too intoxicated to remember what had happened, but no one listened. Frankie made a few calls, got him a lawyer and helped him cut a deal. He pleaded no contest and served one week in prison, agreeing to give up his CPA license in exchange for two years of probation. Frankie had just opened the pub, and Larry came on as manager.

Larry walked into the pub, barely making eye contact with Frankie. He went directly to the back of the bar and grabbed a

Corona. He walked back to the front of the bar and sat at a stool. He popped the top off and took a drink.

Larry looked at Frankie, "You have a lot of cops around here."

Frankie said, "It's how I keep my ears to the ground, and Sydney's a good friend regardless. He keeps me updated on things we would want to know. Things we *need* to know so we don't lose this fucking place."

Larry took out a cigarette. In June of 2004, Massachusetts passed a law banning smoking in restaurants and bars, but since the bar was technically closed, he lit the cigarette and took a drag. He said, "Frankie, I don't want to argue with you about what to do with this place. It's yours, not mine. I've been here to support you since day one, but I feel like there is more to this decision than a subtle warning from a cop."

"There's no such thing as a subtle warning." Frankie grabbed a Sam Adams for himself. He opened it and took a drink. "I never intended to keep the club open."

"Well you should have discussed that with me."

"I didn't know it was that important to you."

"It's not that the club is that important. It's about keeping the books in the black."

"You don't even know anything about the books."

"I'm an accountant. I do know." Larry took a drink. "You think because your little girlfriend came in here and put some receipts into a program that you know more than I do about how we are doing?"

Frankie was getting upset. "So this is about Abigail? What has she done to you?"

"What has she done to me? What has she done to you, Frankie? You've been acting like the world revolves around her needs. You close that club, and you will be making a slim profit. You'll barely be able to pay yourself after all the bills are paid. And with all the free drinks you give away at the bar, you can kiss it goodbye."

"I know, Larry. I won't be making a killing with this place. But I didn't start the bar to be rich. I truly like what I do. And you're right. Abigail has changed me. She reminds me of what's important in life, not to mention that I'm getting too old for this shit." Frankie scratched his head and took a few sips of the beer before he said another word. "My gut tells me our time is up with the club. It's not just Abigail. She's a part of it, but Sydney telling me to chill out only confirms how I've been feeling. I know you love the club. I do, too, so if you want to keep it open..."

"No," Larry interrupts. "No, Frankie. This is the first time we've ever sat down and talked about this. I see the sincerity in you. You want to end it, fine. I'm with you. I just don't want you making this decision because of Abigail. You don't know her. You're not her father."

"I sure wish I was."

For the first time Frankie was honest with Larry about how he was feeling about the bar, the club and Abigail. They talked for another hour before Larry left with a smile on his face. They both were satisfied with the honest conversation which had been long overdue. Larry was glad that Frankie was open about his feelings; but in the back of his mind, his skepticism for Abigail increased. Larry needed to know more about her, what she was up to and where she had come from. He was determined to find out.

BROWN'S APARTMENT

Brown and Finch made love in Brown's bed. Meghan Finch was on top of him. She sat up straight, exposing a large scar on her back from an incident that had happened long ago. When they were done, they laid together naked, barely covered with his gray sheet. He held her tightly. He kissed her on the forehead. She smiled as a tear came to her eye. He wiped it away and kissed her again.

ATKINS' RESIDENCE

Abigail was still hanging out with Roger at his house. It was a relief to get out of the 10 x 8 foot room where she was accustomed to spending her nights. At first, she and Roger were in his garage. He welded something Abigail couldn't identify. She paced back and forth and rubbed the back of her neck thinking about the tattoos she had recently discovered. Roger pulled up the mask he was wearing. He realized she wasn't interested in what he was doing and figured it was time to wrap up this project.

Roger asked, "Wanna call it a night?"

Abigail answered, "Sure."

They put away the materials and went into the kitchen.

Roger and Abigail sat for a while at the kitchen table not saying much of anything to one another. Roger sketched a drawing of another idea that had popped into his mind. Abigail's head tried to piece together her thoughts after the last nightmare, which was more vivid than the last. She made a circle with her finger on the table as she pondered the images Roger took of the tattoos on her spine. Roger stole a few glances but realized she wasn't paying him much attention to him. Ms. Atkins was in the living room watching an Elvis documentary she had recorded days earlier. She never missed a report on her hero. Roger gazed into the room.

"That woman is obsessed." He shook his head and walked over to a cabinet which held a 750 ml bottle of Jack Daniels. He grabbed two glasses, ice and poured a decent amount into the glasses. He handed one to Abigail. She gladly accepted the offer. "We work in a bar and I haven't had a good stiff drink in a long time." He tried to break the cold silence that permeated the room, but Abigail's mind was drifting off into a place of puzzling thoughts and endless confusion.

Abigail swirled her drink around, watching the ice melt away in the warm liquor. Little bubbles formed on the side of the glass. "Tell me about yourself, Roger. Where are you from? What did you do? Your family... shit like that." This is the first time she had made eye contact with him in about five minutes.

Roger was just about to stand up but sat back down and took a short sip of his drink. Clearly it was a little strong for him. "Man, no one has ever asked me that. I'm not sure what you wanna know, but: Hi. My name is Roger, and life for me ain't been no crystal stair." He said with a southern voice. It was the only line he remembered from the Langston Hughes poem "Mother to Son" that his 10th grade English teacher, Mrs. Mackie, read during Black History Month.

They laughed. The liquor slowly seeped into their blood stream, and the quiet moment in the kitchen was once again warm and fuzzy.

Roger said, "I'm kidding. I was born in this city called Agawam, Massachusetts, on the west side of the state. My dad was a teacher in Springfield, but when I was three years old, he died in a car accident on I91 heading south to our exit. He was almost off the exit when two trucks collided. One of the trucks twisted, and the trailer fell on my dad's car. I'm not sure if this is what you wanna hear."

Abigail was excited, "No. No. If you're okay to talk about it, please tell me. I want to know more about you. Tell me about your mom."

Roger had her attention and loved it, "My mother worked at a subsidiary for this company called Global Tech–Gin in northern Connecticut. My mom was one of their lead engineers. They worked on government funded projects, mostly classified. One day she was inspecting a project that she continuously said was unsafe. The company had invested millions into the machine and didn't want to drop the project. They figured it was her team doing something wrong and insisted that she 'make it work!' During an experiment, the damn thing blew up and a huge chunk of it fell on her foot and crushed it to pieces. We moved out here so she could recover at her sister's house, and we never left. She bought this place with the settlement money, and here I am."

Abigail was stunned, "Wow. That's crazy. That's an incredible story. I never knew your mom had gone through something so devastating." She turned the sympathy off in an instant. "So, who are your friends?"

Roger confidently said, "Just you, Elvis. My aunt never had kids. I barely know anyone on my dad's side. High school was a drag. I was 'gifted' so they say. Nerds don't have friends."

Abigail giggled at the fact that he was ever considered to be a nerd.

Roger continued, "A few kids picked on me. People didn't have sympathy for the bullied back in those days. My gym teacher used to yell, 'Chin up! Chest out! Be a man and sock 'em!' Well, Mom put me in Tae Kwon Do for a few months. And I did sock 'em back one day. I cracked John Waterford's skull with a mop stick. That ended that. It was the perfect excuse to remove me from the school. I was rushed out of school and put into a pre–college program at MIT for students who were advanced in math and science. I did well there so they gave me a full scholarship, but I quit. I couldn't deal. I needed a job. Walked into Frankie's and here we are."

Abigail seemed unsatisfied. She was more interested in the mother's story.

Roger said, "Not very interesting huh?"

Abigail shrugged.

"Don't expect a dramatic story when you get your memory back, Elvis. Sometimes people would rather not remember. Maybe subconsciously your mind purposely jumbled things up to keep you out of trouble or something. I think it will come back one day."

"I don't think it's ever going to coming back."

"It will."

They both take a shot.

"If you could know anything about yourself, what would you want to know?"

Abigail thought for a moment. She looked away from Roger and focused on the drink. "I don't think I could narrow it down, but I would like to know about my family and where I'm from. Things like that."

"Shit. I would want to know who shot me and why? Elvis, people out here don't get shot just because. You were shot and you were hiding. You ran from something. Maybe that something or someone is still looking for you."

Abigail agreed, "Yes I have been thinking about that, too. My license says I'm from Utica, NY. Maybe I should go there and dig around. Maybe the library has articles I could search online. Maybe my name will come up."

"There's an idea, but you could be walking right back into the mess you were running from."

Just then, Roger's mother entered the kitchen. She walked in and stared at Roger and Abigail from the lower lenses of her bifocals. "Want something to eat?"

"No thank you, Mom. I'm actually going to take her home in a few."

"Good. I was going to say. One more night, Elvis and I'm collecting rent." Ms. Atkins smiled and turned away.

Abigail smirked and shook her head. Roger giggled as he took another sip.

FRANKIE'S APARTMENT

Frankie was in his apartment above the bar doing bicep curls with 40 pound weights. When his arms were fatigued, he switched to squats and lunges. When he was done with those, he did a few pushups and then he took a shower. The shower was warm and comforting to his aching muscles. He turned on the TV, picked up his computer and entered a few receipts into a Quick Books file named <PUB RECEIPTS>. He had a large pile of receipts that were clipped together by date and stuffed into a manila envelope. He had slacked off a little on keeping up with his finances, but since Abigail had been there, things had been a lot better in the finances department. She kept things in order that he had never considered. She was good at organizing his paperwork and made sure bills were paid on time.

After about an hour, Frankie was done inputting receipts into the program. He saved the file, closed the program and put the computer on a side desk. He pulled his shades close and bent down. Under the desk was a large vent. Frankie opened the vent and pulled out a chest. The chest was a maple 14 x 24 x 10 inch trunk with two gold Master pad locks on the two gold hinges. He threw the chest on the bed and grabbed the keys from a jar on a shelf. He unlocked each lock and opened the chest.

Frankie pulled out four small lock boxes and opened them. One contained a .38 Taurus revolver, the other a colt .45. The last two held Smith and Wesson nine millimeter guns. He gave each one a quick look and put them back in the lock boxes. In another box, he had about $100,000 in cash. He took $3,000 from the stack and placed it on his desk. He closed that box and put it aside.

In a small leather sack Frankie opened, there were three passports of Frankie with a younger face. He looked at one with the name Jonah Thomas. "This one is expired." He tossed it aside. Frankie then pulled another box from the very bottom, which lay under many boxes of ammunition.

The box was thin and made of a cardboard, with a white coating on the exterior. Frankie opened the box and took out a group of photos. These were pictures of him and Amy Chan, the woman from the launderette who had stolen his heart many years before, at a time when Frankie was living a life of corruption. He thought to himself how he hid the truth about what happened to her. Midnight passed and today was the anniversary of her death, which meant he would anonymously send money to her family. He still harbored a guilty conscience concerning the events of her death.

He received a text from Abigail. "SORRY SO LATE. HEADING HOME NOW. DON'T WAIT UP."

CHAPTER 8

BOSTON METRO STATION

Abigail and Roger entered the turnstile for the Orange Line Metro to get back into town. Roger decided to take the train ride with Abigail back to Frankie's and crash on the couch in the common area upstairs. As they waited on the platform Roger and Abigail inspected the Metro map hanging on the wall. Roger pulled his hood over his head mocking Abigail since she always covered her head with her hood.

"I was thinking about getting a tattoo," Roger made one of his famously random statements. "I was thinking of a few robotic gears as a sleeve over here so my arm would look like I was a robot underneath. I had this idea..." he noticed Abigail was ignoring him. He felt bad. "Sorry, Elvis. I didn't mean to be insensitive."

She didn't look at him fully. She nodded and said, "It's cool. I know you don't mean to insult me. Guess I'm just hypersensitive right now. My head is killing me, I'm confused... I'm hungry..."

"Ah, I have some snacks. What are you willing to do for them?"

"I'd rather starve to death."

They laughed as the train pulled into the stop. They waited until it came to a complete stop. The doors opened, and they walked in.

LARRY'S APARTMENT

Larry was in his apartment, sitting on the couch with his feet on the coffee table, his laptop balanced on his thighs while he ran another Google search: "UTICA NEW YORK MURDER SUSPECTS AND VICTIMS." He saw hundreds of articles. He scanned through them quickly, but none triggered a connection with Abigail; and there were too many to read entirely through. He huffed. He tried again: "UPSTATE NEW YORK MISSING WOMEN AND RUNAWAYS." Up popped an open database of no less than 500 names— some coupled with photos; some with baby pictures of women ranging in age from nine to 72 years old who had been missing for many years.

He downloaded the list as an excel file and placed it into a folder he named <PUZZLE PIECES>.

The <PUZZLE PIECES> folder was full of files that Larry had secretly kept on Abigail, starting with pictures of her he had downloaded off the security cameras at the pub. He had pictures of her from all angles. Unbeknownst to Frankie, Larry's curiosity had gotten the best of him. He even had photos of the items in her purse, including a scan of her license.

05101990

"May 10th 1990. This age may not be accurate, but I'll start here." He assumed Abigail was in her early to middle 20's so he narrowed his search to begin with women born in 1987 to 1992 just in case.

"This is better than nothing," he said as he adjusted his glasses. The search narrowed down to 150 or so. He narrowed the search again to women who had gone missing in the past year. The candidates dropped down to 56 names.

"This is more manageable."

Larry was obsessed.

THE ORANGE LINE

The train had about ten other people in their section. Each person had something occupying their time during the squeaky and shaky ride provided courtesy of the MBTA. One woman had a toddler in a stroller. The little boy wore a small Celtics jersey and white shoes. He sucked a bottle and stared at Abigail, smiling and giggling. Roger noticed Abigail's face light up as she waved back at the little boy. She blew him a kiss and the child laughed.

Roger commented, "Wow! He gets a lot more action than I do."

"What can I say? I have a thing for cute faces." She stuck out her tongue at the little boy and waved again. The boy giggled. His mother was totally unaware of the interaction. She was heavily focused on a game on her iPad. Roger was surprised that Abigail was showing a softer side. *Maybe she isn't a machine after all. Probably just an alien.*

Another man on the train was obviously a business man, or at least appeared to be one. He was ferociously texting and grunting. At one point he opened his briefcase and flipped through the papers, then sent another text. His phone rang, and he picked up. "I'm getting off at the next stop. Just wait! I'll have it ready." He hung up the phone, jammed the papers back into a folder before he stuffed a small pile of folders back into the briefcase. He took a few heavy breaths as the train slowed for the Downtown Crossing stop.

Over the intercom a mechanical voice spoke. "Next stop Downtown Crossing." At this stop Abigail and Roger would also get off the train so that they could transfer to the Red Line. The train slowed to a halt and the doors opened. When they had all exited, the man loosened his tie and took off running through the station.

As they stood on the platform, Roger and Abigail noticed an LED sign displaying "THE RED LINE IS NO LONGER RUNNING FOR MAINTENANCE PURPOSES AND WILL RESUME AT 7AM... PLEASE TAKE THE SHUTTLE..."

"Oh great!" Abigail was tired and wanted to get back Frankie's.

"Let's just walk." Roger was frustrated and figured walking for an hour was better than the other options.

"Yeah, we might as well just keep moving."

Abigail and Roger exited the platform through the turnstile. They left the station and walked down the street. It was very late and quiet on the road. Roger insisted that they take a short cut through an alley, which seemed like the most reasonable thing to do. They were joking and laughing as they passed through the smelly, dank passage.

"This smells worse than Frankie's alley."

"This smells like the basement at the end of the week." Abigail suddenly stopped in her tracks.

"What's wrong?" asked Roger.

Abigail looked around. She whispered, "Something's not right. Come back."

"You're just being scary. Come on."

"We can't see through here, Rog."

"It's fine. As long as you can see the other side, then you know which way to go. Come on. I've walked through here a hundred times." Abigail reluctantly followed Roger, watching every dark corner.

Midway through the alley, Abigail grabbed Roger's collar and pulled him back just as a knife swung through the air. The blade barely missed Roger's throat. Roger grabbed his neck and gasped for air. Three men wearing all black emerged from the darkness, barely visible to the eye until they were about two arms' length away. Abigail's senses were heightened.

Everything suddenly magnified around her. She could feel her senses expanding within her body. She could hear another man who was still hiding in the shadows. She looked in his direction and worried that his intentions were worse than the others. Then, she quickly assessed their surroundings.

"There is another one hiding over there. I can smell him."

Roger was completely frightened and perplexed. He couldn't see the man Abigail was talking about, and the other men were closing in on them. He felt extremely helpless but felt the need to do what any other man would do in this situation. He stepped in front of Abigail to protect her. He pleaded to the men, "It's cool. It's cool. We don't want any trouble. We just want to pass through."

"We're taking your money," one of the perpetrators said with a raspy voice. He wiped his nose with his sleeve.

"And the bitch. We're taking her, too," the second man said as he flipped open a knife. "Let her go."

"Move out of the way," the third man demanded. Abigail could tell that he was the weakest of the three. She could sense a bit of fear in his voice.

They waved around their knives. Slight reflections of light sparked of the sharp tips of the blades.

"I can't give you the girl. Just take our money. We won't say anything, we just want to go."

"We're not asking for permission," the first thug was clearly leading this attack. He was the most aggressive.

The three men circled around Abigail and Roger. Roger was horrified but wouldn't allow himself to back down. Though they were outnumbered, Abigail was eerily calm. He mind was calculating distances and depths. Roger knew they were in serious trouble. He was also calculating. He figured he could take out one of them, but knew a full out fight would be hopeless. "When you get a chance, run. Don't worry about me."

"I'm not leaving you."

"You have to. We don't have a choice."

Without warning Abigail, Roger tried a surprise attack method and threw the first punch knocking one man off his feet. Immediately the other men swung their knives. The knives cut through the air slicing Roger's arm. Roger pushed Abigail away just as the men closed in and attacked him. He fought back as much as he could. Punch after punch flew through the air but Roger was beginning to lose steam. Abigail didn't want to run, so she tried to pull the men off of Roger.

"Let him go!" She pulled one man by his jacket. Two of the men tossed her off like a rag doll. Abigail hit the ground with a hard thud, keeping her eye on the corner where she was sure she heard another person. Just then, someone pulled her hood, choking her. The man dragged her to the other side of the alley. She was kicking and tugging back on her collar in her attempt to catch her breath. The other two men were pounding on Roger; it was hopeless. The man let her go. She lay on the concrete for a brief moment, trying to catch her breath. Abigail quickly gained back control and pounced onto her feet. Roger was barely moving. Two men stopped beating Roger, and the first perpetrator who had started it all approached Abigail.

Roger found just enough strength to utter the word, "Run!"

Abigail looked at the end of the alley but refused to run. The other two men held down Roger as they rummaged through his pockets. The first perpetrator backed Abigail against the wall. He grabbed her face and smiled. He suddenly slapped her in the face. All went silent. His hand also popped her in the ear and a ringing sound echoed through her head. Her heart was beating a mile a minute. She was afraid and fearless at the same time. Part of her told her to run, while the other part made her feel like she had to stay and fight. Roger was yelling something to her, but she couldn't hear anything except the beat of her own heart. The other man who was hiding in the dark emerged.

"Why are you fools still playing with this little girl and her faggot friend?" He spit on the ground as he walked closer. The first perpetrator saw him coming. He released her face, allowing the man from the shadows to take over. He looked at Roger and told him, "Yell again, and I kill her without a second thought." He looked at Abigail. He placed a knife against her nose. He harshly grabbed her hair and cut it. He took a chunk of it off the left side. He smelled it and rubbed it across his face. He ran the knife up the hoodie, cutting it loose. He ripped off her hoodie. "This is gonna be fun." He turned to Roger. "You can watch if you like."

Unexpectedly, the man from the shadows punched Abigail in the face, and she saw a spark. Her head slammed against the brick wall causing her to go into a daze. She lost consciousness for a second as everything became a blur. Her body slumped, and she slid down the wall. She could still hear the ringing in her head, which only intensified.

Behind the ringing, she heard one of her attacker's voice say, "Get up and turn around." He intended to rape her and pass her off to his buddies who were still holding Roger to the ground with their boots.

Roger was badly beaten but managed a few words. Softly he mumbled, "Please let her go."

The attackers were ready to rape. One looked at Roger with a stiff evil look and said, "Don't worry. After the show, you're next. Some of my brothers like boys, too."

Roger squirmed to get away but their hold was too tight.

Abigail straightened herself up as much as she could. She looked at Roger, pleading with her eyes for him to find a little strength, whatever he could muster up, and get away. They caught each other's glance for a moment before the man from the shadows reached back and punched Abigail in the stomach, knocking the wind out of her. The men laughed. She lost her breath and with that, the world was spinning. The perpetrators were all laughing as she gasped for air but it would not fill her lungs. Her nose was bleeding. Her sight was fading. Staggering, she took a few steps forward. Her face was bruised and blood dripped from her mouth. Her eyes were watering. Roger shouted her name, but she could only hear the pounding thud of her heart beat. It slowed down and slowed and slowed until it stopped. She was not breathing heavily but her body went cold and stiff.

Suddenly, she gasped for air; but it was an inhale as if the breath of life had been returned to her body. Her face extended towards the sky. Her arms stiffened and stretch firm down towards the ground. A wave of heat emitted from her head and flowed into her mouth. As she sucked in the air, her chest expanded. The veins in her arms popped. When she opened her eyes, they were illuminated to the color of ocean blue. They were like two blue glowing bulbs. Her canine teeth extended ever so slightly. The men's laughs slowly but surely ceased. She snapped her head down to look around. From the lenses of her eyes she could suddenly see everything, almost as if the lights had been turned on in a very dark place. Her head turned to the left, then quickly to the right. Instantaneously she absorbed and analyzed everything around her, calculating the men's location, Roger's location, the escape distance, their weight and height. Within a few seconds she analyzed their muscle mass, speed, and potential stamina. She also analyzed and sensed a growing fear surrounding them. The cruel men suddenly stepped backwards, slowly releasing Roger. Roger was too surprised to get up to his feet. He too, was afraid.

Abigail walked as if the perpetrators did not alarm her. She walked past them over to Roger and picked him up with supernatural strength. She set him on his feet. Her head whipped around. She looked at the men. She ran toward them

128

so fast that she became a blur. She took the perpetrators one by one into the dark and broke their necks, ripping them from their shoulders, tossing their limbs across the alley. She moved so quickly they didn't have time to get away. Each stood there in shock and could not move as they watched the others come and go. *Three down, one to go.*

The perpetrator from the shadows had been the last to participate in the attack. *And he will be the last to go down.*

He stood there, frightened, unsure of what to do. He urinated on himself. She watched him for a few seconds, then disappeared into a shadow. He backed up, unsure where her attack would come from, but he knew it was coming. "WHERE ARE YOU? YOU FUCKING BITCH! FUCK YOU!" He screamed at the top of his lungs, but no one could hear him. She breathed, growled and drooled stalking the man. "Where are you?" He mumbled. Tears flowed down his face. He had never been so afraid.

She suddenly appeared from the other side of him, creeping out of another shadow. *How did she get over there?* She walked around, stalking him, slowly approaching. He couldn't take the pressure and pulled out a gun. She ran directly towards him. He fired and missed. He fired again. She came towards him fearlessly. He was too sick to run. She reached him but instead of smashing into him she hopped onto the wall. On all fours she gripped the wall climbing around, as he fired at her. She ran in an arch over his head. He tried to run when suddenly she appeared behind him and snapped his neck. She tore him apart limb by limb.

Covered in blood, Abigail saw Roger standing across the alley, holding his groin. She walked over to him. Her breathing was fast. Her chest went up and down like a pump. He was mortified. "Abigail?"

She didn't answer but walked closer and closer.

"ABIGAIL! Abby. Elvis?" She kept coming until she was directly in his face. He pleaded, "Ok. Maybe Elvis was a bad idea. Wait, wait. It's me!" He gripped his crotch, trying to hold back from urinating on himself.

Abigail showed her teeth as she growled at Roger.

"Me... Roger. Me good. Me, friend! Me, friend!" His pleading was ineffective. She did not answer but sniffed around him like she was inspecting another potential meal. The glow of her blue eyes dimmed, but her eyes were still blue. Roger backed up toward the building behind him. She followed him and placed herself nose to nose with Roger. "What the fuck. Me, Roger. Me, Friend! Me good! Don't kill me! Don't kill me."

Suddenly, Abigail backed away, reached her arms towards the sky and pulled them down quickly. She breathed out heavily, and the heat she had inhaled released, going back into the air, surrounding her head and seeping back into the crown of her head. One more gasp and she returned to herself. Her eyes were brown again. She shouted, "Roger!"

"ELVIS MOTHER FUCKIN PRESLEY!!! What the hell was that?!"

"We have to go!"

"No shit! Can you run?"

"Hell yeah!"

"RUN!" Roger insisted. Abigail and Roger began to run. "Wait, wait, wait." Roger went back to where the chunk of Abigail's hair was. He found it next to her hooded shirt. He scooped up as much as he could, grabbed Abigail's hoodie; and they took off. "Let's go." Roger and Abigail ran toward the street and disappeared around the corner.

CHAPTER 9

SLIPPING AWAY
EARLY MORNING

Early morning at about quarter past three, the sun had not yet risen. Finch crept out of Brown's apartment while he was asleep. He didn't notice. She had quickly slipped on her clothes, gotten into her car and left to go home.

Finch walked into her house, sat on the couch and took off her shoes. She played with the engagement ring on her finger. Her eyes watered. She got up from the couch and left the living room. She went into the bathroom and washed the tears and make up from her face. She went back into her room, changed her clothes and lay in the bed. No sooner had she closed her eyes to get in a couple hours of sleep then she snapped her body up straight. She knew she had heard something or someone. She tip toed out of the bed and grabbed her pistol off the dresser top. She checked to make sure it was fully loaded. She cocked the trigger back.

Finch walked quietly through the house with her gun raised. She peeked around each corner as she stepped through to the front door. She checked the door. It was locked. She walked through the house to the back door. It, too, was locked. She looked to see if any windows were open, but nothing was abnormal. She could sense someone was in the house but could not find anyone. She was frustrated. Fear grew in her heart. She prayed this wasn't one of Pearson's goons coming to get her after a long silence. She went back into her room and upon entering, she opened her mouth wide and dropped the gun on the floor.

She asked, "Why are you doing this to me?" She cried, placing her hand on her forehead.

ABIGAIL'S ROOM

At about 3:30 am Abigail and Roger arrived at the bar. They entered through the back door in the alley. She and Roger were both bruised and covered in blood, both theirs and their assailants. Abigail and Roger tiptoed into the kitchen and grabbed a black bag. She ran hot water in the sink. Roger was shaken up. Abigail was strangely calm. *She had done this before.* When Roger had first met Abigail, she was cold and hard. In the past few months she had softened up, becoming more personable and less introverted. That cold stranger was back looking at Roger the way she used to, like he was an empty, meaningless shell.

She went into the closet and grabbed a bottle of bleach.

She demanded, "Take off your shoes."

Roger complied fearfully. She looked at Roger without an ounce of sympathy. He was distraught but yet again holding on very well. He was in shock. She plugged up the sink so that the water would collect. The two of them stood in their underwear, covering up the mess they had created.

"Get a mop," she ordered again.

Roger grabbed the mop without hesitation, totally trusting in Abigail's direction. He thought, *Maybe the SUPER BEAST will return if I refuse.* He didn't know what else to say or do, so he complied without objection.

Abigail dropped the mop into the bleach water and soaked it again and again— not sparing an ounce of bleach. She told Roger to mop the floor from the door into the kitchen. He did as he was told. He brought the mop back. She rinsed it in the bleach again and told him to do it again. He did this three times. In the meantime, Abigail dropped their clothes into the water to soak. She finally let the mop and the clothes sit in the bleach water– the color of their clothes faded before their eyes.

Next, Abigail took the shoes and grabbed a lighter and a butter knife. She lit the gas burner and heated up the knife. Roger was totally mystified.

"We are not keeping these clothes. It would be best to burn them, but we will draw too much attention. We will split them up and discard them in the morning," she told Roger.

She then took the heated knife and made marks in the bottom of their sneakers by melting parts of the rubber soles. "Police look for distinct wear and tear marks in shoes that match prints left at crime scenes. I'm going to change these up a little. Go shower."

Roger didn't hesitate a second. He went upstairs, showered and went into her room. He sat on the edge of the bed until she came in from her turn taking a shower. He expected the next list of demands would follow except that the confident, demanding, controlling, deadly Abigail had turned soft again. She looked worn out and drained of energy. *What have I done?*

In her underwear and socks, she climbed into her bed shivering. Her head was pounding so badly, she couldn't completely open her eyes. Roger sat down next to Abigail and tucked her in. He rubbed her back, her arms and gently touched her hair, comforting her. She closed her eyes. He grabbed a pillow and a foot blanket to lie on the floor. She grabbed his arm and pulled him towards her to lie with her in the bed. Roger climbed into the bed. He moved cautiously, sliding under the covers. He lay next to her, pressing his body against hers.

In bed Abigail innocently wrapped her body around his to get warmer. She threw her arms around his neck and mixed her legs in with his. She didn't mean to tease Roger or entice him; she needed to be held to relax her racing heart. He put his arms around her torso, pressing his hands against her back. He rested the side of his face against hers and squeezed her closer. He rolled on his back and put her head on his chest as he pulled her closer. She fell asleep to his rhythmic heart beat, which raced for another 15 minutes before it slowed to normal pace. He fell asleep 20 minutes after she did.

The night brought about a hurricane of memories, thoughts, pain and emotions. Abigail's strength had also returned after months of dormancy. She felt a painful jolt rush through her body. Her veins bulged as if they were being pumped with adrenaline and some type of super stimulus, causing heightened senses and awareness. She woke and jumped out of the bed. Her eyes were glowing blue. She wanted to scream from the burning sensation running through her body. Her skin crawled. At first she wasn't sure if this was another nightmare. She soon realized she was not dreaming when she saw Roger shift in the bed. Roger was so tired that he didn't awake in the presence of her animalistic fit.

Abigail ran down stairs to the bar, out the back door and into the alley. She needed air. She grabbed at her throat, her face and scratched the brick wall outside. Bursts of pain and heat throbbed in her body. She gritted her teeth as her canine teeth slightly extended. Her body rapidly shook and trembled as her muscles bulged. She clenched her fists. She was overloaded with energy and couldn't control or release it. She threw her body against the wall and sucked in the cool air as she grabbed her head. Her eyes glowed blue. She looked up and immediately gripped her claws into the brick wall and climbed to the top of the building next door.

Thunder cracked against the black sky. She stood their grunting, breathing intensely, until she calmed down. She was still full of energy, but she and whatever was within negotiated an agreement, and she was at peace. She climbed back down and exhaled. Her eyes turned brown again. Just as she entered the side door, the first drop of rain came down crashing against her heel.

She went back into her room and slipped into the bed with Roger again, turning her back to him, falling asleep within minutes. Her heart raced for a few minutes, beating against her chest. She slept nightmare free for the first time in months. The rain came down hard and fast, just in time to wash away a significant amount of evidence at the crime scene. It came quickly and stopped after 20 minutes of pounding against the earth.

MORNING

The sweet scent of morning after a night of rain filled the room. The sun streamed through the window as it did every morning. Abigail slept like a baby after her secret late night rage in the alley and on the rooftop. She woke up and was slightly startled when she saw Roger sitting in a chair across from her, watching her sleep. He wore a shirt and shorts. He had taken another shower and returned to the room to watch her sleep.

She grabbed her head, aware of the raging headache that continued from the previous night. "Good morning, Roger." She reached through her hair and remembered that a large section of it was cut off the night before.

Roger was frustrated, "We need to talk." It was the first time he had ever expressed his frustration with Abigail.

She attempted to deflect, "UGH. My head hurts so badly. I need a coffee."

Roger insisted that they speak and raised his voice, "Can we talk about what the hell happened last night?" He was upset for more than one reason. Besides the situation in the alley, his involvement in the killings and the release of the *SUPER BEAST*, his emotions and feelings were all over the place. He knew that Abigail must have been traumatized after the transformation. He watched her tremble and shake herself to sleep, but it took every bone in his body to resist the urge to sleep with her that night. He *and* his penis had a bone to pick with Abigail.

Abigail knew this was a huge burden for Roger yet replied, "I can't talk about it right now." She got out of the bed.

Roger stood up and grabbed her arm, "Do you even remember? Do you remember *anything* from last night?"

She ignored the question.

"What the hell was that!? You turned into an 'I don't know what that was' thing, then you ripped those men to pieces like they were made of putty, then..."

Abigail spoke softly, putting her finger over her mouth, reminding Roger that Frankie was in his room. "Okay. Okay. Yes I remember... a lot more than you think– a lot more than I want to remember and it's too much to talk about right now. I didn't mean for that to happen. I don't want to involve you in any of this. I couldn't control it. It just happened, but it helped me remember a few things."

"Wait. Did all of your memory come back?"

"Not all of it. There are a few gaps I need to fill in but I can't do it here."

Roger's curiosity outweighed his anger, "Well, what do you remember?"

Abigail thought for a minute before she answered, "I can't talk about it. I have to get out of here. I'm putting you, Larry and Frankie in danger."

"How are we in danger?"

She didn't want to scare him, but after last night, Roger was worthy of the truth, "Roger, there are others... others like me. They're out there looking for me. They're the ones I came here to avoid. They shot me. I remember now, and I have to go. I should be in hiding and here I am living out in the open. They are close. I can sense it." She left the room, and Roger followed her. Abigail entered the bathroom with Roger following her.

With a concerned voice he said, "Talk to me."

Frankie heard the arguing and was curious to see if the two were okay. He noticed Roger spent the night and wondered if they had been sleeping together all along. *Maybe this is a lover's quarrel.* Then he noticed cuts and bruises on their bodies. Frankie asked, "What happened to you guys?"

They both stared at Frankie offering no answer. Frankie inspected them. Each second that passed, Frankie's anger increased exponentially. He belted out in a voice neither Abigail nor Roger had ever heard. Frankie had almost forgotten he had it in him. "What the hell happened?!"

Roger was terrified so he answered, "We got jumped. It was my fault."

Frankie moved over to Abigail as she inspected her chopped hair and busted lip in the bathroom mirror.

Frankie was concerned like a father, "Are you okay Abby? Come, let me see." He reached out his hand to touch her.

She pulled away and said, "I'm fine. I'm fine."

"Fine? You two look like shit! What happened, Roger?"

Roger knew Frankie would never understand if he tried to explain everything in detail, so he summarized. "We cut through an alley and some thugs jumped us. They held me down and threatened to rape her. They beat us up a bit, took our money..."

Frankie immediately picked up his phone to contact Larry, unaware that Larry would have used this as a "told you so moment."

Frankie said, "Tell me who. I'll take care of it."

Roger didn't want to lie and knew Frankie's help was necessary, but the trouble they were in was a lot more than Frankie knew. Roger said, "Frankie, it's more complicated than that. We're in some serious trouble."

Frankie asked, "What do you mean?"

Roger replied, "They were kicking our asses. This guy punched her in the stomach and..."

Abigail interrupted Roger, "Roger!" She gave him a vicious stare. She wanted him to keep quiet. It was better not to involve Frankie.

Roger cut the story short, "We... We got away."

Frankie was dissatisfied with the abbreviated story, "You just got away huh? Yeah right. Move, Roger." He pushed Roger aside and decided to try again with Abigail. "Abby, just tell me who it was. I'll take care of it. What did they look like? Where did this happen? Give me some details. I'll make some calls and take care of it. You have to tell me."

Abigail answered, "I don't know. We don't know who they were. It was dark. You shouldn't get involved."

Frankie backed away in frustration. He shook his head. Abigail and Roger stood looking around with guilt. Frankie paced back and forth. He thought about calling Larry but decided against it in his effort to respect Abigail's privacy concerning attempted rape. *These matters are sensitive for women. Maybe this is why she is being shy.* His gut told him that something else was up and just wanted them to ask for help, but he knew he couldn't force the issue. He finally asked, "Okay. Does this have anything to do with what's been all over the news this morning?"

Roger asked, "What? What's been on the news?" He looked at Abigail nervously.

Frankie reached over turning on the 20 inch TV in the room. He clicked through the channels until he found the local news station. Samantha Callahan once again reported, "...between the two buildings. This is a gruesome scene. Three men were decapitated and one man's neck was broken. The remains are spread all over the area. The police say they are collecting DNA, but as you know, back alleys are subject to a lot of night traffic, violence and loitering. There's going to be tons of DNA out here that officers will have to sift through. Currently, they have no suspects but..."

Frankie turned off the TV. Abigail kept a straight face, grabbed a towel and turned into the bathroom to shower, shutting the door behind her.

Frankie looked at Roger with the utmost sincerity and said, "I'm not the one you guys should be hiding things from. You know that more than anything. I don't keep secrets from you; but if you can't tell me, I'm sure there is a good reason why. Go clean up and come down when you're done. Get some clean sweats out my closet." Frankie tapped Roger on the back of his head and went down into the bar.

FINCH'S HOUSE

Another sleepless night passed for Finch. "Why are you doing this to me?" was the last thing she remembered saying before Anthony's presence left the room. He was always there reminding her of the most painful memory of her life– losing him. He knew just when to show up. It was like he sensed the hole she carried in her heart was filling up with love for someone else, and he refused to allow it. Anthony was no longer a person she dearly missed, but a being she despised and began to hate. Was he really haunting her, or was she hallucinating? She couldn't tell what brought him to her, but she was sick of it.

There is no acceptable therapy for these things, she thought to herself. *People will laugh or think I am mentally unstable. I can't have that.* She was very concerned about what others would think, knowing she was borderline schizophrenic and walking around town with a gun. She decided that going for early morning runs and marijuana would be her medication for now.

Finch put on her Adidas crops and a pink tank top. She headed out the house and took on a three mile run, finishing just after the sun came up. When she arrived at home she showered and dressed. She plopped herself on the couch and watched the morning news. She also checked email.

For breakfast, she had a GNC vanilla protein shake. As she sucked it down she received a text from Brown saying, "GET DOWN HERE ASAP! FOUR JOHNS IN AN ALLEY." Finch spilled the shake on her chin as she read the text. She wiped it from her face and rushed into her room. She changed, grabbed her things, and headed out to the police station.

CRIME SCENE ALLEY

Brown and Finch arrived on the scene where Abigail had killed the four men in the alleyway. Both sides of the alley were taped off with caution tape. Officers parked their cars on the other side of the tape to prevent the media and onlookers from getting too close to the scene. Once, an on looker dropped a straw from a fountain soda, which was then carried by the wind into the crime scene. The straw was taken in as evidence where his fingerprints were identified. It took two weeks to resolve the matter.

Reporters, including Samantha Callahan, were on the other side of the police cars. Lead Forensics Detective Tammy and Coroner Michelle Cox were already on the scene when Brown and Finch came on. Brown had a thermos full of coffee. Finch took out her phone, ready to take notes.

Brown greeted her first, "Good morning, Alicia."

"Good morning," she replied. "I want you to take a look at this." She walked them closer to one of the displaced limbs. She used a pointer to point. "Now check this out." They move to another section of the scene. "Anything look familiar to you guys? Look at how this head was severed from the body. As if it was torn. Same tear patterns, same scratches..." They walk to another piece, "Look at this guy, torn limb from limb..."

Finch interjected, "Like the Robert Benson arm!" Her eyes lit up as she took notes into her document.

Tammy said, "I wouldn't put that connection on the shared drive yet, but make a personal note. It's *exactly* like his arm, except this victim was beheaded too. Actually, maybe Benson was beheaded and it's sitting on a window sill in Puerto Rico for all we know."

"Or on a building around the corner." Finch added.

Tammy asked, "You guys have any luck speaking with his wife or with the new CEO? Did anything come up from the check of hospitals in the area?"

Finch answered, "Nothing from the hospitals. No reports of amputees that fit the description. They are all lawyered up the ass and refuse to speak but are currently preparing a statement. We should get it soon they said, but I'm sure it will be very general and elusive."

Brown strayed away for a moment. He took a personal tour of the alley before he returned to Finch and Tammy. He commented, "This alley is a DNA buffet. There has gotta be piss, hair and blood from about a thousand John Does out here."

Tammy responded, "And the rain last night... This is really frustrating. We'll still swab and dust what we can and see what we can find, but we're looking for a needle in a haystack.

There weren't any cameras directly facing this area but Chris is working on some footage from another angle we can look at later."

Brown was excited, "Awesome! Tammy, hold this down for me. Can we get a full report in an hour? I have to follow up on something."

"Yes. I got it. You guys are dirtying up my scene anyway."

He smiled, "Ok, We'll meet you in the lab."

Sydney and Meghan got into Sydney's Wrangler. Sydney pulled off. Meghan didn't understand why he wanted to leave so hastily. "Where are we going?"

Brown sipped his coffee one more time before putting it into the cup holder in the center console. He said, "I'm not satisfied with a few things about that Benson case. We have a murderer on the loose and these fools at Chapel and Case refuse to speak. The wife of a missing armless man won't comment, and everyone else around is oblivious? I don't like it."

"I agree. Someone is covering things up."

"That's clear to me, but why?" Brown asked.

"Oh, I'm sure there are a myriad of reasons …investors, stock prices, secrets, children, insurance. I'm sure they are shuffling their feet behind closed door trying to prepare for the worst."

"But the connection between Benson, Chapel and Case and these random killings eludes me and the fact that people are not talking is burning me up." Brown sipped his coffee.

"Well, people don't talk out of fear of intimidation by someone else or if they are personally involved." Meghan looked out the window again and asked, "So where are we going?"

FRANKIE'S PUB

142

Frankie made home fries, grits, turkey sausage, and omelets with chicken, tomato, onion, chives and cheese. He placed the food on three plates and entered the main floor. He placed a plate in front of Roger, one at an empty seat, and the last plate he took for himself. Roger devoured the food immediately. Frankie inspected Roger's face as he ate the food from his plate. Roger knew Frankie was looking and thus kept his eyes locked to food on the table. He was ashamed that he was keeping such a huge secret from Frankie. Roger kept his head low. They did not speak. They could hear Abigail descend from the upper level. She came down quickly. When she turned around the corner, their mouths dropped.

Abigail cut her hair into a sexy Mohawk style with the sides low. She added dark makeup around her eyes and a dark brown pigment to her lips. The top level of her hair swooped across her face. The sides of her hair were shaved down, exposing more tattoos in her scalp. She found an old pair of sun glasses and a black leather jacket in a box in her room, so she put them on. She walked over to the men and slapped $1000 on the table in front of them. It was money she saved from tip money and wages at the pub.

Abigail said, "For the jacket and ... for everything else. It's not much but it's all I have."

Frankie received the gesture as an insult. He slid the money back over the table and said, "I don't want your money."

She didn't argue. She took the money back and walked towards the door with all her things stuffed into a backpack. She didn't say goodbye. She turned her back without hesitation.

Frankie asked her, "Where are you going?"

She didn't respond.

Her hand pressed against the cold metal bar on the door. Frankie stood up and yelled at her with a stern voice, one reminiscent of a father reprimanding a stubborn child, "Where the hell are you going?!"

She stopped in her tracks and she turned around.

Abigail respectfully responded to Frankie, who she knew cared about her, "If I tell you, it will only make things worse. I have to get outta here. Frankie, thanks for everything. I really appreciate you. You too, Roger."

Frankie calmed down, "Come sit down for a minute. Please."

Abigail gave in. She walked back and sat at the table where breakfast had been waiting for her.

Frankie continued, "If something is wrong, this is the place to talk about it. You're family, Abigail."

She responded, "I just don't want to bring trouble to you, Roger or the pub. You guys don't understand. I wasn't shot in Boston. I was shot about 50 miles from here. I was chased... and ran here— the entire way on foot. There are things about me that are not natural. It's not just the people looking for me. It's me. I could hurt you too. You're a big guy, Frankie but you can't comprehend the strength... There are still some things I don't remember. I can't explain so much of what is happening. It's not fair to involve you guys. And the things I *do* remember..." she stirred her fork around on the plate.

Roger looked guilty, dropped his head and said, "I can help you, Abigail."

She first thought that Roger's suggestion to help was a simple and kind gesture. Then she looked deeper into his expression and realized there was more to the comment than she initially thought. She tilted her head, looking curiously into Roger's eyes as he lifted his head to further explain. She sensed there was a certain level of truth in his voice that made her believe he had something worth listening to on his mind. She nibbled on her split lip and exhaled.

Roger said, "We should talk. I need to be honest with you about something. We should probably head back to my house and talk."

Abigail nodded. They quickly finished eating and rose up from their chairs, heading towards the door. Roger grabbed his things and followed her. Frankie picked up his keys and tossed them to Roger. He trusted Roger more than he wanted to. Frankie said, "Take the truck." Frankie didn't get the whole story from Roger, but at that table, while waiting for Abigail to come down for breakfast, Roger had told Frankie a few things that were almost unbelievable. He told Frankie about the incident in the alley and that Abigail had saved them. He didn't give a complete description of her rage, but Frankie knew something sacred had happened in that alley. And lastly, Roger had explained to Frankie what he was about to tell Abigail on the ride back to his house.

FLASHBACK (EARLY MORNING)

About two hours after Abigail had slipped back into the bed from her late night fit, Roger woke up to a text from his mother, "CALL ME NOW!!"
The phone sounded like a woodpecker, buzzing against the wooden floor. He left the room and called his mother. With a sleepy voice he asked, "Hey Mom. It's late! Are you okay? What's going on?"

Ms. Atkins sounded serious as ever, "Bring your ass home, Roger."

She never usually bothered Roger about staying out late or coming home by a certain time. Roger knew that something was bothering her, but the sense of urgency in her tone was one he hadn't heard in a very long time. The last time he remembered her being overly nervous about things was when they first moved from Connecticut to Boston.

Terry Atkins, a disabled mother of one, would hear voices at night and would run into Roger's room to make sure he was okay. She would lay in the bed with him and cuddle next to him as if they were in danger during a thunderstorm, hurricane or even a mild wind that moved a few plants around on the porch. Before bed time, she double locked all the windows and doors. She closed the shades and blinds and always kept the TV going at night. She slept with a knife under her pillow and gave Roger a knife to keep in the night stand. Her paranoia lasted for about three years after the move to Boston. It took her many years to explain to Roger why she panicked so often. This reminded him of those days.

She repeated herself, "Roger, please... come home now!"

Roger was still waking up, "What... Why?"

She explained, "Your friend Elvis is in a heap of shit. I saw some pictures on your bed..." She took a deep breath before she continued, "I haven't seen those marks in years, but I will never forget them. Never!"

Terry Atkins continued to tell him a few things before she decided that speaking on the phone was a bad idea. *I'm forgetting basic no no's of discretion. Phones are not secure.* She reemphasized to Roger how important it was for him to make his way home as soon as possible. Then she hung up the phone. She scratched the back of her neck and paced through the kitchen. Ms. Atkins spied through the window curtains. Her state of paranoia had returned with full force. She was perspiring and mumbling. Terry walked back and forth in the house as her anxiety increased.

Roger couldn't wait to get home to get more answers and he couldn't wait to tell Abigail that maybe his mother held the key to finding long overdue answers to her questions.

CHAPTER 10
LARGE CORNFIELD
FOUR MONTHS EARLIER

The night was seasonably warm, with a cool tickling breeze. Overhead, the faint cry of a crow echoed over the hills of grass and trodden earth. Silence and mist fell upon clearing on the other side of a forest, which opened to a 100–acre farm. There was a small house and large barn with cracking sides which hadn't been painted in years, but the updated tractor in it suggested that the farm wasn't abandoned. It was off season until spring when plowing and planting would resume. All lights were off in the house. A small stream of smoke ascended from the chimney.

The former corn rows were still visible after a season of a few winter storms and heavy rain. Suddenly, coming out of the forest edge, bare feet splashed through the muddy old cornfield. The feet belonged to a woman. She stopped. She looked around and listened carefully. It was Abigail. Her eyes were blazing blue and her muscles were tightly flexed. Her mouth bled as she breathed heavily. Then, she held her breath and listened. She could hear her enemy near. She bent her knees and slipped one foot back. She growled and burst into a sprint. Within three or four leaps she was taken off her feet by a man also with glowing blue eyes. He pounced upon her, ripping at her body. They fought like wild cats scratching, punching and hissing at one another. They tossed one another to and fro.

Abigail managed to loosen his grip and ran again, dashing towards the edge of the woods on the other side. A helicopter could be heard approaching in the distance. *It must be about a mile away.* They were looking for her. She needed to reach the woods for a better chance of escaping. Just as she reached the edge of the woods, she was suddenly knocked down on her face. She turned around and saw her enemy before her. She and the man fought, rolling and growling in the muddy mash of dirt, grass and fungi. They punched and kicked, blocked and scratched, fighting for their lives. The loser would surely die.

Abigail felt minimal pain, and though her strength waned, she was winning. Every blow was precise, aiming for soft spots and major blood vessels. They were wrestling on the ground when, without warning, she heard a sharp sound behind her. She turned to look and was taken off guard by a fierce blow to the head by her opponent. The sound was the cry of a wounded deer about 300 yards away. The screech sounded like a rusty door hinge creaking. It was a sound that demanded Abigail's attention, but also caused her opponent to gain the upper hand.

The blow created a fuzzy world of spinning mist and dust before her. She could barely see. The man she fought with stood to his feet and pulled out a gun. She had only seconds to think of a way to regain control — maybe kick his legs so that he would lose his balance and most likely miss his target. The chopper was getting closer. Abigail was doomed, but rather than plan out an attack strategy, she gave up. Abigail sat up Indian style folding her legs one under the other. She exhaled a long painful exhale as her blazing blue eyes returned back to black. Instead of attacking, she made peace with God the only way she knew how. She remembered someone say it once, and now she understood why. *Pater, ignosce mihi,* she whispered to herself, and closed her eyes.

The male exhaled. His eyes turned black again. Pointing his gun directly at her head, he stood over her for a moment, confused. There wasn't much time to think and nothing left to negotiate. He shot twice and darted off into the darkness. The farmhouse lights turned on.

BOSTON POLICE STATION

When they arrived at the police station, Finch noticed a few news reporters buzzing around. Finch asked, "What the hell are they looking for now?"

Brown answered, "No clue!"

Brown and Finch walked directly onto the second level, heading straight for Finch's desk. They split up. She went to her desk as Brown went to his. When Finch arrived to her desk, she squatted down and opened her file cabinet. The office buzzed with ringing phones, fax machines, and Xerox copies running all morning. Detective Chris Duffy saw Sydney Brown flipping though papers at his desk. He seemed to be in a hurry.

Detective Duffy called over to Brown, "Hey Brown."

Brown responded, "Hey Duff. How's it going?" He never gave solid eye contact. He was busy.

Duffy asked, "Where's the old lady?"

"Who?"

Duffy smiled, "Finch! Where's Finch?"

Brown pointed in her direction. She was squatting on the other side of her desk and could barely be seen, "She's right there looking for something."

Duffy could never start the day without teasing Brown about something; he decided to pester Finch, "Good morning Finch. Actually working?"

Without raising her head over the desk, she stuck up her middle finger as she continued searching for a few files she needed.

Brown was getting annoyed, "What's going on, Chris? You actually have something to tell me or you just get a kick out of fucking with me on a daily basis?"

Duffy giggled, "Both actually, but I guess I should keep you updated." He turned serious for the first time in a week, "I'm still working on that memory card. I have some kids coming in from MIT."

Brown was concerned, "Official police business goes out the window."

Duffy said, "Listen Sydney, we can sit here and let the damn thing rot in an evidence file or try something new. It wasn't just water that window cleaner's phone fell into. We're talking about a toxic mix of dirt, bird shit and cleaning solutions. The files are jumbled like a jigsaw, but we still have a chance. These kids at MIT are working on software that will restructure the memory files."

"I guess we have no choice."

"That's what I was thinking. We don't have the equipment or the brains to figure it out. OH... I have something better for you."

Finch found what she was looking for and joined in on the conversation. She said to Brown, "I got it! What did I miss?"

Brown filled her in saying, "Well your buddy Duffy has some data recovery experts at MIT looking at the memory card using some software to recompile the pictures and hopefully get us something we can work with."

Duffy interrupted, "Yes and something else too. It was so random. Jiang's mistress called up here this morning. She wants to talk. She wasn't sure who she should talk to, but she asked for Homicide."

Finch was excited, "Where is she?"

Duffy answered, "I really don't know. She called from a payphone in Framingham. Then she called again from a phone in Worcester. I convinced her to leave us a cell number. She said she is willing to meet. She's on her way to the station now. She should be here in about 20 minutes."

Finch didn't like the sound of this. She made a suggestion, "Convince her to meet us at Starbucks on the Commons instead. There are too many ears around here, the media is buzzing about outside. I don't want her flaking on us."

Duffy said, "I wonder if someone found out she was on her way. Hmm." He paused for a minute and said, "Oh one more thing. The footage from the alley murders is being downloaded to my drive now. It's gonna take another hour or two. When we get back, we'll check it out."

"Great. Call this Jennifer woman and meet us outside. Finch, you drive. Duffy, follow us there."

Duffy nodded and led them out the main door.

ATKINS' RESIDENCE

Roger and Abigail entered Roger's house. They felt guilty and shameful after a long night of murder and deceit. They were fugitives, Roger thought. They hid evidence of their involvement as best they could, but Roger couldn't stop thinking about all the technological advances made in modern science that could detect the most minuscule particles of evidence. He couldn't imagine them being foiled by bleach and a hot knife. He prayed the police department lacked in monetary funds to invest in such equipment. He prayed the police would thwart the investigation by their lack of organization, their own stupidity or sheer human error.

Ms. Atkins was sitting at the kitchen table sipping tea as she looked again and again at the photos of Abigail's tattoos. She couldn't believe her eyes, but a spark ignited in her lethargic body. She ran her index finger across the paper, tracing the lines in the designs. Memories of many years ago came to the forefront of her mind. She had vivid memories of her past—memories that she had blocked for about a decade had resurfaced thanks to Elvis.

Terry saw Abigail and Roger walk in and immediately stood up, leaving the tea on the table. She gestured Abigail to come closer. Abigail walked closer.

Ms. Atkins straightened her glasses and said, "It's ok. Come here, Elvis. Come let me see."

Abigail turned around and took off her top layer of clothing. Ms. Atkins ran her hands over the markings. Her hands were warm from the tea. Ms. Atkins scanned Abigail's back with the tips of her fingers and her eyes. She adjusted her glasses to get a better look.

Ms. Atkins mumbled, "This is Paltee's work. Dr. Paltee, that son of a bitch."

Roger asked, "Doctor who?"

Abigail put her shirt back on. She draped her leather jacket over the back of the chair and sat down. Ms. Atkins poured Roger and Abigail each a cup of tea. She paced for a moment before she remembered to grab sugar and cream from the refrigerator. She placed them on the table next to the tea kettle. She put her hand over her mouth and tapped her cheek with her index finger. She paced again. Roger and Abigail didn't ask again. They knew these must be hard memories that had resurfaced. Anything she was willing to share would be welcomed. She may never share it all and may never share again.

Roger got out of the chair and put his arm on his mother's shoulder. Her anxiety had returned after years of remission. He guided his mother to the chair and kissed her on the head to reassure her that he was there for her. Ms. Atkins thought for a moment before she said another word.

"Dr. Paltee. Oh my, I haven't said that name in years. It's been about 15 years, but I remember his work. He made these marks. That's his mark. Right there." She pointed to a photo on the table.

Abigail looked at the photos but wasn't sure to which photo Terry was referring. Ms. Atkins shuffled through the pile of photos. She selected one and showed it to Abigail.

Ms. Atkins explained, "This one. He stamped everything he ever did with it– letters, drawings, and I guess you. I wasn't around long but..."

Abigail was stunned and interrupted, "Wait. How do you know about this? What is your involvement?"

Each mark was tattooed in black ink. They were circular tribal style designs. Each circle was smaller than the next as they stretched from center of her shoulders to the small of her back. The inner designs were constructed of various combinations of shapes, varying line thicknesses, symbols and shading. Four of the tattoos centered on a main animal figure in the center. The smallest tattoo was a simple circle about the size of a fifty cent piece. There were three concentric circles with the circumference of each circle, getting thicker towards the center. In the middle was a small tribal butterfly that Dr. Paltee used to signature his work.

The marks in Abigail's head, the ones she could see, were different. Through the shortened hair on the sides of her head, the tattoos were visible. On the left side, the tattoos looked like ancient symbols or an unknown language. They were written in the shape of a 3 x 3 inch square. There were about 15 lines of symbols, some repeating, some only depicted once. On the right side of her head, was a larger design that disappeared under the longer hair that striped down the middle of her head. What was visible showed a bar code and a hieroglyphic style picture. There were various images crowded together in layers. Only the bottom three levels were showing. She would have to shave her head to get the full image.

On the bottom level were four animals standing about an inch and a half tall, the same animals in the tattoos on her spine. They were standing side by side with locked arms. The animals on the farthest left and right held weapons. One held a spear, the other held a bow. They had animal heads and human bodies. They were accompanied by other symbols and artistic designs. The second level centered around eagle wings. On either side of the wings were clouds with smaller birds and four more animals similar to those on totem poles. The third level was partially covered, but of what was visible, there were pictures of spears, spiders, skulls and bones accompanied by more symbols.

GLOBAL TECH–GIN TESTING FACILITY

Global Tech–Gin consisted of three buildings. Building A was a 100,000 square foot, three story facility constructed of gray concrete and steel with tinted windows. Building B was a smaller building at 70,000 square feet, constructed in a style like that of Building A. Building C was built eight years later and was made of mostly glass and steel. It also stood ten floors high. All three buildings were connected by underground tunnels and above ground walkways. The buildings were located on a private 100 acre lot surrounded by iron fencing, bushes, short grass, a few trees, a helipad, and a manmade lake in the rear. The facility was guarded 24/7 by the Guardsmen Security company, which employed armed ex police and military officers trained in their nationally awarded training school. Because of the success of the company, a plaza consisting of small shops, restaurants and a gas station were erected. By the time Ms. Atkins had arrived, Building C was almost completed and the company employed about 1,000 employees.

Ms. Atkins sipped her tea as she thought about where to begin. Roger and Abigail sipped their tea as well, patiently waiting for Terry to answer. Many memories flowed into her mind. She didn't know which memories were worth mentioning or ignoring. It had been so long since she talked about the place. She thought for another moment, sipped her tea again and finally began talking. She told the story with every detail she could remember.

"Back in 1994, I worked for an engineering firm in northern Connecticut. The town was uh… Windsor. There were many companies in the area like mine, building and designing various parts for the aerospace industry. We mostly focused on airplane and shuttle engines, wings, and propellers, but that year they decided to branch out and invest in the production of smaller military equipment per order of the US Government."

Abigail didn't understand the connection and asked, "What did you do there?"

"My unit consisted of the best mechanical engineers in the Northeast. We got word that the unit was commissioned for a 'special project' which required special attention and detail. There was a board meeting that consisted of my team, the company president, shareholders, other CEOs of subsidiary companies and military personnel. They explained that tension with the Saudis was running high and the only way to suppress their advances was on the ground level and some other mumbo jumbo they explained. I can't remember. They wanted to create an elite squad of ground troops and wanted my team to create a classified "super armor" of sorts that amplified human strength and agility, but could still be disguised under clothing."

"We worked on the suits for a long time, building one prototype after the other. We eventually settled on a design for the suit and ran a few animal tests. The problem was that we made the damn thing so powerful that unfortunately it was not safe for humans. But the government insisted on trying them anyway and the first few prototypes killed the men and women who wore them. They created some story about a helicopter crash in Kuwait. The theory was that the neuro–sensors in the suit were supposed to stimulate the nervous system to increase reaction time to one tenth of average human response time. Unfortunately, it ended up pinching nerves and flexing joints in the wrong direction. The suits even broke a few necks and suffocated a few men. Some even defecated on themselves due to many uncontrolled neurological responses. We were devastated. The project was a disaster and was shut down."

Ms. Atkins grabbed a bottle of gin from the refrigerator and mixed it with orange juice. She took two sips before she continued talking. "About five years later, I was called into a meeting where they decided to revive the project. My unit was totally against it, but we wanted to hear what they planned to do, so we pretended to be interested in its revival."

Roger already knew the suit story and asked, "Can you explain what this has to do with Elvis?" That was the part of the story he *didn't* know.

Ms. Atkins continued, "The plan was not to change the suit, but to change the human. They wanted to make a human that could respond to the demands of the suit. The project was secretly moved to Plum Island, off the coast of Connecticut. They tried everything– steroid injections, cross breeding, but the humans created were irregular looking or so dumb that they couldn't follow basic directions. They had to put many of them down, which I was totally against. Our job was to continue working on the suit. We worked on the project for three more years. The suits we made were getting more advanced and we still couldn't produce a human fast enough and smart enough to handle it. The project was a disaster."

Abigail asked, "What does all this have to do with me?"

Terry answered, "After constant disappointment, one of the members on our team, Travis Smart, did some research of his own and stumbled across some vital information. He made a few phone calls and set up a meeting with the same CEOs, the company president and military personnel that were overseeing the project. The next day a man was flown in from Boston. We sat in the conference room anxiously waiting to hear what his solution would be. After about 30 minutes of waiting, in walked a tall handsome Native American man— a neuroscientist from Harvard. His name was Dr. Colin Paltee. He explained that the suit would never work on humans because human reflexes cannot adapt to the neurological demands of the suit— kind of like putting a Chevy Cobalt engine into a Porsche shell expecting the same results. He said that even the most trained highly trained human had insufficient ability for optimal performance of the suit, and it would only work if we were to decrease the ability of the armor which was not even discussed as an option."

She continued, "I left the project a month later when my foot was crushed. Last I heard… the project was shut down. You must have been in the facility when I was there. I remember seeing some children but I figured after they shut down the project, they would ship you guys out, but I guess they didn't. I'll be damned."

Abigail asked, "Me? I was at Global Tech–Gin? For what?"

"That's for Paltee to explain to you. I can't even go there." Ms. Atkins wiped sweat from her brow, using her sleeve.

Abigail asked, "So this Dr. Paltee. Where is he? How do I find him?

Ms. Atkins answered, "Oh. I can get you Paltee, but I wanna show you something first." The three stood up and left the kitchen.

CHAPTER 11

FRANKIE'S PUB
MORNING

Frankie spent the morning shuffling around the kitchen, cleaning and prepping food for lunch and dinner service. He chopped onions, cleaned and seasoned meat, and started peeling and boiling potatoes.

After he was done, he grabbed the broom to clean the onion skins and pepper seeds off the floor. He pulled the broom with wood bristles towards him, sweeping the debris in his direction. As he pulled it, he saw a red streak, run across the floor. "What the…" He knew right away that it was blood. His mind ran around the possibilities and knew right away who the culprits were. He took a few paper towels and Fantastic with bleach, sprayed down the floor and broom bristles. He wiped the blood away and tossed the towels into the sink. He then took the head of the broom and lit the paper towels and broom on fire until most of the broom was burnt to ashes. He washed the ashes down the sink and tossed the rest of the broom into the trash just as Larry arrived.

Larry walked into the kitchen door startling Frankie. Frankie hadn't heard the door open. "Hey, Larry."

"Damn it's smoky in here!" Larry waved the air in front of his face and coughed.

Frankie was a good liar and said, "My clumsy ass dropped a rag on the stove and it hit the pilot light. It caught fire before I could pick it up, but it wasn't anything serious. What's going on?"

"I came by to see if you needed any help prepping food for the day." Larry said.

"No actually. Thanks. I got up early and took care of it. I'll need your help later on though when we open. I don't know when Roger is coming back and I can't say if I know whether or not Abigail is coming back," Frankie said.

Larry was taken aback by Frankie's comment. "What do you mean? Is Abigail leaving?"

"I don't know! She has a lot going on right now and she isn't sure if this is the place for her." Frankie was sad. "She's been dealing with some things from her past that are popping up suddenly."

"Really? Like what?" Larry was all ears.

Frankie wasn't sure what to say but responded, "I think if Abigail wants to share this with you, that's her call. I respect her privacy. You and I haven't talked much about her because I know you aren't very fond of her. I personally don't think you ever gave her a chance. She clearly has issues. One minute she's giving evil stares, the next minute she's joking at the bar. She's an awkward person for sure. I get that, but that's not enough reason for you to hate her."

"I don't hate Abigail, Frankie. I just don't get her. You just opened up to her and you immediately trusted her. Why?"

"I didn't immediately trust her, but I gave her a chance. She's like a daughter to me."

Larry shook his head and said, "Frankie, but she is not your daughter."

Frankie gave Larry a sincere look and said, "But I wish she was. All this time I avoided having kids. Now I realize having one, or even something close to it, makes me feel more complete. I'm getting old, Larry. Who am I going to leave this place to if something happens to me?" Frankie paused for a moment before he finally said, "I'm closing the fight club this week."

Larry knew the day was coming, "So have you figured out how you're going to make a decent profit?"

"I'll figure it out."

"You kind of sprung this on me. You should have told me sooner."

"I made the decision just now. Why prolong the inevitable? Let everyone know. It's over. Friday will be the last day." Frankie walked out onto the main floor leaving Larry in the kitchen. Frankie felt bad saying it, but telling Larry the fight club was closing for good was a huge burden lifted off his back.

Larry shook his head again in disbelief. He was steaming with frustration. *This is how he tells me this shit?* Larry was so disappointed in Frankie that he couldn't stand it. He wasn't sure if Abigail was coming back nor did he care, but he knew Frankie was becoming preoccupied with Abigail's happiness and safety over his own financial security. He attributed the soon to be closing of the fight club to Frankie's desire to protect her. *Maybe if she doesn't come back, we can keep it open.* But the thought was futile. Frankie was tired of the club with or without Abigail's influence. There wasn't a thing in this world to make Frankie change his mind. *Now Frankie is thinking of leaving the bar to her?* Though Frankie didn't exactly say that, Larry was sure it's what he meant. *I'm gonna expose that bitch!*

Larry's obsession with getting Abigail out of the picture was only fueled by the newly found information that the *bitch* was possibly leaving. *Frankie wants her to return.* Larry's goal was to make sure this didn't happen. He also remembered Frankie's comment about certain aspects of her past resurfacing and he couldn't wait to learn what that meant. Larry couldn't imagine how messed up she truly was and figured she had made up some excuse to break the news to Frankie that it was time to move on. Larry took her for a user with a seductive smile that drew men in for a greater ulterior motive.

Secretly Larry had been doing his own private investigation of Abigail, which had turned up one dead end after another. In frustration, Larry took a photo of Abigail and made a missing woman advertisement and placed it into a missing person's database which focused on upstate New York and metropolitan areas within a 300 mile radius. The missing person file had the picture he scanned from her license. The headline read, "Missing Mental Patient." He felt it was a more than suitable title for the young woman he believed to be a nut case.

STARBUCKS – BOSTON COMMONS

Jennifer Kalis Martin arrived at the Starbucks around noon, just in time to get in line before the lunchtime rush. Seconds after she got to the counter, the line filled up and went out the door by about 10 patrons. She ordered a Mocha Coconut Frappuccino and a blueberry scone with a side of butter. After she received her order, she sat at a table in the corner where she could have a full view of the front door and her car, which she had parked in metered space. She didn't know she would need more than three chairs because she was unaware of who was coming with Duffy. As she waited, she checked her phone, sent out a few text messages and looked at her eReader.

When Brown, Finch and Duffy walked into the store, Jennifer knew immediately who they were. They stuck out like sore thumbs with their ties, blazers and side arms sticking out. She had hoped they would have been a little more discreet. She knew Duffy was coming, but she didn't know about the other man and woman who showed up with him. She figured they thought a woman's touch was needed and must have brought her as a tag along. She couldn't be that important. They noticed Jennifer and walked over. Brown realized they needed an additional chair, so he grabbed one from another table and slid it over. They sat down.

Jennifer, Allen Jiang's mistress, sat at the table with Brown, Finch and Duffy. She had a big tan Michael Kors bag with a silver buckle on the strap. Sticking out of the opening were a few file folders, some paperwork, and a rolled up magazine. She wore heels, jeans, a tan leather jacket and a floral patterned scarf. Her eyes are covered with big black sun glasses. She crossed her arms and leaned on the table. She had an attitude to go with her Frappuccino.

Duffy decided to start the conversation and said, "So... Miss Martin."

She interrupted, speaking with a funny upstate New York accent. "Just call me Jen. Jen is fine. I didn't expect you would bring company."

Duffy responded, "This is Detective Meghan Finch and Detective Sydney Brown. It's protocol that we bring another detective, just in case things get complicated. I need to be sure that we properly document this and I don't miss any important parts."

She nodded, but wasn't exactly thrilled. She looked at her car and watched the door. It was obvious that she was anxious about the meeting and wanted to leave as soon as she could.

Duffy said, "Ok, Jen. You said you wanted to talk. We're here to listen. What would you like to share with us?"

Jennifer was upset with Duffy's last minute request to change locations. She kept her voice low as she complained, "I wanted to talk at a police station, not a damn Starbucks in front of all these people. I don't like this."

Finch interrupted, "I'm sorry, Jen. I have to be honest with you. Coming here was my idea. I often meet people here so there is nothing to hide and you can feel empowered to just walk out the door if you need to. We apologize for the late notice, but we wanted to keep you out of the station. Someone may have gotten wind that you were coming and sent the media over. We saw them around the station and they would have swarmed you."

Jen looked at Duffy and said, "You could have just said that on the phone." She fiddled with her sun glasses and played with the end of her scarf. "Next time, let me know, ok? This has been a stressful time for me. I don't like this."

Duffy apologized, "I'm sorry about that and didn't mean to inconvenience you. Sometimes explaining things over the phone can be just as risky. I didn't want to chance that your phone would be bugged and they would know we were on to them. I can check that for you later, but let's get down to business and get you out of here."

Jen understood. She said, "Anyway, I just wanted to explain some things that may help a little, you know."

Finch said, "We really appreciate that and I'm sure the loss has been difficult, so take your time. Just start wherever you think you need to start. If we need clarification, we will ask. Is that ok?"

Jen nodded and adjusted her sun glasses. She had tears in her eyes as she explained. "I know I sound like a silly girl, but he promised me he would break it off with his wife and marry me. He said it a few times before but I never took it seriously. I figured it was just his way to keep me interested. After a while, I wanted it all to be true. He told me that after he returned from this particular business trip at his cabin, he would break things off with his wife and marry me."

Brown asked, "So this was a business trip? I thought it was a fishing trip."

She explained, "Alan was always working. He would take me to the Bahamas and meet with clients in the mornings or they would meet us for dinner. Knowing him, he didn't tell the kid he took with him that it was a business trip."

Brown asked, "Why wouldn't he tell the kid it was a business trip? What was that kid's name again?"

Duffy answered, "Dennis Matthews."

Jen answered, "Alan was very private and didn't trust his own left foot to follow him forever. He didn't want the people around him talking about what he is doing. I'm sure he wanted to go fishing, which he loved to do, but I'm sure he told the kid that's all it was yet planned a meeting anyway."

Finch opened up her cloud based files and began typing in notes.

Jen continued, "I didn't know Alan was taking Dennis up there or else I... I've been to the cabin a few times and I had the key so, I went up there early to surprise him. I couldn't wait for him to come home. I was desperate to see him. He didn't know I was coming. He went fishing before I got there, I saw the boat was out and waited."

Finch, "So you were at the house the whole time?"

Jennifer was crying a little. She continued to explain, "A bad storm came down. I heard thunder rolling and it began to pour. I watched out the back window to make sure he was ok coming up the boat ramp. Suddenly the boat pulled in. I didn't notice at first, but Alan showed up with that kid. They pulled up to the dock; they were in their fishing gear. When they were tying down the boat I figured they were ok since they were off the water. I didn't know Alan was going to have company with him and I knew he would be upset with me, but I didn't really care."

"So they made it to shore? I thought they drowned at sea!" Duffy said.

"That's how the media made it seem, but no. The last time I looked out the window they were walking down the dock toward the house. A few minutes passed and I couldn't understand why they were taking so long. I looked out and there was the boat, but they were gone," Jennifer said as tears fell from her face.

Duffy asked, "Gone? You mean like disappeared gone?"

Jen spoke softly and said, "Yes. Just gone! I looked around and around and suddenly I saw these people running very quickly, like someone was fast forwarding a movie. They moved so quickly and quietly like they were hunting. I ducked down out of site, terrified as all hell. There were two of them moving back and forth around the area. Another man in a suit came over. I saw one guy jump straight up into the air and land on a tree branch like a... a kangaroo, straight up!"

Brown asked, "Wait. Did you say, 'Like a kangaroo'?"

Jennifer was aggravated, "Yes I said a kangaroo. I don't know any other animals that jump like that. I don't know. He went up in the air about 15 feet without a running start."

Brown responded, "You gotta be kidding me. Is this a joke?"

Duffy added, "This sounds odd. I'm not sure what this has to do with our case."

Duffy and Brown tried to keep from laughing.

Jen removed her sunglasses. There were subtle streaks in her makeup and her mascara was beginning to run. She asked, "Are you mocking me? I didn't come here for that."

Duffy giggled as he asked, "Well then Jen, what did the kangaroo do in the tree?" Duffy and Brown laughed. Finch was highly frustrated with the two men.

Though she wasn't sure if she wanted to answer the question, she answered anyway and said, "He looked around, scoping out the scene or something. So I ducked down and on all fours I crawled into the room and hid in the closet."

Duffy joked, "On all fours like a doggy or like a kitty?"

Jen had it with them and said, "You're a jerk! Fuck you I'm outta here. I don't need this. Good luck with your case." Jen grabbed her stuff and walked out. She stormed out of the door and didn't look back.

Finch was pissed off with Brown and Duffy, "Are you two trying to solve this case or wreck it? We have nothing! Nothing at all. Brown, I ought to…" She squeezed at his head in a motion to crush it. "We are investigating a homicide. If she thinks she saw bunnies and elves on our crime scene, then we better fucking listen because it's a lot more than *anyone* has told us thus far. You guys are such assholes. If you blow this case…"

Finch jumped up out of her seat to follow Jennifer and hopefully catch her before she got in her car. Finch caught up to her, "Wait! Please wait."

"I don't have time for this," Jen shouted back as she fumbled her car keys.

Finch got closer and said, "Jen, wait. Please wait. My partners are being idiots."

"You guys think this is funny? I'm not an idiot. I'm a fucking full time pharmacist. I must have some brains."

"I know. I know. Men can be jerks even when they don't mean to be."

Jen stopped fidgeting for a moment. Finch put her hand on Jen's shoulder. Even though Jen didn't want to be touched, something about that touch made her feel a certain level of calm that she hadn't felt in a long time. Finch knew what it felt like to be ridiculed or mocked by a bunch of jocks and immature men. When Meghan had been attacked at the concert, many of the male cops told her she should not have been there. Others laughed and told her that her cheek bone broke because it was too dainty. Someone even put pink boxing gloves in her locker. She knew that Brown was being a dick because of Duffy; otherwise, his behavior was unfamiliar to her.

Finch wanted to hear the rest of Jennifer's story. It was the only new information they had in a desperate attempt to solve a cold case. Meghan looked sincerely at Jen and said, "I believe you. Take a ride with me."

FINCH'S CAR

Finch's gray Honda was two blocks down the road, parked in the opposite direction. Finch lightly jogged across the street to her car. In the meantime, Jen added another hour to her time on the meter. Finch got into her Honda and pulled up to where Jen was standing. She unlocked the door. When Jen got into Finch's car, Finch pulled off and turned on a little cool air.

Jen pulled out a cigarette and asked, "Do you mind?"

Finch answered, "No. Go for it."

Jennifer continued, "You would think as a pharmacist I would know better. I can't seem to kick the habit. I hadn't smoked since I was an undergrad but after Alan's death, I've been smoking a pack a day. Now, I stink of Marlborough Lights and coffee." She opened the window a little and lit the cigarette. She took a drag and exhaled with her eyes closed as if she had just felt the best feeling in the world. The small crack in the window let in a breeze that blew Jennifer's hair back as she leaned her head against the headrest.

Detective Finch was eager to know where the story was going before Brown and Duffy screwed things up. She waited until Jennifer looked settled and said, "Tell me about these men you saw at the dock."

Jen continued her story, "I know it sounds crazy, but I know I saw those guys move like lightning and one of the men jumped from standing still... straight up about 15 feet. I know what I saw. I'm not crazy."

Finch sympathized and said, "Jen, that's not crazy at all. Every day I go home and I see visions of my fiancé.

168

Sometimes he stands directly in front of me blocking my path. I can see him clear as day. He never says anything, but it's very stressful to come home to that every night. I never told anyone this so consider yourself lucky. He's been dead for two years now."

Jen apologized, "I'm sorry."

"Me too. He was a great man and I loved him very much."

"What happened to him?" Jen asked before she took another drag from her cigarette.

"He died in a car accident a couple blocks away from home and I've seen him just about every day since the accident. So when I say I believe you, I mean it."

"I can't imagine having to deal with that."

"I'm dealing with it day by day. You will, too. You just have to give it time. So now… Let's take it from the top. What happened at the dock?"

Jennifer began to explain but Meghan decided to stop her until she could take notes. They both agreed to talk over lunch.

ROGER'S HOUSE

After Ms. Atkins shared her story with Abigail, Abigail was distraught. There was so much more to this woman, she thought to herself. And by the finagling of fate, Abigail found her way to the woman who held an important key to the mysteries of her beginnings. There was still so much she didn't know. What she *did* know is that she was connected to a suit but wasn't exactly sure how the tattoos, her nightmares and her supernatural experiences all tied together. She had an idea. She was tempted to ask more questions, but could barely get her head around everything she had just learned. Her memories were not piecing together the way she expected. Ms. Atkins offered to show Abigail something and brought Abigail down into the dank basement. Roger reached down to the floor and opened a trap door hidden under a place rug. There was a hidden lower level in the basement.

Roger opened the door about an inch before he said, "I have to show you something." Roger opened the door and climbed down the steps into the room. Roger's entire body was in the black hole in the floor before he turned on the light. Abigail tried to peek in but could not get a full view of what was hidden beneath her feet. "Elvis, Come on!"

A cool gust of air puffed out of the room and ran up Abigail's ankles. Abigail looked at Ms. Atkins. Ms. Atkins held her hand out signaling for Abigail to go down after Roger. Abigail took the steps down into the room. Ms. Atkins slowly followed. The room was a 13 x 40 foot rectangular enclosure with white cinder block walls. On the walls were a series of military grade weapons, gadgets, sketches and project schematics made by Roger. Abigail ran her hands across some of the pieces. She was stunned. *What the hell are Ms. Atkins and Roger doing with these things?* Roger waited for her by the back of the room.

Roger said, "We've been working on this for years."

Roger pulled a sheet down, revealing a replica of the experimental armor that Ms. Atkins highlighted as being the center of this entire controversy. Abigail gasped for air; she couldn't believe what these two had done. *Roger can't fix the dishwasher but he can build a high tech super suit body armor with bulletproof nerve stimulating electro sensors? Bullshit!*

The suit was a shiny charcoal gray with black stripes along the sides of the arms, legs, around the neckline, the wrists and ankles. The black stripes also lined the zipper going up the front. The texture is reminiscent of flexible tiny fish scales. There was a certain elasticity to it. The arms, legs and back were reinforced with thin Teflon plates covered in the scaly material. The interior was covered in electrodes that connect to the skin of the person wearing the suit. Their purpose was to increase neurological response time, reflexes and stimulate muscular contractions.

Abigail was physically attracted to the suit. It magnetically drew her in, pulling at her flesh and tugging at her soul. She didn't understand why, but she could not help circling the suit and studying it. When she reached her hand out towards it, her eyes turned blazing blue. She pulled her hand back and they returned back to normal. She took in a deep breath, stretched her body, her fangs extended and her powers were turned on. Roger jumped back. He walked slowly over to his mother, guarding her. Ms. Atkins had never seen Abigail like this, but she was not afraid. Abigail continued circling the suit. She smelled the suit and touched it like prey she had just killed and was ready to devour.

Ms. Atkins didn't show much emotion but could hardly stand it. She was so excited that she would have jumped out of her skin had it been possible. Her life's work was finally going to have a purpose. She smiled at Roger and said, "It's calling her."

CHAPTER 12

SEPARATE WAYS

After Meghan and Jennifer had left Starbucks, Brown and Duffy returned to the police station. They didn't say much along the ride, Brown knew that he would pay for his immaturity later. Brown sat at his desk, going through papers, looking for something to do as he waited for Meghan to give him an update. He thought about Meghan and figured it was time to check in. He took out his phone and sent her a text message: "SORRY ABOUT EARLIER. MISS YOU. CALL ME WHEN UR FREE." He put down the phone. He knew she wouldn't respond.

Meghan wasn't much of a joker when it came to official police business. He couldn't believe that he let his ego get in the way of getting the job done. He didn't really want to joke with Duffy at the interview but Duffy had that effect on him from time to time– the betting, the joking. If Meghan knew the things the men said about her, she would never allow their relationship to be public. The first time, Meghan and Sydney came back from a drive she said to him, "Thanks for the ride." The men in the room snickered like 15 year old boys and "Thanks for the ride" was the joke of the week. *Men will be men*, he thought to himself. But he never wanted to let Meghan down. He loved her. What was important to her should also be important to him. He knew this would never happen again.

He just hoped he didn't have to spend weeks or months explaining this to her.

Duffy walked over to Brown's desk and asked, "Is she still mad?"

Brown shrugged, "Yeah. I feel like I should have set a better example."

"She'll get over it. We're gonna grab a bite to eat at Tony's. They have a soup and sandwich special today. Wanna ride out?"

"No, I have a lot to do."

"Wanna see that tape?"

"I would love to, but I think it would be better to view it when Finch gets here. I'd rather wait."

"She would be mad as hell."

"I know!" Brown smiled.

"I'll send you the footage anyway. View it when you're ready. And, if you change your mind, call me and I'll pick you up a sandwich or something."

"I'm not really hungry, but thanks."

"Hey, Brownie. Don't let your girlfriend twist up your head and mess up your day." Duffy smirked.

Brown wasn't sure how to respond to the comment. He couldn't tell if that comment was a joke, or if Duffy was letting him know they were on to him and his affair with Meghan. He could just imagine if their cover was blown, all the gossip floating through the airwaves. Any officer with a hot female partner faced locker room jokes and ridicule about budding relationships and sexual intercourse, but Sydney was actually guilty of it. His guilt didn't allow him to utter a piggish comeback or even a simple denial. All he could say was, "If you're that concerned about making sure I eat, grab me a turkey on wheat... with a pickle and a Snapple. Any kind will do, but not diet."

"You got it." Duffy left the desk.

Brown breathed a sigh of relief, sat in his chair and leaned back. He looked through his phone at some pictures he had taken at the crime scene. He connected his phone to the computer and uploaded the pictures to the cloud server. Then he remembered that Meghan was very diligent about taking notes and looked to see if she had made any updates to the file on Jen which she had begun in the Starbucks. He opened the file labeled <JENNIFER K. MARTIN>. No updates since she left. He opened a few of the other files and saw that Meghan hadn't added any new files. He thought to himself that either Meghan hadn't continued the notes, or she created a new file, but hadn't given him permission to access it. He was thinking it must be the latter. He was a little disappointed in himself.

He decided to review more files from the logs on the Robert Benson case, hoping that there would be a connection somewhere that he may have overlooked. Something was missing and Jennifer was the key, but he had to wait until Meghan returned. He looked at his phone again to see if he had received any new messages. There was one. It was a spam email for beauty products from a company called *Face it Fabulously*. He erased the email and decided to pass the time playing *Bejeweled* on his phone. He could never make it past level 11.

FRIGO'S RESTAURANT

Meghan Finch and Jennifer Martin decided to complete the interview over lunch at Frigo's. Frigo's was a small Italian family restaurant that had originated in Springfield and recently opened a chain in Boston. They ordered their food and carried it back to a booth on the right side of the restaurant floor beside a hanging Italian flag. They both ordered soup and salad combos with buttered bread. Once they began to eat,

Meghan decided to take notes the old fashioned way. She took out a flip notebook from her inner pocket and sneakily turned on a recorder while her hand was in her pocket. She didn't want to miss anything.

Jennifer had a few bites of the salad, but wasn't very hungry. The two women sat calmly. Meghan waited before she asked another question. They could barely be seen through the window from the outside. Jennifer continued explaining the dynamics of her relationship with Jiang, how they had met and how Katherine fit into the picture. Jen explained that she knew Katherine was never involved in her husband's business affairs but that she knew about Alan's relationship with Jennifer. She knew that Katherine was a powerhouse at work and that she was called *The Kraken* behind her back. She also explained that Jiang loved his wife, and she wasn't exactly sure why he had changed his mind about being with her. Soon there was a moment of silence.

She decided to break the silence, "What do you know about Dennis Matthews?"

Jennifer answered, "He was an innocent party in this, but I can tell you that Alan's wife, Katherine, paid his family half a million dollars. She said it was for funeral expenses, but I'm pretty sure it was hush money."

"Really? How do you know?" Meghan asked as she took notes.

"She told me. She had her lawyer visit me at work, which was rather embarrassing. I went outside and she was sitting in a limo. A limo in the parking lot of CVS. She's a nut. I went inside the limo and she said that if I needed to be paid to keep my mouth shut about her husband's private life, then she was willing to pay me the same amount that she had paid to Dennis Matthews' family. She had a check for $500,000 pre–written with my name on it. I refused and told her that she didn't have to worry about me writing a book about a man that I loved. She wanted to keep everything hush, hush."

"Hush about what?" Meghan asked.

"I'm not 100% sure. I know that Alan used to be extremely private. Even about things other people wouldn't think were necessary to be private about. He mentioned a few times that this was the one lesson that Dennis struggled with. He told his mother everything. If I know that, then I'm sure Katherine knew as well."

"Do you think she had anything to do with the murder?"

"No. She's not like that. She likes stability. She totally knew about our relationship and didn't let it drive her mad. As long as he came home, she let it go."

"Ok. So did she know that he planned to leave her? If she had gotten wind of it, that would be a motive for murder."

"No. I don't think she knew. I think she paid Dennis' mother so that whatever she knew, if she knew anything, she would just leave it alone and move on with her life so that Katherine could sort things out without a conspiracy. Same reason she figured she better drop me off a check."

"Hmm," Meghan said as she took more notes on the pad.

"I know something else."

Meghan was all ears. "What's that?"

Jennifer looked around and whispered, "When I saw the men at the dock, one of the men I saw was Robert Benson. I'm pretty sure it was him."

"Benson was there?"

"Yes. He was there, but when I saw the men grab him, I jumped back and hid. I wasn't sure if they were going to come into the cabin. They never did, but I wasn't sure. But yes, Benson was there."

Meghan was excited. This was important information to note. "Do you know why they were there?"

"I'm *sure* there was a meeting," Jen said before she took a sip of water. Jen continued, "Have you ever heard of Indigo, Inc.?"

"No. What kind of company is that?"

"I'm not sure. I think they do some stuff with research and development. I know that Alan and Robert were not seeing eye to eye about dealing with the company. They were supposed to meet about something concerning the company. Alan told me that Robert would see things his way but he needed to show Robert some numbers. Maybe that's why they were there. When the other men showed up, I assumed it wasn't just a chat over numbers and maybe it was an informal meeting, but a meeting none the less. I'm not sure if it was just an investment deal or a purchase but it was a big deal and Alan wasn't very interested in any of it. Robert was."

Meghan's hand was hurting. She wrote a mile a minute and then she remembered that her recorder was on. She relaxed a little.

Jennifer reached into her big tan purse. "I scraped up some of the files Alan left at the house. Maybe you would like to have them. I can't promise that they will help you solve the case, but I'm assuming that whatever happened to Alan is probably going to happen to Benson."

Meghan knew that Jennifer probably had heard that Benson was missing but didn't know anything about the arm they recovered on the ledge. She said to Jennifer, "This is very helpful. Thank you." Finch opened the files.

Jen pointed out a few things and continued explaining the paperwork. Finch received a text from Brown. She read it, lightly smiled and continued talking to Jennifer for a few more hours. Jennifer provided more details about the event. Meghan asked her to repeat what she saw at least three more times to make sure her story was consistent each time. Meghan thought Jennifer to be a very smart woman. They had gotten along fairly well and exchanged phone numbers by the end of the meeting.

Meghan took Jennifer back to her car where Jennifer managed to get a $41 ticket for an expired meter. Meghan promised to take care of the ticket before she drove off. As she drove away, Meghan thought about Brown. She had forgiven him by now, and was excited to share this information with him, but she decided to go to the library to do some research first before heading back. She needed a break and wanted to make Brown suffer a little before they reconnected. She also needed some time alone to write her report. She knew that meeting up with Brown was going to begin with at least an hour of wasted time fooling around.

In addition to the fact that she had just received information which filled a few holes in the Benson case, Finch could not stop thinking about Sydney. She also couldn't stop thinking about Anthony. His presence was all over her house and she could not get him out of her mind. She had packed away most of his belongings but hadn't found the strength to tell his mother to take them. Finch wanted to move on with her life, but Anthony was still haunting her. She knew she was hallucinating but sometimes his presence was too real to deny. She knew she could never move on unless it stopped. She couldn't figure out if it was his anger with her that kept him there or her guilt that kept bringing him back.

She pushed the paperwork aside to think for a moment. Her relationship with Sydney was a bit inappropriate, but there were no rules against dating coworkers. Or was she making excuses? It happened from time to time. This wouldn't be a first. It would have helped if she weren't a hot topic in the locker room. Unfortunately for Brown, Meghan was well aware of the THANKS FOR THE RIDE jokes and other smart comments the men made about her. She had made a decision to ignore the jokes and to keep working hard. If she complained, she knew the men would make her look like she was just bitching, looking for attention. The only parts of her reputation she cared about in that place concerned her ability to outperform her peers, which she did frequently. Dating Brown would just be the icing on the cake, the final nail in the coffin. Was he worth it? She played with the ring for another minute and went back to work.

FRANKIE'S PUB

Frankie worked the bar with Larry. It was packed. He served dinner after dinner that afternoon. It seemed that a break would only come when the bar closed that evening. Larry and Frankie were a little overwhelmed by noon, so Larry had called in his friends, Marty and Frita, to run the bar for him while he and Frankie worked the kitchen. They had recently lost their bar around the block and had told Larry and Frankie to call whenever they were short on staff. This was a night they were needed. Abigail and Roger were out of town, and a Red Sox/Orioles game played on the big screen.

Frankie watched the 20 inch flat panel TV in the kitchen. The Red Sox scored. Frankie cheered with the crowd when they scored, but in the back of his mind he could not stop thinking about Abigail and Roger. *Where are they? What have they discovered? Are they coming back?* He wanted them to return, expressing their inability or exhausted desire to find something more. He wanted Abigail to be content with her new life and forget about whatever haunted her. He wanted her to forget about digging into her past or seeing where the rabbit hole went. He thought that one day she would get over the nightmares, forget about everything that didn't make sense, and think of him as a father.

He also wondered what kind of trouble they had gotten themselves into. He knew that young folks sometimes did silly things, but he felt that this time it was serious. They had come home bloody and bruised. Abigail was almost raped. Roger was shaken up and there was blood on the broom in the kitchen. He thought about what he had seen on the news. He could not imagine that Roger or Abigail would have the ability to pull off a stunt like that. He had only turned on the news to shake them up a bit, but for some reason, they seemed guilty. *Why? Could they manage to pull off something this horrific?* Frankie couldn't imagine it, but wondered, *If it were possible, how the hell did they do that?*

"I need those fries, Frankie," Larry yelled into the kitchen.

Frankie had lost focus for a moment. He snapped out of it and dropped some fries into the fryer. He flipped a few burgers on the grill and got back into watching the game. He served up the burgers. Marty grabbed them off the counter and passed them to Larry. Frankie checked his phone, but no messages. He thought for a moment and couldn't resist. He made a funny face, took a picture and sent the photo to Abigail followed by the text: MISSING YOU AT THE PUB—FRANKIE! He looked around to make sure no one had seen him and got back to work.

FRANKIE'S TRUCK
FINDING PALTEE

Roger and Abigail left Ms. Atkins at home while they ventured off to find Dr. Colin Paltee. Ms. Atkins had pulled out an old phone book and prayed the man still had the same number. She called and to her amazement, the number worked. She spoke to Dr. Paltee and explained as much as she could without saying too much on the phone. Paltee understood enough of her clues to get the point and told her to send Abigail to his home in Hampden, CT, right away. They drove off that afternoon hitting the Massachusetts turnpike heading west towards I84.

It was lightly raining. The wipers went back and forth across the windshield leaving streaks from the worn blades. Roger was driving. Abigail had packed the armor suit into a duffel bag and planted it in her lap. She rested her hand on the bag, keeping guard over it. Suddenly she received a text message. The vibration broke her concentration on the suit folded meticulously in the bag. She looked at her phone. She saw the picture Frankie had sent and for the first time in a couple days, she sincerely smiled.

She said to Roger, "So… the fact that you can build this suit and can't seem to fix anything else perplexes me."

Roger knew this was coming and said, "Playing possum isn't easy, Elvis. I can do a lot more than you think. All the bullshit gadgets in my house... it was just a front so no one would suspect anything."

Abigail asked, "So what was the point of having me come over to help you work on your 'inventions'? They didn't work and you never intended for them to work. I don't get it."

Roger looked at Abigail and smiled. "I told you to come because I figured you needed to get out. And… I wanted to spend time with... I guess you don't get it but anyway… We didn't want them to think we had the capacity to rebuild the suits. They stalked our home because they thought she stole the plans."

"Which she obviously did."

Roger nodded, "True, but you know how the government is sometimes. They watched our house for about eight years after we left CT. I fucked up by going to MIT. It made them watch even more. I pretended to have a nervous breakdown. We hoped to leave them with the impression that my unstable mind and disabled mother weren't capable of fixing a toaster. I intentionally failed classes at MIT so they would leave us alone."

"So you stopped educating yourself to get the government off your back?"

"The government, Global Tech–Gin and all the other goons they had working on the project. According to my mom, those people were up to no good. She didn't trust their intentions and sabotaged her own lab before she left. She blamed it on an electrical fire. She left behind some bogus plans for the suit and got out of there." Roger pulled into the right lane.

"My mother was being modest, Elvis. She was the brainchild behind the suit. Those were her schematics and her ideas. She designed the suit. Yes, the rest of the team helped, but don't let that woman fool you. She is a genius. She felt totally responsible for the men it killed. She couldn't let them have it. That suit would have been left in the wrong hands, so she took the plans and taught me everything she knew about engineering and math when I was young."

Abigail asked, "Have you ever tried it on?"

Roger answered, "Hell no. Didn't you hear what happened to the other men who wore the suit? We've made some adjustments but I'm not willing to risk it. The suit now has a processor located in the collar. I created software that reads heart rates, analyzes body temperature and movements so that the suit understands that the human wearing the suit is boss and will know not to overexert itself. It will know when to shut itself down if necessary. It now reacts after the human body says react and not before, which had been a major problem. I also added in a tracking device and can remotely monitor the suit's activities from home or... my iPhone." He shrugged. "I designed the app three weeks ago. Don't worry. It's not on iTunes."

Roger shifted lanes.

"Ok so no one has ever tried it on. How do you know it works?"

Roger confidently responded, "Trust me. It works. We'll find out soon enough."

"And the guns and weapons?"

"Abigail," Roger said, "There are people around us willing to kill for this armor. Willing to do whatever it takes to get it and or the plans. If they come, we need to be ready."

Abigail looked out the window. "How far are we?" Abigail wondered. She looked at the Garmin GPS.

Roger asked, "What does it say?"

"40 minutes to Hampden." She put the GPS back in the center console and pulled the bag in tighter and unzipped the bag. She wanted to try it on but hadn't got up the nerve to do it. She looked in the collar and could see sensors sewn into the fabric.

"There are sensors all over the suit, but the brains of the suit are right there."

Abigail didn't want Roger to know how impressed she was. She squinted her eyes, nodded and zipped up the bag. Then, she tossed it into the back seat like it didn't matter anymore.

A couple of minutes later, Abigail leaned her head on the window. It lightly bumped against the glass as they drove down the freeway. She was tired and was starting to doze off. She closed her eyes. Little by little she drifted into another haunting dream.

She was running through a jungle in a black tank top and khaki shorts. She heard drums as the black leaves on the trees screamed in her direction. It sounded like children on fire. She thought she saw a face in the dark mist surrounding the path underneath her feet. Once again she was being chased by men in black suits. A black oily substance crawled from her feet, up her legs, across her back, over her neck and onto her head. When it reached her head, it burned into her scalp. She stopped and grabbed her head in agony. The screaming increased in volume, piercing her ears.

Suddenly, four beasts jumped onto her pinning her down and licking her flesh. Each one bit into her wrists and ankles, holding them in their mouths, stretching her body above the ground. Black blood oozed from her mouth and the bite wounds. She could not focus her eyes enough to make out what the beasts were, but she could see their fangs. One had wings. She could hear their thoughts but could not make sense of them amongst the screams in the jungle and her own screams. They were speaking a language she didn't understand. Soon the men in suits caught up to her. They stood on either side of her and ripped her shirt off.

Her breasts were exposed. She was paralyzed. One of the men pulled out a gun and pointed it at her. The beasts pulled harder, pulling in four different directions, as if their desire was to rip her body into pieces. The man with the gun had blue glowing eyes. He said something, but his voice was muffled. He fired twice.

Abigail's body jerked in the seat. Roger noticed but continued driving. He tried to watch her and the road at the same time and realized it was a dangerous attempt. He looked for the closest exit. Abigail's body jerked again.

Abigail's weak body dropped to the ground. The beasts and the men were gone. She slowly got to her feet and ran. They were all once again chasing behind her. Once again she jumped off a cliff to get away. She fell into a bed of red fog. It turned into a hospital bed where she was suddenly strapped down, lying on her stomach. She had electrodes attached to her body. The room was dark and steamy. She heard a muffled voice. The words sounded like a chant. Incense floated in the air. She could see candles, mirrors and low lights. She heard knocking. A man whose face was painted white tapped wooden needles into her back, creating the tattoos using an ancient method. Her mouth was bound. She stretched her body to scream, and suddenly she was awakened by Roger.

He gently shook her and called her name, "Elvis. Wake up sweetie. Wake up." They were at a rest stop.

Abigail jumped up opening her eyes. Roger ran his hands through her hair. She was shivering.

Roger asked, "Are you okay?"

She nodded and pulled him over to her. He held her tightly and kissed her lightly on the forehead. She looked up at him. He kissed her head again and then her cheek. She smiled but turned her head down and took a deep breath. She held him tighter. The soft rain beat against the metal truck.

BROWN'S HOUSE

It was early evening. Brown decided that waiting on Meghan was not going to help, so he left the office and headed home. When he arrived home, he immediately took a shower, threw on a t–shirt and sweats and walked barefoot into the kitchen. He grabbed a bagel, coffee and some grapes from the refrigerator. He moved his paperwork and laptop into his home office, turned on the computer and went on the shared file drive to check if Finch had uploaded any new files. *Nothing. She must be pissed!*

He spent about a half hour reviewing papers and drinking scotch. His eyes were heavy. He thought about calling it an early night but he continued working anyway. Then, he received a text from Finch. "KNOCK, KNOCK!" Simultaneously he heard a knock at his front door. He walked over to the door. It was Finch. She entered the house. Brown closed the door behind her.

Brown said, "I was really stupid earlier."

She responded, "Don't worry about it. I got a lot of info from her that I think you should hear. She gave me some..."

Brown interrupted, "I don't want to talk about work just yet. Spend some time with me." He kissed Meghan. She dropped her bags and kissed him back. They took each other's clothes off and began to make love. He tossed her down on the couch. She moaned as he pressed his body against hers. She pulled him closer and bit him on the ear.

CHAPTER 13

COBALT ROAD
DR. COLIN PALTEE'S HOME

1129 COBALT ROAD was written in faded white paint on the side of the red mailbox at the edge of the driveway. Roger didn't initially see the house but turned into the driveway. In the distance, they could see the house was recessed behind a small wooded area and a large front yard. Roger pulled the truck down the long cobblestone driveway that led to the front door. The ground was not level. The older truck bounced roughly as the tires eased over the damp stones and splashed through little pools of water from the rain.

The place was not very welcoming. The yard had not been kept up. Old leaves from last fall were scattered across the yard. Spring grass had no chance of flourishing. In the yard were a few rusty old cars and trucks from the 50s with various parts removed. There was a pile of tires and a pile of hubcaps on either side of the house. Organized clutter. There was also a shed off to the right side of the house, a lawnmower and rake leaning against the side. There were three rainwater collection barrels on the left side of the house and another against the shed. As Roger drove closer to the house, the cobblestone driveway slowly turned into gravel, then sand, then grass. A six foot tall light post stood at the end.

The home was a wood sided Victorian built in 1918. It had two chimneys, a white door, a wooden white painted porch, white shutters around the windows and a slate roof. Hanging from the windows were empty flower baskets. Along the front of the house was a series of perennial flowers and untamed shrubs that had grown up past the bottom of the first floor windows. They hadn't been trimmed in at least a couple years. A sparrow had made a nest in a crack by the drain attached to the roof and slipped into the hole just as Roger and Abigail shut off the engine. A silver wind chime hung from the roof of the porch. The light wind blew just enough for it to create a soft melody that set anyone at ease. The stairs were cement with a white railing.

Abigail and Roger exited the truck. Roger walked over to Abigail as she investigated the exterior of the home. Neither of them were completely comfortable with visiting strangers, but Roger trusted whomever his mother trusted. Too bad it wasn't the other way around. They walked past the dirty old trucks and over the leafy yard. There was a dead black bird lying in the leaves. Abigail felt no sentiment and stepped over it as if it were an object. The only thing she felt was the dry crunch of leaves under her heels as she walked to the house. They reminded her of the leaves she ran over in her dreams except they were not lush and green. She could hear mice and squirrels shuffling in the woods, around the house and by the shed. They reached the edge of the porch.

Roger asked, "Ready?"

She replied, "Let's do it."

They walked up the porch, reached the door and knocked. Within seconds a tall, older man with salt and pepper hair opened the door. The smell of incense rushed out the door and into their faces.

Dr. Colin Paltee was more than six feet tall. Under his left eye, he had a birth mark shaped like the state of Florida. It was darker than his natural skin tone. He sported a long ponytail that was braided in the back, gathered together with a leather strap. He had a mustache, glasses, and wore a beaded necklace and bracelet. "Abigail? So that's what they are calling you now. Abigail! Yes!" He was excited. "Well look at you! It was long ago, but I remember you. Come in."

They entered the house through the front room to see Native American artifacts and artwork which decorated the walls of the home. He had many books piled onto shelves and tables. His house was full of his research. There were faded pictures on the wall of an older Native American male and female. Abigail would have guessed that they were Paltee's parents. There was another picture of a young woman that Roger thought resembled Abigail. She had two long braids that stretched over her shoulders. She was beautiful. The picture was dusty. It was clear there were no women or children currently in his life, possibly because Paltee was completely submerged in his work. He walked Roger and Abigail around the house, showing them a few things they were not very interested in seeing, before they made their way to the living room on the back side of the house.

Dr. Paltee said, "I haven't heard from Terry in a couple years. But when she told me about you, I had to meet you again. Have a seat."

They all sat in the living room on a very comfortable couch. Dr. Paltee had tea ready on the coffee table. He asked, "Tea?"

They shook their heads. Roger placed the pictures of the tattoos on the table. Dr. Paltee looked at them. "It's been a while since I have seen these," he said in reference to the tattoos. "Oh such beautiful work," he said as he examined the pictures. He had a curious smile on his face as he fumbled through the various images of Abigail's back.

Abigail also pulled out her little bible and dropped in on the coffee table. Paltee picked it up and was confused. Abigail opened it and showed him the handwritten the note: E2 ON THE FIRST FOURTEEN.

Abigail said, "Someone wrote this but I don't understand."

Dr. Paltee read aloud, "EZ on the first fourteen."

She said, "No E2 on the..." then she realized what she thought was a two was a fancy letter Z. "EZ?" she questioned.

"EZEKIEL?" Roger shouted out. Roger didn't know why he knew that.

Abigail grabbed the book and turned to the book of Ezekiel. The first four verses had nothing of interest she could connect to. It was verse five that made her stomach drop.

Verse 5: Also out of the midst thereof came the likeness of four living creatures. And this was their appearance; they had the likeness of a man.

Verse 6: And every one had four faces, and every one had four wings.

Verse 7: And their feet were straight feet; and the sole of their feet was like the sole of a calf's foot: and they sparkled like the color of burnished brass.

Verse 8: And they had the hands of a man under their wings on their four sides; and they four had their faces and their wings.

Verse 9: Their wings were joined one to another; they turned not when they went; they went every one straight forward.

Verse 10: As for the likeness of their faces, they four had the face of a man, and the face of a lion, on the right side: and they four had the face of an ox on the left side; they four also had the face of an eagle.

Verse 11: Thus were their faces: and their wings were stretched upward; two wings of every one were joined one to another, and two covered their bodies.

Verse 12: And they went every one straight forward: whither the spirit was to go, they went; and they turned not when they went.

Verse 13: As for the likeness of the living creatures, their appearance was like burning coals of fire, and like the appearance of lamps: it went up and down among the living creatures; and the fire was bright, and out of the fire went forth lightning. **Verse 14:** And the living creatures ran and returned as the appearance of a flash of lightning.

Abigail was astonished, "Ezekiel, the first 14 verses in the book. It speaks of human/beast hybrids. These are the beasts I've been dreaming about."Abigail handed the book to Dr. Paltee and asked, "What does this mean?"

Paltee closed the book, "Whoever wrote this was trying to remind you in case you forgot." He looked sad and sipped his tea. "You obviously have forgotten, haven't you?" He adjusted his glasses before he spoke again saying, "I'm not sure what you know and what you don't know about project Flutter."

She asked, "Project what?"

Dr. Paltee was happy to explain and said, "Project Flutter. Flutter was the code name for the military based project that *you* were the product of. There's so much to this project that no one knew, not even Atkins. She was dealing with it from a different end. We only met occasionally. She told us what needed to happen for it to work. It was my job to deliver a human specimen that fit the criteria and your marks... may I see them? Do you mind?" His heart raced in anticipation. He remembered making the marks using an ancient method of tattooing using sharpened bones, wood and ink using a *hand poking* technique. The bone, with ink on the sharp edge, is repeatedly tapped into the skin.

Abigail didn't mind. She shook her head. Abigail and Dr. Paltee stood up. Roger watched closely, waiting to see what the man had planned. Abigail took off her shirt and she turned around. Dr. Paltee lightly ran his fingers across the marks on her back. He said, "Yes. You were one of the unique ones.

This is your totem on the spine leading up to your brain— the god of your nervous system." He looked in her scalp and asked, "What is this?" He roughly grabbed her head with his two hands turning her head side to side. "These, I don't know. The marks on your spine, I did those, but your scalp that is not me. Hmm." He stopped for a moment to think. Paltee paced the room tapping his head trying to remember if there was something he missed.

"I can't imagine who would have done those marks there. But they, too, seem to have a connection with the bible passage... and the marks on your spine."

Abigail and Roger hadn't photographed the marks on her head for Abigail to get a proper look. They touched the marks on her head after he let go.

Roger asked, "The marks on her spine. What do they mean?"

Dr. Paltee looked at Abigail's sad and confused face and said, "It's an interesting story. Sit, Abigail. Let me explain." Dr. Paltee walked over to a shelf. He fiddled through some books pushing a few aside and piling others on the floor. He grabbed an old leather book off the shelf and handed it to Abigail.

Abigail opened the book to see that it was a journal. Paltee reached over and closed the book in her hands.

"Wait!" he said. "You will never understand unless you listen first. You must hear me out before you open this book."

Paltee scratched his head and sat down. He took his glasses off and cleaned the lenses with his white cotton button–up shirt. He put them back on his face. He took another sip of the tea and poured a little more into his mug from the kettle as he explained, "Project Flutter didn't become Project *Flutter* until I got involved, but it had been around for about five years before me and was known as Project Gray Scale. As you know the government wanted to make a super armor that could increase a soldier's skill, speed, agility and strength. It had to be durable enough to withstand gunfire and small explosions and light enough to wear as undergarment. It had to be sleek, water resistant, fireproof and safe. Thanks to Atkins, this was all accomplished, but they couldn't find humans strong enough to wear the suit. Our bodies could not naturally react with the speed necessary to make the suits work. So, to make a long story short, we had to make humans have the ability to adapt. We didn't need a genetically altered human but one with heightened neuro–senses."

Abigail and Roger sat quietly listening as he explained.

"Around the time when you came in, I was brought in to try something different– a creative, unconventional method to adjust, let's say, insufficient human ability. But right after we thought we had made a few years of progress, the president shut down the program and ceased all funding. A private company picked up the program; but I didn't agree with the purpose, and I left the project."

Abigail asked, "What did you do to me?"

Dr. Paltee answered, "The purpose wasn't to hurt you. As you can see by looking at the interior of my home, I am Native American; the same as you. Well half anyway. My last name was a name given to my great grandparents many years ago. The Shaman in my culture played with the spiritual world for thousands of years. They were very much in tune with earth and nature. Many times, their work with the other side placed them right on the edge of our world and what you would call the underworld or the afterlife or... you know what I mean. They played along the edge of that boundary between our world and theirs, often welcoming spirits to dwell among the living and within the living as well, offering their own bodies as vessels to accept the spirit temporarily or permanently. When a human is possessed, that spirit taps directly into the neurological system of the host."

Roger interrupted, "Wait a minute. Did you say possessed? What are you saying? She was demon possessed?"

Paltee answered, "Demons are bad spirits that cannot be controlled. And to possess a human with a human spirit would be pointless. For some reason, human spirits are stronger than us, but not strong enough for the suit. Human spirits can carry grudges, pain, and too much opinion. They are not easily controlled" He smirked. "We used animals."

Abigail asked, "Animals?!"

"Yes. Only an animal can respond with the 6th sense needed to survive the suit. The strength and agility of animals far surpass what a human could ever accomplish. You Abigail were different. You were my little experiment within the experiment. You have multiple, which was against the orders of the design team, but I couldn't resist pushing the envelope. Our biggest challenge was the ability to control the outbursts of your inner animal spirits… and you have four."

Roger shouted, "FOUR!? Jesus Christ!"

"Four? What are they?" Abigail asked.

Dr. Paltee explained, "Yes. Four, Abigail. They live in you, nestled within your totem, and when you need them, when you call them, they come forth. Look." Dr. Paltee spread the pictures of the tattoos on the table and placed them in order. He pointed as he spoke. "This icon, as you know, is mine. This is where the name *Flutter* came from. This here," he pointed to another, "is your first possession, an eagle."

"That would explain the eagle in my dreams? And the winged figure I dreamt about on the way here." Abigail tried to make sense of it.

"That could be the case. An eagle can read the wind like no other animal in the sky. It is fearless of heights and can predict changes in the wind. It's a very sharp animal. This was a subtle possession since the soul of any bird is rather small. The second… the Taurus. Not to mention it's your zodiac sign—

we needed your determination to be so powerful that even in the face of death your goal would be to complete the mission. No animal is as stubborn as the bull and it is also very strong. The bull has a big spirit but is more reactive and takes a lot of stimuli to project its abilities."

"That explains a lot," Roger mumbled.

Paltee continued, "The white tail deer, your third spirit, a very strong spirit and very swift. We needed you to have that speed and agility. It would have been your dominant spirit but that ended with the presence of your fourth possession, the jaguar. When you get in your element, this is the spirit that dominates all others. The rest pick up where he leaves off. This is the animal we experimented with. Most others have bears or lions or deer. No one was given multiples, let alone the jaguar. It was a fragile experiment, but it worked." He piled the pictures and handed them to Roger.

Roger suddenly felt sorry for Abigail, "Do you think that it's okay to use someone's life and experiment this way?"

Paltee tilted his head in shame and said, "No. I don't. I was young then and didn't have the experience I do now. I was trying to understand the science of my family traditions. I wanted to see if they could be used to... I'm sorry Abigail, for any pain I have caused you. This is why I am here to help you. Are you having trouble remembering things?"

She answered, "Yes. I have dreams..."

"Nightmares!" Roger blurted.

"Nightmares..." Abigail corrected herself, "all the time, but I have lost most of my memories. I recently remembered a few. I had an episode not too long ago."

Dr. Colin Paltee said, "Your memories are within you, Abigail. You haven't lost them. They are stored wherever your spirits have placed them. The eagle can place them in one place and the deer another. They store memories according to their needs so that they can adapt for the next time. Your personal memories will get jumbled in the mix. All will collide and come forth in your dreams."

Abigail, "I remember your face from them."

He nodded and said, "That is probably so."

Roger asked, "So what *do* you remember Abigail?"

Abigail paused for a moment, thinking of where to begin and said, "I remember a car accident. I was being followed by others like me. The car spun out and I ran to an old farm. I was losing a lot of blood from the accident, so I stopped to quickly tie down the wound on my leg when I heard them closing in. I ran to the backyard through a cornfield. Eventually one of the men caught up. We fought. I was on the ground. He shot twice and whispered, 'Run!' I picked myself up and took off faster than ever before. I heard another shot, but I kept going. I just kept running. I don't remember the details. Everything was a blur." And a blur it had been. Abigail ran into downtown Boston, into the street and was hit by a car. She banged her head on the hood and went out cold. No one else was on the road at the time. The driver and passenger were both extremely drunk. They looked around and knew no one had seen what happened. They got out of the car and quickly dragged her into alley and covered her body with trash. "I woke up with bullet wounds, a bruised head and no memory of what had happened," she continued.

Dr. Paltee said, "They will be looking for you Abigail. I'm sure they are close. They will find you. You have to run or confront them, but you have already decided, haven't you? You will not run." Dr. Paltee sipped his tea, "It is not in your nature to run. You are a trained killer from a young age. You have been trained to stalk, attack, kill, and disappear without a pinpointing trace. You will fight to the end." He looked at Roger and said, "And what do you plan to do, Roger? These men are highly skilled and trained to rip you both, limb from limb. I don't mean to sound negative. I am here to help you, but I'm not here to give you false hopes about the enemy you face."

Roger was offended initially, but he knew the man spoke wisely. He thought to himself, *What can I do?* He could barely fight off the four men in the alley. He was well trained with weaponry and was an excellent shot with handguns, compound bows and knives, but his hand skills were lacking. He couldn't fight very well. He imagined how different his skills would have been if he had taken a little time to practice with Frankie and Larry in the fight club. How could he be worthy of Abigail if he couldn't protect her or even hold up to her enemy? Roger felt a lump of shame grow in his throat and made a promise that this would never happen again.

Abigail also had a few thoughts running through her mind. All this talk about spirits and possession of animals. Now she knew that her exotic looks were because she, too, was partially Native American. She had never known anything about her past or origination, her heritage or her real family. But she did know that her enemy was strong. She didn't feel hopeless. She was concerned for Roger for a moment, and then she remembered the artillery in his basement and his strong arms and hands. He had the build to be a strong fighter, but he lacked training. She could fix that. She knew she needed him as much as he needed her. His only weakness was his lack of confidence, and it would take more than encouraging words to build that.

Abigail was hungry for more information. Her questions about her origin could wait. She said, "Tell me more about the company that picked up the project."

Dr. Paltee responded, "Remember, I told you I left the project because I didn't agree with the direction it was going? They said they wanted the research for some bullshit. It didn't even make sense. I think they were creating corporate killers to take out the competition or… Oh my. I just thought of something. Alan Jiang. He was murdered recently. His partner is missing. His firm just invested in a firm called Indigo Inc. I remember that company poking its head around the facility. I'm pretty sure they were the company that took over the project. Yes. I think so. Let me check something."

Dr. Paltee walked into the kitchen and grabbed his laptop off the kitchen table. His head was pounding with thoughts and memories and guilt. He was so overwhelmed. He remembered Abigail's face, but didn't remember her by that name. He didn't remember her even having a name but rather having a label. Seeing her was like seeing a ghost. He thought they had killed the prototype hosts. They never said they would, but he felt it was inevitable. Yet she was here, sitting on his couch, strong and alive. He turned on the laptop and rejoined Roger and Abigail in the living room. He began to type in some phrases on Google. He pulled up the Chapel & Case company website. "See here. This is Alan Jiang. This is his partner, Robert Benson, who is missing. I don't know who that guy is, but I bet Indigo had something to do with Jiang's death and Benson's disappearance."

Roger said, "Makes sense. Look here. They said his body was dismembered when they found him washed up on the shore. This reminds me of when you fought the men in the alley. The bodies..." They look at Abigail.

She said, "Don't even...I didn't have anything to do with that."

Dr. Paltee said, "Maybe not, but your friends may have, which means they are here."

Abigail asked, "What happened to the other suits?"

Dr. Paltee said, "They were all destroyed and the plans were destroyed... or stolen." He looked skeptically at Roger and asked, "Did your mom know anything about that?"

Roger, "No way. She barely wanted to talk about what happened. She can't even walk straight."

It didn't really matter to Paltee. He said, "Hmm. Well, young lady, there is still much to discover. Keep my notes as long as you need to. They are very thorough. You may discover some things that you would have wished you never turned over the stone to uncover. Go through the journal. Study my notes and figure out things for yourself."

Abigail asked, "You said they must be near. Are you not afraid of helping us?"

"If they come for me, I will deal with it when it happens. *If* it happens. For now I suggest you lay low until you decide what you are going to do." Dr. Paltee handed Abigail another journal. "Take this one, too. These journals will not answer all of your questions, but they will put you closer to knowing who you are and what happened."

She hugged them tightly to her chest.

Paltee escorted them to the door. "Take these," he took the beads off his wrist. "They're supposed to be for good luck. You will need it more than I will." He smiled and shut the door as soon as they turned their backs.

Roger and Abigail returned to the truck, got in and drove off. In about five minutes, they were back on the two–lane Merritt Parkway heading north to Interstate 91 North. Not many words were spoken on the way back. Abigail was eager to get home. She wanted to go through the journal, but she knew there was too much information to absorb and couldn't focus during the bumpy drive home. She took out a cigarette, cracked the window, lit it and began to smoke. Roger didn't like the fact that she smoked, but he figured he would work on that with her later. In the meantime, he tried to keep his eyes on the road but the way Abigail's lips curled over the cigarette took his attention away from the white and yellow lines.

He imagined for a moment what else she could do with her lips before he felt the car drift to the left and a horn beeped at him. He swerved to get the car back between the lines. Abigail gave him a strong stare. He shrugged, smiled and kept his eyes on the road from that point forward.

Abigail thought about Frankie. She missed him. She knew the attitude she had given him earlier was a foul but necessary move because telling him how she had ripped those men apart would have been a mistake. She hadn't meant to be so evil, but she knew he wouldn't understand. The cigarette put her at ease for a moment. She looked out the window through her faint reflection and saw a deer carcass resting on the side of the road. A deer: one of her spirit possessions. She thought for a moment how this could even be possible. *Why me?* She wondered, but the answer to that question was lost for now.

The sun set as they crossed from the Merritt Parkway to the short drive on I91 North, then to 84 east, and back onto the Mass Turnpike, Abigail and Roger both had an entanglement of reflections in their minds. This string of intertwining thoughts consisted of the gruesome murders in the alley, today's discussion with Paltee, the infamous suit, Frankie, and their physical attraction for one another. Though Abigail fought hard to ignore it and often denied it, she caught herself drifting into a subtle image of being wrapped in Roger's arms, a place she had been before; but this time she imagined stealing a kiss. She was suddenly reminded of her attraction for him that she had felt before all this mess started. She snapped out of it as fast as it had popped into her mind. She gave him an evil stare to make up for her mistake. *It was just a thought, nothing more.* She lit another cigarette.

CHAPTER 14
BROWN'S APARTMENT

Night had fallen, and the streets around Sydney's place were calm and quiet. This was unusual since his place was in a more populated area than Finch's home in the suburbs where quietness around the house was expected. Brown and Finch were stretched out on the couch, wrapped in a thin blanket. Their bodies were intertwined as the soulful sounds of James Morrison played softly in the background. There were a few candles lit on the counter and two glasses of wine, with melons and pineapple slices in a bowl next to Sydney's glasses on the end table. They kissed and massaged one another for a while, pressing their naked bodies as close as they could. Brown took a piece of the pineapple and rubbed it against Meghan's neck. He then licked away the juice that streamed down to her collar bone and then ate the fruit.

Finch smiled, "You're such a freak."

Brown said, "You haven't seen freak. I can put this pineapple somewhere else and do the same if you like." He winked as he chewed.

Finch thought Brown was cute when he didn't have on his glasses. He squinted like a little mole and sometimes pretended to see better than he could. Finch had her papers sprawled out on the coffee table. Every time she wanted to review them, she was distracted by her insatiable desire for Sydney's body. Brown kissed her head, back and neck while she spoke. She said, "You are the biggest distraction of my life. I'm never going to get any work done," and laughed.

Brown said, "I can distract you for the rest of our lives. How does that sound?"

She answered, "It sounds like I will be fired and jobless, eventually homeless; and I would have to kill you."

"You would not be homeless. You could just stay here with me," he said.

Finch thought to herself, *Here he goes again with this conversation that I'm still not ready to have.* It spoiled the mood. Finch got up off the couch. She walked her fit naked body across the room. She retrieved her clothes off the floor and went into Brown's room. She yelled out, "I'm stealing some sweats." She searched through the closet and found a pair folded on a shelf. She knew where they were; she had borrowed them so many other times. Then she said, "Oh by the way, I got some important information from Jen which we should discuss before morning."

Brown knew he had killed the mood once she mentioned work and said, "Okay, okay. What was she saying?" Brown sat up and put on his pants and glasses.

Finch dressed in his room. She spoke loudly so that he could hear. "She retold me what was going on that day and all the weird stuff she had seen. Most you already heard. Her story was the same. I asked her three different times in three different ways. We went out to lunch, and she started pulling out these files. Alan Jiang and Robert Benson were meeting about some business deal with a company called Indigo Inc."

Brown was surprised, "Did you say Benson?"

"Yes! She said he was there."

"Interesting. What else?"

"She said she didn't know what kind of business deal they were discussing, whether it was an investment or a purchase. She gave me a lot of paperwork that Jiang left in the cabin. She said that he also had told her that he wasn't interested in the deal anymore and that the company wanted to discuss other options. He wasn't interested in any new options."

Brown asked, "But I thought this was a fishing trip."

Finch replied, "Yes and no. She said Jiang was extremely private about his affairs. She said Dennis Matthews, his mentee, probably didn't know about the meeting, but Jiang must have wanted him there. Jiang would often disguise meetings as vacations. She believes this was the case again." Finch walked back into the main room dressed in sweatpants and a t–shirt.

"Did she say anything else about Robert?" Brown scrunched his forehead and asked.

"She said he was more interested in Indigo, Inc. than Jiang was, but she wasn't sure that he had all the facts. She knew that many of their colleagues had invested in the company so Benson thought it was the smart thing to do. After our meeting I did some research. The crazy thing was, after Jiang's body was found, their stock dropped 40% and got bought up by a private firm in Salt Lake City. The new CEO, Erin Moore, stepped in and within two weeks the price was back where it was before Jiang's disappearance and murder. Something is also telling me that the murder in the alley way is also connected."

"The men we found? You think they know Benson?"

She said, "No. I don't, but the kill pattern seems to be similar. I know Jiang's body was dismembered, but I don't know what that looks like. Maybe he fell out the boat and was chopped by the blades."

Brown said, "Duffy is going to take the lead on the dead johns in the Alley case, by the way."

She was upset, "WHY!? Since when?!"

Brown knew she wouldn't be happy about this and said, "Since today. Chief Downy called and told me he wanted us to focus on the Benson case. Duffy said he will keep us informed on all major points. But he sent me this."

Brown pulled out his laptop. It had the surveillance footage Duffy had sent over earlier. Finch walked over. The camera was facing the alley on a slight angle, but the camera was situated a distance away at another building. Brown played the video. Initially there wasn't much to see. Then Brown saw dark blurs moving in and out of view but was unable to pick out much.

Brown commented, "Hmm, not much there but there is another video." Brown played the next video. It showed two frazzled youths cutting across the street in the distance.

Finch asked, "Can we link anymore surveillance to that time?"

Brown said, "I can ask Duffy, but I believe this was all we could get. It looks like a male and a female, but they look like they were running away in fear. Maybe they saw something."

Finch said, "Maybe they did it. Zoom in."

Brown paused the footage and zoomed in on the figures. The only face that could possibly be recognized was Abigail's. But it is so unclear it was hard to get a sure match. The image pixilated as it enlarged and the particular details of the face were losing shape and distinction. Finch huffed in frustration. Then she looked closer, squinting her eyes. She said, "I feel like I know that face. They don't look like they would be mixed up with the Robert Benson case. They look like kids. Snapshot that face and forward it to my phone."

Finch walked over to a chair and plopped into it. She opened up the shared file drive on her phone and finally uploaded her notes. Brown sent her the photo in an email. She uploaded that to the drive as well. "I guess I'll give you access to my files on Jennifer Martin. But only you. I'm not sure I'm ready to share this information with anyone else until I know if it's going anywhere." She put her phone on the coffee table.

"Did you get any news from your MIT boys on that memory card?"

Brown answered, "Not yet. I will call them in the morning. I'm not sure why it's taking so long, but I don't know anything about what it takes to get this done."

She looked out the window and saw a man pass by. "Well I have to..." Meghan was suddenly distracted. She looked up and was certain she saw Anthony looking through the window. She shook her head and looked again. There was nothing there. Her nerves were worked up. She was ready to leave. "I have to go. I'm gonna check out Indigo, Inc. Please stay on that memory card at MIT."

Brown was confused by her sudden desire to go, "Why leave? You can research here."

She answered, "You are my biggest distraction remember? I'll never get a damn thing done. You know it's true."

Brown agreed, "I guess you're right." He stood up, walked over to her and kissed her on the shoulder. She kissed him on the lips, grabbed her things and rushed out the door.

When Meghan reached her house, she went directly to the back porch and had a quick smoke. She started to think about what it would be like if she and Brown moved in together. She wondered how the department would view it. She liked working in the city, but figured she could always get a job on the Cambridge police force instead. *Is he worth all of this?* She couldn't imagine that having an open relationship and working for the same force would work for them. She had to admit that she was in love with Brown. They had crossed every line possible, and their feelings were only getting stronger.

She twisted her ring around her finger, and finally slipped it off. She took a deep breath, A few tears fell from her face and she put it back on. She went into her kitchen. She made a turkey and tomato sandwich and poured a glass of whiskey.

She sat at the table with her laptop and began running searches:

ALAN JIANG
ROBERT BENSON
INDIGO, INCORPORATED

A few items surfaced about the Alan Jiang investigation, but some of the files were clearly missing, mostly the graphic details of the murders. She knew that she needed more information about it including more on Dennis Mathews. She found out that Alan was Dennis' mentor and found articles highlighting Jiang's corporate career. One interview was conducted with Dennis. It was clear that his answers were pre–engineered to ensure Dennis didn't say the wrong thing. There was a lot of information Meghan didn't know about Jiang, but since she was recently discovering how strong the connection was, she was all over it. She only wished she had acted sooner. Her biggest complication was that Portland, Maine, was completely out of her jurisdiction, so getting information out of them would take some networking. She kept browsing link after link, hoping that the media could provide more info, but she realized quickly that they, too, were lost. She thought to herself, *I bet Katherine was involved in keeping this quiet.* She thought for a moment and swallowed the rest of the whiskey in the cup. She poured another shot just as she received a text message from her mother in law, "WE HOPE ALL IS WELL." She ignored the message.

She then focused her research on Robert Benson where she mostly found trivial information about him and a few things about his wife. He played Harvard Football from 1993 to 1996 but didn't play his senior year. She found a few old pictures of him from sports highlights in the papers and saved them to her files. Benson had worked for Bank of America for eight years before he returned to Harvard to get his MBA. He had dated a black woman named Diana Hines during his two years at Harvard's MBA program and had married her the day after graduation. It seemed Diana and Robert last saw one another a year earlier when she decided to leave the country to do research in Kenya. Diana was currently in Meru doing research on the progression of infectious diseases in Kenyan villages. She was featured in a segment on *Newsviews*. An article with a videotaped interview popped up when Meghan searched Diana Benson's name. She was very confident and slender, with her hair worn in a long black braid. Her eyebrows were thin. She had high cheekbones and long fingers. She could have been a model when she was younger.

The interview was about five minutes of questions and answers. She seemed very passionate about her work. She spoke gracefully until the end of the interview when she had been asked about how her husband felt about her being gone for so long. In a British accent she commented, "Beside the fact that I am a professional and have a duty to work and grow in my profession, providing factual findings from thorough research that will benefit the public, no one asks me what I think when my husband goes on elaborate business trips. Thus, his approval or discontent is not my concern nor should it be yours. Frankly, I don't think his opinion of what I am doing and where I am matters at this point in our relationship." She made her statement bold and clear, signifying tension in the relationship.

The interviewer ended the interview with a shaky, "Thank you," and wrapped up the segment with an outro and uneasy smile. Finch was sure Diana must have stormed out of the room as soon as the director said, *Cut!*

Finch wondered if Diana knew anything about Robert's disappearance and concluded that she wouldn't care but made a side note to find out one way or another.

As Meghan searched on, she realized there was one sad story after another. Benson's parents had died in a helicopter accident when he was 29. He had just been accepted into the MBA program, but wasn't able to share the news with them. The fact that he was missing had never made the news. Anything that was mentioned was mostly speculation but no one could say exactly why he hadn't been seen in business meetings. There were a few proposals he had missed and people started to talk, but no one had filed an official missing persons report. Brown and Finch wanted to keep as much out of the media as they could. One brave reporter speculated that he had gone to visit Diana in Kenya to rekindle their dying love for one another.

Robert began working at Chapel and Case four years earlier. Meghan looked to see what type of business deals Chapel and Case had been involved in during his employment, but nothing out of the ordinary surfaced. She created a new document named <INDIGO> and placed it on her laptop. She took a sip of whiskey. It was strong. It reminded her of Anthony and Sydney at the same time. Strong and relaxing. She stretched her body and rubbed her eyes. It was getting late, but she was wrapped up in figuring out what was going on. She knew there was a connection between the recent occurrences.

Meghan spent the next few hours working diligently into the wee hours of the morning, researching, copying, pasting and printing information on Indigo Inc. By the time she was satisfied with her progress, the sun was peeking over the treetops. She knew she needed rest but was also elated about her thorough acquisition of information through research. *Thank you, Google.* She packed her files away, shut down the computer and climbed into bed. She put on three alarms to be sure she would get up on time for work. She opened her phone and took another look at the blurry picture of the alley murder suspect and thought, *Why does this face look familiar?* It bothered her the same way trying to remember a word that was on the tip of her tongue. She put the phone away and rested her head on the pillow with only a few hours remaining before she had to get up. A few hours of sleep were fine. She would be okay with that. Her mind raced for a few minutes, but she was sleep within five. She slept well.

MORNING

Erin Moore ran six mornings a week. Today was no different. She spent the morning finishing up her daily run at the local health spa about two blocks from her apartment in downtown Boston. She usually ran for an hour a day and occasionally engaged in light weight lifting but wasn't interested in bulking up in any way. She already had a natural strength. Her muscles were naturally formed without much effort. She liked her slender, feminine physique and thought herself to be envied by the women from the various aspects of her life: colleagues, coworkers, family. She refused to be overweight by any standard.

Moore worked hard to maintain her lean body and grunted as she watched people in the office pile the sugar and cream into their coffee. She rolled her eyes every time she saw workers return from lunch with a McDonald's bag and a shake. She considered bad eating habits to be a lack of self control and poor judgment, which in her mind was a statement of weakness. She was even more repulsed by people who were naturally smaller than others yet ate like pigs. She knew that being thin was not an excuse to overindulge. She saw them as an implosion waiting to happen: indigestion, bad cholesterol, heart disease... *Disgusting!*

As she ran on the treadmill, her mind slipped back to her more pudgy years of life, the things she ate, and her refusal to be in that shape ever again. *How could others not care?* She didn't mean to judge others, but in her own way she used her judgments of them to stay motivated and work out in the gym.

Erin was from Ontario, California. She had two sisters. Geraldine and Sandy. Her older sister, Geraldine, had moved to New York, and she sought an excuse to get to the east coast as well. Sandy was also back east attending George Washington University in DC, so Erin was highly motivated to get a new position on the east coast as well. That opportunity came when an executive suddenly quit. He had walked right out of the office, taking only one box with him. He lit a cigarette before reaching the elevator, smoked his way down to the ground level, and walked out. He never returned.

At the time, she was working as COO of a company in Utah. She received a call from Jusford Chillings, the head of the board of directors. He told her that she was recommended by a former board member who had worked a few projects with her in the past. The next day she flew in for an interview and was hired on the spot. She was very sharp and witty. She answered questions thoroughly and without hesitation. She had poise and would be a great image for the company. She worked as Robert Benson's assistant COO. It was a slight pay cut, but she was closer to her sisters and happy to move on with her life.

After the murder of Jiang and the disappearance of Benson, without hesitation the board voted unanimously to move her up to CEO.

Erin ended her workout and walked out of the spa. She noticed a text message from Darren Hall, her lover and coworker, "CALL ME AFTER YOUR RUN." She dialed his number. It rang and he answered.

"Yes love?" Darren said sarcastically.

"Oh so you love me now," she joked though she was still a little winded from the workout. Hall could hear it in her voice.

"Of course I do. How could I not love you?" He said.

She asked, "Did you workout today?"

"Yes. I exercised a little earlier so I could do some work before getting in. I wanted to run some things by you. Some of the numbers in the deal are not where they need to be. I can show you what I mean in person. What time are you coming in?"

"I can get there by 7:30 if you need me to," she said as she looked at her watch.

"Perfect. I will be in by 7:15. We have a few meetings today, so I wanted to get some time with you before that started."

"Thanks," Erin said as she wiped sweat off her forehead.

"How about dinner tonight? My place. I'm cooking," Darren said.

"I wouldn't miss it. Salmon?"

"Your favorite. I can do that!"

"And a massage?" She asked as she approached her apartment building.

"You're pushing it, boss lady."

She laughed, "It was worth a shot. Well, I'm home; I will see you in about an hour then." She hung up the phone, cracked a quick half smile and went in to her apartment. She had a protein shake, showered, dressed and headed out to work.

CHAPEL AND CASE INVESTMENT COMPANY

Erin Moore's office was on the top level of Chapel and Case, directly across from the elevator. It was the only office on that level with two high–tech conference rooms on either side. In front of the office was a waiting area with couches, chairs, a small refrigerator, a bathroom and wet bar. Cameron Myles was Erin's executive assistant. She used to work for Jiang and now happily assisted Moore. Inside the office, the back wall was constructed completely of glass. The side walls were constructed of a dark gray, smooth concrete with cherry wood shelves. The wall to the left held track and field awards from college, her degrees and a few family photographs. The wall to the right had a wet bar and a door that lead to a private bathroom equipped with a shower, mini steam room and a bidet.

In the office, Moore and Darren Hall sat at a small table by the window looking over figures that he had promised to show her. He had a laptop open and a stack of papers with Excel spreadsheets and charts. She wasn't very surprised by the findings but she knew that Darren didn't pull any punches when it came to his calculations. He was very thorough. It was one of the reasons she was attracted to him. If things were not in the company's favor, he would be the first to prove it numerically. This was not the news that Erin wanted to hear; but the numbers didn't lie, and Erin trusted Darren's work without question. They reviewed the findings for about 30 minutes before Darren left for a meeting. Erin had a string of meetings and conference calls that morning. Just as Hall exited the room, he saw Cameron escorting a group of executives from other companies into conference room 19A. He smiled at Cameron, walked in and took a seat, waiting for Erin to enter.

A couple hours later at the front of the building, a black limo followed by two black Escalade trucks pulled up to the firm. The men in the Escalades exited the trucks, walking rigidly and uniformly. There were a total of six men, three in each vehicle. They were wearing all black European cut suits and black sun glasses. They were clean cut and moved mechanically over to the limo. One turned around and a tattoo on the back of his neck became visible. It was small and circular. The tattoo was similar to Abigail's. One of the men opened the limo door. An older man, Jason Dewey, exited the limo. He looked around before he too placed sun glasses on his face. Dewey led the way to the lobby. Two of the men in the suits walked with Dewey into the building. The others stayed behind, keeping watch.

ERIN MOORE'S OFFICE

The two mysterious men and the older gentleman barged into Erin Moore's office. She was on a video conference call. Cameron Myles tried to block the door but they easily brushed her aside. Their strength was too powerful for her. She said to Moore, "I'm sorry they..."

"Let them in," Moore said. She was very upset but refused to show her emotions.

Mr. Dewey shut the door in Ms. Myles' face and said, "Excuse me Ms. Moore. It's always a pleasure to see my old friend."

"Likewise," she replied sarcastically. "What brings you here this morning, Dewey?"

"We have a few things to talk about, Moore. You haven't been returning my calls, so I thought it was best to pay you a visit and don't give me shit about being busy. I know your schedule."

"Then you would know that you picked a terrible time to interrupt." She said to the executives on the video conference, "Excuse me." She muted the conversation and said, "Mr. Dewey. I'm in an important meeting right now and..."

He interrupted, "They can wait." He sat down in a chair and removed his sun glasses. He took out his glasses and placed them on his face. "We have serious business to discuss. Now, you can unmute the call and let them know what we've been up to, or you can reschedule. Sit your ass down and listen."

"How did you get past security in the lobby?"

Dewey smiled, "My men can be very persuasive." The two men stepped forward in a threatening manner. Moore could see their guns bulging in the side holsters behind their jackets.

She knew what they were capable of. She was frustrated that she hadn't been watching the live lobby footage. She looked at the monitor. She saw the guards at the front desk sitting at the desk with two of Dewey's men standing behind them holding weapons to their backs. Moore was shaken up. She unmuted the call and said, "Sorry folks. Let's pick this up in about an hour."

Mr. Dewey said, "Make it two."

"Two hours. Let's make that two hours. Grab a lunch. We'll reconvene at noon." She hung up on the call.

Mr. Dewey slammed his briefcase on the desk. Erin Moore completely shut down her computer and drew the shades on her windows. Dewey opened the case, and Erin slammed her palm on it and shut it back. She was still afraid but wasn't keen on being embarrassed in front of her colleagues.

With a stern voice Erin said, "In order for me to run this company and be taken seriously by clients, you need to show me some respect. You do not own this company. You do not *run* this company. It is my ass on the line. Not yours. If I decide not to drop another penny into your fledgling account then that is my decision. Do not come in here shoving your way through my firm, roughing up my secretary, threatening my..."

Mr. Dewey snatched his case from under her hand, "I am not asking you for more money. You are so uninformed. You have no idea what mess I have been trying to clean up. I came here to talk about one of our joint investments which seemed to have 'misplaced' and the fact that my company is being heavily researched by a two bit cop who has a... hunch. Believe me, if they can connect you back to the company in Salt Lake City, your ass will be sitting in cell block eight receiving the Martha Stewart special. I came here to warn you."

"What do you mean by lost?"

"She escaped?" he uttered sarcastically.

"She?" Erin had only seen Dewey with male guards but never heard of females.

"Oh yes. A she. She is a trained killer on the loose. She's a special one unlike the others. We tracked her here. In your backyard. Would you believe it?" Dewey took out a cigar but decided to just chew on it.

Moore was nervous, "Why would she come here?"

"We don't know and don't care. Some idiot posted her picture as a missing person. We will need to pay him a visit if we cannot locate her exact whereabouts. We need her back ASAP. I need to run tests and she needs to finish her training."

Erin picked up her cell phone, "Get me a name and picture. I'll put my contact on it. They'll find her."

Mr. Dewey smiled, "Good. I'm also going to send my boys out to retrieve that investment and take care of that nosey cop. An old buddy of mine, Jackson Pearson... Do you know the name?" Moore nodded her head. "Seems he has a bone to pick with this same cop or detective or whatever she is."

Jackson Pearson had offered Detective Finch a half a million dollars to foil the evidence against his son Sean Pearson and she had refused. His son was convicted and was sent to prison for a year on bribery charges. Dewey and Pearson had made a few shady business deals. Dewey knew that Pearson had contacts within the police force so he made the call. It just so happened that Dewey was looking for information on the same detective who had helped Pearson lose millions. Pearson wanted to help, but he was still on probation and knew he was being monitored.

Dewey continued, "My boys are going in to handle this. Call your contacts. Keep the rest of the police squad off the case; let them do what they came to do, and we will be on our way out of town as soon as possible. Make some calls and make it happen so I can get out of your hair and back to my business endeavors."

"I will make the call now." Erin began to dial a phone number.

"If things go well, I will get you a pair of Ezekiels as a show of my appreciation." He smiled and walked out.

He called them the *Ezekiels*. It was the nick name Dewey gave the men and women of the Project Flutter program. He didn't know what else to call them so he made up the name in reference to their hybrid combination of human and animal abilities. They had names like just Abigail did. His two favorites were Ben and Saul, the two who followed him just about everywhere he went. They were the most loyal, emotionless and least opinionated. They did as they were told, killed without question. They protected Dewey and often called him *Father Dewey*. He was their creator. And they were his angels of death, taking the lives of anyone who infringed upon his vision or the visions of those who hired him to eliminate obstacles.

CHAPTER 15

FRANKIE'S PUB

Frankie spent the morning prepping food, cleaning and ordering supplies. A few shipments came in so he spent the morning also packing things away and rearranging the kitchen area. Not many people came into the bar before noon. Larry was on his way. Today would have been a good day for Abigail and Roger to return, but he wasn't sure what was going on. She hadn't returned his texts and Roger hadn't checked in either. He was worried. Unknown to him, the two were on their way back to the pub. Frankie mopped and hummed a random tune in his head. He made it up as he went along. He opened the pub at 11:05am. The first patrons entered by 11:15. One of them was Detective Brown. He immediately ordered a coffee and sat down with his briefcase.

Roger and Abigail had spent the night at Roger's house and drove back to the pub. About noon, they arrived at Frankie's Pub. They parked the truck in the back and walked around the building, heading to the front. It was a warm day. The foul stench of rotting garbage lingered through the air. This had never bothered Abigail. She never complained about the smell of bad meat and festering foods. Roger fanned a few flies from his face. They didn't speak but Roger watched Abigail, as she seemed disconnected from the world, placing one foot in front of the other, heading toward the front door. She was almost dragging her feet. She wondered what she should say to Frankie. He was being a lot more understanding than she had imagined he would be, but she didn't want to have to answer questions. Her only defense to this would be to put up a wall, her regular tactic to avoid conversation.

Detective Brown and a few other patrons were in the pub. Brown sat at a table by the window, drinking a coffee. He looked through a few papers and sent Finch a text, "STILL COMING TO FRANKIE'S?"

A few moments later Meghan Finch responded, "I'LL BE THERE IN A FEW. DRIVING NOW!"

Brown wrote back, "X THE TXT!" a reference to an ad campaign to end texting and driving.

She wrote back, "SHUSH!"

Frankie saw Abigail and Roger coming in and opened the door. Immediately, Roger handed Frankie the key to the truck. They walked in. Roger sat down at the bar. Abigail went into the kitchen without saying a word.

Frankie went over to Roger and said, "I didn't think she was coming back. Is everything cool?"

Roger replied, "More complicated actually. We've got some work to do but we didn't want to keep your truck this long without checking in."

Frankie wanted to be discreet, knowing that Brown was in the room, "It's fine. I don't use that thing enough to miss it. I'm glad you guys are okay. I know you are being secretive for a reason, but I need to make sure all is well. You can keep to yourselves for a while, but at some point we should talk about what happened the other night and we should talk soon."

Roger nodded. Frankie poured him a Coke just as Abigail walked out of the kitchen and joined Roger at the bar. Frankie looked at Abigail and immediately felt her anguish. She was distracted with thoughts of everything. Instead of haunting her dreams, these thoughts were now affecting her daytime consciousness. Anxiety was settling in. She felt her temperature rising. Her hand rubbed the back of her neck where her first tattoo rested. Her eyes were dark with worry and sadness. She had a rough night, tossing and turning in the bed next to Roger. Her mind raced with images of the beasts from the bible passage. She couldn't get them out of her head.

Frankie passed her a double shot of Crown Royal, her favorite. She took it and tossed it back with ease. The burn in her throat was eerily comforting, especially the warm sensation that followed the harsh burn. Frankie walked away to serve a customer who waited at a table by the window.

Roger noticed Brown sitting by the window and spoke softly, "What are we gonna do, Elvis? We're back where we started, back at Frankie's."

Roger broke Abigail's concentration and she replied, "We are so far from where we started, Rog. How can you not see? We know so much more today than we knew yesterday or the day before. I have the suit. And I have these." Abigail pulled out Paltee's journals and placed them on the counter. "Paltee said they would be looking for me. Let them find me. It's the only way I will get more answers. In the meantime I need to go through these and do some research. I could use some help, Roger." She hated to admit it.

Roger was happy to assist, "You don't have to ask." He gently grabbed the back of her neck and rubbed his thumb across her hairline. She gave a soft smile. He smiled back and asked, "What about if we look into that company Paltee mentioned– Indigo, Inc.? I'm sure we'll find out something or at least someone to talk to." Feeling dehydrated, he gulped down the Coke Frankie had poured for him earlier.

"Do you have any plans for this suit?" Abigail lifted the bag with the suit in it and draped it over her arm.

He answered, "I dunno. We built it about three years ago and spent the rest of the time enhancing the technology. I don't even know what to do with that damn thing."

"Shit. I do. And you can start by building another."

Just then Finch walked in. Her badge was exposed. Abigail saw it and was ready to go upstairs. Finch and Abigail locked eyes for a moment. Finch squinted her eyes, drawing her head back slowly, and then Abigail turned away. Frankie whispered to the two, "Why don't you guys go upstairs? I'll be up in a few. We'll talk then." Abigail and Roger walk up the stairs, leaving the main floor.

Frankie looked over to Finch. She looked tired, "Hey Finchy!"

Meghan smiled and said, "Hey Frankie.

Frankie said, "Well, don't you look like you had a long night. You work too hard." He walked back behind the bar and asked, "The usual?"

She said, "No thanks, Frank. Not while I'm working. Just coffee would be great."

Frankie said, "No problem. Anything for you."

Finch sat down at the table across from Brown. He said, "Long night?"

She nodded and said, "Sorry I'm late. I was so wrapped up in researching this company, Jiang and Benson that I couldn't sleep."

"Did you find anything good?

"A few things of interest," she said, "but my research is incomplete and only raises more questions that need exploration."

"You don't have to put the pieces together alone. You work so exclusively. I can help you more than you allow me to."

"I don't mean to be... I'm sorry." She knew he was telling the truth. She liked to work alone. She respected his skill, but still felt the need to prove herself as a competent detective.

Brown touched Meghan on the hand and said, "It's okay. I understand." He knew the feeling. When Sydney began his career as a detective, he had shadowed Detective Cado Briggson who people used to call ROBOCOP. The man was an ex–Navy Seal. He was more into the action side of things than the research and actual piecing together of clues. Upon the conclusion of his shadowing of ROBOCOP, Brown and Briggson found themselves in a shoot out with a suspect they had followed for weeks. At the end, the suspect was apprehended after killing two hostages and wounding ROBOCOP, shooting him in the neck and thigh. Brown had landed a precision shot that saved the last hostage and took down the suspect at the same time. The suspect was in critical condition for five weeks but recovered, stood trial and was sentenced to life without parole. Briggson retired but not before he gave Brown a stellar recommendation and evaluation.

"I've been working on your evaluation, anyway. It's about that time," Brown said.

"Anything good to say about me?" Finch asked.

"In fairness, you'll get a full evaluation meeting soon enough; but as your mentor, it's been an honor."

"Don't just say that," she said.

"You know I don't say things I don't mean. You're intelligent, precise and thorough. It gets no better than that."

"I appreciate it. I try my best." The end of her training period brought on the inevitable thoughts of, *Now he will expect us to be open about our relationship*, but it was a complicated decision. People might think he gave her an amazing evaluation because she was sleeping with him. Even though it wasn't true, it didn't matter. That's how people would see it. It would take a good year or more before an open relationship would be acceptable to have without anyone scrutinizing her evaluation. She knew Brown was willing to risk it. He felt that anyone on the force could speak on her behalf and validate her ability.

Brown added, "I'm going to also ask Tammy, Chief Downy and Duffy to fill out evals for you. I want to make sure your evaluation is solid."

She smiled, "Thanks," but knew the additional evaluations were an attempt to cover the tracks of his personal feelings for Meghan Finch.

Frankie brought over the coffee and placed it on the table. He swiftly walked back into the kitchen. Meghan took a quick sip of the hot, dark liquid just as Larry walked into the pub.

Larry waved at Brown and Finch. They nodded. He asked, "Where's Frankie?"

"He's in the kitchen," said Sydney.

Larry walked into the kitchen as well.

Brown said, "Duffy sent me a text this morning. He'll meet us in the lab. Oh, and the MIT boys got the data cleaned up on that memory card. They are sending it later."

Finch said, "Good. Tammy called me this morning and said she has some info for us. We should go check it out as soon as we can."

Brown said, "Then let's go!"

Finch left a few dollars on the counter. Frankie nodded from behind the counter. Brown and Finch stood up and walked out the door together. Finch paused, turned back to look in, shook it off and continued forward. She suddenly felt uneasy about Abigail. She had seen Abby many times before but for some reason, Finch felt like something was odd or different about her now. *Maybe it's the haircut.* Abigail was being her usually quiet and disconnected self, but Finch's sudden curiosity about Abigail steadied in her mind for a moment, then was gone.

Abigail and Roger were on the upper level. Abigail was in the shower. Roger walked over to the bathroom door, ready to knock, but decided against it. He walked away, turned on the TV and sat in a chair. As the water ran over Abby's head, she tried to think and hoped that more of the mysteries of her life would reveal themselves. At that moment, she declared herself to be on a mission to find the men who were possibly looking for her. She was sure they were getting closer so her nerves were rattled. But she was not afraid.

She thought about the danger that loomed ahead for Roger more than herself. *What if they find out where I am staying? Or where Roger lives?* She knew Frankie wanted to help but couldn't bring herself to involve the man who saved her life. She at least owed him that much. It burned him up inside how much he wished he could help her, but she didn't invite him in to be a part of her secret life– not yet. *I will tell him when things have settled down.* She finished her shower, dried off, got dressed and went into her room where Roger was waiting for her. She grabbed the journals. Roger opened his laptop and the research began.

Back on the pub floor, Larry walked around, wiping tables and doing regular chores to keep the establishment tidy. His private investigation of Abigail made him feel a bit guilty that he had been hiding this from Frankie. As soon as the activity on the floor settled down Larry joined Frankie behind the counter.

Larry asked, "Should I call in Marty and Frita to work this evening?" He tried to break the silence between them.

Frankie said, "Yes. That would be a good idea. I think Abigail and Roger need a break."

"Again? It's hard to run a business when employees can come and go as they please. Marty and Frita may not always be available. Maybe we should get a definite answer from them as to what they want to do," Larry commented as he wiped down the bar.

"You're right. I will talk to them tonight and get a better feel of how much time they need. I'll get a concrete answer, and then we can plan accordingly." Frankie picked up at few glasses from the dishwasher. He wiped them down and hung them above the bar.

Larry was obviously frustrated and asked, "Does this have anything to do with Abby's past resurfacing? Is she still trying to figure things out?"

Frankie hated to have this conversation with Larry again. "I told you, Larry, Abby's past is her business. I feel like I've told you too much already because now you are questioning me about it. You act like you have answers to things I don't even understand and things I know you don't understand yourself. I don't want to argue with you about this again and again."

Larry shook his head and said, "Well I may not know any answers, but I will find them. I'm getting close to..."

"What are you talking about, Larry?" Frankie gave Larry a stiff stare and slapped his hand on the bar.

Larry grabbed a glass and wiped around the brim. He didn't answer.

Frankie grabbed his shoulder and asked, "What have you been up to, Larry?" Frankie folded his arms.

Larry answered, "I've been doing my own research on your girl, and Abigail Paige does not exist. That ID is fake! She's a fraud! She..."

"Keep your voice down!" Frankie interrupted. He looked around to see if anyone was paying attention. They weren't. "What do you mean Abigail Paige doesn't exist?"

In a soft voice Larry said, "I looked her up. I spent a few days trying to see if there were any reports of a missing woman and didn't find one. So, I ran a background check and *nothing* came up under that name. Nothing! So then I placed a missing persons report."

"WHAT!?" Frankie shouted in the pub.

Frankie was clearly not happy with this information. He threw a towel on the counter and stormed into the kitchen, pushing the door open. A few of the customers noticed. Larry smiled and put his hand up as if to say, "It's okay."

Larry followed Frankie into the kitchen.

Frankie yelled, "Are you out of your goddamned mind? Why would you do that?!"

Larry said, "Don't give me that, Frankie. You act like you don't know how this works. This is what we do! You are a king at this. You know how to run checks without detection, so don't play dumb. You should have run that ID months ago. You should have searched her thoroughly, and you didn't."

Frankie bit his lip until he broke the skin. His eyes were red. He said, "You are in violation, Larry. You should have *never* done that without telling me first."

Larry rolled his eyes and walked away. He said, "Someone has to know the truth about this girl. You don't even care to know."

"I don't want to know, Larry. Is this all about this pub? Is my happiness up for trade over saving this business?" Frankie asked with a disappointed look on his face.

Larry quickly answered, "Your happiness, Frankie? What about mine? I haven't been happy since she got here," Larry's eyes watered.

"What the hell does she have to do with your happiness? You would be totally fine if I hadn't closed the fight club, and you're taking it out on Abigail because you attribute my decision solely to her when I'm just over it!" Frankie paced the kitchen for a while and said, "I don't know exactly where she comes from, but if my common sense were to decide, someone from her past was trying to kill her. You know this. They are probably looking for her and you... you lit a fucking beacon for them to find her. You selfish son of a bitch."

"Son of a bitch? That's where this is going now? Okay, I'll take down the ad." Larry felt disrespected and was hurt by the insult, but Frankie didn't care.

"Yes you will. Take it down right now!" Frankie shouted. He wanted to wring Larry's neck.

"No fucking problem, boss man. Anything else?" Frankie didn't answer. Larry said, "You are so narrow minded, Frank. You wouldn't know a concerned friend if you saw one. And you know what, I may be wrong about her. That's possible, but at least I was trying to protect you and this good thing we have going here. I was trying to be a good friend, that's all. Sorry that in the process all I am telling you are things you don't want to hear." Larry turned to walk away.

Frankie leaned on the counter, and with a calmer voice he said, "Larry, I know you mean well; but you have to trust me. That's all I asked. God, Larry. You just shouldn't do things like that without telling me."

"Okay, Frankie. You win. I'm done. I'll take the ad down and leave you and Abby alone to figure things out; but don't say I didn't try to warn you, Frankie. And if I'm wrong, trust me, the repercussions of me being wrong will never amount to the repercussions if you are." Larry walked out of the kitchen.

POLICE STATION
FORENSICS LAB

Detectives Brown and Finch met up with Detective Tammy. She was in the Forensics Lab in the south corner on the 3rd floor. The lab was cold, with dim lights. There were two other lab technicians in the room photographing and sorting the remains from the alley murders. The walls were covered in white subway styled tiles. There were two commercial sinks by the back wall, a shelf of various tools, vials, bags and storage cabinets. There were vents and eight, 5 x 20 inch translucent windows resting 11 inches from the ceiling. The old windows were transparent until a brave reporter had rappelled down the wall to steal pictures of the room. He wanted to get an image of a female serial killer who had stalked and killed priests. In the process he accidentally fell, broke both legs and laid on the ground until he was discovered four hours later. Soon after, the windows were replaced to let in only light and nothing more.

Tammy worked with her assistant, Maria Sanchez, who took notes as she spoke. She saw Finch and Brown walk into the room. She smiled and nodded as they walked over. She said, "How's it going?"

Brown answered, "As well as it can. Meghan's been busting her ass trying to put some pieces together and has only stirred up more unanswered questions. But we feel good about the connections we've made so far."

Meghan smiled. She took Brown's comment about her work ethic as a compliment.

Tammy said, "Sounds good. Did you guys talk to Duffy?"

Finch answered, "Not yet. We came straight to you. We figured we would come ask about the murders in the alley and see what you've found out so far. Did you have anything more to add?"

Tammy was happy to answer, "Yes! Well, let's start with the Benson arm. See here. These fingers were pried open."

Finch was taken aback, "What do you mean pried open?"

Tammy responded, "Once the hand was disconnected from the body, rigamortis would set in and stiffen up the hand in whatever position it was in. Who ever found the hand first, didn't find it with the fingers open."

"So they opened the hand," Brown said.

"Exactly," Tammy said. "When prying the hand open, a few of the ligaments were torn. I did an X–Ray to be sure. I can tell the ligaments were torn *after* the arm was severed because of the lack of swelling and bruising. If you were to tear all these ligaments in your hands, they would look like sausages with plums for knuckles."

Brown added, "And the only reason to pry open a hand..."

"Because you want what's in it," Tammy finished. "From what I can tell, this hand wasn't in a tight fist but it was closed and had something in there. I wiped down the hand and found paper fragments that had stayed attached to the skin from oil and moisture."

Finch said, "We know his ring was stolen, but what else? What was on that paper?"

No one had an answer. Suddenly Brown received an email and said, "I just got an email from MIT." Brown checked the email. They sent the images from Eddie Cons' cell phone memory card.

Brown shouted, "Son of a bitch."

Finch leaned over to view the photos and said, "What? What is it?"

Brown turned to a picture with a better view. He said, "The hand *was* closed. And it looks like something *was* in it." Brown showed Tammy the images.

Tammy shook her head and said, "I hope that's not a ring I see on the finger there."

"Yes it is!" Finch chimed in. She was furious. "Cons is a liar!" She took out her phone and made a note but didn't upload it to the shared drive. She said, "So now that we know I'm gonna kill Cons later... I know Downy wanted Duffy to take over but, what about the alley slayings? Anything you can share with us?"

Tammy's assistant pushed the cart with the Benson arm on it closer to the body fragments of the men found dead in the alley. Tammy used a pointer and said, "Look over here. Compare these two. The tears, scratches... identical. The bones have clean breaks. There wasn't any DNA we could use to link the two. We tried but nothing."

Brown added, "These weird patterns here are identical."

Duffy suddenly walked in and said, "Taking over my investigation?"

Brown said, "Sorry, Duff. We were just making comparisons."

Finch said, "Duffy, do you think we could get Alan Jiang's autopsy report? Do you know anyone up there that can hook us up without a shitload of drama?"

Duffy thought for a moment and said, "No, I don't think so. I can make some calls."

Tammy butted in and said, "I can dig it up. I have a few favors owed to me over up that way."

Brown said, "Great! We're gonna follow up with Cons and get back to you. Please call us as soon as that info becomes available. Keep it low key please; I don't want to hear anything from Downy about this."

"I'll make that phone call right now," Tammy said. She pulled off her gloves and picked up the phone.

Duffy, Brown and Finch walked out of the lab into the hall. They reached Duffy's desk.

Brown said, "We're gonna follow up with this Eddie Cons guy."

Duffy said, "I have some work to do here. I'll be here when you guys get back. I'm trying to ID these Johns from the alley. None were carrying ID' on them, but we matched prints on two of them. There were two missing persons reports filed yesterday for men who, if we could piece them back together, would fit the description of names we pulled. I'm hoping Tammy can get the bodies presentable for the family members to come in and give a positive identification. I'm also hoping that they know the other guys, too."

"Did you get any possible names?" Finch asked.

"Oh. Yes. One was uh..." he fiddled for a paper on his desk. "Scott Baine. The other we think is Caesar Gibbs. I know you guys are looking for a connection here but I don't think these guys knew Alan Jiang."

"But the murderer probably did." Finch said.

"Very true." Duffy added.

"Okay. We're heading out." Brown and Finch walked off and out the door. Just as they walked outside, Brown received a phone call from the Chief Downy. He told Brown that they were cleared to search Benson's home, but only under the supervision of Benson's lawyer Attorney Kasper Coltrain. They agreed. They decided to check in with Cons later on. Finch called Tammy to join them with her assistant.

Duffy went back to his desk and sat down. He looked at pictures of the murdered bodies in the alley. He was sickened by the photos and began to sweat. He wanted to vomit. The images were so grotesque he couldn't believe that someone was capable of such horrible acts. He closed the binder with the images and wiped his brow. He then turned on his computer. On his desk he had a picture of his wife and daughter in a picture frame. He took a sip of coffee from his thermos.

As he waited for the computer to boot he received a text message. "HOW'S IT LOOKING?"

He replied, "STILL WORKING ON IT. I WILL LET YOU KNOW AS SOON AS SOMETHING COMES UP."

"MAKE IT FAST AND GET BACK TO ME."

He clipped his phone back to his hip. His computer was ready. He checked his work email. Nothing new came up. He checked his personal email account and erased a few spam messages. Next, he decided to open the shared drive. He clicked on the <ROBERT BENSON> file folder and opened it. He saw a few new documents inside and said, "Interesting."

He tried clicking on the <JENNIFER K. MARTIN> file but was not allowed access. He giggled and said, "So they suddenly want to be private. Hmm." He saw another file named <DIANA HINES BENSON>. He could not open that file either. He checked the folder to find the date of the last modification and it was that morning. He checked the files in the folder and noticed that none of the files had been modified. Then he thought for a moment, right clicked and hit <Show Hidden Files> and a ghost file named <INDIGO> showed but was also locked.

Duffy closed the folder. He picked up his phone and began texting someone. "THERE IS A HIDDEN/LOCKED FILE ON A SHARED DRIVE I WOULD LIKE TO GET ACCESS TO. CAN YOU DO IT?"

The person responded, "SEND THE INFO. I'LL SEE WHAT I CAN DO."

Duffy closed the drive, leaned back in his chair and smiled. He took another sip of his coffee and went back to the lab where Tammy was preparing the bodies to be viewed by family members who should be arriving within the hour. Duffy cleaned up his desk, sorting papers and clearing off unnecessary files. He threw away old candy wrappers and receipts. He knew that body viewing was difficult for families so he didn't want to look too sloppy, like he didn't care.

After about 30 minutes, the families had arrived and gave a positive identification of the bodies. They only knew the nickname of one of the other men, Scissor, but the fourth man no one knew. Duffy decided that he would do more research on SCISSOR later. In the meantime his mind was bogged down trying to figure out why Finch and Brown were being secretive. *Or maybe it's just Finch.* He wasn't sure if Brown knew or not; but either way, he assumed Finch was the mastermind. He was determined to keep an eye out and stay on top of her.

CHAPTER 16

BENSON'S RESIDENCE AND IRIS

Meghan Finch and Sydney Brown arrived at Robert Benson's home in Melrose, Massachusetts. They had also called in Alicia Tammy and Maria Sanchez who pulled up in a car behind them. The house was a light gray 2,500 square foot Colonial styled home with four bedrooms and an in–ground pool on a full acre of land. The house was on a hill with a two car garage under the main level. The driveway was constructed of flagstone blocks that circled in a path around to the back of the house. The stones also continued up the stairs that led up to the main entrance made of a mahogany door. The shrubs were slightly overgrown and the grass needed clipping, but it was obvious that someone had been maintaining the ground. Sanchez took out her camera and quickly snapped a few pictures of the exterior. There was a car in the driveway.

Attorney Kasper Coltrain had parked in the driveway. He noticed the detectives approach the house and exited the front door to meet them. He was a short Jamaican man whose friends called him Duppy. Coltrain had an interesting story. Rumor had it he entered the United States when he was 15 years old on a school trip to visit the United Nations. Coltrain never made it back on the plane. He and his friend, George Fenton, walked out of the building, crossed the street and never returned to the field trip. They had planned it for months; but his family and school officials had no idea.

Jamaican students disappearing while on school trips to the United States was nothing new. It had happened in the past on a few Disney World trips and trips to Washington, DC. It happened more often when students traveled to Great Britain. Coltrain and Fenton quickly blended in, forged paperwork and graduated from high school with honors. They both ran track at the University of Connecticut. Coltrain stayed for law school. Fenton was killed at a bar in Hartford a week after school reopened.

Coltrain descended the stairs full of confidence. He had only agreed to the search after speaking with Diana the day before. She had given permission and was happy to cooperate. He saw Sanchez taking pictures and said, "Please, ma'am. Not out here." He wanted to be discreet. Sanchez lowered her camera. He continued, "I'm Kasper Coltrain." He stretched out his hand to Detective Brown.

Brown said, "I'm Detective Brown, these are Detectives Finch and Tammy and Sachez who will be assisting us."

Coltrain shook hands with all of them and said, "This way." They followed him up the stairs and through the front door. "I've been trying to keep the property up myself. I sent over some landscapers, but I need to do a better job staying on top of this."

Once inside, Tammy and Sanchez walked off through the house taking pictures. Coltrain didn't bother them. He was interested in helping.

"What discoveries have you made so far?" Coltrain asked.

Finch answered, "Unfortunately, most of what we know hasn't given us enough to locate a body or find him. No one is speaking. He was extremely private; his wife has been out of the country, and his closest partner is dead. We have a few theories but nothing leading us to a direct answer."

"We are trying to connect this case to another one," Brown jumped in. Finch's eyes widened. She felt it was too much information to share but she let Brown take the lead and trusted his decision to let Coltrain know a little more. "If we can connect him to that case, then we may even be able to connect him to Jiang's murder. But as she said it's mostly speculation."

"Have you found anything at all?" Coltrain asked.

"Yes, we have; but we cannot say much more about it. I hope you understand," Brown said.

Coltrain nodded, "Indeed I do."

Finch asked, "When was the last time you heard from Benson?" Meghan had her phone open and ready to take notes. She started a new file in the ROBERT BENSON folder:

KASPER COLTRAIN
ATTORNEY

He answered, "About one week before he went missing. He called me about trying to look over some paperwork. I got the impression he wanted to start an LLC or a corporation. He wasn't sure which did what so I wanted to remind him of the differences between the two and the tax benefits, protection of his personal assets, stuff like that."

Finch asked, "Did he tell you what type of company it was?"

"No," he said. "I wasn't sure what it was about. I do know that he and Alan Jiang had had a disagreement about some investments, and I assumed he was ready to leave the company and do his own thing. I didn't want to ask over the phone. We never got a chance to meet about it."

They walked into the living room and then into Benson's study. Meghan went through some files on the desk. She opened a desk drawer and fiddled through a few files. She asked, "Did he keep a computer?"

"He had a laptop that he carried everywhere. I haven't seen it. Maybe he took it with him on his trip."

Brown said, "Trip?"

"Yeah. He said he needed to get away and do some work. He needed to be alone and sort some things out."

"Did he say where he was going?" Finch asked.

"He said he had to go to somewhere in upstate New York. It was around the same time Alan was murdered. Right before, actually." Coltrain added.

Brown asked, "Do you remember the city?"

Kasper thought for a moment, "Oh it's on the tip of my tongue. U– U..."

"Utica." Brown asked.

"Yes! Utica! That's where it was." This caught Meghan and Sydney's ears. "He said he was going to book a hotel room up there and take some time to himself. I figured it was bullshit, but what do I know? I figured he was covering for something else."

"Covering for what?" Brown asked.

"I'm just speculating based on his behavior and the questions he asked. He was covering for whatever business he was investigating. Benson never takes 'personal' time. My hunch is that he was cutting a side deal with a company and may have needed to meet with them. I'm just not sure which one."

"I think I have an idea," Finch said. She opened the new file and typed in one last entry:

INDIGO, INC. UTICA, NY

Tammy and Sanchez returned after taking numerous pictures throughout the house. They took fingerprint samples and filed them away. They checked the beds, the bathrooms and the backyard. They checked the refrigerator, but Kasper had already removed the spoiling food. They would have preferred he left in order to get an accurate count of how long it had been since he left the house. Finch and Brown took a few files with the permission of Benson's attorney. They stayed there for about five hours, sifting through everything. Finch and Brown left, parting ways with Coltrain, Tammy and Sanchez and decided to return to their plan to pay a visit to Eddie Cons.

EDDIE CONS' APARTMENT BUILDING

It was early evening. Meghan and Sydney left Benson's house, discussing their notes. Their biggest find was the possibility of a connection between Benson and the company called Indigo Inc, whose name had surfaced once again. Finch and Brown took another look at the pictures from MIT which only served to refuel their rage while on their way to Eddie Cons apartment. When they reached their destination, they parked in front of the apartment complex and looked up. They could see Cons' lights were on. They went up the stairs and knocked on the door. Detective Brown banged on Cons door vigorously. No answer. They stood there for a moment. Brown banged on the door again.

Cons finally answered, "YES YES YES! WHAT DO YOU WANT?" There was a commotion on the other side of the door. He must have tripped over the clutter.

Finch yelled back, "It's Detectives Finch and Brown. We want to follow up with you. Can you please open the door?"

"Give me a minute please." Cons shuffled around in his place for a while. Meghan was losing patience. Brown grabbed a piece of paper out of his pocket. After about a minute Cons opened the door. His apartment was a mess. He held up a sandwich on a plate and said, "I made lunch. Want a bite?"

Detective Brown was furious. He pushed a printout of the pictures of the severed arm into Cons chest and pushed him backwards into the apartment until Cons fell back onto the couch. He managed to keep the plate balanced and the sandwich intact. Brown asked, "What is this?"

"What are you talking about?" He didn't understand until he saw the pictures. Cons inspected them and knew he was in trouble. "Ok... I can explain."

Brown said, "You better have a damned good explanation for this one."

Finch tried to calm the situation down, "What did you do with the ring, Cons?"

Eddie looked down in shame and saw the sandwich on his plate. He decided to take a bite of the sandwich.

Brown was so upset he slapped the sandwich out of his hand and yelled, "WHERE THE FUCK IS THE RING?"

Cons was terrified, "I uh... I pawned it," he said, with a mouth full of turkey, grape jelly, cheese and wheat bread.

Finch said, "You pawned the ring!? Are you stupid? You're a real piece of work. All this talk about being sick and throwing up. You're a fucking liar!"

Eddie swallowed the food in his mouth and said, "It's true. I was sick, I just..."

Brown said, "Fucking idiot. You better give me a reason not to arrest you right now." Brown reached in his jacket and pulled out his cuffs.

"I can explain. I can explain. Just give me a second," Eddie said. He held his chest as if he was having chest pains.

Finch said, "Cut the shit, Eddie. Start talking."

Eddie took a hard swallow and said, "I saw the arm and freaked out. The guard just so happened to be passing by the room so I knocked on the glass in a full panic. I didn't know what to do. We both looked at the arm and... It was the guard. He told me to take the ring."

Brown asked, "Why would he do that?"

Finch answered, "To raise suspicion around Cons."

"And not himself," Brown continued. "Let's go. And Eddie, you stay in town. Tampering with police evidence during an official investigation can mean some serious jail time. You'd better get a lawyer. A good one."

Finch and Brown walked out and slammed the door behind them.

FRANKIE'S APARTMENT

Abigail sat in her room looking at the black bag which contained the suit. Abigail and Roger spent the afternoon looking up the keywords: Plum Island, Project Gray Scale, Alan Jiang and Indigo Incorporated. They printed page after page of articles and pictures, looking for connections. Abigail opened Dr. Paltee's journal. Initially she hesitated, unsure of what she would discover, but her curiosity overpowered her apprehensions. She flipped through the pages of the first book, looking at notes and pictures of various children documented over a few years.

She saw the man she remembered fighting until he let her go in the cornfield. There were pictures of him as well. "FLUTTER 14" was written underneath his profile picture. She flipped through and saw a few more faces of boys and girls. She suddenly began to remember more about her past but not everything. She remembered FLUTTER 25a and FLUTTER 25b– twin brothers with dark, short hair. They looked withdrawn. She flipped through a few more until she saw a black and white photo of herself.

She felt her eyes meet the eyes of her younger self in the photo, expressionless and disconnected. She was younger. Her hair was cut off. Underneath the narrow figure, the title read "FLUTTER 43".

Roger walked over and removed the photo from the sticky flaps that kept it in place. He could tell that Abby was feeling a pain he could not understand. He said, "This is you."

Abigail said, "Yes. I think I remember a few of these kids." She flipped back and showed him the twins and the man who had let her go. The one who saved her and sent her on her way was probably killed for doing so, yet here she was. She remembered.

"You look so drained. How old do you think you were here?" He asked.

"I look about 14... 15... I'm really not sure."

"Are you okay?" Roger asked. He was getting better at reading her. He didn't want her to withdraw again. He saw that she was making progress and didn't want her to slip back into an anxious or depressive state. He could tell her heart was heavy.

"Killing and dying is so easy, Roger. It's giving life and living that costs so much. I am a killer, Roger." She wasn't sure why she said that, but it came out amidst an influx of memories resurfacing. Memories of different elimination assignments she had done in the past.

Abigail had once killed a lawyer to keep him from filing a case against a company in Arizona. She had entered his office undetected and slipped poison into his coffee. By the time he reached the parking lot of the courtroom he suffered a seizure. His brain exploded and leaked out his mouth and ears. His files mysteriously disappeared. She took out the witnesses and a few others disappeared. Another time, she had killed four executives who were set to testify against a Wall Street banker who allegedly ran a multimillion dollar Ponzi scheme. She killed another in his office late at night. She broke his neck in the men's room. She had suffocated two others as they shared a hotel room, hiding under the protection of the FBI. Her last victim had disappeared without a trace.

Abigail was also a keen shooter, the best they had. Many of her cases involved killing closely guarded men and women whom she would have to kill within a window of opportunity of seconds and inches. She once had 15 seconds to shoot a 30.06 rifle bullet through a hole the size of a quarter after running for six miles straight. Then, after successful elimination of the target, she had to run another four miles to the rendezvous point, undetected, where her ride awaited her. She was always given the most difficult assignments.

She had no fear of heights. Abigail would scale buildings and trees and leap from them without hesitation. She could leap ten feet in the air without a running start. Her senses of smell and hearing were highly developed. Abigail was fast, poised and disciplined. She trained four hours a day, running, shooting, archery, and strength training. She would spend an hour a day in meditation. She also spent a significant amount of time learning computer programming, some electrical engineering, lock picking and working with explosives. She outperformed most of the other *Ezekiel* candidates in training and could not be taken down lightly in hand–to–hand battle.

Abigail once fought a security detail of 26 men. She killed the first 11 within the first 30 seconds and fought the rest of the armed men until they were all eliminated. She ripped them limb from limb. Her target was a woman named Iris Campbell who had hidden in a panic room. Abigail placed bombs on the weakest wall, set the charges and walked away. When the bombs failed to get through, Abigail cut the communication wires to the room. She piled the dead bodies against the rear wall and began to wait. She was cut above her eye going through her eyebrow. She let the blood run and drip down her face. She sat Indian style outside of the room and did not budge or speak for four days. She sat without food, water and only walked away to urinate in a bucket. Her cold eyes stared at the opening, waiting for Iris' inevitable surrender. Iris watched her every move from a camera inside the panic room. Abigail stalked Iris from outside. Iris was afraid for her life.

On the fourth day Abigail was feeling dehydrated and began to feel dizzy. Her dizziness was visible to Iris through the screen. The dead bodies were beginning to smell, but this didn't bother Abigail. Iris had water and food. It was enough to last for two, maybe three weeks. She pressed the speaker and asked, "Are you hungry?" Abigail snapped out of her delusional state. She realized that she had missed her pick up and no one had checked on her. No one was coming until she made the call, and she was not ready to make the call because Iris was still alive. She was on her own and determined to complete her mission. "Are you hungry?" Iris asked again.

Embarrassed, Abigail nodded. It was the first time she remembered feeling an emotion other than satisfaction. The blood flushed to her cheeks. Suddenly an orange fell from an opening in the side of the panic room. Then a bottle of water. Without thinking Abigail ate the orange without peeling it and drank the water quickly. Then another orange fell out of the opening. Abigail grabbed it and tucked it close to her side. She didn't understand how the target she wanted to kill could have compassion for her potential murderer. She never knew what compassion was or had ever felt it before. She didn't understand this target's actions. She was intrigued.

Then, again, the soft voice spoke through the speaker system. "Who are you?" the voice asked. Abigail did not answer. "Why are you here for me? What did I do?"

Abigail didn't want to answer but she couldn't subdue the overpowering sense of curiosity she was feeling. She said, "They never tell us why. They just tell us who and when... sometimes how."

"How old are you. 16? 17?"

"I'm not quite sure. 17, I think." Abigail answered. And she truly did not know, but that's what she had been told at the time.

"What's your name?" Iris asked.

"They call me sister; sometimes daughter, but mostly, they call me..." Abigail stopped herself before she said too much. "This information is not for you to know."

"What are they paying you?" Iris asked. "I'm curious to know what I am worth. Can you tell me that?"

Abigail answered, "You cannot bribe me out of this assignment. No amount of money will suffice. I live a very comfortable life. They pay me nothing extra for these services. I do it because I am told. I do it for pleasure. Nothing more. They tell me what to do, and I do exactly as they say."

"Who are 'they'?" Iris asked curiously.

"My creators. My Fathers. The people tell them who needs to be eliminated, and I eliminate them. I don't know anything more than that," Abigail wanted the conversation to end. She had never spoken to a target. She was told they were soulless and evil, that they had no purpose. This Iris woman seemed soft and innocent. She seemed polite and caring. *Maybe she is trying to trick me. Maybe she is trying to get into my head.*

Abby had never had a conversation with a target. She wondered what they were thinking. The most she ever heard them say was, "Please don't," or "I can pay you," or "Pater, ignosce mihi," but not much more. Most of it was begging or screaming from agonizing pain, – the only sounds she craved to hear. Iris was confident and realistic. She feared and respected Abigail. She would probably get on her knees and accept certain death rather than prolong the inevitable with begging and drooling.

"If I open the door, will you kill me?" Iris asked.

"I am not to return until I have your head in that bag," Abigail said without flinching. She was being honest.

Iris said, "I appreciate you sharing this information with me and I will never speak of it again. I appreciate your honesty. And I appreciate you. You've shown me a discipline I have never known. You also showed me that my life is bigger than these four walls, and it is short, and I need to make amends with some people and reconnect with others because I would never want to be as lonely as I am now. As lonely as you must be. And since you have taught me a lesson, I will also tell you that this panic room has a timer on it. If it is locked for 96 hours without reopening, an alarm will sound, I will push a red button signaling danger, and then my men will come for me within 20 minutes. All 200 will come. These men will attack you, and they will succeed in killing you. They will be here in five minutes. I am only telling you because I feel sorry for you. You have an evil inside of you that is almost unnatural, but for some reason I feel it is not your fault."

Abigail stood on her feet. She believed Iris. She turned her face away from Iris' view and walked toward the door. Her eyes turned blue and she listened. She could hear vehicles and a helicopter approaching. Her eyes turned brown again. She felt desperate.

"I will tell them you fled after a day or two. Here!" Iris tossed a bag full of food out of opening. "Take this and run. You will not kill me today."

"No need to lie to them. They will not find me. But you will die, Iris. I cannot stop this. I have failed, but they will find you and eliminate you."

"Who wants me dead?"

"I don't know."

"Then what should I do? How can I change this?" Iris pleaded.

"I do not know that side of the business. I never negotiate; but whatever you are doing or whatever you *were* going to do...

don't do it. In the meantime, run. They will regroup and come again once I am gone."

"Then I will have a head start." Iris then asked, "What will they do to you for failing to kill me?"

"They will starve and beat me for a week. If I live, I will retrain and promise never to fail again." Abigail heard the chopper closing in. She wrapped her bag and took the bucket of her urine and poured it onto the bodies. She then poured gasoline on the bodies and the bucket and lit them on fire. Before she left, she went back over to the panic room where Iris could see her and said, "By the way, you will find that your enemy is always someone you think you can trust. Start looking there. Good luck." She exited through a window in the rear of the building and ran for 10 miles south. She sent a signal and was picked up within the hour from an old gas station on a dirt road.

******

As Roger and Abigail conversed in her room, a subtle breeze cooled the sweat on their shoulders. She told him the story of Iris. He could tell that this was someone she cared for, probably the first and only person until he and Frankie had come along. He rested his hand on her knee as he sat next to her on the bed. He said, "I know that you can kill without a second thought. But, are you a killer? Would you consider yourself a killer?"

"Of course I'm a killer, Roger. You saw what I am capable of," she said as she picked at her fingernails.

Roger plucked a small feather from her ear that must have come from the pillow. She smiled as he flicked it away. "Abigail. You were defending us. That's different. A killer is cold blooded and heartless. I don't see that in you. Just because you can kill doesn't make you a killer, Abigail."

"Roger. The word killer doesn't truly describe who or what I am. Yes. I *am* a killer. And a thief! A liar! A manipulator. I have done some insidious things. Being cold blooded and heartless are just the side effects of years of enduring beatings, being told what to do... and stealing the souls of the innocent. I don't even know why I killed all those people. I just did it. I did whatever I was told to do." She couldn't look him in the eye.

Roger felt bad and said, "But you are not who you *were*, Abigail. The Abigail I know is nothing like the person you describe. And you don't *have* to kill. You have a choice."

Abigail giggled and said, "Roger. You don't get it. I am a byproduct of something that cannot be undone. I am who I am, Roger. Nothing will change that. I feel pleasure from killing. When I killed those men in the alley, I fed that hunger. My nightmares ceased only when that hunger was fed. It's what you would call... withdrawal. It's painful. The smell of fresh blood and the squeal of dying men should not be stimulating to anyone."

Roger understood "withdrawal," but only as far as caffeine headaches that resulted from drinking coke and coffee every day. He continued with another question, "Why were you running away then? Why leave?"

Abigail thought briefly about the night she had run away and ended up in Boston. Her memories played backwards in her mind. Things she hadn't thought about or remembered in a long time came forward. Abigail stood up and walked to the other side of the small room. She leaned on the table and said, "Because I broke the rules, Roger." She then told Roger the story of Iris Campbell. She told him every explicit detail she could remember. When she had failed at that task, her creators were very disappointed. They limited her food rations to water and wafers once a day. They moved her from her apartment into an 8 x 8 room and beat her for an hour a day. This torture lasted for ten days. On the tenth day she was returned back to her apartment where she slept for two days and healed from her wounds. She knew they would make a second attempt at killing Iris, but they could not find her. As far as she knew, Iris had totally fallen off the face of the earth. She knew that Iris must have taken her advice. *Run!*

Three years went by and Iris Campbell was discovered in Montreal. Her father had passed away, and she attended the funeral. Abigail figured Iris didn't care anymore. Abigail wasn't put on the assignment, but she knew it was coming. She explained to Roger that she felt compassion for Iris and wanted to give her a second chance. She snuck out, put together a package for Iris and slipped into her motel room. She drugged and kidnapped Iris, taking her 1000 miles west before she placed her in a motel. When Iris woke, she was frightened, she thought Abigail was there to kill her, but Abigail was there to protect her.

Abigail handed her an orange and winked. That was when Iris Campbell understood. Abigail spoke quickly and told her if she wanted to live, she had to do everything that Abigail told her to do. Abigail gave Iris strict written instructions to follow before she took off for good. They set up a communication system for emergencies only. Abigail slipped away into the cold misty night. She returned a few days later and realized she had been caught. Abigail went rogue against the agency but eventually, they caught up with her.

Abigail told Roger, "Iris was the first stranger I ever felt love for. Frankie was the second and... you. You are the third. I don't know what I would do if I were responsible for losing you." She fought the emotions that flooded into her body and turned to the window. Roger stood up and held her from behind. She closed her eyes accepting the warm embrace. He smelled her hair and took in the moment.

"Have you lied to me? Or Frankie?" Roger asked.

"No. Never. I never would." She turned around, looking Roger in the eyes, and said, "I promise." Abigail put her slender hand on Roger's face. He kissed her on her scared eyebrow, then on the right side of her face between her nose and cheek, then on the corner of her mouth. Her heart beat against her chest like drums. He kissed her again, directly on the lips and she immediately felt something similar to the feeling of drunkenness.

No one had ever kissed her and meant it. Abigail had pretended to be in love with many targets, dressed as a hooker or dolled up in gowns for corporate banquets. She kissed a few men in offices who were looking for a fling with a hot seductress only to realize she was there to put a bullet in their head or knife in their gut. This kiss was different. *He's in love with me.* It was everything she needed, wanted and hated at the same time. It was too much. She needed a diversion and thought about something, abruptly changing the subject. She asked, "Did you ever hear back from your mother?" She turned away leaving Roger holding the air.

"Now that I think about it, no. I haven't." Roger looked at his phone.

"When was the last time you sent her a message?" Abby asked.

Roger answered, "30 minutes ago, but she should have responded by now. I sent her four messages before that one. Maybe she's sleeping."

Abigail said, "Maybe. But let's still go check up on her." Abigail started packing up her stuff to go with Roger to his house.

Roger said, "No. I'll go. You stay put. I don't want you out there like that."

Abigail said, "You've been supporting me all day. I'm going. I'm not gonna hide here. If they are looking for me, then they will find me no matter what I do. I wouldn't want them to find me here anyway."

Roger, "So, no more hiding?"

She said, "No. Let them come. I'm not running anymore." She grabbed Paltee's journals and hid them in a corner. She grabbed the bag with the suit in it and a few other things, including a knife. She flipped it around her palm before she put it in her side pocket. They put on their jackets and went down to the main floor.

On the main floor Frankie, Marty and Frita were working. Frankie saw Abigail and Roger heading out. As he finished ringing up a drink he said, "Hey guys. Kitchen," signaling the two to meet him in the kitchen before they head out. They all gather around the stove area.

"Where's Larry?" Roger asked.

"He got a call and stepped out. He said he'll be back. What's going on with you two?" Frankie asked.

They didn't answer.

He said, "I don't know what you guys are doing. I mean, I try to talk to you, but... you don't tell me anything. So, I'm gonna leave it alone for now and get to my main point. Larry and I had a long talk and I need to know what's going on. I wanna give you time to sort things out, but I've had to call in help for the past few days, which is cool, but I can't operate efficiently if I'm not sure when you guys will peek in. I have a business to run. I don't mean to sound funny but, Abigail, my heart tells me you aren't coming back. One day you will close that door and never return..."

"I don't mean to screw up your business plans. My head isn't... together. But I understand what you're saying. Take me off the clock for good. I can't say what's going to happen and..."

Roger was shocked, "Are you leaving?"

"If I have to leave, I will." Abigail sadly had to say. She adjusted the bag draped over her shoulder.

Frankie was sad and said, "You'll always have a key here, Abby." He looked at Roger and said, "You get yourself straight. I'll get you back on the clock for... how does Monday sound?" Roger nodded. Frankie said, "Good!" as he slapped the truck key on the counter and walked out with a lump in his throat. He was angry, but he needed to calm down. He took out his cell phone and called Larry, but there was no answer.

CHAPTER 17
POLICE STATION
6:49 PM

It was getting late. Things were quieting down in the previously noise filled, buzzing station. Finch, Brown and Duffy were in the police station reviewing evidence. Detective Tammy received the Alan Jiang autopsy report from a friend in Portland. The email and scans had just come in. Tammy printed the reports and pictures, and then posted the pictures up on a bulletin board. She pointed out the similarities in the dismembered bodies. They were all stunned. "The consistency is remarkable! The power it takes to rip these bodies like this... they look like they were done by hand. If that's true, we're talking about a superior amount of strength," Tammy said as she pointed at the pictures of the bodies.

"But how are Benson and Jiang connected to the men in the alley?" Finch asked.

"That seems to be the biggest puzzle piece here," Duffy said. "I checked up on Scott Baine and Caesar Gibbs, the two Johns we ID'd from the alley killings, and nothing. There was not one significant connection. Scott used to work for about three weeks at a mail delivery service that delivered once or twice to Chapel and Case, but that was about a year ago. He's been to jail a few times for aggravated assault and armed robbery."

Brown said, "Then maybe it was random."

Finch replied, "Maybe unintended. Maybe the Johns mistakenly crossed paths with the killer?" She pointed to the image of Abigail and said, "I can't see these two frail things here pulling off something this vicious."

"You're right, but they were there. Maybe they saw something. Maybe they saw the killer or killers and ran away," Brown added.

"That's plausible. We really need to find out who they are. I need better footage or something. Until then, we have nothing to trace back to them." Finch took out her phone and took pictures of the Alan Jiang murder photos just to have them on hand. "What about Caesar Gibbs?"

Duffy said, "Oh. You'll love this. That boy had a rap sheet as long as he was tall. And he was a sex offender. He had just got out of..."

"Sex offender?" Brown said.

"Yes! Big time. There were three complaints. Only one was solid. Sex with an eleven year old boy. He was in jail from the age of 18. He just got out a year ago. He should have been about 25 now," Duffy added.

"So... a sex offender... in an alley with a convicted armed robber, and I'm sure the other two Johns weren't Mormon saints," Brown added. He pointed at the digitized picture of Abigail and Roger and said, "They were attacked by those men, and whoever else was in that alley probably helped them get away."

Tammy said, "Maybe it wasn't the same killer as Jiang and Benson's. Maybe..."

Duffy interrupted, "Impossible! That type of strength in more than one person? I can't see it."

Finch said, "That may not be a far off idea, Duffy. Give me a minute." Finch turned to her computer. She began typing as Duffy, Brown and Tammy continued to discuss connections or possible scenarios.

Brown eventually noticed Finch was completely focused on something else. Brown asked, "Everything okay, Finch?

Finch was shaking her head as she looked at an email she had just received, "Well, first off, I contacted the HR department at Chapel and Case to see if we could come in and talk to the security guard who thought it was a good idea to tell Cons to steal Benson's ring. They told me that they outsource their security to a company called Guardsmen Security. I called Guardsmen. They told me they would look into it and get back to me. They just sent me an email in response to my inquiry. They don't have any record of him."

Brown sipped his coffee and rubbed his head in frustration, "Why am I not surprised? I bet he hasn't shown up for work since we left."

Finch said, "I doubt it. I asked, but they refused to give me work schedules. Even more interesting, I'm looking up this company Indigo Inc. that Jen told me about. Alan and Robert were supposed to be meeting about it the weekend Alan was killed. I keep getting all these whacked out conspiracy theories and a supposed connection to research facility in CT called Plum Island."

Duffy had been secretly listening and butted in, "Yes I heard about Plum Island. I saw this thing on the History Channel about it. Some stuff about testing bio–warfare initiatives and human DNA alterations and testing. There was this… thing that washed up on a beach a few years ago, a crossbred animal…"

Brown said, "Yeah. I remember hearing about that. It was called the uh… the Montauk Monster. It was really creepy looking. Then there was another one. Some sort of dismembered and distorted human figure. It had elongated extremities, the witnesses said. And when people tried to get copies of the police report about the dead body, the police pretended not to know anything about it."

Tammy said, "This sounds interesting."

Finch continued, "So, Indigo received a shit load of money from the government for research and development to take over a project called Gray Scale. Investors didn't know much about it but they made a ton of money. When the government invested in the company, the stock price increased by 25% in a month. So being that Project Gray Scale was first class, top secret, the details of the project where hush hush. But thanks to WikiLeaks, the facts on a Project Gray Scale were leaked to the public, but no one was concerned about it because no one knew to look for it. Until now."

Launched in 2006, WikiLeaks was a non–profit organization that received recognition by releasing and publishing classified government documents on its website.

Finch handed Duffy a paper which was a print out of a top secret document dated back in the early '90s. He read, "Project Gray Scale... creating super soldiers... tests 1 through 62... failed, resulting in 24 deaths of marine soldiers... blah blah blah. President orders cease and desist. Project Gray Scale failed... blah blah blah. Government no longer funding. Project orders reassigned to Indigo Inc. under the direction of Jason Dewey. Dr. Colin Paltee... Reignite Project Gray Scale as Project Flutter... inconsistent results... cease and desist."

Finch said, "Then, as years went on, Indigo suddenly lost a bunch of money, investing revenues from other projects into Flutter; and they requested additional funds from the government. The government declined and from there, they sought out funds from venture capitalists, angel investors, etc. So, guess who recently dropped a huge sum of money on Indigo Inc.?"

Brown said, "Chapel and Case."

Tammy said, "Ok let me sum this up so I can see if you agree with where I see this going. Indigo is connected with Chapel and Case and connected with Plum Island– known for human and animal testing. And, they wanted to create *super soldiers*... At some point Chapel and Case invested money..."

Brown said, "And Jiang and Benson were supposed to meet with Indigo again."

Finch said, "Don't forget Jen's account of what she saw. Men that could leap 15 feet in the air, moving around as fast as lightning."

"Sounds like they would have enough strength to rip a man apart with their bare hands," Brown said. He wiped sweat off his brow. There was a brief moment of silence. Brown walked back over to look at the pictures on the board. He took a sip of coffee and scrunched his face as he thought a little more. Tammy watched over Meghan's shoulder as she scanned through more memos, photos and articles on WikiLeaks.

Duffy broke the silence and said, "Awesome work guys. Really! I have to step out for a moment. Nature calls." He smirked.

"Thanks for sharing," Brown said.

Duffy walked out of the room.

Tammy said, "He's right Meghan. This is great work. I was a little worried for a minute. It looked a bit bleak for a moment."

"Tell me about it!" Finch said.

Brown added, "I can't even take credit for all of this. You've outdone yourself, Meghan. You should be proud."

Meghan smiled and blushed a little. "Thanks but the case isn't solved yet, Sydney," Finch said.

"True indeed. We should talk with Downy and keep him abreast of everything," Brown said.

Suddenly an alarm went off on her phone. Finch immediately started packing up her things and said, "Yes, but in the morning. I'm gonna get outta here. I want to follow up on something. It should be quick." But she knew it wouldn't be quick.

Brown was taken aback and said, "Whoa! Where are you going? You make these connections and then boom. Gone!?"

Finch continued packing and said, "I'll text you." She just shut down the computer and tucked it back into her bag. She took off out the door so quickly that she scratched her knuckle on the lock. She didn't even finch, she just kept it moving right out the door and down the hall.

When Meghan got into her car, she took a deep breath. She rolled down the windows and let the breeze flow over the mist of sweat on her brow. It felt refreshing, reminding her of her younger days playing in the meadow with her brother, hiding in the shade from the sweltering summer sun. The cool breeze offered a comforting coolness that helped to calm her nerves. They were on edge.

Meghan had finally answered her mother–in–law's text message that morning after months of ignoring her messages and phone calls. She wasn't sure why she answered this time, but the woman's persistence made Finch feel guilty. Meghan promised to meet up with her for a late dinner. She was about to get there. She really wanted to go home, shower and change, but knew she wouldn't have enough time to do all that. *Should I go or come up with an excuse?* Meghan tossed the idea around in her head, unsure of what she should do. She thought, *Technically, she was never my mother–in–law in the first place. I don't have to be there for her, do I?*

Meghan knew she was avoiding the things that would feed into her memories of Anthony, starting with his mother, who was never friendly towards Meghan. Anthony was still haunting her and she needed to move on. And, now that she could admit to herself that she was in love with Sydney, she didn't want to take any steps backwards by digging up old wounds. But she had made a promise to meet Anthony's mother; and though it made her nauseous, she decided to follow through.

She didn't tell Sydney about the meeting. She didn't want to stir up anything or answer any questions. She didn't want advice or judgment. She decided to see how it would go and tell Sydney only if it were necessary. Sydney was intimidated by Meghan's lingering feelings for Anthony. He knew that anything referring to "Anthony" took Meghan ten steps backwards in progress. Telling him now wasn't the best idea.

Meghan plugged in her iPod. She scrolled down to Adele and played the first track. She pulled off the road, deciding to make a stop at the store before heading out so that she wouldn't arrive too early.

******

Duffy left the men's room and walked to his desk. He received a text message, "CHECK THE DRIVE. ALL FILES VISIBLE AND UNLOCKED." Duffy looked around and made sure no one was peering over his shoulder. Most of the men in the office had left for the evening. He opened the shared drive and saw the two folders: <JENNIFER K. MARTIN> and <DIANA HINES BENSON>. He clicked on the JENNIFER MARTIN folder and saw scans of photos of her and Jiang, he saw Meghan's hand written notes which she had scanned and then typed out from the meeting he had missed. He saw files and memos between Chapel and Case and Indigo. He copied all the files onto a jump drive. Then he opened the DIANA BENSON file. He didn't see much, but since he wasn't sure what he was looking for, he took copies of those files as well. He tossed the drive in his pocket and left the office.

ATKINS' RESIDENCE

Roger and Abigail took Frankie's truck and headed off to check on Ms. Atkins. As they drove, Abigail could hear

Roger's heart beating against his chest. She analyzed his anxiety levels, breathing speed and depth and watched his eyes. He was in total panic but was holding steady. She wasn't very good at being affectionate, but she knew she had to try. Roger was about to lose his composure. He held back tears, and negative thoughts came to his head. *Why am I panicking? She's okay,* he kept telling himself, but he didn't believe it. He never went this long without hearing from her. She had always returned his messages, but he couldn't have imagined what was really going on.

Roger became more and more concerned as they got closer to the house. Abigail called Ms. Atkins a few times but there was no response. She said to Roger, "I can't get through."

He replied, "Please keep trying. If it's not going straight to voicemail, then the phone is still ringing, which means she should hear it."

"Maybe she stepped out, Roger," Abigail said. She tried to offer an alternative to what she knew Roger was thinking.

"My mother NEVER leaves the house. She rarely goes outside; and if she did leave the house, she would have contacted me. I just need to get there soon as possible. I don't want to speculate about what's going on," Roger said with his hands shaking on the wheel. Roger's feelings were valid. He knew how his mother functioned.

Roger knew his mom slept a lot, but she was not a hard sleeper. If she heard the slightest noise, she would wake up. After years of paranoia, she learned how to listen in her sleep. Roger knew that even if she had missed the first call, she would wake up for the second call. A third or fourth call would not be necessary. He tried to stay positive. Abigail sensed his anxiety and knew it was her turn to comfort him as he had been comforting her for some time. She placed her hand on his thigh, softly rubbing her thumb from side to side. She would have held his hand had it not been on the wheel.

He picked up the speed, going 20 miles per hour over the speed limit.

Abigail thought of the day she had warned Iris that they were once again coming for her. She had slipped out that evening from her apartment which was shared with other Ezekiels in the same building. After reaching the desired skill level, Dewey let the Ezekiels live on their own in apartments he chose for them, but he would usually make them live in what he called "clusters". Abigail lived in the Alpha cluster with four other Ezekiels including Adonis. She lived in a posh two floor apartment with two bedrooms, two bathrooms, a small office, a personal gym, and a pool. There were black marble tile floors throughout the apartment. Her living room had a leather ivory sectional sofa with a matching chaise and ottoman where she often sat eating Thai noodles with chopsticks. On the wall hung a 60 inch LED HD TV over a gas fueled fireplace. Unknown to anyone, Abigail had installed surveillance into the other Ezekiels' apartments. She would turn on her TV and study footage of each of the apartments where she had installed six cameras and microphones in key locations. Abigail didn't watch much TV. She mostly spied on her counterparts.

One night as she returned from an assignment, she looked out the window to see Dewey entering the building with Ben and Saul. *His pesty pets!* She rushed to the TV dropping her weapons and supplies on the floor. She flipped through the channels, unsure who he was visiting. When she realized he was visiting Adonis, she put in her headphones and carefully listened to the conversation. Dewey was completely unaware of the surveillance and spoke freely about the next target, "Adonis, we've located a target that eluded us a few years ago. She's been in hiding ever since. I'm sure she is receiving assistance." He pulled out an envelope. "Here is her photo and information. This will require your special, immediate attention and comes with Red Level 10 discretion requirements."

Adonis looked at the picture and said, "This was 43's target," referring to Abigail as *Flutter 43*.

"Iris Campbell. Mission failed years ago. 43 has not been the same since that day, I can't trust her to follow through with this elimination after what happened last time. I would prefer if we left tonight. We think she will make a move in a couple days and I don't want to lose her again. Can you be ready in an hour?"

"Certainly, sir." Adonis placed the photos and files on the table.

They mumbled a few other words that didn't matter to Abigail. She rushed around her apartment gearing up. Her heart pounded against the back of her chest. Her hands were shaking. She had to calm herself down. Abigail shut everything down and disguised her surveillance with a few switches and buttons on a controller. Montreal was approximately four hours away. If she left now, she could get there before they did. *How did they find her?* She didn't know the answer to that question at the time, but she would sort it out later. She put on an all black combat outfit with a black vest. She packed a back pack and pulled out a sack of money.

She knew Dewey had cameras in the halls and lobby, so she slipped through a trap door she had constructed in the closet and crawled through the vents to the roof. She hopped across to the next building and descended down the fire escape. She ran four blocks to a storage facility where she stored a black Hayabusa. She jumped on, clicked the starter on the key, and sped off. She had a 45 minute lead.

Abigail easily crossed the border using an alias ID card and continued into Montreal where she arrived at the motel where Iris had stayed for the past month. She had warned Iris about slipping up. She wasn't sure what happened, but there was plenty of time to find out. Now was not the time.

It was 3:00 in the morning. The *Ezekiels* were on the way. Abigail slipped into a side door of the motel. She used a tracker that she had given Iris and located her on the second floor in room 222. Abigail knocked on the door. Iris was stunned and pulled out a gun from her bag. She looked out the window. Abigail knocked again. Iris came to the door. "Who is it?" Abigail did not answer, but knocked again. She stood off to the side so Iris couldn't see her. "I said who is it?" Iris cocked back the gun.

Abigail said, "Pizza. You ordered Pizza!"

Iris swung open the door only to receive a chemical mist sprayed in her face which knocked her out cold. Abigail rushed through the room and packed Iris' bags, slumped Iris over her shoulders, carried her down the stairs and slipped out the side door. She put Iris over her back, strapped Iris to her and sped off just as Adonis and another Ezekiel arrived in the lobby. Abigail knew she was in for trouble if she were to be caught, but she didn't care. All she could think about was how Iris saved her from dehydration even though she had planned to kill Iris. *Compassion.* A new emotion was also added to the list. *Love.* It was now Abigail's weakness. Ezekiels were not trained to deal with this. The idea of Love was eradicated and replaced with Duty.

Abigail thought about her panic level that night. It's different when you are concerned for a person you love. A person whom you know is helpless. She totally understood what Roger was dealing with in his head. *Love.* How oppressive it can be to love someone. He was crippled from the sickening feeling of having no control over the possibility of losing a loved one.

Roger and Abigail pulled up to the house. Everything looked normal. He was still confused, frustrated and angry. He parked the truck directly across the street. They could see a television flickering in through the window. Roger let out a sigh of relief, but Abigail was not fully convinced. They exited the car. Right before they crossed the street. Abigail put up her arm to stop Roger from going farther. She began to breathe heavily.

This shocked Roger so he asked, "What's going on, Elvis?"

A mist rose up from the crown of her head. She stretched out her body and inhaled. Her muscles flexed, her CANINEs extended slightly, and her eyes turned blue. She took out her knife.

CHAPTER 18

RECAPPING THE DAY
LARRY'S HOUSE
4:40 PM

Earlier that afternoon, Larry had received a phone call on his spare prepaid cell phone which he carried around for more "private" calls. He didn't want to take the call on the floor, so he hurried into the kitchen. Unfortunately he missed the call, but the person left a message. He went into the back corner of the kitchen to hear better. It was the voice of a man.

"Good afternoon. My name is Jordan Levy calling from the New York Department of Child Services. I'm sorry it's late, but we've been swamped with numerous phone calls coming in today. I was responding to your missing persons report on Abigail Paige. I would like to speak with you. You may be unaware, but this is a very sensitive case that will require your discreet assistance. Please give me a call on my private line." The man left his contact number and hung up. Larry scribed the number on a piece of paper and placed it in his pocket. He had taken the ad down when Frankie asked him to, but someone must have seen it before it came down.

Larry called the number and the man answered. He had an old raspy voice and cleared it often. He told Larry that he was in the Boston area following up with another case and said that he would like to meet with Larry as soon as possible. Larry was ecstatic. Finally, he would get answers which would unlock the mystery of this *Bitch Abigail!* He couldn't wait. Larry told the man to meet him at a diner that was located 10 blocks from his house. They agreed to meet in an hour.

He walked back onto the restaurant floor where Frankie was serving a few guests.

"Hey, Frank. Something came up. I got an important call and have to run out for a minute," he prayed Frankie didn't ask too many questions, and Frankie didn't. His mind was too busy thinking about Abigail and Roger upstairs.

"Are you coming back?" Frankie asked.

"Yeah. Give me about an hour or two." With that, Larry grabbed his things and rushed out the door.

Larry ran home and grabbed his research. The one thing he promised himself was that he wouldn't let Levy know anything about Frankie's Pub or Frankie's relationship with Abigail or that she worked there with him. He knew Frankie would be upset with him if he knew Larry led them directly to Abigail, so his plan was to tell Levy that Abigail recently disappeared and let Levy figure things out from there. He mainly wanted to get more information about Abigail. *But why should we be this discreet? Is she wanted? Is she a runaway? Is she an escaped convict?* Larry's curiosity took captive his senses. Everything was shady about this meeting, but he put his common sense aside for the sake of answers.

Larry wasn't totally foolish. He used his secondary prepaid phone for the contact number to his advertisement. He regularly cleared it and never kept contact information or stored texts or images or recent calls. He never told the man his real name. He used an alias that he had used in the past, complete with a fake ID and bogus credit cards. His name for the night was Talbert Sullivan. He walked the ten blocks from his apartment to the diner where they had arranged to meet. When he reached the diner, he saw a black Escalade parked with a man standing outside of it. By the way Larry looked at him, Levy could tell Larry was the man he was waiting for.

Larry got closer and could see Levy's face clearly. Unknown to Larry, Levy was really Mr. Jason Dewey. He said, "Are you Talbert?"

Larry stretched out his hand and said, "Yes I am. Levy?"

Dewey said, "Yes you can call me that if you like." They shook hands. "How about we take this conversation into the car? We will need privacy. It's a sensitive matter."

Larry eagerly hopped into the car. Saul and Ben were in the front seat. Ben was behind the wheel. Once Larry got into the car he knew something wasn't right with the situation and wanted to get out of the car, but felt that opportunity had passed. Dewey lit a cigar. Ben pulled the car out of the parking lot. Dewey didn't say anything for a few minutes. He wanted to make Larry as uncomfortable as possible. Dewey finally spoke and said, "Talbert. I see you have done some research. How do you know my Abigail?"

Larry already had a story prepared, "I met her one day at the Supercoin Laundromat on Winchester Street. She was hungry and cold, so I gave her some money, clothes and some food. I went there regularly to check up on her and one day she took off. I put up the ad to try and find her."

"How did you know to post the ads in New York?" Dewey asked.

"She was reluctant but eventually she came around. We talked a few times. She couldn't remember much about her past but she had an ID so she let me borrow it to look her up." Larry hoped Levy wouldn't ask too many questions, but he knew by the questioning that Levy was not convinced of his lie. He decided to switch gears and do the questioning. Besides, he wanted to know what the hell was going on. That was his main purpose. "What's the deal with her? Was she a runaway? Escaped convict? Who is she?"

Levy said, "Oh, Mr. Sullivan it's very complicated and classified, so how about you cut the shit and tell me what you really know?"

Larry knew then that Frankie was right. *Leave it alone!* He would say. And that is all Larry could here in his head. "I'm not sure what you mean." Larry said in an unconvincing manner. It was true that Larry didn't know much, but he knew a lot more than this story about an occasional rendezvous at a laundromat.

"I see you have done some digging. And what did you find out?" Dewey said teasingly as the smoke from his cigar filled the truck. Larry didn't answer. "Well, since you cannot seem to put things together, let me tell you." He soaked in every syllable; every word and punctuation mark was clear in what would be the last paragraph he'd ever hear in his life. "My name is not Levy. As I am sure your name is not Sullivan, but that matters not. You are more irrelevant than I hoped and not even worth torturing. I will take your materials and kill you. But before I do, listen carefully. Your Abigail Paige is a creature like none other, similar to my sons here." He referred to Ben and Saul. They smirked. "Only, Abigail is a unique creature. She was carefully crafted under the auspices of myself and a few other geniuses in a fashion you wouldn't understand. But if you must know, she is a killer ordained by... well, me. You could say that I am her father."

Dewey continued, "You are very foolish. I don't sense concern for Abigail in you. I sense a rage, a discontent. She sickens you. Am I correct?" Mr. Dewey smiled. He knew he was right. "Oh yes. So now I wonder what she has done to you."

"What has she done to you!?" Larry yelled out. Larry knew these would be the last words he would ever hear.

"Disobedience. Lying. Treason. All worthy of elimination. But it matters not. And you led me to her. I know she is here. But where exactly? Where is my disobedient little daughter?"

"I truly do not know." Larry wasn't lying. Abigail was all over the place.

"And if you did know, you wouldn't tell me anyway, would you?" Dewey asked.

Larry shook his head. Dewey said, "You would have been better off leaving things alone, my friend." The car slowed in a dark place. Larry had no weapons, no help. He wasn't the fighter Frankie was. He couldn't even try. It was hopeless. They are killers! He didn't have a chance in hell. Mr. Dewey took the materials away from Larry. Ben and Saul dragged him out of the car and shot him in the head. Each of them delivering fatal wounds to the skull. They left Larry lifeless on the side of the road and pulled off.

Dewey made a phone call. "How are things looking?"

A black Ezekiel named Adonis with green eyes and a low haircut answered, "We are walking to get him now."

DR. PALTEE'S HOUSE
6:11 PM

The cool air outside had changed and the wind picked up as heavy dark clouds made an appearance over the tree enveloped Victorian home. Dr. Paltee was in his house having tea in front of his fireplace, reading a book. Suddenly he glanced over and saw on a surveillance screen on the table a dark figure walking slowly up the cobblestone driveway. A few weeks earlier, he had installed hidden cameras at the entrance of his driveway and around the home. He stopped and watched, and then he saw another figure walking behind the other. *Ezekiels!* He dropped the tea on the table and ran into his basement. He grabbed a bag that was pre–packed and went back up to the main level. For one reason or another Dr. Paltee knew this day was coming. *If Abigail could find me, they will be soon behind.* Since that day he had prepared an exit plan. He had given Abigail all he had left of his research on Project Flutter and Gray Scale. He took a few more books and tossed them into the fireplace. They began to burn. He rushed around the house and packed a few more things into a second bag. He grabbed a few books and tossed them into a suitcase. Just before he left, he gave his house one last look. He closed the door.

He looked around but didn't see them. His older body struggled to pick up the heavy bags. His car was only a few steps away. He quickly shuffled over to the car and opened the back door. He threw the first bag into the back of the car. He stopped. He heard something. He looked around. He picked up the second bag and tossed it onto the back seat. He closed the door. He stopped again. He heard something again. He saw something coming quickly in the distance. Just before they reached him, he smiled and pressed a button on a black device he had pulled from his pocket. There was a light series of four beeps and his house exploded.

They were all thrown to the ground. Paltee's body was weakened by the blast. He momentarily lost his bearings and hearing. His eyes were out of focus. The explosion only knocked the two dark figures off their feet for a few moments. He made an attempt to make one last phone call, but he was too late. He didn't get a chance to press SEND. The two mysterious men approached Paltee, then jumped on his body and immediately ripped him to pieces. The pain was agonizing but his screams only lasted for a moment. The two Ezekiels checked Paltee's belongings, grabbed the two bags from his car and found his phone dangling from his hand. They searched through the phone and immediately knew the next target. They walked back down the cobblestone road and faded away into the darkness. Suddenly two red lights of a car appeared in the darkness. There was the sound of opening and then closing car doors.

Once inside, Adonis called Dewey. Dewey picked up the phone and Adonis said, "Target eliminated."

Dewey said, "Excellence as always, Adonis. I expect nothing less."

"Thank you, Father," Adonis was proud. "We did have a minor kink. He must have known we were coming and destroyed his house before we reached it. We took care of him and fled as quickly as possible. It was a huge explosion which would easily alarm authorities. We needed to move quickly."

"Shit! Were you able to recover anything?" Dewey asked.

Adonis said, "We grabbed a briefcase and a few bags from his car. We didn't go through any of the bags, but we got his phone. He attempted to make a call to someone named Atkins, before we killed him," Adonis said.

Dewey smiled and said, "Atkins!?" Dewey remembered her. He remembered the intel on her said that she was clean, dysfunctional, slightly insane and incapable of being an issue. He wondered how Atkins and Paltee had reconnected. He wondered how their communicating had slipped under his radar. Paltee made a major mistake looking up Indigo, Inc. the night he and Abigail met. A Google search for Indigo is not unusual unless it comes from an IP address that is on their watch list. Paltee should have known better. Dewey was immediately made aware and Paltee became a target, just in case. Thus *Ezekiels* were sent in, but he never suspected that Paltee and Atkins had been keeping in touch after all these years. *How did that slip by me? We must tighten loose ends.*

"Terry Atkins. Now that *is* a pleasant surprise. After all these years they've been keeping in touch. Hmm. I should have checked up on that but, whatever."

"There's one more thing," Adonis said. "It seems Paltee met with Abigail. He snapped a picture of her on his cell phone. I don't think she noticed."

"So, he reunited with Abigail? How did he manage that? Probably Atkins. Hmm. Well, I guess we know our next target. Ben, quick change of plans. Drop me at the hotel. I have a new assignment. It just came in." He referred back to Adonis saying, "Good work. I will see you in a few hours."

They hung up the phones and drove off.

DEWEY'S HOTEL ROOM

Dewey reached his hotel room and immediately changed his clothes into a white cotton shirt and cotton slacks. He sat at a table and looked through Larry's papers and said softly, 'What do you know Mr. Talbert Sullivan or whatever your name is?" He flipped through the files and only saw information that he already knew. He also found a pile of missing person's reports of young women that fit Abigail's description and would be about Abigail's age at this point. "Oh I think you were on to something!" Mr. Dewey found a report of a missing young girl named Savannah Paltee.

Savannah Paltee was Dr. Colin Paltee's daughter. Her picture used to hang on the wall next to the picture of his parents. She favored Abigail. They looked like they could have been sisters but Savannah was a few years older. Paltee volunteered her into the program after his wife left him for another woman. When he realized the direction of the program had changed, he quit but they refused to release her, stating she was now intellectual property. Paltee fought hard, but was denied visitation due to a contract he had signed but hadn't read, thoroughly due to his initial excitement for the program. She had disappeared three years earlier and was never recovered. Seeing the post brought back many memories for Dewey.

Dewey had his assistant post the report, but nothing came of it. Savannah had completely vanished without a trace. She had gone on assignment, eliminated the target and never returned to the rendezvous point, nor did she call in. They spent the next two years searching for her but they determined that she was either dead or in hiding. Dewey believed the latter. Larry had found the posting and thought the girl in the picture looked a bit like Abigail and printed it out, but he was never able to make any additional connections. Dewey took the posting and placed it off to the side.

Dewey took a sip of water. He then took Larry's phone and opened it. He was disappointed at the lack of a memory card and the lack of contacts, call history and missing text messages. Dewey took out his cell phone and made a phone call. When the person answered he said, "I have a number here. I will need the numbers called from this phone as soon as you can." Then he listened for a moment and said, "$5,000 is fine. I will give you another $5,000 if you can get that to me in three days or less." He listened again and said, "Goodbye."

Dewey closed the phone. There was a knock on the door. He opened the door. It was Detective Duffy. Duffy took out a drive, handed it to Dewey and said, "Chris Duffy. Erin Moore sent me." Dewey greeted him with a smile and a stiff pat on the shoulder.

CHAPTER 19

ATKINS' RESIDENCE

Abigail sensed something was irregular. She stopped Roger in his tracks, blocking his way with her arm. Roger was too eager and anxious to follow his senses and piece things together. He was ready to bolt into the house until Abigail stopped him. Abigail's eyes were blazing blue like a high temperature flame. Though she cared about Ms. Atkins, she refused to lose control of herself. *Protect Roger!* She thought. She told him, "You can't go in." Abigail could sense that Ms. Atkins was not alone.

Ben and Saul were in the house standing over Ms. Atkins who was bloody and barely breathing. She had been beaten and tortured and was hanging on for life. They questioned her about Paltee, Abigail and the suit. Though they didn't know she had managed to build a suit, they knew she must have access to the plans. She was suspected of stealing the plans years ago, but now they were sure she was guilty of it. She refused to speak to them. She refused to tell them anything about Abigail, and she refused to answer questions about the suit. They had beaten her badly in response to her noncompliance. They were even more frustrated that they hadn't recovered her phone.

When they first kicked in the door, she was in the kitchen. She had received a call from Paltee earlier and heard him scream, then suddenly go silent. She had listened for a moment before hanging up. Next she had turned off her phone's ringer and tried to send Roger a text message, "DONT COME HOME TONIGHT! GET ELVIS OUT OF TOWN!" but she was so jittery and nervous she had forgotten to press SEND. Paranoia set in. She tucked her phone in the refrigerator behind the eggs. Then she went back into the front room, attempting to lock down the house. But they had kicked in the door within 15 minutes of the call from Paltee, and her attempt at securing the door had been no match for their strength.

As they stood over her, harassing her and searching her house, they suddenly stopped in their tracks. Saul and Ben's eyes turned blue. Their fangs grew slightly. They recognized Abigail's presence. Saul looked up and said, "Ben, it is our sister. She is here!" Saul smiled.

Ben said, "Yes, brother. She *is* here, isn't she?"

Saul said, "Just as we knew she would be."

Ben looked out the window and looked at Ms. Atkins, "Seems your son is here, too." Ben and Saul smiled at Ms. Atkins. She was tied up, sniffing blood through her nostrils. Her mouth was gagged with cloth covered in tape. She was splattered with her own blood which was coming from various parts of her body.

Roger and Abigail were in the street. Abigail was heating up with anger. She could smell the blood but couldn't tell if Roger's mother was dead. She assumed she was. She didn't want Roger to know and freak out on her. Roger said, "Someone else is in there."

Abigail nodded. She didn't know what to say. She looked at Roger. She was breathing heavily and struggling to speak. "Do as I say, Roger. Get in the basement and get to the weapons. Put dirt in your hair and cover your mouth so it's harder to smell you. They may already know we are here." She dug up a handful of dirt from the grass on the side of the road and rubbed it in his hair.

Roger took a bandana out of his pocket. He tied it around his mouth and nose. Roger then ran around the back of the house and disappeared into the dark. He decided to try and sneak in through the back door. Abigail, confidently and fearlessly, walked up to the front door. The door was slightly ajar. She opened the door and walked in.

Abigail slowly walked down the hallway, taking in the scenery. She peered her head around the corner and saw Saul and Ben standing there over the sad–looking Terry Atkins. She pretended not to be affected by the condition of the woman. Abigail recalled a quick memory of them training together. She also saw flashing memories of their photos in Dr. Paltee's journal– "FLUTTER 26" and "FLUTTER 19". She fearlessly entered the room.

Abigail said, "26 and 19." She stood firm.

Ben smiled and said, "Sister. You remember."

Abigail said, "I am not your sister."

Saul said, "But you remember. We came here to retrieve you. Won't you come home with us? Our Creator, our Father, he wants you to come home."

Abigail shook her head and said, "No. He will kill me."

Ben said, "No, 43. He will reprogram you. You need to be cleared. Your mind must be cleaned. You have been confused."

Abigail softly growled and said, "No. I have been delivered." She saw that Atkins was within inches of her death. She asked, "What have you done to this woman?"

"Why do you care?" Saul asked.

Abigail struggled to speak and said, "Settle your business with me. Not her."

"This is not about you," Ben insisted, "This woman is a small assignment we must take care of. She has something we want. We are here to get it. And since you are here, we will take you home with us as well."

Abigail smiled and said, "I will not go anywhere with you, and you know that." Her muscles flexed and she hissed at them. She clenched her fists.

Saul said, "Always so rebellious." Saul smirked and said, "I guess we will have to make you come with us." He took off his eye glasses and placed them into his inner pocket. "We don't want to disappoint our father." Saul hissed at Abigail. She hissed back. Both Ben and Saul ran toward Abigail. They fought.

The three of them ripped at one another, but Abigail tossed them across the room. They punched and kicked and tossed her when they got the chance. Abigail could take down two men easily, but these were not regular men. These men were just like her. And though she was possessed with more than one animal, she never was able to call on all of them at once. She was faster than they were. She was smarter than they were. She knew she would eventually win the fight, but it would take time.

Saul had been Abigail's biggest rival on the wrestling mat. They had fought for 20 minutes once before. Abigail had eventually won, and Saul hated her ever since. *Hate* was one emotion that *Ezekiels* were allowed to have. Abigail used to think that they must have forgotten to eliminate *Envy* in the brainwashing unit. As she became wiser, she understood that *Envy* could be the most powerful driving force behind the desire to win, encouraging competition and an untamed desire to defeat another. It was perfect. This fight was Saul's opportunity to settle unfinished business.

In the meantime, Roger snuck into the house using the trap door in the back. Once he got into the basement, he ran over to the hidden door. He was trying to be quiet as possible, but the wind had slammed the trap door shut. Abigail, Saul and Ben heard the noise. It stopped them all in their tracks. Protect Roger! Abigail knew they would pursue him. She fought even harder. Ben immediately slipped away from the brawl and headed toward the basement. Abigail tried to follow, but Saul prevented her from leaving.

Roger got the door open and saw Ben descending quickly down the stairs. He shut the door just in time to lock himself in. BANG... BANG! Ben repeatedly banged on the door. Roger put on a protective vest and began collecting weapons, picking up guns and strapping them to his body using the belts and straps on the vest. He tried to catch his breath. All he could think about was his mother. He loaded up with ammunition, grabbed a few explosives, and took a deep breath.

FINCH'S CAR

Finch was in her car, fighting back and forth in her head, looking for excuses not to go to the dinner or to be able to leave early. She thought about convincing Brown to call her and fake an emergency. She knew she was being cruel, and the woman didn't deserve this. She knew Anthony's mother was going through hell, and Meghan was her last connection to Anthony. Finch was driving slowly through the streets when she heard a call on her police scanner. She didn't use it unless she was off duty. She liked to know what was going on in the streets. The call was coming from dispatch, "We just received a call. There seems to be a domestic disturbance at 161 Wallace Street. Anyone in the area?"

Finch knew she was not far away. She was on her way to meet up with her mother–in–law and what better excuse than to show up late and have to rush through dinner. *I got called in to check out a domestic dispute.* Finch called in and said, "This is

Finch. I am about two blocks away from there. This is not my regular thing, but I'll check it out for you."

"Roger that. Let me know if you need back up," Dispatch responded.

"Stand by." Finch made a sudden U–turn and turned on her flashing lights.

ATKINS' RESIDENCE

Abigail and Saul fought as if they hated one another. They were destroying the house bit by bit, busting holes in the walls, tossing furniture across the room, and breaking glass. They both had scratched one another in various places. They growled like animals. Sometimes they would stop fighting and circle one another before pouncing on each other again. Ms. Atkins was too weak to move. She was losing too much blood, and the blows to her head kept her vision blurry. She slipped in and out of consciousness as the two fought. Saul finally got a good grip on Abigail and tossed her clean through a wall into the kitchen.

Saul said, "Give up, 43."

Abigail slowly pulled herself off the ground, "You have never beaten me 19."

"I've been training while you've been off in Lala Land, you idiot!" Saul was clearly bitter about Abigail's comment. *Envy. Hate. Revenge!* "And after I kill you, I will make a sandwich out of your friend. If Ben hasn't yet." He smiled.

Abigail growled. She walked around from the kitchen back into the living room. When he threatened Roger, a fire burned deep within her. Saul knew he had flicked on a switch but didn't understand the fuel that fed the fire he had ignited. *Love.* Abigail ripped across the room, beating on Saul and tossing him around like a rag doll, through the wall and into the kitchen.

Roger was locked in the lower research room. He found a duffel bag in a supply closet and tossed a variety of weaponry into the opening. Ben continued banging on the door, trying to pry it open with his bare hands. The door was giving in. Roger took a deep breath and cocked the gun.

Finch reached the home. She saw lights flickering as she pulled up. When she got out of the vehicle, she heard loud banging, growling and glass breaking. She took a walkie talkie out of the car and placed it in her pocket. She removed her gun from the glove box and placed it in into her side holster. She went up to the front door. It was slightly open. She placed her hand on the gun and entered the house.

The house was trashed. Live wires hung from the ceiling where a fan and light used to hang. Abigail and Saul were now fighting in the kitchen. Finch slowly crept down the hallway. She saw Ms. Atkins lifeless on the living room floor. She tiptoed over to her. Finch grabbed her walkie talkie. Saul sensed another person in the house. He left the fight with Abigail and went dashing into the living room. Finch was surprised by his attack. He grabbed her and threw her across the room. Finch hits the wall. Her gun and walkie talkie hit the floor. She was completely stunned.

Saul headed toward Finch and Atkins when Abigail ran into the room. Abigail immediately noticed Finch, who was a regular patron at Frankie's Pub. She pushed Saul away from her. They continued to fight. Saul kept trying to get to Finch, but Abigail protected her. They wrestled until Abigail got her hands on the gun. Saul backed away and pulled out his gun.

Saul said, "Move out of the way."

Abigail said, "Don't move, Saul." Her blue eyes flickered as the broken TV lights reflected on their surfaces. "You're empty!" She said referring to his gun. He was bluffing and knew he hadn't reloaded after shooting Larry and Atkins a few times.

Saul smiled and said, "Are you sure about that?" Saul knew that his shooting skills were not up to par, and Abigail always delivered a deadly shot. She knew his gun was empty because he would have used it already.

Finch finally got her eyes to focus. The two figures became clear. Clear as day. Then her face flushed with embarrassment and confusion. Immediately, she realized who had saved her. *That mysterious girl from Frankie's. That's her. She is the one in the photo! The girl from the footage, in the alley!* It finally clicked. She thought the male figure must have been Roger. *What have they been up to?* She was terrified. This girl had been sitting under their noses the entire time. She wanted to cry, but she had to get away first.

Detective Finch felt completely helpless and weak. She tilted her head to get a better view of the scene to try and make a run for it. She needed to get out. Abigail and Saul stood in a stalemate. Finch was weak and vulnerable. She knew that her life was in Abigail's hands. Abigail saw Finch moving. For a brief moment, Abigail took her eyes off Saul and saw Meghan struggling to straighten herself out.

"Don't move," she told Meghan. Meghan complied for two reasons. She was frightened, and she couldn't move anyway.

Abigail wanted to help Finch but Saul was ready and waiting for her to slip. Suddenly she heard gun shots coming from the basement. Their focus was broken; and Saul took off, running out the front door. Abigail didn't bother to follow him. Abigail bent down at Meghan's side.

"Sit up." Abigail helped lift Meghan with ease. Meghan looked into Abigail's flaming eyes. Abigail's muscles bulged. She hissed at Meghan and scared her. Abigail checked Ms. Atkins' pulse. It was very faint. Abigail handed her the gun and said, "Take this! Protect her." Abigail jumped up and took off to the basement.

By the time Abigail reached the basement, Roger had somehow shot Ben in the chest. Roger stood over the failing body. Ben was weak, losing blood very quickly. Abigail walked over to Ben. She picked Ben off the floor with one hand. She backed him against a post. His toes were barely touching the floor. Blood streamed from out of his mouth. "Who sent you, Ben?"

Ben choked, coughing up blood. It squirted onto Abigail's face. She didn't mind. "Father... sent..."

"Not him! Who asked him to send you!?" She yelled at him.

He coughed up more blood. He was getting colder and colder. He managed to get out the words, "Indigo... and Robert Benson. They want you and the plans for the suit." She dropped him on his feet. She wasn't familiar with the name Benson but knew Indigo very well from her research. Then she remembered... Dewey, the Creator, the Father, was on Indigo's board and was the mastermind behind the Ezekiel Project. Memories fluttered in like wildfire embers, the little bits of memories had had been piecing themselves back together each time something from her past resurfaced. Ben used his last bit of power to try and fight her. She fought back, easily overpowering him. She ripped his limbs from his body just as she had done to the men in the alley.

"I used to like him." Emotionless, she turned to Roger and said, "Go say goodbye to your mother. We are leaving for good."

Roger almost forgot. He rushed up the stairs, dropping everything. Abigail grabbed the bags of weapons and followed behind him. Her blue lit eyes floated around in the dark basement. When Roger reached the room his mother was in, Finch turned her weapon on him.

Finch shouted, "DON'T MOVE!" but Roger ignored her.

Roger went over to the body. It was too late to say anything. His mother was dead. "MA! No! No no no!" He kissed her and held her tight. Her blood soaked his clothes. He sobbed.

Abigail entered the room to see the sad scene with Roger crying over his mother. Finch lowered her gun. Ms. Atkins was dead. Abigail picked up Finch with one hand, placing her on her feet. Finch asked, "Did you kill Jiang? Matthews?"

Abigail said, "No."

"The men in the alley? Did you kill them?"

"Self defense," Abigail said.

"And Benson?" Finch asked.

Abigail said, "He is not dead. He sent them."

"What?!" Finch was angry. She had spent all of this time looking for a man who wasn't even dead. "He's not dead? What the hell is going on? How did you get involved in this?" A whirlwind of questions came into Finch's head. So much had happened.

Abigail ignored the question. She walked over to Roger. Suddenly her body stretched out and she exhaled. The heat from her lungs released back into the air and she became her normal self again. Her brown eyes returned. Finch was totally amazed, afraid and shocked. She could not believe what had happened before her eyes. The murders in the alley. It all made sense. Finch tried to assess the situation. She scanned her eyes around the crushed interior of the house and rested them upon Roger with his mother. He was crying. He kissed his mother again and got up. He laid her down and folded her arms over her chest. He covered her with the afghan she used to cover her legs with as she watched TV. He and Abby began to leave. Finch pointed the gun at Roger and Abigail. She said, "STOP! I have to take you in."

Abigail said, "I'm not going to let you do that. And who will protect you if I am locked away? They will come back for you. You know too much."

"Who will come back for me?" Meghan asked.

She remembered what she said to Iris. "You will find that your enemy is always someone you think you can trust. Give me your phone." Finch knew she was right. She reached into her pocket and grabbed the phone. She handed it to Abigail who programmed her number into the phone. "I'll tell you everything I know in exchange for your secrecy and Frankie's protection. He doesn't know about this. I'll tell him when I'm ready." Meghan held steady. "You have no choice but to comply. I will not let you take us in. You will have to shoot me if that's what you want to do." Abigail stood there, ready to take a bullet.

Reluctantly, Meghan lowered her weapon and said, "UGH!!! I can't do it. Get out of here. Now! Both of you. I radioed in about three minutes ago."

Abigail pulled Roger by the collar. Roger struggled to stay on his feet. His knees were weak. Abigail said, "Now you know who I am, and you know where to find me. I will answer your questions later. This house is going to blow up in one minute. You should leave. Oh and maybe you can get some answers with this." Abigail tossed Ben's phone over to Finch. She had taken it after the fight in the basement. "You should get out now." Abigail and Roger ran out of the house. They jumped in the truck and drove off.

Finch stood on the porch for a moment, still stunned from the event. As she began to hobble over to the car there was a large explosion, and she was blown off her feet onto the front lawn. Police cars arrived on the scene. Finch could not see and her hearing was gone. Her vision was blurred. Eventually, she looked up, hearing muffled voices. Her ears were ringing. Slim black figures walked all around her. Someone touched her neck. *Anthony?* She saw blurred police lights. Red, blue, white. All went black.

CHAPTER 20

THE RIDE HOME: FRANKIE'S TRUCK

Abigail and Roger drove back to Frankie's in the truck. Abigail was driving. Roger stared out the window with tears running down his eyes. He had to remind himself to breathe. He thought about every breath of air that passed through his nose and into his lungs. He was sick to his stomach. He never understood the danger of his mother's involvement in this project. He never understood how much these people wanted the suit. He was just getting to understand how powerful Abigail was but wanted to choke her. She had revived the dormant secret he and his mother held together. As he filled with anger against Abigail and Ben and Saul and Finch and Frankie and the entire world, he then thought about how Abigail also brought life back to his world. A volcano was erupting within. The heat seeped out of his nose.

Roger and his mother were a sad duo. Working in the basement on a project they knew no one would ever see or use. He hadn't seen his mother that excited and alive in years! She had felt a sense of purpose again. She felt needed and useful. She was walking around again, talking to someone other than Roger, talking to Paltee and Abigail. *Abigail made my mother smile. That nutty woman!* He thought. He smiled. *I couldn't even do that.* He wanted to blame Abigail for everything that had happened, but he was just as much to blame for encouraging Abigail to dig deeper and rediscover who she was.

He couldn't be mad at her. He couldn't be mad at himself. He now had a new problem. Indigo.

That was the longest car ride of his life. He had left his mother in the rubble. A decision that was necessary, but it would forever be hard to live with. It was the best decision at the time, but he would never forget how she laid there, lifeless. Roger was still angry.

They finally reached the back alley of Frankie's Pub and parked the truck.

FRANKIE'S APARTMENT

Abigail and Roger went upstairs. Roger paced the room. He started throwing things around the apartment and hitting the punching bags. Abigail watched. She didn't try to stop him. Frankie could hear the ruckus from the lower level. Abigail slowly walked over to Roger and touched his face. He wanted to hit her too. *Don't touch me!* He thought, but every time she touched him, his heart melted. He would never harm her. She helped settle his anger and nerves with one touch.

Abigail said, "This is my fault. Roger. I know it crossed your mind. I could sense your anger with me on the ride. You are right to be angry with me. It's your right to wish me harm, but if you allow me to be forever in your debt, I will do my best to fix this for you." The blue eyed Abigail would have told him to get it together and strap up! But this Abigail was gentle and warm. She was reassuring and sensitive. She was not good at being sensitive; this was the best she could do.

On the outside, Abigail was calm. On the inside, she was filled with rage and ready to strike. But, it made no sense at this moment for the two of them to scream and shout and throw things. She held in her true feelings and her true thoughts. She, too, caged a volcano within, and it was filled with molten HATRED bubbling up against her innards. She wanted revenge, and she wanted it NOW! She could go out and find them and kill them all, but she knew Roger would never let her go alone; and if Roger was going to help, then she needed him to stabilize. Truth is, she wanted to cry, but instead she said, "When you're ready. We know what we have to do."

Abigail grabbed the bag with the suit in it. She was heading to her room when she heard someone coming up the stairs. It was Frankie.

Frankie entered the room and said, "What the hell is going on?" He had heard the banging and things breaking.

Abigail said, "Roger lost his mother tonight."

Roger blurted out, "They killed her!" He had tears dried to his face. His eyes were red and swollen.

Frankie didn't know how to respond to this news. Frankie walked closer to Roger. He said, "Roger, are you serious? Who did this?"

Abigail answered, "The people who are looking for me... and this." She removed the suit from the bag. She said, "I need to show you something." She inhaled and her eyes began to glow as she gripped the suit. Frankie had never seen anything like this. Abigail, the *Super Beast,* stood in front of them. Her eyes are blazing blue like little hot flames. Her muscles increased in mass. Veins popped out of her neck and arms. Her teeth extended. Oddly, Frankie was not afraid, and he didn't understand the importance of the suit. It looked like a simple wet suit from where he was standing. As he got closer, he could see that the suit was more complicated than he first thought. Abigail's chest pumped up and down as she breathed heavily. Frankie went up to her and touched her face while she was in her fit. She growled and tilted her head closer to him until her forehead was an inch away from his. She locked her eyes onto his.

Frankie stood his ground and said, "My Abby. Where are you?" She did not answer. She had never met Frankie in this state. It was like her possessions needed to examine him and give him the okay before they allowed her to speak.

She said, "Abby is here," In a strong raspy voice. She touched him on the chest.

Frankie smiled. He could feel her strength from that simple touch. He reached for the suit and gently took it from Abigail. He was not afraid. She let him take it. He examined the suit and said, "Who made this?"

Roger answered, "My mother... and me. That's what they wanted. They killed her for it."

Frankie handed the suit back to Abigail. She grabbed it back. He looked down at the bag on the floor and realized it was full of weaponry. He reached into it and pulled out a handgun. He checked it for ammunition. It was loaded. He handed it to Roger. Abigail, the beast, stood there breathing heavily. Frankie asked, "What's the plan?"

MASSACHUSETTS GENERAL HOSPITAL (MGH)

Finch was picked up by EMTs and placed in an ambulance. They sped along the 30 minute ride to get her to the hospital. She was taken to Massachusetts General Hospital and placed in a room on the 7th floor. Finch was in stable condition but in terrible pain. She had a fracture in her left shin and a variety of other sprained and bruised parts. Her left arm was in a sling. The blast caused significant damage to her ears which would take weeks to heal.

She lay in the hospital bed, unaware of what was going on. Finch eventually woke to see Duffy and Brown standing over her. Her eyes were in full focus within a few seconds. They noticed her eyes were blinking. Brown said, "Meghan... Meghan..." as he softly held her hand.

She said, "My head." She let out a grunt and touched her head with her hand. "My head is killing me!"

Brown asked, "Are you okay?"

"Pssh!" Meghan rolled her eyes.

"What the hell happened over there?" Brown asked. But she didn't have the strength to go into the details. He would never have believed it anyway.

Duffy added, "Dispatch said it was supposed to be a routine domestic disturbance? Why did you even take that call?"

"I don't know. I was right there. I thought it would be simple..." a tear rolled down her face. Finch looked confused; but actually, she was not confused at all. She was overwhelmed. She had seen things that no one would understand. Duffy and Brown stepped outside of the room to converse. Suddenly she heard a cell phone vibrating. It was Ben's cell phone. Abigail had given her the phone on her way out of Roger's house. Finch saw the cell phone hanging half way out of her pocket. She opened it. Her eyes widened in shock. She saw a text from Dewey that said, "ELIMINATE HER EXPEDITIOUSLY!" She also saw phone calls and text messages from Ben to Chris Duffy.

Duffy had sent a text, "ELIMINATED?" but Ben had never responded because he was dead.

After seeing the text, she remembered Abigail's words, *You will find that your enemy is always someone you think you can trust.* Finch snapped out of her fuzziness, took a swift look to make sure they hadn't seen her, reached over to her jacket and grabbed her gun. She slid the gun under her thigh and lay back down. She reached for her cell phone and tucked it under her pillow.

Duffy and Brown returned after their brief conversation. Duffy somehow convinced Brown to leave. Brown reentered the room. Meghan lay in the bed, pretending to be resting.

Brown said, "In a few, I'm gonna go back over to that house to follow up with Tammy. Duffy's gonna stay here until I get back. I made him promise to keep you safe." Brown winked. Meghan gave him a fake smile. Duffy looked in and smirked at her. Brown kissed Finch on the forehead. They talked for a moment but she never mentioned anything about the explosion or about Duffy's treason. She didn't know who to trust except for Abigail.

When Brown left the room, Meghan sent Abigail a text, "MASS GENERAL. 7th FLOOR. THEY ARE COMING!"

FRANKIE'S APARTMENT

Abigail had eventually returned to her normal self with brown eyes and normal breathing. Then she received the text from Meghan. She showed it to Roger and Frankie. She quickly told Frankie about Meghan. He had already known her from the pub, but she had somehow gotten involved in the matter at Roger's house. And now she was a target. Abigail moved quickly. She tore her clothes off as quickly as she could. She slipped her legs into the suit. Her heart pounded. She pulled it up over her thighs. Her eyes were glowing. Her muscles bulged. She put her arms in and zipped herself in the front. She walked out of the room. Frankie and Roger stood amazed. Roger had never seen anyone wear the suit. He knew Abigail took a risk putting it on, but she trusted his work. She was more powerful than ever.

Roger asked, "Are you sure you want to try the suit? It has never been tested. I can't make any promises that..."

Abigail cut him off and said, "Roger. Believe me. It will work. Let's go." Her eyes flicked from blue to brown. She was struggling to keep herself from going into beast mode. The suit pulled at her possessions making them want to come forward. Within a few minutes she was in control, and the brown eyed Abby was consistently there.

Abigail slipped on black cargo Dickie pants over the suit. Roger strapped up with a vest and a variety of weapons. He attached a few guns around Abigail's waist. She put on her leather jacket. They loaded up on ammunition.

Frankie asked, "WAIT WAIT! Are you sure you want to do this?"

Abigail said, "They are looking for me, but I'm not gonna wait until they find me. I'm going to them. And they are going to kill Meghan if I do not get over there now."

Frankie asked, "Who are 'they?'" a question asked of Abigail many times."

Abigail answered, "The man who made me and my brothers. We have to go, Frankie."

Frankie said, "Take this." Frankie reached into his pocket and handed her a knife. He continued saying, "It was my father's. Bring it back to me."

Abigail said, "I will. I promise." She touched Frankie's chest and turned away. She said, "Roger... Let's go. If they're going to go after Finch, we've got to get to her first."

Abigail received another text from Finch. She read it and tossed Roger her phone. He opened it. The text read, "I DON'T HAVE MUCH TIME HURRY!" Roger and Abigail reached the truck, got in and drove off.

DEWEY'S HOTEL ROOM

Jason Dewey was sitting in a recliner, chewing on the end of a cigar and reading the paper when Saul was far enough away from the commotion to contact him. The news was not exactly what Dewey had wanted to hear. Saul was completely out of breath when he explained what had happened at the Atkins residence. He explained that they went to get Atkins and pressure her about her communication with Paltee; but she wouldn't speak, so they tortured her to get answers. Then they had questioned her about the experiments going on in the garage and in her son's room. "They were building things," Saul insisted. He explained they weren't constructing anything overly complex, but they were complicated enough to raise suspicion about their ability to create something more useful. So on a hunch, they questioned her about the plans for the suit and she looked guiltier.

He gave explicit details of what they did to her and no matter what they did or how they threatened the life of her son, she refused to speak. Then, to their surprise, Abigail had shown up. Saul wasn't sure of the connection. He assumed that Paltee and Abigail may have kept in touch after all these years and had slipped under everyone's radar because in Saul's mind, it would never be pure coincidence that Abigail would find the Atkins on her own. Dewey agreed. "He must have sent Abigail to Atkins for the suit. Atkins has no other use in this matter," Dewey said.

He explained the fight and the nosey cop showing up. Then Saul explained that Abigail and the Atkins boy had killed Ben, and Saul had fled, at which point Dewey's temper went straight through the roof.

He stood up and threw down the cigar and said, "Get your ass here, NOW!" Saul was already in a cab heading to the hotel.

MGH: FINCH'S ROOM

It was late in the day, and the nurses were transitioning between shifts. The night guards were coming in. Most of the doctors were leaving for the night. The hospital was quiet, and the hall lights had been dimmed a bit. Duffy had been sitting outside of Finch's room for about 40 minutes when the nurse entered the room for the last time for the night. As she checked Finch's vital signs, Duffy walked in. Meghan was pretending to sleep.

He asked, "How's my champ doing?"

The nurse smiled at Duffy and said, "She's fine. She just needs a little rest. You can leave if you want. She's fine here."

Duffy said, "Oh no, no. I'm gonna stay here. She'd be happy knowing someone she was close to was right here making sure she was okay. Plus I have a lot of questions to ask, so when she wakes up. I want to ask them while the answers are fresh in her mind."

The nurse shrugged and said, "Ok well... I see a few of her wounds are bleeding through so I want to clean her up a little. I'm going to have you step out for a minute."

Duffy said, "Oh sure. Sure. No problem. I'll be right outside. Take your time." As Duffy walked out of the room, his phone buzzed. It was a text from Mr. Jason Dewey. "WE NEED TO FINISH THIS TONIGHT AND CLEAN UP THIS MESS BY MORNING! I'M ON MY WAY TO MAKE SURE YOU DON'T SCREW UP!"

Duffy replied, "COMPLICATIONS. NEED 30 MINUTES." He sent the message. He then sent a text to Detective Brown, "ARE YOU ON YOUR WAY?"

Brown responded, "COMING BACK NOW."

Dewey was so angry he picked up the phone and called Duffy on the spot. Dewey stepped away for more privacy and answered the phone. He said, "I'm doing the best I can."

"Your best is not good enough. When Moore referred you, she told me you were reliable," Dewey explained. "So, my disappointment is inevitable."

Duffy angrily responded, "Do you know what I have at stake here? What I have risked? You said you wanted Finch, and I faked the dispatch call to get her to your boys. They failed. Not me. If they can't take out a female cop, then discuss that with them."

Earlier that evening, Duffy had Barkley "Duck" Duckworth, the officer who usually worked the front desk, and Detective Fisher follow Meghan when she left the office to meet with her mother–in–law. She didn't know she was being followed, and Dewey didn't know that Finch would end up in the same area as the Ezekiels; but when she did, Duffy immediately came up with the idea of luring her to the house, calling in a domestic disturbance. It had worked! Duck called in the disturbance.

"There was another distraction we didn't account for," Dewey added. "I'm sure she is on her way to the hospital, so you have to act fast. I'm on my way. My boys are coming, too. You get those halls clear; and if you get a clean shot on Finch, take it! I don't give a fuck about what you have at stake." Dewey hung up.

Duffy knew he would need to act fast if he was to kill Finch before Brown returned and figured out he was behind it.

Abigail and Roger pulled up behind a high rise building that sat near the hospital. Roger took out his computer. He hooked it to an electronic device. He attached the device to the electrical unit that controlled the electricity of a few blocks in the area. Abigail said to Roger, "You know what to do. I'm going in."

Roger nodded. He looked away for a second, then he looked back at Abigail; but she had already disappeared up the side of the building. On all fours she climbed up the high rise. Roger packed up his things and quietly moved closer to the hospital. He saw four black trucks pull up. Indigo had sent in more men like Ben and Saul. Saul stepped out of the front seat of the truck. Roger watched from a dark shadow. Abigail had reached the top of the building. She took out a cigarette and quickly lit it. She took a strong drag and flicked it to the side. She walked up to the edge of the building and watched her prey from above.

BACK TO THE BEGINNING

Abigail was angry. She inhaled and turned into the *Beast*. Her blue eyes zoomed in on the little black figures circling the building, planning their attack against Meghan Finch. She wasn't going to let that happen.

There she was, standing at the edge, thinking of life's mysteries that had created this kink in her path– her choices, decisions driven by her fears and uncontrollable desires. They all had changed the meaning of her existence and everything around her. This is where she committed to regain control of everything. She threw off her leather jacket.

Abigail turned around, jogging away from the edge. The only sounds were the sounds of her pounding heart and the chilling wind squeezing through her hair and riding past her ears. Her fast hard footsteps got louder as she got closer and closer to the edge. She ran full speed toward the edge and when she ran out of roof, she jumped.

Abigail stretched out her arms and wind gliders appeared between her arms and sides and between her legs slowing down her decent. Roger had installed them as a feature on the suit. *Eagle*. She soared down towards the ceiling of the hospital. She then released a short parachute and quickly, she tossed out a rope. The parachute slowed her from a deadly fall to a soft, safe glide. The rope wrapped itself around a cell tower at the top of the building. She swung around a few times and detached the parachute as soon as her feet hit the cement. The landing was perfect. She talked into a wire in her ear.

Abigail said, "Roger, I'm here. Take out the lights."

The wind took the parachute around to the front of the building where her enemies awaited. They looked up. Slowly the black silk chute floated to the ground. Saul picked it up.

Saul looked up and saw Abigail peering over the edge. He said, "She's on the roof!" The men dashed into the building.

MASS GENERAL HOSPITAL

After Roger shut off the electricity, the emergency generators came on, turning on machines and emergency light strips in the halls and stairwells. The low lit lights flickered from the inconsistent power offered by the generator. Telephone and Internet communication was disabled courtesy of Roger Atkins. Roger then took three of his radio controlled cars and placed them on the road. Earlier, he had strapped explosives to their tops and clicked their fuses into the "live" position. He turned on the cars and directed them with a remote control, driving each one straight ahead. Each car crept forward to the trucks in the front of the hospital and rested underneath. Once Roger got them all in place, he hit a green button, and they exploded.

The four Ezekiels outside of the hospital were thrown to the ground. They were completely stunned and temporarily out of commission. Roger loaded up a sniper rifle and took them out, one by one. They didn't have the strength to run and couldn't see where the shots were coming from. They were rendered helpless from the blast.

Jason Dewey smoked a cigar as he sat in a car hidden in a dark corner across the street. He yelled to the driver, "Get out of here now!" He was utterly disgusted with the fiasco brewing outside.

FINDING FINCH

As soon as Abigail's feet touched the floor of the room, she was attacked; but her attackers were no match for her. They were a mixed group of Ezekiels from Project Flutter experiments and a few soldiers. She moved very quickly. The few bullets that did hit her bounced off the suit. She unloaded her weapons on the attackers, twisting and turning with inhuman speed. *Deer.* In hand to hand combat, she hissed at the men, fighting and thrashing through them, ripping them to pieces. All was quiet again on the roof. She took out a cigarette, lit it and confidently walked to the door that led to the stairwell.

Finch saw Duffy leave his post to take the phone call. She knew that her body was too weak to outrun him. She laid there for a moment, hoping that Abigail had received her message. Then the lights had gone out and explosions and gun fire erupted. *They're here!* Meghan's knees quivered and her hands were jittery as she tried to get out of the bed. She was extremely nervous. The lights going out, explosions and the gunfire meant mayhem. *Maybe I'm putting too much faith in Abigail! She's not coming. I can't lie here and wait for them to kill me. Maybe Brown is on his way.* She wasn't sure, but she knew that she had to guard herself. She slipped her arm out of the sling. It was too restricting. When her arm dropped, a pain shot up through her left side and rested in her collarbone. She bit down on her teeth to shield the yell she wanted to release. Finch was extremely weak but managed to drag herself to the door and lock it behind the nurse who had left. She closed the shades to the room and turned off the lights. She ducked down in the corner on the other side of the bed.

Duffy returned and tried to open the door. It was locked. He banged on the door and yelled, "Open up, Finch! It's me, Duffy."

Finch ignored the request. She clutched her gun in fear in the corner of the room. He continued to bang on the door and yelled, "I just want to help you."

Meghan's silence alluded to the fact that she must be on to him. *How did she figure me out?* Duffy thought. *No matter now.* He loaded his gun as lights flickered all around. Finch was almost in tears. Suddenly her floor filled with ten Indigo agents. Behind the pack was Saul. Abigail reached the floor on the opposite side. Roger had entered from the ground level and ran up the stairwell taking out the few Ezekiels he saw in the halls. The agents shot and charged toward Abigail. She took out the knife Frankie gave her.

Abigail spoke into the wire in her ear and said, "Roger get your ass up here!"

Roger was out of breath but responded, "Coming up now, Elvis."

The men shot at Abigail and approached her full force. The bullets were no match for the suit. Any that hit her slid off to the side. She quickly moved around them. The men were close. More hand to hand combat was required. She threw the knife, hitting one Ezekiel in the throat. She had killed him. She fought another. Before the man with the knife in his throat could hit the floor, she took the knife out of his throat and used it to slit another agent in the throat. They were no match for the suit. Her movements were fast, slick, strong, and precise. Saul approached. She had taken out all of the agents and dismembered most of them. She tossed the knife around in her hand as Saul got closer to her.

Saul said, "So you have a suit after all. And here we were looking for just the plans." Abigail didn't respond. Saul was even more frustrated and said, "You don't give up, do you."

She smiled and said, "Taurus." Then she spoke softly into her wire, "Roger, get Finch." Saul charged in, and they fought.

Roger reached the room on the 7th floor. He saw Duffy trying to break into the door. Duffy turned and saw Roger, and he immediately fired. Roger pulled back behind a corner. He and Duffy shot at one another. Their bullets flew past Saul and Abigail. Eventually Roger was shot in the arm, but his last shot was a deadly blow to Duffy. Duffy hit the floor, and his body bounced one time. Abigail and Saul continued fighting, and Abigail was winning. Roger kicked Finch's door. He needed to get it open. Finch sat on the other side of the room with the gun pointed directly at the opening.

Detective Brown pulled up to the hospital seeing the disturbance. He pulled out his gun. He entered the lobby where a few late workers were hiding. He tried the elevator but it was not working. He began running up the stairs. Roger kicked Finch's door repeatedly. He yelled, "Detective Finch, It's me, Roger. Open the door so I can get you outta here."

She was relieved to hear his voice. She hobbled over to the door but couldn't get it open. She yelled back, "I can't open it. I jammed it."

"Back away from the door," Roger said. He had an idea. Roger backed away and shot the lock off the door. He entered and picked up Finch and backed out of the room. He leaned her against the wall.

Saul knew Abigail had the upper hand. He retreated, running quickly toward Roger. Roger was holding Finch. Abigail took the knife Frankie had given her and threw it. The knife zipped through the air, piercing Saul in the back of his neck severing his spine. He was about six feet away from Roger when it happened. Saul's body plunged forward knocking Roger over and Saul exhaled his last breath into Roger's face. Saul's possessive spirit fluttered into the air and entered into Roger's air passage. Roger inhaled. The timing was fateful. Roger coughed and coughed grabbing at his neck. His body jerked. Abigail watched in awe. Roger couldn't breathe at first, but when he opened his eyes, they were blazing blue. Abigail reached forward, touching his face. Roger growled. She picked him up, setting him on his feet. They grabbed the guns on the floor and Abigail retrieved the knife from Saul's neck.

Brown reached the 7th Floor and shouted, "Drop your weapons!" Brown was stunned when he realized the last two men standing were the two youths from Frankie's Pub. "What the...?" He was confused, "Drop 'em NOW or I *will* fire!"

Finch yelled "NO! They are okay. They saved me. They saved me."

Brown was confused, but didn't care. His heart was broken when he saw the love of his life had been badly injured, yet was relieved that she was still alive. He put his gun aside to help Finch who had slid down the wall. He immediately held and kissed her. She kissed him back without a second thought of who may be looking. Once he was satisfied that she was ok, Brown looked up, but Abigail and Roger were gone. They had both slipped out of sight. Exiting through a window, they climbed down the side of the building. Abigail had to help Roger a little; he was slipping. Once they reached the ground, they ran with superhuman speed into the darkness. Abigail had to slow down. Roger didn't have a suit to run as fast as she could. They got a few blocks away and covered their heads with hoodies from a bag they had stashed. They backed away into a dark corner and disappeared.

CHAPTER 21

FRANKIE'S PUB
MORNING

It was early morning. The sun emerged from behind the building tops, drying up the night's moisture and warming the air. Frankie was downstairs cleaning tables at the bar. He looked out the window and saw Abigail and Roger coming towards the bar. Abigail walked in first with a battered Roger struggling behind her. She dropped the knife and keys to the truck on the bar. Frankie smiled and continued wiping. Abigail and Roger went upstairs to the apartment. Although Abigail was exhausted she stayed alert as she observed the new man before her.

Roger's body ached. He had never felt this way. He felt his skin crawl, something was living inside. Abigail knew that he and that possession were going to have to learn to live together; but until then, Roger will seem almost bipolar, frantic, paranoid and schizophrenic. She laid him down on the bed and tucked him in. Roger was going to need rest for the inner spirit to settle down in its new host. Roger lay down and slept for eight hours without waking. Occasionally he growled and moaned in his sleep, but nothing too loud or worth worrying about.

Abigail sat in the room the entire time. As she sat there, she reviewed Dr. Paltee's notes. He outlined his method of possessing humans in great detail. Abigail took notes until she saw Roger wake.

Frankie knew the two youths were upstairs. He was so busy downstairs, working the bar with Marty and Frita that he hadn't thought to bother them with questioning. By 9:00 pm, Frankie decided to close down and pay them a visit. As he ascended the stairs, there was a soft buzzing sound coming from the room. He was familiar with the sound of a tattoo gun. Frankie stepped into the room to see an interesting and striking scene. Roger had cut his hair into a stylized Mohawk. He sat backwards on a chair with his arms folded over the back of the chair. Abigail was giving him a tattoo. *Lion.*

They finally explained to Frankie what happened from start to finish. She explained the tattoos, the possessions, the Ezekiels, but the suit she left for Roger to explain. It was his baby. Frankie was dumbfounded. They talked that entire night until the sun rose again the next day. Frankie couldn't believe that fate had brought these two into his life and brought them together.

Samantha Callahan came on TV a week later with breaking news. Larry's body had been recovered from a ditch a week after the fiasco at Mass General Hospital. The media swarmed the area, taking photos and live footage of the murder scene. At the time they had no information about the body. No ID was found on or near the body. After scanning his prints, the body was identified as belonging to Larry Crawford. Frankie was extremely upset. He cried for a week, thinking about his best friend being shot in the head and left for dead. He wondered who would have done this and why. Abigail and Roger made it point to break into Larry's house and confiscate whatever they could find, including his computer. After studying his records, they realized what he had done. Larry was the reason the Ezekiels knew where to find her, but now Larry was dead and that's all that mattered. Frankie held a grudge.

Vengeance was all he could think of; and so he, too, was determined to make Indigo pay.

Now, it was Frankie's mission to help them. He thought about the closing of the fight club and had an idea for a new routine. In the day, they would work at the bar. After midnight, they would train. The former fight club was converted into a lab for Roger and a training gym. The lab had all types of equipment Roger could use, including two computers and a total of four monitors. Abigail helped him with his projects. Frankie promised to find a better space in the future. Frankie invested in free weights and a few exercise machines and replaced the mats on the floor for combat training. Abigail used it daily to teach Roger and Frankie the defense and attack moves she remembered from her training.

Frankie spent his spare time refurbishing a used car he purchased for Abigail and Roger. The truck wasn't good enough for them, Frankie figured. Once a rusty mess, the used car was transformed– completely redone, painted and polished black with silver pinstripes on the hood and silver stripes on the sides. It was an all black 1967 Ford Mustang. They named it Terry. It was Frankie's baby.

And Roger had a baby of his own. When Roger was not working the pub or training in the gym, he was in the basement with Abigail, working on his next project — another suit. It took him three months to complete the second suit. This suit was just like Abigail's, but it had gunmetal gray accents on the sides of the legs, under the arms and around the neck. It was larger to fit his body. He showed Frankie how to monitor the suit's activity on his iPad and gave him a wire to communicate with them as well. Some nights, Abigail and Roger would put on their suits for outdoor training, climbing up buildings, leaping from roof to roof, and dashing through streets at lightning speed.

Occasionally Meghan Finch and Sydney Brown stopped by to visit. Finch hadn't quite explained the entire story to Brown, but he hadn't pressured her to do so. He figured she would explain things to him in due time. He didn't ask many questions about it. The incident at MGH was classified as an act of terrorism by unknown assailants. It sparked a media frenzy and public outcry for more gun control. Chris Duffy was dead and labeled a hero to avoid further speculation. Robert Benson's body was never recovered.

CHAPEL AND CASE
AFTER THE DISCOVERY OF THE FOREARM

Rewinding time back to the day the arm was discovered. Sam Petit, the guard from the office, left the building after his interview with Finch and Brown. He was extremely hot and exhausted by the hours of questioning that had resulted. He didn't feel well and needed to get out of the office. He finally got away and sent out a text message, "I NEED TO GET OUT OF HERE."

He received a quick response, "COME NOW."

Leaving the building was a dizzying experience. The rooms were caving in around him. People looked like zombies. He felt everyone was looking at him. The patterns in the rug spiraled in circles around his feet as he took each step. *Sinking sand?* He thought he was sinking into the floor. He was convinced everything around him sought to swallow and devour him. His ears clogged as if water was rising over his head. He couldn't breathe. *Panic Attack!* He had to get out of there.

He eventually made his way to the main floor, shuffling his fumbling feet over the marble tiles. He tried his best to stand upright, but his stomach cramped. He wanted to vomit. The sour stomach acid sat at the back of his throat. He left the building through the side door entering the garage where a black Escalade awaited him. He entered into the truck. He sat in the back, breathing and sweating. He tried to calm himself down. He looked over to see Mr. Dewey who was in the car, smoking a cigar. Saul was in the passenger seat in the front, and Ben was the driver. The guard removed a facial disguise and took off his jacket, revealing a prosthetic arm. He said, "This better fucking work."

Jason Dewey said, "Mr. Benson... you have nothing to fear. All is well." Mr. Dewey exhaled smoke into the air. The car pulled out of the garage and travelled down the road.

ABOUT THE AUTHOR

L.E. Green is an educator in Springfield, Massachusetts. She is a graduate of Springfield Central High School and the University of Massachusetts Amherst. She is an avid fisherwoman and a part–time artist, or so they say. Green has been writing various genres of fiction for many years and recently has decided to make *Flutter* her first self–published novel.

COPYRIGHT

Printed in Great Britain
by Amazon.co.uk, Ltd.,
Marston Gate.